GERALD GRAY'S WIFE AND LILY: A NOVEL

Gerald Gray's Wife

AND

Lily: A Novel

BY SUSAN PETIGRU KING

With an Introduction by Jane H. Pease

and William H. Pease

Duke University Press   Durham and London 1993

INTRODUCTION

Susan Petigru King wrote and published virtually all her novels and short stories in the years during which her native state severed its ties with national politics, seceded from the federal union, and endured a bloody civil war. Her fiction, with the exception of a single passage in *Gerald Gray's Wife*, deals with none of this directly. Like those whom Mary Kelley has called the literary domestics, King chronicles courtships and marriages, love and jealousy—but, unlike them, provides few happy endings. Almost always fortune hunting triumphs over love; marriage proves to be a "prison house"; and jealousy among women is a fully justified proclivity. She openly criticizes the institution of marriage while her fellow women novelists praised it as woman's highest calling or masked their criticism as miserable exceptions to the rule. Nor does King preach the work ethic so common in the stories of *Godey's Lady's Book* editor Sarah Josepha Hale and of her Massachusetts-born Charleston neighbor Caroline Gilman. Indeed, she ignores routine domestic duties and gives worldly advice rather than moralistic instruction. Like most contemporary writers, North or South, male or female, she almost entirely ignores the issues of race and slavery that Harriet Beecher Stowe and Lydia Maria Child tackled. And unlike her fellow southerners Caroline Lee Hentz, Augusta Jane Evans, and Mary Virginia Terhune (Marion Harland, pseud.), King puts no women authors or other bluestockings into her stories to speak for women's literary creativity. Indeed, her voice, at its most evident, is that of a hard-headed, somewhat cynical woman educated by experience rather than books.

In setting almost all her fiction in Charleston, South Carolina, and its surrounding low-country plantations, King wrote out of her own social experience. Born Susan DuPont Petigru on October 25, 1824, she lived in Charleston virtually her entire life. Nonetheless, because her parents were relative newcomers and she, by temperament, somewhat of an outcast, she cultivated the perspective of an outsider while she enjoyed the familiarity of an insider writing about her own social circles. Her father, James L. Petigru, the son of a minimally prosperous farm family in the remote western corner of the state, had, by virtue of his education at South Carolina College, his success as a lawyer, and his engaging personality, risen to prominence after he had moved to Charleston in 1819. Indeed, within three years of his arrival, when he was only thirty-three, he became his state's attorney general. Sue's mother, the daughter of a modestly placed low-country planter, had been suitably polished by a year at a Charleston finishing school, and as a young woman had been much lauded for her wit and beauty. Nonetheless, as her husband steadily rose in social prestige, Jane Amelia Postell Petigru ever more noticeably declined in health, becoming so emotionally explosive and so eccentric in her behavior that she provoked shame and hostility in her daughter.

The youngest of the Petigrus' four children, Sue grew up in a large household, which, after the accidental death of her older brother when he was only eight, still included a brother and a sister as well as three of her father's sisters, the youngest of whom was only eight years older than Sue. Because James Petigru stood so well among the established as well as the aspiring elite, all five girls came to maturity and married in the world of Charleston "high society." Additionally, Sue's education introduced her to other would-be belles. At home, she attended Mme Ann Talvande's school with Mary Boykin, who, as Mrs. Chesnut, would write her famous and somewhat fictionalized Civil War diary. When she was fourteen, Sue was sent off to Mme Guillon's finishing school in Philadelphia, where she polished the French she already knew and with which she would garnish so much of her writing. Just as important, she enhanced her understanding of her own world through the novels that, from her earliest childhood, she read constantly—even, perhaps, compulsively.

No sooner had she ended her schooling and returned home, intent on following her sister Caroline's example as a Charleston belle, than her family fell on hard times. The aftermath of the panic of 1837 left her father so deeply in debt, even after he had sold his recently acquired rice plantation, that, in 1842, he surrendered to his creditors all his possessions, excepting only his house and his law office. To their father's financial failure Mrs. Petigru responded by pressing both daughters to marry money. Caroline complied more readily, marrying William Carson, a man twice her age with whom she had little in common and to whom she felt no emotional tie. Sue, who spatted constantly with her mother, first resisted the "advantageous" marriage proposed for her, but then, in 1843, at age nineteen, she did marry Henry C. King—short, stout, and physically unattractive. The son of a prominent lawyer of great wealth, Henry had been educated for the law at home and in Germany. But until his father-in-law took him on as a partner, his practice was minimal. Neither he nor Sue met the other's spousal expectations very well. Their only child, Adele, was born in 1844 while they still lived with Henry's parents. Not until 1846 did they establish their own home, for which Sue had yearned but which she then left whenever she could—to summer with her parents on nearby Sullivan's Island, to visit aunts on their plantations, to spend time in Philadelphia and New York, Saratoga and Newport. Usually it was ostensibly to accompany and assist her ailing sister that she traveled in the North. But the prolonged absences of both more often than not openly defied the wishes of their husbands.

At home, Sue King devised stylish entertainments and had, at least by 1850, established her reputation as an outrageous flirt if not the "fast woman" William Thackeray had heard she was. At least once accompanying her father and her by-then widowed sister to Washington, she attracted attention in the political society to which her father's extensive acquaintance introduced her. Wherever she was, she made a point of meeting the notables: lawyers, writers, and scientists, as well as politicians. At the same time she began to write seriously.

When in 1853 the northern firm of Appleton brought out her first book anonymously, Charlestonians did not wait for Professor Frederick Porcher's review to conclude that *Busy Moments in the Life of an Idle Woman* was the production of a fellow townswoman. And it offended others as it did Porcher because it not only "unequivocally condemned" "our Charleston Society" but also taunted the cultural inferiority of "our wives [who] devote themselves to family care."[1] Yet, despite persistent gossip about the real-life models that, so relatives and neighbors believed, underlay her characters, *Lily,* published by Harpers in 1855, drew greater praise from the local press. Lauding it for its "subtle observation" and "delicate irony," one reviewer almost perversely deplored the theatricality of its ending, that part most clearly inspired by local lore of a "poisoned bride," Harriet Mackie, who had met her fate in 1804, calling it a decline from "the air and sunshine to the sickly glare of footlights."[2] And in 1859, when *Sylvia's World* and *Crimes*

Which the Law Does Not Reach were issued in a single volume by yet another New York firm, Derby and Jackson, local praise, though sparse, was still less reserved. Whether because each had been previously serialized—the former in the *Knickerbocker Magazine,* the latter in Charleston's own *Russell's Magazine*—or because the book came out when Carolinians' attention was focused on John Brown's recent raid on Harper's Ferry, or simply because King's novelty had worn off, the reviews were short. But one local reviewer, calling the book her best work, now praised King for confining herself to "the domain of social existence, as modified by a peculiar convention," and to the "character and the philosophy of motive" played out by "inward" rather than "outward" action.[3]

Whatever public acclaim and attention she received, Sue was minimally satisfied with her private life. Henry's income did not stretch to fund the travel and entertainments she demanded. Men whose attention she cherished married others. Her sarcasm and arresting style offended both strangers and friends. Her relations with her mother were downright hostile; controversies with her sister occasionally left even them at odds. Her daughter was increasingly alienated, depending on father and grandparents more than on mother for intimacy.

Then came the Civil War. Henry enlisted in a Charleston militia unit and was fatally wounded at the nearby battle of Secessionville in 1862. But even before that, Susan and Adele had become refugees: in Columbia with a friend who ran a girls school; at the Petigru homestead near Abbeville; and with the King in-laws at Flat Rock, North Carolina. Under these inauspicious circumstances she finished her last novel, *Gerald Gray's Wife,* which, in 1864, was her first to be published in the South. Widowed with a minimal inheritance, King realized at the end of the war that she must now work to support herself. When giving public readings in northern cities produced little income, she became a clerk in the Post Master General's Washington office; and thereafter, except for a single novella published in *Harpers Magazine* in 1868, capped her authorial pen.

In 1870 King married Christopher Columbus Bowen,[4] a South Carolina congressman and the Radical Republican boss of Charleston County. Born in Rhode Island in 1832, raised as an orphan, trained as a mechanic, Bowen had moved to Georgia in 1850 where he first wandered from town to town as a journeyman, then farmed land not his own, and, along the way, acquired a reputation as a professional gambler. Court-martialed and dismissed from the Confederate army for forgery and extended absence without leave, only the Yankee occupation of Charleston saved him from criminal prosecution for planning his commanding officer's murder. In 1871 he was saved from his conviction as a bigamist only by a presidential pardon.

Whether because her new life with Bowen so far exceeded the scandals connected with her past life and writing or because it cut off all social intercourse with her family and former social equals in Charleston, Sue never again wrote professionally. Totally isolated from the society that had been her world, she comforted herself with Bowen's spacious Charleston mansion, at least six servants, a carriage, and an elegant summer house on Sullivan's Island. But they were empty trappings. "The deadly loneliness of my existence is hard to stand," she wrote in 1874. "Of what constitutes 'society,' I have none. My parties are all given by myself; my guests are, for the most part, old & poor & forlorn—less friendless perhaps than I, but a great deal more destitute than I ever was."⁵ Worst of all, her daughter, now her "bitterest foe," refused even to see her. On December 11, 1875, she died of typhoid pneumonia.

Susan Petigru King set all but one of her novels and most of her short stories in antebellum Charleston and the surrounding low country. In exploring the social life and sexual politics of privileged South Carolinians, however, she largely ignored both the cultivation of rice and cotton that made planters' fortunes and the trade in those staples that underlay the prosperity of urban merchants and professionals. Nor did she people her fiction with African Americans, although they comprised half the city's population and up to 90 percent of some coastal plantation districts. Those few black people who do appear briefly in her fiction are not, moreover, called slaves; and, with a single exception, they are all domestic servants. Still less visible, except as an occasional vulgar foil for elite gentility, are poor or middling whites. She focuses, in short, on that narrow spectrum so frequently romanticized in tales of the "Old South."

Collectively, King's characters lived in a languishing economy. In 1825, the year after her birth, the bottom fell out of the cotton market and Charleston's commerce plummeted. Thereafter, except briefly in the 1830s and 1850s, Charleston's economy remained in the doldrums. The city sank into second and then third place among southern ports and increasingly depended on northern capital to provide the shipping, credit, and insurance that its trade with distant markets required. At the same time, thousands of rural Carolinians annually deserted their state to plant cotton on the rich, virgin bottom lands along the Gulf coast and the Mississippi River. Furthermore, many of those low-country planters who stayed faced ever decreasing productivity on both rice and cotton land.

The anxiety generated by the state's relative economic decline was further exacerbated by northern abolitionists, whose increasingly vehement attacks threatened the slave labor system on which any remaining prosperity depended. In response, a unique Carolina politics evolved, in which the state in 1832 first nullified a federal tariff law and then in 1860 led the South in seceding from the federal union. Similarly, the low country's social style, first shaped when South Carolina was Britain's richest North American colony, changed markedly after old ties with England had been severed. Until the Revolution no Americans had surpassed the wealth accumulated by successful rice and indigo planters. No colonial city-dwellers had displayed their wealth more elegantly than the planters and merchants who built their mansions in Charleston. They had filled their houses with locally made but ornate furniture and silver; decked their walls with family portraits in oil; cultivated gardens filled with exotic plants; patronized the theater and concert hall; established a substantial library society; and supported a variety of schools. As open to new wealth as to old, this distinctive upper class had gradually evolved as descendants of families who had migrated directly from England or had come by way of Barbadian sugar plantations had then mingled and intermarried with Scots and French Huguenots.

As their city's economic vitality flagged in the early nineteenth century, however, those who already were the upper class began to close ranks. Yet they never shut the gates altogether. Wish though they might to entrench a waning past, they, like other Charlestonians of European ancestry, realized that in a city where Caucasians were a bare majority sharp class divisions would put at risk the social cohesion needed to control a vast African American slave population. In addition, grand old families stalked by financial difficulties positively wooed vulgar new money. And so fortunes made by unpolished fathers in trade could turn a son into a distinguished planter, a daughter into a sought-after belle. Furthermore, in Charleston, the cousinage that so frequently determined social contacts and marriage partners in the countryside lost much of its power, for in the city the spring and summer social seasons enabled resident and visiting young people to meet and mingle at horse races, parties, and balls where they flirted, courted, and preferably with family consent, often agreed to marry.

Yet only King's first novel, "Edith," and her very last published story follow the pattern Nina Baym[6] described as central to nineteenth-century woman's fiction, wherein an orphaned and impoverished young woman achieves financial independence through her own efforts but then marries a wealthy and honorable suitor, presumably to live happily ever after. Yet even "Edith," published as part of *Busy Moments*, has a subplot introducing the darker theme developed in most of King's subsequent work, how men exert unfair and deceitful power over women. Here it is the plight of a young widow much in love with a poor man whom, because of the terms of her late husband's will, she cannot marry without losing the large income she now enjoys. Moreover, the five short stories that complete *Busy Moments* explore, as the initial novel does not, the physical incarceration and psychological trauma that marriage and husbands inflict on women. Most shocking to contemporary critics was the heroine of "Every Day Life," Mrs. Mordaunt, a worldly wise widow of forty-three whose mother had pressured her to marry money, whose jealous husband had abused her, and whose wit and determination to enjoy life had gained her a scandalous reputation. Sufficiently tough and self-centered to survive all this, she is, in this story, ready to sacrifice herself to rescue a young girl on the verge of a similarly loveless marriage. King's assertion in this story that "if love be not there before the knot is tied, small is the chance that that capricious blind boy should enter the dwelling afterwards" provoked one reviewer to accuse her of ignoring a wife's "positive duty of *atonement*, or of making *the best of a bad bargain*."[7] On the other hand, King's adherence to the social norms of her day despite her exposés of domestic wretchedness is played out in "Old Maidism v. Marriage," in which the heroine defies the devastating testimony of all her married friends to follow their example.

The futility of their warnings defines King's central irony. In real life, she was the constant flirt, reputedly "fast," drawn especially to younger men, and ready enough to venture a second marriage to a womanizer eight years her junior. Yet her fictions lay bare the sinister motivations of the cads who toy with women for their own amusement or enrichment. But almost as persistently, Bertha St. Clair, Mrs. Mordaunt's successor in *Sylvia's World* and *Gerald Gray's Wife*, warns the young women she befriends against the designing women who would destroy their loves and reputations as well as against duplicitous men. In proffering such help, Mordaunt/St. Clair distances herself from the relationship among most of King's young women characters that mire down in jealousy and double-dealing and those between other older and younger women—generally mothers and daughters—that founder on the naivete or selfishness of the seniors just when their juniors desperately need nurturing guidance. Indeed, except for Mordaunt/St. Clair and her many ingenue heroines, King is no more sanguine about women than she is about men or marriage. Among the stories in *Crimes Which the Law Does Not Reach,* one about a woman's flirtation with a man whose sole attraction to her is the opportunity it affords her to destroy his fiancée, parallels narratives of male flirts who, for their own amusement, play on the emotions of innocent girls only to lose interest in them once they are entrapped.

Although King follows Sir Walter Scott and Charles Dickens in dramatizing differences between dark and fair women, for her it provides a readily visible means to dissect female jealousy in a world more clearly defined by William Thackeray's Becky Sharp than the reciprocal strengths of dark Rebecca and fair Rowena or the fragility of darling Dora. In *Lily* the blond heroine's jealousy of her diabolically dark cousin Angelica, like the jealousy that white Lily inspires in a woman of color, both contribute to Lily's melodramatic fate. In *Gerald Gray's Wife,* it is tiny and fair-haired Cissy on whom large and brunette Ruth vents her jealousy. Yet, however much these are hostilities among women, they feed and contribute to the deceptions that male characters practice on female.

As removed from feminist notions of sisterhood as from the many popular sentimental romances that Jane Tompkins believes are rooted in nineteenth-century evangelical religion,[8] King draws far more than other contemporary American women writers on French models of social and sexual intrigue, especially those of George Sand, which she read extensively and repeatedly. Not for her, either, the parochial defense of regional values and institutions that Elizabeth Moss[9] finds central in the novels of antebellum Southern women. After the heroine of her first novel marries her wonderfully wealthy planter cousin to regain her Southern heritage, King's sectional comparisons value New York and Saratoga ways over Charleston stuffiness and European sophistication above Southern provincialism.

In tracking these themes and patterns, it is easy to connect them with Sue King's own life. Her unhappy first marriage, her persistently flamboyant behavior, her frequent fallings-out with friends and relatives doubtless shaped her writing. Family members acknowledged as much as they discussed the limits that King's restricted experience imposed on her fiction, fictions that all admitted were rooted in her immediate world. Charleston neighbors were alternately fascinated and infuriated as they identified characters in what all agreed were romans à clef. Nonetheless, her novels and stories were not just thinly veiled reportage. While Mrs. St. Clair serves frequently as the author's voice, the character who knows the "real" situation, King vests some of herself, her aspirations, and her interests in each of her young heroines. On the other hand, her first critical attention to the question of women's paid work coincides with her own experience of government employment and writing more as a necessary means of support than a busy moment for an otherwise idle woman. In "My Debut" a privileged Southern woman, after having lost her wealth in the Civil War, undertakes to support herself by working. While ultimately she finds a romantic solution to her economic problems, a commonplace in so much woman's fiction, she also expresses King's frustration with a gender-defined work world. Through Elizabeth Leighton King laments that "working for my living" is "a prosaic and difficult thing." Her wages are "miserably scant," less than half what would be paid a man. "To this dead level of presumed inferiority my petticoats alone keep me down. In masculine attire I should have been paid according to my powers; in feminine garb I could form no such pretensions."[10]

But she also qualifies what might otherwise seem a nascent feminism seldom associated with Southern belles. "Let me pause to say that I neither wish to vote nor preach, nor practice medicine or law, but I *should* like not to be damned into eternal mediocrity in those few lines where a woman may modestly assert herself."[11] Here is perhaps King's strength as well as her weakness as a social critic. She was very much of the society about which she wrote. Hers was a world in which all people were ranked by class and race, a ranking which she never challenged. Except for the variations in fortune that might elevate or diminish the standing of individuals, she assumed an uninterrupted social stability. And when war, emancipation, and efforts to reconstruct a different world had destroyed that stability, she stopped writing.

Yet King also lived in a world and was part of a class that, like most others, restricted women's lives and personal freedom far more than it did men's. Its economic and political ideology encompassed a patriarchy in which the husband-father-slaveholder presided over an extended family of his wife, his children, and his labor force. Their wives and daughters, by comparison with their slaves and with most other women, were privileged. They lived surrounded by physical amenities; they had access to education; they might expand their world by travel or reading. But in the ordered system of their society they were inferior to men. And it was at this juncture and only here that King became a social critic. She attacked women's dependence in marriage; she stripped away the pretenses of romantic love. But she still saw marriage as central to women's lives, their sole access to economic security.

On the other hand, in the novels reprinted here, the heroine of each is a wealthy woman in her own right,[12] theoretically at least free to choose or reject marriage and to choose among suitors without concern for their ability to provide that security. *Lily,* the best known of King's works, follows the courtship and education of a young woman born to "old wealth." Set first at Chicora Wood, bearing the name, location, and characteristics of a plantation owned by King's uncle, Governor Robert F. W. Allston, then in a Philadelphia finishing school, and finally in Charleston, this novel is played out in territory with which King was intimately familiar. But the heroine's wealth and beauty, like the novel's seemingly improbable conclusion, are the author's imaginative devices for addressing the vulnerability even of those women best equipped to assert themselves. Lily Vere is an orphan, devoid of any guidance from a mature woman. Barely fifteen when the novel begins and twenty at its close, she is naive, inexperienced, and left to make her own decisions. Lacking any defenses against the rituals of courtship and her own romantic yearnings, she is weak despite the potential power her extrinsic assets might have given her.

Ruth Desborough, who is twenty-six when *Gerald Gray's Wife* begins and thirty when it ends, has grown up knowing that only her millionaire father's money attracts the bevies of men who woo her. Plain in appearance and icily reserved in personality, she is, when Gerald Gray first appears, the apparent opposite of Lily Vere. Her lineage is humble, even crude. She suspects the motives of both the men and the women around her. She maintains a distance from all of them as her surest protection from being exploited. But, like Lily, she has grown up without a mother's guidance. And in a moment when her defenses are down, she is attracted by the external attributes of a man handsome almost to feminine beauty and preternaturally sophisticated—almost exotic—in bearing. Perhaps most compelling, she wants the love and marriage that both heroines consider the desideratum of a woman's life. She becomes, when she permits herself to be courted, putty in the hands of her suitor and when married, putty still more malleable.

But the continuity and resemblance end there. Ruth Gray, in a denoument almost as melodramatic as that found in *Lily,* regains autonomy and uses the power her father's wealth gives her to make the independent best of personal tragedy, albeit with great suffering. Her choice thus defines less an assertion of power than a return to her earlier defensive shell. It is rather Bertha St. Clair, possessing worldly experience and a "saucy"—as King repeatedly puts it—personality rather than either wealth or beauty, who can play and win at sexual politics. And all we know of Mrs. St. Clair's husband is that at one time she must have had one.

Technically, we have kept textual editing to a bare minimum. *Lily* is reproduced directly from the 1855 Harper edition. *Gerald Gray's Wife*, set in worn type on bad paper by obviously inexperienced typesetters working under wartime conditions, resisted modern copying technology. It had, therefore, first to be transcribed from the original, for which we thank William Manning of the University of Charleston. In proofing that transcription for accuracy, we have made some silent variations from the 1864 copy to make it more readily intelligible. We have inserted quotation marks where they were missing and have adopted current American usage governing single and double quotation marks. We have corrected misplaced apostrophes in contractions. We have altered when the original seemed obvious the typesetter's guesses at the handwritten French in the manuscript from which he worked. But French words transposed in ways we could not fathom we have left as they were but followed them by [?]. On a very few occasions, where an English word that makes no sense is an obvious misreading of King's chirography, we have made silent corrections. We have also made spelling of proper names consistent with the version most frequently printed in the original. All else we have left as it is in the 1864 copy. The absence of copy editing will therefore be evident, most frequently in inconsistent punctuation and the erratic hyphenation and separation of compound words.

Jane H. Pease
William H. Pease

NOTES

1. F[rederick] A. P[orcher], Article VIII. "Busy Moments of an Idle Woman. . . ," *Southern Quarterly Review*, XXV (January 1854), 212–213.
2. "[Review of] Lily. . . ," Charleston *Mercury*, November 21, 1835.
3. "[Review of] Sylvia's World, and Crimes which the Law does not reach. . . ," *Russell's Magazine*, VI (October 1859), 95–96.
4. Because all her published writing was done before her marriage to Bowen we have not followed common library practice of calling the author Bowen. Also, though she was christened Susan, she was consistently known as Sue, in part to differentiate her from Henry's sister Susan King.
5. Sue Petigru King Bowen to Caroline Petigru Carson, February 2, 1874, Vanderhorst Papers, South Carolina Historical Society.

6. Nina Baym, *Woman's Fiction. A Guide to Novels by and about Women in America, 1820–1870* (Ithaca: Cornell University Press, 1978), 11–12.

7. "Busy Moments of an Idle Woman," Charleston *Daily Courier*, January 5, 1854.

8. Jane P. Tompkins, *Sensational Designs: The Cultural Work of American Fiction, 1790–1860* (New York: Oxford University Press, 1985).

9. Elizabeth Moss, *Domestic Novelists in the Old South, Defenders of Southern Culture* (Baton Rouge: Louisiana State University Press, 1992).

10. Susan Petigru King, "My Debut," *Harper's Magazine*, XXXVII (1868), 532.

11. *Ibid.*

12. Here King differs markedly from the authors treated in Anne Goodwyn Jones, *Tomorrow is Another Day: The Woman Writer in the South, 1859–1936* (Baton Rouge: Louisiana State University Press, 1981). Their heroines all gain their independence and self-reliance through paid work.

Lily: A Novel

BY SUSAN PETIGRU KING

"She was not very beautiful, if it be beauty's test
To match a classic model when perfectly at rest;
Said I she was not beautiful? Her eyes upon your sight
Broke with the lambent purity of planetary light."
—N. P. Willis

To LOUISA,

who, with a more brilliant mind than

LILY,

is yet her equal in purity, sweetness, and gentleness,

I offer this imperfect representation

Of a Lovely Woman.

CHAPTER I

The droning voice of the lawyer's clerk slowly continued,

"—of which I die possessed to my honored friend, Hugh Clarendon, Esq., in trust for my beloved daughter, Elizabeth Vere, sole offspring of my late lamented wife, Mary Elizabeth Vere. Such a sum as the said Hugh Clarendon may consider proper shall be yearly set aside for the maintenance, education, and support of my said daughter, who, with the permission of her guardian, Hugh Clarendon, thus appointed, shall reside with his family so long as she desires it. The balance of my yearly income shall continue to be invested, after the payment of such legacies as I shall presently name, until my beloved daughter be of age or marry, at which time she shall come into immediate and entire possession of my whole estate, without restriction.

"In case of her death before either of these events come to pass, I hereby devise my whole estate to the said Hugh Clarendon and his heirs forever."

Then followed numerous legacies to friends and public charities, for Andrew Vere was a man of large heart and immense fortune, with no relations except his only child, and possessing a character so just that he considered it necessary to return, in a measure, to the city of his adoption, a portion of that wealth which he had acquired as a successful merchant in Charleston, South Carolina.

"Right," he said, in a feeble tone, as the clerk finished his task. "Thank you, Mr. Corbett; you have explained fully my wishes. You accept this charge, dear sir?" turning to the gentleman at his bedside.

"My dear friend," answered Mr. Clarendon, to whom Mr. Vere spoke, "you are too generous. I do not allude merely to your legacies to us, which are princely, but the confidence you repose in me is exceedingly gratifying. God grant that I may be enabled to act a worthy part by your little girl, and my wife's tenderness and interest in Elizabeth will, I trust, lead her in time to look upon us as her family."

"She will be happy with you," said Mr. Vere; "and she is so young, that before many weeks are over, my darling will have forgotten that I ever lived. Lift her up, Clarendon; let me see her in your arms; I would like to give her my last blessing there."

Mr. Clarendon leaned over the bed, and, drawing down a shawl which was closely wrapped about what had seemed a large bundle, he softly laid upon his shoulder the fair head of a lovely little girl of five or six years. She was not yet awake, and her rosy mouth all puckered up, her disheveled curls, and flushed cheeks, which showed traces of tears, looked as if she had probably cried herself to sleep.

The dying father passed his weak hands caressingly over her smooth, childish brow.

"I may well call her Lily," he said, smiling; "is she not white as any lily that ever grew? Oh, cherish her, Clarendon! deal gently with her. Perhaps you doubt the wisdom of making her so young independent, or of putting no check upon her choice in marriage; but I have every confidence in Lily; she has great judgment. Don't laugh at that word, applied to a baby. She deserves it."

Mr. Clarendon silently pressed his friend's unoccupied hand, and there was a pause of several moments.

The lawyer, Mr. Corbett, and his clerk had noiselessly withdrawn to the adjoining room. The solitary candle, burning amid the phials and gallipots on the table near, cast a wavering, flickering light, now illuminating the wasted features of Andrew Vere, then flashing upon the strong, hearty, honest face of Hugh Clarendon, and sometimes gilding with double gold Lily's light ringlets.

"She looks like her mother," continued Mr. Vere. "Poor Mary! as earnestly as I recommend Lily to your care, did she charge me to watch over her two-weeks-old infant. Mrs. Purvis wished to take the child from me. She will be very angry now that her granddaughter should pass into your hands; but they never liked me, those haughty Purvises, and there is no love lost between us. I can forgive them for despising me as a low-born Scotchman, but I can not forget their persecution of Mary. But these are not proper words for the lips of one who must turn his thoughts to heavenly things."

A fit of coughing seized Mr. Vere, and the sound aroused Lily.

She opened her large blue eyes, slid down from Mr. Clarendon's arms, and, without bustle or noise, went to the table and prepared some medicine for her father. It was curious to see the tiny hands and grave little face so absorbed and quiet.

Mr. Vere swallowed what she gave him, and then, the paroxysm over, laid back upon his pillow exhausted and death-like.

Lily replaced the glass and snuffed the candle with the composure of a matron, and then, smoothing the bedclothes, took her stand at her father's side.

"You are a real little nurse, Elizabeth," said Mr. Clarendon, kindly.

"Dr. Barton said I might stay with papa all the time if I would be good, and not cry or make a noise," answered the child, with a sweet voice, full of tears.

"When I die, Lily, you will remember that I bid you love Mr. and Mrs. Clarendon, and look upon Willie, George, and Alicia as your brothers and sisters:" this was slowly and with difficulty pronounced by her father.

"Yes, papa." The large tears rolled down the child's face, and she shook with an inward tremor, but no sound escaped her: one small palm was closely locked in her father's, and she tried to find her handkerchief with the other. Deeply she dived into her little pocket: it was not there; so, lifting quietly the hem of her short white dress, she wiped away the scalding drops, and stood patiently and sadly, ever watchful and perfectly still.

So the hours wore away. Dr. Barton came, looked at his patient, patted Lily's head, advised her being sent to bed, but could only persuade her to resume the shawl and the place by her father; and at daylight the spirit of Andrew Vere passed from this earth.

🌰 CHAPTER II

"Who shall be queen?"

"Sara Purvis."

"Oh no! we must draw lots."

"Let the boys choose—let them vote for queen."

"No, indeed. This is a fair field, and we shall have no supremacy of men— in round jackets at that. We shall all vote," said Grace Meredith.

"Lily ought to be Queen of May. In her own house, too! And see how tall and stately Lily looks! Just like a queen, as she walks down the steps."

"Very well; Lily shall be queen, for all that I care," said Sara Purvis, curling her lip.

"Thank you, Sara," said Lily, advancing. "And precisely because it is in my own house I would rather not be queen, Nora."

"Nonsense," exclaimed George Clarendon. "Sara, you are always making a fuss. Here is my cap, and there is a sheet of paper and a pencil: each of you young ladies and young gentlemen, without distinction of petticoats or—or—etcs., write the name of any young lady you choose on a scrap of this paper, throw it in the cap, and when you have all voted, we will count the result, and, of course, majority takes it. The elected queen may have a king chosen by herself if she likes, and if she has any sense she will confer that honor on me."

"A King of May! what an absurdity!" cried Grace Meredith. "No, George, you shall be chief executioner to the queen, and cut off the heads of rebellious and revengeful subjects. Sara," she continued, maliciously, in a half whisper, "has so small a throat it will not be a troublesome case, any more than that other poor lady's of ancient days who wanted to be queen and was not popular enough."

George Clarendon, who enjoyed such thrusts at Lily's supercilious cousin, laughed out.

"Very well. I resign the office. 'Uneasy lies the head,' and so on. Now let us to business. Young ladies, if I might be permitted to suggest one caution: don't each of you write your own name. It may create confusion, and will certainly be found out. Miss Sara, can you write legibly?"

"George!" exclaimed Lily, laying her hand upon his arm, while her sweet blue eyes at once implored and commanded him to be quiet.

"Oh yes, Lily—oh yes, certainly. Miss Purvis, here is my pencil; you must begin."

Sara Purvis haughtily took the pencil and scribbled a name. She was too angry by this time to attempt to retort, and surely it was a wise part, unconsciously assumed, for she could not cope with her teasers. A prettier dunce did not adorn all Christendom.

The balloting went slowly on, for some wrote, and then changed their minds, and wrote again. The halfgrown boys, with all the fickleness of full-grown men, were even more capricious than the young girls, and countless ends of paper strewed the green turf before their decisions were fairly inscribed.

Meanwhile Lily, after depositing her vote, left the group to give some order in the house, soon returned, and, pausing on the threshold of the door, gazed around and about her.

Calm, beautiful, and luxuriant was the scene. The sun was just sinking. It was the last day of April, and the growth, the vegetation, the wide-spreading lands in their Southern loveliness smiled back at their fair mistress, as she, with a deep-drawn inspiration, thanked God for having bestowed upon her so much power for doing good and making others happy.

Chicora Wood was the name of this plantation. Chicora being the melodious Indian word for mocking-bird, and for these American nightingales every tree seemed as a colony. The house was spacious, built in a rambling, old-fashioned, disconnected manner—very comfortable, but very queer. There were curious little closets of all odd shapes, and a window projected here, and a piazza was added there, without much reference to any fixed plan. But the effect was not ugly, for glorious old oaks surrounded it, and the moss waved its gray banner over the gable ends, a fresh verdure covered the lawn, and beautiful baskets of osier, filled with roses and flowers of every sort, like huge fairy offerings, were scattered about wherever a vacant spot among the oaks gave sunshine enough to warrant their cultivation. Two fragrant beds of violets and mignonnette flanked either side of the broad stone steps, and a woodbine, with its brilliant red blossoms, climbed up the pillars of the piazza. Orangetrees, with their deep amber fruit, and here and there a lingering white flower spoke of poetry and bridal tokens; and far in the distance was seen the forest, now all green, and cool, and sombre. Turning her eyes in the opposite direction, Lily could perceive the gently flowing Peedee (not twenty yards from the house), her own rice-banks, the negroes coming in from their daily task; through a vista cut in the forest, the white gleaming cottages in which they lived; beyond, the barn, the mill, the poultry-yard, kitchen-garden, and other offices. From afar off came a murmur of life and work (but not of misery nor grinding care); in the empty rooms behind her, not a sound; on the lawn, beneath the largest and most venerable of the oaks, one known as the Traitor's Tree (from the tradition that on its branches during the Revolution a Loyalist spy had been hanged), laughed, jested, and frolicked her youthful guests, about fourteen in number.

Lily herself had just kept her fifteenth birth-day. She was well-grown for her years, and threatened to be a tall woman. She was not strictly handsome. Her mouth was large, her nose short, but her complexion was the most exquisite you can conceive; no pastil, which gives such softness, such brilliancy to its pictured beauties, would be exaggerating my heroine's skin. Her color was variable—tender, but always rich; and the mouth, as I before said, though large, was of the most beautiful carnation, and closed over teeth small, white, and even, like little seeds. The eyes were her decided feature; so deep, so blue, so clear, opening with that honest fearlessness so rarely seen, and differing essentially from a stare. You could never fancy Lily a coquette, "making eyes," as it is called. They were simply to her mind useful articles, kindly given her by that God to whom she was so grateful, for the purpose of seeing. If their lustrous mirror reflected faithfully the thoughts which filled her heart, it was by a process wholly unknown to herself; she merely looked through them. Her hair was no longer worn in childish style upon her white shoulders as when I first presented her to you in the last chapter. A rich roll of it was round about her head, and long, glossy, actually sparkling ringlets smoothly but carelessly framed her face. These glittering "prisoned sun-beams" were the only womanish sign of Lily's advancing years. Her dress was white, and simple in the extreme, gathered in at the throat and waist (which were slight, and girlish, and graceful) with statuesque plainness; her bare, still slender, but well-shaped arms displayed no bracelets, nor was there a ring or other sentimental signal upon her fingers.

Such was Lily: do you like her? Every one called her Lily; she preferred it; and what Lily liked was pretty sure to come to pass. Her father had now been dead nine years, and Mr. Clarendon had spared no pains to make his friend's loss as lightly felt by the daughter as Nature would allow. Lily's childhood had been very happy. Mrs. Clarendon was an excellent, worthy *Southern matron*. She was by no means an ornament to society, but she was a liberal, hard-working housekeeper. Her very soul was devoted to her husband; her children came next, then her house and household duties, finally her religion. She was a strict Churchman, relieved the poor, visited the sick—when she had the time—and tried not to believe the gossip that her old cronies whispered after morning service, or during a very occasional tea-drinking. Though she had been quite a belle, and Mr. Clarendon had carried her off from many competitors, no one would have believed it, she was so plain and fusty now. The pretty, delicate features were embrowned by exposure to the sun; the hands were hardened by washing up cups and dusting shelves; and the once rounded figure had quite disappeared, refusing, I suppose, to stay where it was so put upon by ill-made gowns. The children had been sent to good schools chosen by the head of the family, and Mrs. Clarendon had always been careful about their lunch, and that the doily which enveloped each child's portion should be clean, and should be regularly brought back every day. They were very fond of her, and though, of course, each year separated their pursuits and pleasures more and more from hers, and though they already began to feel and see that her views of life did not march with the progress of time, and that, consequently, her judgment could not be entirely relied upon, still her ear was always open to their wants and wishes, and her heart never was closed against their incursions. But the time was approaching for a more active exercise of her affection. Good waffles, excellent corn-bread, and well-mended clothes were all admirable in their way; but the moment had arrived for sympathy. Willie, when he returned for his first college vacation, and began to entertain manly views about society, said one day,

"Mamma, what will you do when Alicia is grown up? You will surely go to balls and pay visits with her?"

Mrs. Clarendon, who had not found herself in a ballroom since the winter she was married, shuddered at the very thought.

"Why, William, I should not know what to do with myself. Mrs. Purvis has long since promised to bring Lily out, and I suppose she won't mind taking Alicia too. One of you boys can always look after your sister, and our own carriage would bring the girls home without ever troubling Lily's aunt."

"But, mamma, you will never know who associates with the girls; you can never become acquainted with their acquaintances; and I have seen so many bad effects from young ladies not having their mothers with them when they are from home—some one who can speak openly and fearlessly when a girl is going too far," and Willie pulled up his cravat like a dandy who might relate adventures to point his remarks. "Besides," he went on, "in Europe, you know, girls never are seen without their mother, or some especially and carefully appointed chaperon."

"My dear boy," cried his mother, quite shocked, "don't speak to me of European women, who leave their own homes to go gadding about as if they had neither homes nor husbands. And my girls are too well brought up, I hope, to need watching. You ought not to speak so before them. Ask your father if he would like to see me out all the morning paying visits to people I don't care a straw about, and dressing myself up at night just at the time when I ought to be going to my bed. No, indeed; a pretty-looking goose I should be, and a nice house I would have, with every servant gone to rack and ruin, while I was coursing round the town with Lily and Alicia. How should I be up in the morning at seven o'clock to see about breakfast, when I got home at one or two? Nonsense, child! you give me a fever to hear you talk."

"Could you not have a housekeeper, mamma, to see about breakfast at that hour? You have always had more servants about the establishment than you knew what to do with, and yet you are always hard at work doing their business."

Mrs. Clarendon laid down the coarse seam on which she was diligently sewing:

"My dear son, where have you got these ideas? Do I look as if I would neglect my duties for parties and visitings? Do I look as if I would give up my time to the world instead of to my family? You surprise me."

Willie might have answered that, in this case, she did neglect her duties; that any woman who fancies that by leaving her young daughters to enter upon the stage of grown-up life without the watchful guard of a parent's eye and presence, is casting away a privilege and disregarding an urgent necessity; that there can be no comparison between the relative claims of scrubbing, scolding, and housekeeping, and the care of one's child; but Willie merely shrugged his shoulders, gave up the contest, invited Lily (who was then twelve, and Alicia a few months younger) to take a ride with him, and went whistling off to order the horses, while Mrs. Clarendon resumed her sewing, and wondered why boys were so foolish.

Mr. Clarendon was a capital planter, an experienced man of business, but had neither literary tastes nor more fondness for society than his wife. He liked a game of whist; he sometimes gave dinners to men, at which Mrs. Clarendon presided (outwardly smiling and inwardly chafing at a bore which, for her husband's sake, she did not shirk), and from which, so soon as the wine began to circulate after the cloth was removed, she hurriedly retired "to the children," and was seen no more. He frequented a summer club, and was a first-rate judge of cattle, horses included.

A portion of the winters was spent in the country; the entire summers in the city. Mrs. Clarendon might have gone north, or she might have traveled in Europe, for her husband was unfailingly indulgent, but she hated to move; and then the servants, "they get so spoiled when you leave them! and as for hiring out my servants, my dear friend," this model lady would say to her confidantes, "*that* is out of the question."

She could not love Lily quite as she did her own children, but she was as devoted to her as any one could expect; and the little orphan was tenderly attached to all her guardian's family. Mrs. Clarendon was a timid woman in some things, and Lily's matter-of-fact, straightforward manner used to startle her. Lily had such a way of putting aside trifles and narrow prejudices. Her heart was so large, so open, and her charity, even at an early age, was so discriminating. When I say charity, I speak in its broad, Bible sense. I do not speak of the mere giving of alms, but that charity which "seeketh not her own; thinketh no evil, hopeth all things, endureth all things, and envieth not."

I do not know if I quote correctly; many of us, besides, can give the letters of the words, but ignore utterly their spirit.

As an instance of how Lily practiced charity, she was sitting one day in the drawing-room beside Mrs. Clarendon, learning to darn stockings, while the latter lady was receiving the visit of a friend high in the Church. The conversation turned very soon upon a young girl noted for her imprudences, and whose sayings and doings were liberally reported. At the close of each anecdote, both ladies would exclaim,

"But, after all, I don't believe that." Little Lily listened attentively. At length, raising her eyes with meek wonder, while a rising blush betrayed her modest daring,

"Why, then, ma'am, if you don't believe it, do you repeat it? It must do Miss Jones great harm to have these things said of her."

Mrs. Clarendon, quite taken aback, was infinitely shocked at Lily's reproof, but, being at heart a good woman, she felt the justice of it, while she blamed her ward for bringing her elders to task.

Mrs. Meredith, the visitor, was not difficult to appease. The heiress, Miss Vere, had a right to speak; and, though she could not promise, either by word or thought, to forego the dear pleasure of picking a rash girl's reputation into holes, still she was so impressed by Lily's speech that she determined to encourage a farther intimacy between her own daughter Grace and the little stocking-darner.

Thus developing in beauty as well as in excellence, Lily's childhood passed away. She had no airs, no pretensions. If she led, it was by the force of her sweet temper, her unwavering truth, and her indomitable courage to pursue the right. She had very little cleverness, no brilliancy. Industrious and diligent, she acquired with difficulty, but retained what she learned. Alicia Clarendon got through her lessons in half the time, but next week Lily could repeat hers, while Alicia's task was quite forgotten.

I have left my heroine too long, however, on the wide stone steps of Chicora Hall; so, after telling you that, by her desire, the family always spent the month of April on this beautiful plantation, which had been her father's favorite, and that on this occasion they had invited a large number of young people to accompany them, I will return to her as she now is.

🏵 CHAPTER III

"Come on, Lily!" shouted George Clarendon, impatiently. "Don't stand like a statue on the steps there. We have all voted at last, and are now going to see the result."

The contents of the cap were investigated, and George, self-appointed poll-keeper, counted the number of heads present to see if the slips of paper tallied with the company.

"How many of us are there?" he asked. "Grace Meredith, one; Miss Leonora Tracy, two; Miss Ella and Miss Kate Jennings, four; Miss Sara Purvis, five (in her own opinion, ten," he muttered aside to his ally Grace)— "five," he continued; "Miss Marguerite Melbourne, six; Miss Julia Melbourne, seven; and you, Lily, make eight young ladies in all. For the gentlemen: three in *tail-coats*, i.e., Clarence Tracy, William Jennings, and Gustavus Purvis; and in the round jackets, which Grace Meredith, still in petticoats above her ankles, despises, I think we are four: John and Edward Carroll, Charley Purvis, and myself."

"Which make," put in Clarence Tracy, "fifteen."

"Just so; and here are fifteen votes. All right. Nobody has cheated, so far."

The little papers were unfolded, and proclaimed "Lily Vere" to have the majority. Sara Purvis looked disgusted.

"Have you counted right, George?" asked Lily.

"Yes, my dear: ten votes for you, three for Miss Purvis, and two for Miss Marguerite."

"My dear Lily," whispered Grace, "nobody wanted Sara for queen except Bill Jennings, yourself, and herself. I would not be dependent on her humors for half an hour. We should expire to be obliged to 'follow her leader' during the whole of to-morrow."

"I shall only consent to be queen on condition that I choose my own crowner. May I do that?" inquired Lily.

"Yes, yes; I suppose you may be permitted that privilege, although it is out of May-day rule."

"Then I choose Sara Purvis," said Lily, kindly taking her cousin's hand, whose beautiful features were overclouded by a deep shade of ill-temper.

Sara reluctantly smiled, and thanked Lily with indifferent grace; but Gustavus, her elder brother, made some warning remark in her ear, and she gradually cooled down.

The gay group now began discussing the spot on which to erect the throne.

Marguerite Melbourne, a sensible, pleasant girl of about Lily's own age, suggested the very oak under which they stood.

"It has so long been known only in connection with that unfortunate martyrized spy, that, grand as it is, it ought to receive a newer baptism, and be henceforward *our* 'royal oak.'"

The suggestion was adopted without dispute, and the boys began to clear away the dead leaves around the roots, so as to prepare a living carpet of pure green for the ceremony.

"How anxious Alicia will be to know the result of the election," said Kate Jennings.

"Yes, poor child!" said Julia Melbourne; "she would much have preferred staying with us at home to taking a ride with that solemn Mr. Langdon."

"Why don't Angel ride with her own betrothed?" asked Ella Jennings; "eh, Sara?"

"Because," interrupted Grace, "Angelica doesn't choose to be so selfish as to keep all her happiness to herself."

"Because," said Lily, "Angel does not know the road to the Pineland settlement, which Alicia has so often traveled, and which Mr. Langdon wished to visit."

"Then why did not Angel go along with them?" persevered Ella Jennings, who was fond of a little malice.

"Because," again pursued Lily, "she can only ride Alicia's pony, being timid on horseback; consequently, my uncle" (this was the name she gave Mr. Clarendon) "bade Alicia go with our guest alone."

"And where is Angelica?" inquired Gustavus.

"Speak of the devil, and an angel appears," exclaimed George.

At this instant a young lady advanced from the house with a book in her hand, and approached the party. She was a very peculiar-looking person. At the first glance you thought her plain, she was so sallow, and the lower part of her face was heavy and coarse, but a nearer inspection brought to light undeniable beauties. Her eyes were very large and deep set, with thick black lashes, which lay in a massive fringe upon her cheek, and through their dark curtain they sent forth fitful rays of dazzling brilliancy, or else of still more dangerous softness. Her hair was intensely black, kept with the greatest neatness, and so glossy, that its large bandeaux, which adorned each side of a broad, moderately high forehead, shone like polished jet, and were as smooth and unwrinkled. Her dress of rose-colored barege, with wide and flowing flounces, set off a figure of the most voluptuous proportions, and the sallowness of her face was undistinguishable in the dead whiteness of a pair of arms exquisitely moulded, and a bust and shoulders of corresponding perfection. Over her head she had thrown a long gossamer scarf of white lamb's-wool, through which gleamed the profuse braids of hair at the back, and which rested like a fleecy cloud around her face, and was wound gracefully about her person. Altogether she was very striking; and besides, the nose and mouth, which I mention as heavy, were of the same cast as

Lily's, only the expression was so different that the likeness was not percepti-ble at a casual glance. This was Miss Angelica Purvis, or, rather, Miss Purvis par excellence. She was the eldest daughter of Lily's mother's brother, and, consequently, a first cousin of my heroine.

Mr. Clarendon had not rejected the overtures made by Mrs. Vere's family to his orphan ward. He permitted no interference in her concerns, either personal or pecuniary, but he rather encouraged a friendly feeling from the very beginning. The Purvises were constant guests at his house, especially since the death of the old lady, May Vere's mother, who had been a mar-velously disagreeable and exacting individual. They were none of them very conciliatory or particularly congenial companions. Mrs. Purvis was a had-been beauty, with weaknesses, vapors, and a morphine bottle; Mr. Purvis was ostentatious, purse-proud, and stingy; Angelica's character I shall leave to develop itself; Sara has already shown a few touches of her peculiarities; Gustavus was a well-meaning, gentlemanly lad of eighteen, two years older than Sara, and two years younger than Angel; and Charley was a quiet, plain-featured boy of fifteen. But Mr. Clarendon, standing in the position, by her father's will, that he did to Lily (next heir, to the exclusion of her relatives), thought it most prudent and generous to give them a chance of knowing and being appreciated by the young heiress. It was thought by the world generally that Gustavus was to recommend himself to Lily, and many were the scolds that the otherwise spoiled Sara received from her parents touching her behavior to her cousin.

"Well, jeunesse!" cried Angel, "have you elected your queen?"

"Yes; Lily is Queen of the May."

"Lily! Ah! that is right!" and Angelica kissed Lily condescendingly on the forehead. "What are you all doing now? Is that gnarled trunk of the old oak to serve as a throne?"

"Yes; it will be wreathed with flowers and moss. If Alicia were here," added Grace, significantly, "she could go, before the sun sets, to find us some beautiful party-colored leaves which she spoke of, and which we could keep fresh till to-morrow."

"No doubt," said Angel, composedly; "but I fear Mr. Langdon finds Alicia so entertaining that he will not be inclined to let her shorten her ride. I wish that Willie were at home. I wonder if he could enjoy this calm scene and Lily's royalty instead of his present European views?"

"Willie's absence is voluntary," remarked Grace.

"Dear Willie!" said Angel, sentimentally: "it is now so many years that we have been intimate with these two families, and with Lily as a sweet connecting link, I always forget that we are not relations, and I love Willie as if he were my brother."

"If you don't love him more than you do Charley, Angel," called out George, who was hard at work, "I don't think he need hurry home to live on your affection."

"Poor Charley!" exclaimed the young lady, smiling, and patting his close-curled red hair with the ends of her fair fingers; then turning to Clarence Tracy, who had sidled up to her, and was looking over the book she held, "Master Clarence," she continued, coquettishly, "do you wish to take me a row on the river?"

Lily, who had not moved away from her cousin, blushed and started slightly.

Angelica perceived it, and winding one of Lily's long gold ringlets around her wrist, where it shone like a bracelet,

"Let us go to Dr. Hatton's plantation, Lily's next door neighbor, and beg some roses for our beauteous queen."

Clarence Tracy was the oldest of the juvenile group. He was nineteen, very clever, had already distinguished himself by being "first honor man" at his late graduation, and was the only son of a once rich but now impoverished family. He and his sister Leonora were orphans. Nora lived entirely with a maiden aunt, and was a sweet-tempered, enthusiastic admirer of Lily's perfections. Since she was twelve years old, a grave friendship had subsisted between Miss Vere and Mr. Clarence Tracy. While he was at college, in every letter to Nora there was mention of Miss Lily. He sent her regularly the "Nassau Monthly," which was the Princeton receptacle for the overflowing genius of those hard-working students; and on his final return, after a hurried embrace of his aunt and sister, he flew to receive the congratulations of his cherished friend, the staid little school-girl.

Mr. Clarendon never noticed the intimacy at all. Clarence was the son of an old friend, and it was natural he should come to the house. Mrs. Clarendon thought them mere boy and girl, and there was the end of it.

"Oh, Clarence, don't go off!" cried his sister; "you ought to begin to write Lily's address. This business has been got up in such haste! We have so little time. And Mrs. Hatton is very precious of her flowers."

"Don't keep him, Nora," said Lily, gently. "If you wish to row with Angel, Clarence, you had better go at once," but her eyes said plainly "don't."

Clarence wavered, and William Jennings offered his services.

"It does not matter," Angelica murmured, her white teeth just visible in a half smile which parted her full red lips, and she glanced sideways at

Clarence; "I interfere with nobody, I hope; and I did not know that it was poaching on my neighbor's manor to ask for a few roses."

She hummed a tune and walked away, her dress caught up with one hand to protect it from the stray leaves, her deeply-embroidered petticoat sweeping the ground, and her little feet, so daintily laced in their tiny brown boots, "peeping out," as she moved with a firm, elastic, but undulating tread across the lawn. She was so stylish, and carried herself with such an air, Clarence thought she must look like those dangerous Andalusians of whom he had read and thought so much. How pleasant it would be to float down the river in such delicious company, with a young May moon to light them back, and snatches of song warbled by Mr. Langdon's fiancée!

Heavens!

"I sha'n't be long," he exclaimed; "Miss Purvis can't go alone," and off he darted.

George shrugged his shoulders; some of them were indignant at the desertion, and this time Lily made no excuses for her cousin.

CHAPTER IV

Presently two men-servants began to prepare the tea-table in the piazza. The weather was so warm, and the nights so beautiful, that the young people had for the last week petitioned Mrs. Clarendon not to immure them more than was possible in the house, so that recently they had been taking their evening meal only protected by the sloping roof of the piazza and the clustering vines which encircled its pillars.

Two more footmen, by Lily's order, placed under the royal tree a large rustic chair, and some benches which had been originally installed in other parts of the grounds; and by the time that these preparations were completed, the carriage was seen approaching through the great gate in the distance, meekly followed by Alicia and Mr. Langdon, who had come up to them a few moments before.

In the carriage were Mrs. Clarendon, and Mr. and Mrs. Purvis.

They stopped in front of the oak, and Mrs. Clarendon and Mr. Purvis, by their united efforts, dislodged from amid her pillows and disentangled from her shawls the wife of the latter, who sank in her usual state of syncope upon Lily's destined throne.

"Sara, dear, how flushed and burned you are!" were her first languid words. "My dear friend," to Mrs. Clarendon, "I really can not undertake such a severe drive again. I am quite *épuisée*."

"Did you invite every body, ma'am?" inquired Lily of Mrs. Clarendon.

"Oh, every soul," murmured Mrs. Purvis, who, in spite of her weak state, always did more talking than any body else; "we have driven round the whole neighborhood, and I believe fifty people will be here to-morrow, so that the queen, whoever she is, will have a crowd to face."

"Who is queen?" demanded Alicia, eagerly, as she sprang from her horse, scarcely touching Mr. Langdon's offered hand. She appeared to have had enough of his society already.

The answer delighted her.

"You will look the queen so nicely, Lily!"

"Has Angelica been seen?" again prattled Mrs. Purvis.

"She has gone rowing with Clarence Tracy," answered George.

Mr. Langdon's brow darkened.

"I thought Miss Purvis had a headache; I was informed—"

"Oh dear me!" ejaculated Mrs. Purvis, "there is such a breeze blowing up, I must go into the house. Mr. Langdon, might I trouble you for your arm? Mr. Purvis—where is Mr. Purvis? He is always going off. William Jennings, do come on this side. Never mind, Gustavus, stay here and help Lily and the girls. Lily, love, just arrange my shawl. Julia, my handkerchief; thank you— that's all. Don't stay out too late; the dew is very unwholesome;" and, amid a general confusion, the invalid got under way for her journey of twenty yards.

The tea-urn was sending up clouds of steam, and Mrs. Clarendon was dispensing cups of the strongest fragrance, when Angelica and Clarence sauntered in, their hands full of flowers.

"I trust your head is better," said Mr. Langdon, sharply.

"Much better," answered Angel, sweetly; and, depositing her bouquets on one of the window-sills, which "gaze," as our French friends say, into the drawing-room, she removed her scarf, and asked for a cup of tea.

"Not too much sugar, dear Mrs. Clarendon. I like a little sourness some-times; it 'tells' in the midst of the profusion of sweets which your bountiful housekeeping spreads before us."

She looked very handsome. The lamps were lit in the drawing-room, and joined their brilliancy, shining through the open casements and muslin curtains, to the moon's pale radiance, which shed so picturesque a light upon the landscape and the party. Her complexion, not now exposed to those terribly unflattering sun's rays, was creamy white; she could do what few women accomplish—eat well, and with perfect grace helped herself to various good things which abundantly covered the table.

"Where is mamma?" she asked, balancing a spoonful of strawberries and cream half way between her lips and the saucer.

"Quite overcome by her drive, and gone to her room."

"Poor mamma exerts herself unnecessarily."

"There is her supper-tray; that will bring her up," remarked George, as a smartly-dressed colored woman drawled out to one of the attendant waiters,

"Missis wants a little of ebery ting."

Meanwhile, as this was even a more informal meal than breakfast, most of the girls had carried off their plates to different ends of the piazza, and, in the lingering twilight, were laughing, jesting, sending their boy cavaliers on errands for extra cakes, and making the rafters ring from time to time with their joyous peals.

Sara, who was rather a gourmand, always grew better tempered when eating, so that now she and William Jennings, her warm admirer, sat peaceably together, chatting about a last winter's juvenile fancy ball, and disposing of piles of thin bread and butter and sweetmeats.

Lily was seated on the top step of the piazza, leaning her head against the pillar behind her, with her pure fair brow raised to the sky, and bathing itself in the moon's rays. A great Newfoundland dog lay at her feet, every now and then thrusting his black nose into her hand, or raising himself on his front paws to a level with her face, and gazing earnestly, with wagging tail, as if he meant presently to say something.

What were Lily's thoughts? She could not quite read them herself. She feared Angel was a coquette; and she had noticed for days that Clarence, her friend, her own especial friend, was fond of watching the varied play of Angelica's peculiar countenance; but what then? She could not be jealous of his admiring Angel, and Angel was almost a married woman. Still, why were they now so much together? And yesterday morning, when she had asked a dozen times for Clarence, to give him a book they were to study together, without being able to find him, at last he was discovered in the little darkened boudoir, reading Moore's Loves of the Angels to the future Mrs. Langdon, who was half lying on the sofa, with those deep black eyes partly closed, and her taper fingers listlessly pulling a rose to pieces. Lily did not understand, though, why this should distress her, or make her uncomfortable. It was surely very unreasonable and selfish to require that Clarence should give his whole time to herself. He was four years older than she, and so much more clever, it was very kind of him to devote so many hours as he still did to a comparative little girl. Angel was accomplished and interesting. It was flattering that she should notice a boy, for Angel was very fastidious; and—why soon she would be married, and go to her New York home, and Clarence— Here an involuntary sigh interrupted Lily's train of thought, and Burleigh's cold nose touched her cheek.

She roused herself, patted his long, silky coat, and begged his pardon for forgetting him.

"Burleigh is hungry, Lily, if you are not," said Clarence Tracy, seating himself beside her. "I have brought him some cake, and a cold chicken patty. Won't you eat something? Let me get you some strawberries—a cup of tea?" and he put Burleigh's plate down, and rose again.

"No, I thank you, Clarence. Get your own supper, and I will feed Burleigh myself. Aunt would be horrified if she saw you offering the finest old china in the house to Bur's paws." Her tone was light again, her heart beat more regularly.

Clarence did her bidding, and soon hastened back. While he drank his tea, Lily fed her dog. Often Burleigh's teeth grazed the little white fingers which presented the cake, and she, with the child-like playfulness she rarely exhibited, scolded Burleigh for his greediness, pulled his ears, and then, suddenly repenting of her make-believe harshness, threw her slender arms around him, and gathered his rough head to her bosom.

"Isn't your cousin a flirt?" exclaimed Clarence, presently, with the utmost nonchalance, and a slight laugh.

Lily looked quickly at him.

"It is her vocation," he went on. "I believe she would flirt with me to keep her hand in, rather than be quiet. Look at her now. After getting up a headache to block off Mr. Langdon, when she finds that he is really angry, see how dexterously she is bringing him round!"

Lily's kind nature had resumed its sway. No sooner did another judge harshly than her better self regretted a severe thought, and she inwardly blamed the injustice of her late suspicions. Had she the faintest idea that her friend's indifferent and fault-finding tone strengthened her own good resolve not to pass stricture so hastily again?

"Look at her, Lily!" pursued Clarence. "I wonder if you will ever learn to use your eyes in the way that your cousin does execution. How her tricks amuse me! Now she is singing."

Sure enough, Angel was at the piano between the two windows, and her highly-cultivated and melodious voice gave exquisite effect to a sentimental French *romance*. In her shining black hair she had carefully placed a branch of some drooping wild flower, and Mr. Langdon, leaning through the window, with his harsh features relaxed, was listening, while her whole battery of charms was brought to bear upon his already badly-protected heart.

"Clarence," answered honest Lily, "I do not like your words and your actions to be so much at variance. If you seek Angelica's society, it must be because you admire her, and if you admire her, why conceal it? Moreover, to my mind, there is something dis—not right, in allowing people to suppose that they please you, while behind their backs you cavil at their manners and conduct."

"What a little Mentor it is!" said Clarence, jestingly; but he was young enough still to show a slight flush of shame. "You do not understand Miss Purvis. She does not ask or require the respect and consideration of any man; she demands only their admiration."

"I will not listen to you," said Lily, gravely; and she was about to rise, when Clarence caught her hand and detained her.

"Don't let us quarrel about this, Lily. I shall never say another word against Miss Purvis, if you dislike it."

"It is your thoughts more than your words—your opinion more than your conduct, which distress me. To have gone off this afternoon when we wished you to stay, merely for the purpose of amusing yourself with watching Angel's 'tricks,' was scarcely unselfish. When I thought that you preferred her society to mine—to ours, I mean, I was foolish enough to be put out about it," and the girl's fair cheek was slightly tinged; "but, now that I find that you went only to study her, and to sneer at her foibles, I am really sorry."

Ah! good, but unsophisticated Lily! you never suspected that Angel had whispered to her tractable pupil just after her entrance,

"You to your dove, I to my bear. Both are sulky. I give you leave to abuse me by way of reconciliation."

"Come, come, Lily, I am only jesting. This is almost a first cloud between us. Let us shake hands, and you shall teach me to be as good and wise as your little self, and to think as well of all the world."

Clarence's tone was frank, and there was a great deal of earnestness in the dark eyes which he bent upon hers; so much that she never dreamed of reading the different tale which his thin, sarcastic lips betrayed.

"*I* can not teach you to think well of any one, dear Clarence; but, at least, we all know that, if we have nothing pleasant to say about people, it is kinder to say nothing at all. And that is so easy, we surely deserve no credit for simply holding our tongues, do we?"

The truthful, calm, clear blue eyes, unsullied by a single vicious thought, returned the false rays of Clarence's.

"We are waiting for you, Lily."

"My dear Elizabeth," said Mrs. Clarendon, "come out of the night air. When I was a girl—"

"Yes, aunt."

And, springing joyously up, the whole party adjourned to the drawing-room, where they discussed the final arrangements for the next day; and Grace Meredith, the poetess, and Clarence Tracy, the famous prose writer, were set down to concoct the speeches and addresses of the queen and her court.

CHAPTER V

Brightly rose the May-day sun, and much earlier than they were accustomed to welcome its first beams the young people were astir.

Very soon the garden was rifled of its treasures; the wicker baskets which adorned the lawn were carefully shorn of some of their glowing blossoms, and a party proceeded even into the depths of the woods to gather wild flowers. The shadiest side of the piazza looked as if a flower-storm had passed over it, such piles of gaudy and beautiful leaves and petals strewed the floor.

The breakfast-bell rang; the horticulturists reluctantly left their perfumed task, and turned their attention for a little while to a more substantial repast.

Angel, always late, sauntered in, with her dreamy eyes and white skirts, and heard, with affected surprise, from Sara that they had all been up for hours.

"Then, as you have been 'breathing sweets' so long, none of you need breakfast. Don't you all believe in the 'Islands of Pleasure,' where people feast and have surfeits on perfumes? So, Charley, give me that bun;" and Angel carried off from beneath Charley's hungry eyes an appetizing morsel, to which he was about to help himself.

Mrs. Clarendon was getting fidgety. She wished her guests to leave the dining-room free for her housekeeping operations; but Angel dawdled, and Mr. Langdon wished still another cup of tea. Mrs. Purvis's maid came for more chocolate for her mistress, and George begged that he might have a third "helping" of coffee.

"I have been so hard at work, mamma, I am as tired as Mr. Conway's negroes, who never have any rest, and he gives them half a fish. Think what a mean man, mamma, to cut a fish in half for 'allowance!'

Mr. Purvis glanced uneasily at his destined son-in-law when George made this revelation, and began to disclaim the fact.

"Indeed but he does," said George, swallowing his coffee with eager haste, "and he has a horrid beast of an overseer, who is as bad as himself."

"My dear George," said Mr. Purvis, pompously, "our negroes at the South are as well fed and as well treated as it is possible to conceive. Instances are rare of unkindness or neglect; they are, in fact, happier than any body of people in the known world. They—"

"Excuse the interruption, Purvis," broke in Mr. Clarendon, with a smile; "don't 'talk for Buncombe.' There are many cases of bad masters, just as there are many instances of bad fathers; but we should scarcely argue for the necessity of doing away with parental control. Newspapers constantly bring to light horrid tales of ill-used apprentices: do Christian parents of the lower orders consequently refuse to bind their children to trades? And is an unkind father, or a harsh and cruel blacksmith, carpenter, or other mechanic, taken as a type of their class? As for the peculiar happiness of the negro race, I believe it is an understood thing that not one human being was placed in this world to enjoy happiness, but I know that they have as much contentment in a general way and in their way as we have."

"You forget that strangers with prejudices, and who look at the gloomiest side—"

"Strangers with prejudices come with their opinions, and, for the most part, leave us with these same opinions, just as we go to listen to political views given by our opponents, without the least intention of shaking their original faith. We are curious to hear, they are curious to see; but if we applaud the eloquence of the speaker, and appear temporarily impressed, it is only for the moment. We change when interest or when personal conviction demands it, not sooner."

"But do not you really think that intelligent men who are inimical to our institutions are often brought to a different conclusion by a personal inspection of our system?"

"I do not. Their views may be mollified, but hardly can we expect more than that. Besides, I entirely agree with a certain clever woman, herself a Northerner, who says that any abolitionist wishing to visit us ought to be forced, if he come at all, to stay at least a year in our midst; for a superficial insight, for the most part, only strengthens his belief. It can not graze even the outer coating of human conceit. It is interest which is the great lever to move the weightiest judgment on this point. I will give you a sum, Purvis, for your 'prejudiced friends' to make out. Given the fortune of my little Alicia, with her bright eyes thrown in, and in how many seconds would a 'prejudiced friend' discover that slavery was not so great an evil? unless, indeed, I consented that she should sell out, and invest 'the price of flesh and blood' in wholesome, healthy Northern bonds."

Lily had stolen round to her guardian's chair, and now murmured a word in his ear.

"I beg your pardon, Mr. Langdon. I forgot that probably you have prejudices, and, in fact, if I remembered it at first, it escaped me before I finished speaking. Besides, I am doing what I always condemn. There is no need for us to defend the justice of our position, and nothing gives our enemies a greater advantage than to discuss and argue the propriety of what exists and will exist. Weak writers on the popular topic are the present curse of this country's feeble literature."

"I wish, Mr. Clarendon, that you would finish all this talk in the piazza."

"My dear, it is finished already," and every one rose en masse.

"Mr. Clarendon no doubt fears that some bloodthirsty New Yorker may snap up more than Alicia," sneered Angelica; "you, Lily, will be a great mark for fortune-hunters in a year or two."

"I!" exclaimed Lily, coloring; "ah! Angel, I would rather die than marry a man who sought me for my 'houses and lands.'" She paused; her slight figure dilated: "How foolish, at my age, to talk of marriage! but still, let the man beware who, when I am older, proves to me, however faintly, that my dollars and cents are my attraction! Angel, I should be without mercy."

"Bless the child!" said Angel, affectedly; "how very energetic!"

Lily's passion vanished. She glanced unconsciously toward Clarence, and, with a sweet laugh, said,

"You must think me very absurd, cousin."

"No, my dear, only melodramatic."

"I wish to explain," said the girl, coloring still more deeply. "People are constantly talking in a foolish way to me about my fortune, and prophesying an early wedding, and I dislike the idea so much, it really angers me when I hear it, and irritates me more than such a trifle should. If I ever marry, I trust I shall be as fortunate in one respect as you, Angel—that the man of my choice may love me as sincerely as Mr. Langdon loves you."

Angelica's lip curled, and her eyes shot a glance of fierce scorn.

"Thank you: you appear to have thought a good deal on the subject;" and then, resuming her usual softness, "Is this the topic which Mr. Clarence Tracy and you find so interesting? And when does he have his reward?"

Lily was hurt; the tears started to her eyes, and the sight of them touched the not entirely seared heart of her friend.

"You take Lily at a disadvantage, Miss Purvis; you profit by your years and experience to mortify her. Why not direct her with your taste, judgment, and admirable tact, instead of crushing her by your sarcasm?"

"Why not make wreaths, young gentleman, and not speeches?" replied Angel, haughtily; and she waved her white hand toward the busy group among the flowers; "that better suits *your* years," and she swept away. Burleigh jumped to catch her. "Down, Burleigh!" she exclaimed, striking at him: "school-boys and dogs should be kept in their places."

"Here, Burleigh, come here, sir!" said Lily, as she rejoined her guests and beckoned to Clarence.

"Confounded coquette!" muttered Clarence, as he followed her.

A note of preparation now rang through the house.

Mrs. Clarendon had her hands full of keys, her apron dusted with flour, and her eyes every where. Maum Nelly, her chief captain, was superintending the beating of eggs and boiling of custards. Yesterday's cakes, all dressed with oldfashioned pastry grandeur—gold leaf and colored sugar— were Maum Nelly's delight and pride. She had arranged them in a glorious row on the pastry-room dresser, and took in her favorites, singly and mysteriously, to gaze (without touching) at them.

"Oh, Maum Nelly!" cried impudent Alicia, "they look just like a nigger wedding! That is not the way cakes are ornamented now."

Maum Nelly, too indignant to reply, took Alicia by the shoulders and turned her out, without offering her either a "Shrewsbury" or a "jumble," which had been her token of approbation to the others.

The number of these large fruit-cakes would have puzzled a Northerner, who might have fancied that nothing but a nuptial festival, and the necessity for filling white boxes according to the list of the guests, could have required such pounds and pounds of frosted unwholesomeness; but it is a peculiarity of South Carolina housekeepers of a primitive date that no provision is so important as these cakes.

A Boston lady, who came once to visit a sister married in Charleston, was amazingly struck by these countless pyramids, rounds, and gigantic hearts. When the time arrived for a ball to be given by them, she begged solemnly that one favor might be granted to her.

"Pray, my dear Sarah," she said, "don't have any fruit-cakes. I have already seen enough of them at two parties to last my lifetime."

Mrs. Clarendon never could have been brought to this. She would have refused, no matter how urgently entreated; for she would have considered her guests as defrauded of a just privilege. Accordingly, when, the day before, Lily decided upon this May-day festival, the first idea which immediately struck Mrs. Clarendon was the cakes.

In hot haste, citron, raisins, and currants were sliced, stoned, and washed, and the result shows itself in these wonderful performances, which Alicia, unworthy scion of so painstaking a mamma, declined commending.

The gentlemen wandered about, at the mill and over the river; then Mr. Clarendon went to write letters for the post (for post-day must never be interfered with); Mr. Purvis buried himself in a book on "Political Economy," yawned, and went to sleep; and Mr. Langdon tried to amuse his idol, who was snappish and impracticable.

The boys and girls were busy decking the throne, and making wreaths and bouquets. Every tub which could be begged or stolen from the washer-woman, throughout the establishment, was in requisition to keep the flowers fresh, and the clatter of tongues rose louder and louder.

"Sara, do you know your address?" asked Grace Meredith; "as it is my production, I wish the delivery to equal the beauty of the lines."

"And, Lily, are you perfect in your recitation?" inquired Clarence.

Both young ladies were doubtful, so they were immediately required to go off to a private rehearsal.

Ella Jennings assisted with her taste and theatrical judgment. Many were the discussions and fault-findings.

"Lily, don't be stiff."

"Sara, be more animated."

"Oh dear!" cried Lily, "I do wish Grace were queen."

"Yes, it would just suit me," answered her lively friend; "but I trust my crowner would offer the symbol of royalty to her gracious, graceful, graceless majesty of a Grace with suitable ditto, or else I should seize my crown à la Napoleon, and put it on without waiting for Sara's drawl. Wake up, Sara, *do!*"

"Lily, dear," called out Mrs. Clarendon from the adjacent pantry, "do you wish the oldest wine drawn?" and off darted the youthful queen, thankful of escape, and promising to do better.

At two o'clock a hasty lunch was served; at four commenced the toilet of the ladies.

At six, carriages began to drive up, and Mrs. Clarendon, in much haste and a black silk gown, received the guests. Mrs. Purvis was radiant in pearl-powder, billows of costly lace, and altogether a costume of such united juvenility and magnificence that the quiet sojourners on the banks of the Peedee River looked at her with never-ending surprise.

"What a remarkable lady Mrs. Purvis is!" said Mrs. Hatton to Mrs. Adderly. "It must be her visits to Paris which make her dress up in that style."

"She is old enough to know better," said Mrs. Adderly to Mrs. Hatton; "and she is the most stuck-up piece of affectation I ever saw."

There was quite a crowd, as Mrs. Purvis had predicted. No engagements are apt to interfere with invitations given even at such short notice; if a shower had threatened, the house would have been empty, no matter if you had prepared yourself and your guests for a month previous; but a fine, bright, cloudless afternoon, with a moon in prospect, insured a full attendance.

❧ CHAPTER VI

None of the younger portion of the ladies residing in the house appeared before the time for the *pageant*. They wished their costumes and their little theatrical flourish to be a novelty altogether. Grace Meredith was the instigator. She had been anxious for weeks to get up the affair, and now she bewildered her quieter companions by a constant change of programme, and her incessant introduction of some new feature.

She even tried to impress Miss Purvis into the band; but, though a few adroit flatteries brought that haughty lady to consent to marshal Sara, there was no more to be gained.

The hour arrived; the sun was setting. The guests were scattered about the grounds, in the piazza, near the throne. The musicians (drummed up from the neighboring plantations) scraped their fiddles, played a march, and forth stepped through the library door, upon the green turf, a charming procession.

Lily led the way. Her golden curls, worn at their full length, swept to her waist; her white, girlish shoulders shone like polished ivory, and a faint blush stealing over her cheek gave so modest a charm to her prettily assumed dignity, that she fairly eclipsed the positive beauty of her cousin Sara, who walked proudly beside her, bearing the floral crown.

Grace was on her left, and carried the sceptre; behind them came Ella

Jennings and Marguerite Melbourne, Kate Jennings and Nora Tracy, Alicia Clarendon and Julia Melbourne. They were all covered with flowers; freshest roses formed garlands for their heads and snowy dresses, and it was like a moving garden that they passed over the lawn.

Clarence Tracy began the applause which welcomed them, and it was with many clappings of hands that Lily mounted the first steps of her sylvan throne.

A buzz—a hush—and Sara spoke:

> "With a wreath of simple flowers,
> Gather'd from the spring's bright bowers,
>   Thus we crown thee, dearest,
> While thine eye, undimm'd by sorrow,
> Looketh forward to a morrow,
>   Fairest, brightest, clearest.
>
> "Royalty ofttimes, we know,
> Presseth with a weight of woe
>   On the young heart's gladness;
> Yet we hope the fealty,
> Which we lowly bow to thee,
>   May bring no drear sadness.
>
> "Thus, gentle one! while resteth now,
> The royal crown upon thy brow,
>   We hail thee Queen of May!
> Short though thy present reign may be,
> May joy await your majesty
>   Throughout its gentle sway."*

It was very well done. Angel had drilled Sara carefully. At the words,

> "Thus we crown thee, dearest,"

she placed on Lily's magnificent tresses a circlet of white roses and geraniums. At

> "We hail thee Queen of May,"

her low bow of reverence was artistically managed, and the vain child had the satisfaction of exciting much admiration.

*Written by Miss Rand, of Philadelphia.

She smoothed her dark braids, smiled, glanced around proudly, and retired a step back.

Grace advanced more fully into view. The sceptre was a delicate ebony cane, completely wreathed with the sweetest perfumed and most brilliant flowers. At the summit a single large white lily reared its snowy petals, and around it a hedge of scarlet geraniums set off its virgin purity, and called attention, by its conspicuousness, to the intended compliment.

Grace was not pretty, but she had a great play of countenance, expressive eyes, and a voice of unsurpassed modulation.

"Fair queen!" she said, "we have seen the crown placed upon your royal brow, and to match the only gems which adorn it, fresh and glowing blossoms, we add this other fleeting symbol of your blooming majesty. A moment ago you were our equal; now, our pleasure and our duty is to obey. Wield your sceptre lightly; a hasty touch will cause these buds to fall; and as they droop and perish, so ends your power."

She placed the sceptre in Lily's hand, paused, and then, as if with sudden recollection, continued: "But no! the lily always reigns. Nature has spoken her throne-right; while flowers live, and Flora is cherished, so long will Lily's pre-eminence be acknowledged. I spoke for other queens of May; ours is a life-long queen!"

The little actress bent her knee, and the company applauded.

"Black is the foundation of this sceptre; Nature's brightest colors conceal the dark certainty. Thus will your days pass, O cherished queen! Life's blessings and flowers, perchance Love's smiles and garlands, will ever banish from view the fate of general humanity. Beneath a republican sky, standing upon this patriotic soil, I cry with loyal heart,

"Long live our Lily-queen!"

From mouth to mouth it resounded,

"Long live our Lily-queen!"

Could there be a more popular sentiment? An heiress, a beauty—so young, so sweet, and their hostess!

Tears started to Lily's eyes—tears of genuine pleasure. She bowed her rose-crowned head, and spoke:

"Dear friends! well-loved companions! dutiful subjects! you have conferred upon me an honor which fills my heart with joy and pride. I am Flora's representative—Queen of May! A rosy reign awaits me; a butterfly's life, it is true, but the *recollections* die not.

"In after years, when, with girlhood's visions vanished, we meet again upon this dewy turf, may our spirits be as light, our steps as buoyant with health and happiness as now! No clouds veil our future. Bright as yonder heaven smiles the pathway of our coming days. May the augury be true!

"Mutually loving, always united, let this moment serve to cement the tie which long has bound us.

"Friends! playmates! companions! right royally would I greet you, but the voice of the heart is stronger within me than the voice of position. 'Tis your affection which has placed me here; I see the motive, not the power. Mine shall be a majesty which asks not obedience, but love."

Lily's voice trembled at first, but soon grew stronger, and the final words of her simple address were pronounced with a pathos which gave an air of truthfulness to the whole scene. In the composition itself there was nothing, but the delivery gave it emphasis and originality.

A gleam of sunlight rested like a halo upon her maidenly brow, her blue eyes looked earnestly forward, and her whole appearance and attitude spoke the pure and clinging tenderness of her nature.

"Very good, indeed," whispered Grace, and the plaudits were long and loud.

Lily, recalled to herself, blushed, smiled, and settled her crown more firmly.

The musicians struck up a lively air, the young girls scattered bouquets at the feet of their queen, and many of the guests pressed forward to make their homage.

"Remember, Lily, your dance with me," said Clarence Tracy.

She nodded.

"As if I should forget!"

Angelica came up. She was wrapped in black lace, like the Andalusians to whom Clarence had, in his mind, compared her. I fancy I shall always describe Angel's dress, for it always seemed a part of herself.

"You spoke very well, Lily. It was a very pretty sight. Quite theatrical though. Do you think it was in good taste, dear? But then you are so modest, and can blush so apropos always, that it covers a multitude of doubtful improprieties."

"Did I look like an actress?" asked Lily, quite aghast; "has this seemed too much?"

"Oh not at all," answered Angel, carelessly. "An heiress like you may do any thing; and, besides, you are only a child."

"I did not feel like a child just now," said Lily, thoughtfully; "my mind went forward to our future years, and it seemed to me when I spoke of our next meeting here, though the words had been written for me by Clarence, they appeared to be all my own, and a dreamy sensation stole over me; I was not happy, but it was a calm sadness, as if *I* might be with you but not among you."

Angelica sneered.

"Foolish fancies, my dear," she said; "you are excited—what our French neighbors call *un peu exaltée,* and you have assumed a little sentimental air. Come, let me pay my loyal homage with the others, and let us begin the ball."

Miss Purvis raised Lily's hand lightly to her lips, and her face wore its usual haughty indifference of expression. Merrily sounded the fiddles, and gayly the troop flew to form a quadrille.

Lily's half-spoken presentiments yielded to the spirit of the moment. She danced with Clarence, and her gentle eyes beamed with satisfaction. She played her part very prettily. Though still so young, she was already an object of attention and interest to more people than her immediate circle. The eyes of the whole parish watched her movements, and many a papa casually mentioned to his son or sons,

"What a singularly pleasing young lady Miss Vere is, Harry, or John, or Thomas," as the case might be; "why arn't you a little more devoted?"

They danced in the piazza, in the drawing-room, and on the grass. Her majesty was most condescending, and smiled upon her whole court.

Angelica, Sara, and a few others waltzed. The stricter portion of the society professed to be immensely shocked, but they divided their exclamations between horror and a desire to have a nearer view.

"I am glad, Miss Vere," said Dr. Hatton, pompously, "that you do not take part in this pernicious dance."

"Do not give me undue credit," answered Lily, smiling; "if I danced as well as my cousins, I should not hesitate to do the same."

"Surely you do not approve?" asked the doctor, who was the prosiest of elderly planters, and was striving, as he thought, happily, to talk down to the level of his wealthy little neighbor; "an exhibition of such a nature can scarcely suit the purity of your views."

"My dear doctor," replied Lily, "I am not old enough to discuss the subject learnedly, but I think that with waltzing, as with many other things which we do not ourselves cultivate, we have prejudices which are unreasonable; and as lookers-on we adopt ideas that shock the performers themselves quite as much as they shock us. You forget, moreover, that the principal dancers at present are the Misses Purvis."

"Yes," exclaimed George, coming up, quite breathless, "if you abuse the queen's relations, doctor, I must take you into custody for high treason to the royal family, sir. For mercy's sake, Lily," he added in an under tone, drawing her away, "what *are* you wasting your time on that old fogey for?"

"He looked so forlorn," said Lily, deprecatingly.

"Then set your uncle Purvis at him, and let them mutually bore each other. I declare, Lily," he continued, affectionately, and throwing his arm boyishly, as became his sixteen years, around her waist, "you are the best little girl in the world. You think of every body. That big-eyed Angelica walks over you whenever she chooses, Sara snubs you, Alicia hectors you, Grace orders you, Clarence leads you like a lamb, and I say whatever I please, and you never get angry. And if old Hatton, or Mrs. Winterday, or any tiresome old soul wants a listener, there you sit with as much good-nature as if you liked it."

"That's because I am so stupid, George," said Lily, laughing heartily at the catalogue.

"Not a bit—not a bit," said George, sturdily. "You are *not* stupid. You don't say funny things like Grace, nor cutting ones like Angelica, but you have a deal of sense."

"Thank you," said Lily, still smiling.

"And, now that we are on the subject, do let me beg you to put down Angelica. She talks to you in a way that makes me very angry. Such a tone of superiority!"

"Why, George, how can you be so foolish? that is Angel's manner. She *is* very superior, and very much admired. It is natural that she should treat me and look upon me as a mere child. She feels above most people, her juniors especially."

"And especially Mr. Clarence Tracy.'

"Who calls my name? George, you are accused of a wish to monopolize her benign majesty. Fairest sovereign, deign to permit the humblest of your slaves to claim your dignified attention for two moments. To descend to commonplace, Mrs. Clarendon is terribly afraid that the ice will give out and the cream *unfreeze* if we do not sup early. When will your majesty command the repast?"

"I will speak to aunt," and Lily hastened away, followed by her companions.

Night had now arrived, and the lawn, bathed in its moonlight glory, lay green and tranquil. Here and there a couple sauntered along, unheeding the evening dew and the cautions about "night-air" and "country-fever." Some of the "field hands" had come up to the house, and were peeping unchecked over the piazza railings to see "n'young missus" and her company; the dowagers were installed in the drawing-room, the elderly gentlemen in the piazza; occasionally a distant clatter of plates might be heard through the open windows from the dining-room, and a dishonest Paul Pry would have discovered Maum Nelly flourishing about in the tallest of head-handkerchiefs superintending the preparations for supper.

Here again flowers abounded; they surrounded those time-honored cakes, they encircled the candelabra, they perfumed the room, and adorned the supper-table more than spun sugar or fruits glacés could have done.

When a respite was needed by the musicians, and even the young ladies wearied of dancing, the doors were thrown open, and in great array the guests were marshaled in.

A suitable time was given to stay the appetite on sandwiches and salad, then Dr. Hatton rose to propose a toast, and gave, amid stunning applause,

"The Lily of these waters. May she never be transplanted to bloom on other banks."

"You owe that burst, my dear," whispered George, "to your patience a while ago."

Mr. Clarendon, with much humor, replied for his ward: something he said about flowers not being appreciated in that part of the world. Rice-planters had nothing to do with buds or blossoms, and so on.

"What a mercy that Lily's name is what it is!" said Miss Purvis, "for it strikes me that it has done all the wit and brilliant allusions of the day."

Just as Mr. Clarendon had concluded his little speech, the gray-haired butler touched him respectfully on the arm, and announced the arrival of the post-boy from Georgetown (the nearest post-office), whose delay had occasioned many inquiries and much uneasiness on the part of his master.

"You will excuse me," said the host, turning to the mountainous lady whom he had escorted to supper, and whose size and age had entitled her to that respect; "you know, Mrs. Murray, that gentlemen are always anxious about their letters, and I am on the look-out for some important ones."

Mrs. Murray, with her mouth full of pâté, nodded her consent.

"This hog's-head cheese is so good, sir, that it will keep me busy till you come back."

Mr. Clarendon enjoyed the joke, and whispered to his wife as he passed her on his way to the door,

"My dear, your excellent friend, Mrs. Murray, is running risk of a surfeit on pâté de foie, which she takes for your admirable hog's-head cheese."

"Well, I am sure, Mr. Clarendon, I shan't undeceive her, for it would almost kill the poor soul if I were to tell her that she is eating diseased goose-liver. I am sure that I should be very sick if I were to do it. These new-fangled notions don't suit old-fashioned people."

Among the letters which Mr. Clarendon rapidly examined, there was one for Clarence Tracy, marked on the outside "important," so he carried it in and gave it to Clarence, with the hope that nothing disagreeable was contained in it.

"But," he said, "I give it to you now because if there is any thing which requires immediate attention the post-boy can be off again, and catch the mail before it starts at daybreak."

Clarence broke the seal, and a rapid flush crossed his brow, an exclamation of delight escaped him, and he crushed the letter triumphantly with sparkling eyes.

Lily watched him anxiously.

"No bad news at least," remarked Mr. Clarendon.

"I beg your pardon, sir," said Clarence, his countenance changing, and throwing into his eyes a melancholy look, "my godfather, Mr. Clarence, who has long resided in New Orleans, is just dead, and this letter from his lawyer informs me that I am left a legacy which amounts to fifteen hundred dollars a year. My immediate presence is requisite; and, moreover, it is my godfather's wish that I spend the two ensuing years in European travel."

"I congratulate you heartily," said Mr. Clarendon; "and Henry Clarence is dead! He was an admirer of your aunt Purvis, Lily. I wonder if she will have a fit of hysterics if I announce this suddenly, eh Lily?"

"Very much indeed, sir."

"What, my dear?"

"I—did you not ask if I congratulated Clarence, uncle? I do most heartily," said the gentle Queen of May.

He was busy with his letter.

"Where is Nora? She must pack my trunk for me. Could you lend me the buggy, sir, to take me to Georgetown to-night? I shall then take the steam-boat, which, fortunately, goes to-morrow."

"Nora is yonder," suggested Lily, "standing near Angelica. Do you not see her?"

Clarence strode across the room, making his way through the crowd with eager haste. He spoke rapidly to Nora. She was filled with surprise, asked questions which he cut short, and, at his bidding, left the room.

Miss Purvis had heard the conversation. She turned round, gave him one of her deep lustrous glances, and offered her condolences on the bereavement with mocking grace.

"Can I speak to you?" he whispered.

She shrugged her bare, creamy shoulders, indicated Mr. Langdon by a movement of her full eyelids, retired a step into the embrasure of the window, and discovered that her gold cassolette was missing.

"Mr. Langdon, might I trouble you to look behind the bronze pastille-burner on the drawing-room chimney-piece for the little cassolette that you gave me? Now," she continued, "say your say, for it will not take my future lord very long to hunt behind the pastille-burner for the pretty toy which is in my pocket."

"Angel," murmured the boy, with passionate eagerness, "you hear of my good fortune. I have now two thousand a year, adding this windfall to my original five hundred. It is a pittance—it is comparative poverty; but if you can decide to reject this cold-blooded Yankee, who does not possess one throb of your heart, and wait but a little while till I have made myself a name among lawyers—a power in my native land—you will yet be placed, as my wife, among the richest and most influential women in this country. With you as a hope—a treasure to be gained—this addition to my income to keep me out of debt, I will renounce the European tour, devote myself to my profession, and be the happiest of men."

A smile, so transient that it instantly faded, ruffled the broad curve of Angelica's lip.

"My dearest Clarence," she said, with melting intonation, "it can not be. I have too much unselfish love for you to consent to your wild project. I am eighteen months older than you—a vast difference when it lies on the woman's side. You fancy that you are very desperate about me now, but it is only because you have no one else with whom to compare me, for I do not count these little girls. If I were to agree—to break with Mr. Langdon—to wait till we had enough to marry upon, by that time I should look ten years your senior; and, though your strict sense of honor" (here the sneering smile played again, and belied the soft accents) "would force you to keep up the semblance of devotion, my heart would read the change, and would suffer even more than now.

"No, my dear Clarence, pursue the destiny which awaits you, as I do mine. Lily loves you. With her immense fortune to gild over her deficiencies" (Clarence winced), "you will be very happy, and learn to thank me from your very soul for what I am now saying."

"Happy, Angel!"

"Yes, happy. You are yielding to a youthful, evanescent impulse, which fills me with tearful joy, but which I must not encourage. I shall satisfy myself with thinking that I have done what was right, and, though Lily may possess your hand, shall I not have a place in your heart always?" her voice sank, and she looked tenderly in his eyes. "Now you love me with boyish passion; when we meet again, after your Continental experiences, and when you are the heiress's husband, your fancy will have sobered down to a sweet friendship lasting through all time."

"You are cruel. I love Lily, but not as I love you. She is a child. I have listened during these past ten days to your advice about her, and I felt that it was kindly meant, and arose from your interest in me, because every one is aware that your family wish her for Gustavus; but then I had no hope of winning you. It was madness to think of it. Now, it is different."

"It is not different," said Angelica, hastily, and resuming her languid haughtiness of manner. "I told you to-day, when you came to ask an explanation for my crossness this morning, that I was jealous of Lily's influence, but that you must not allow that to change your intercourse with her. Here comes Mr. Langdon. Give me your address. I will write to you before you sail for Europe. To Europe you must go." She hurriedly pressed his hand in her velvet fingers while pretending to arrange the flounces of her dress.

"Your flacon is not there, Miss Purvis."

"No?" she inquired, glancing up at Mr. Langdon's gloomy brow: "then come with me, and we must hunt for it. Some tiresome old woman has it, no doubt, dangling from her glove;" and, while Clarence's blood was yet tingling in his veins from the effect of her thrilling touch, she nodded slightly to him, and disappeared in the crowd that was now leaving the supper-room.

"He shall marry Lily," were her scheming thoughts, "and will always, through his enormous vanity, think that I am pining for him. Their house will be a better Southern *pied à terre* for me than if I owned it. No bills to pay for its maintenance, and the doors open to myself and my friends. As if I should decline marrying this rich goose, whom I shall soon reduce to order, for the dear pleasure of being Mrs. Briefless Barrister Tracy on two thousand a year!"

"She is not true; she is not sincere; she is a thorough-going, heartless, unprincipled coquet; but, such as she is, she can make a man forget the whole earth for her. Lily is worth fifty such detestable exponents of worldly wisdom; but oh! Lily is insipid as orange-flower water after the piquant, scornful, tender, delicious charm of her cousin; and I am sure she does love me. I could master her, fickle and haughty as she is."

"Bravo, Clarence," cried a party of young men, interrupting his soliloquy; "behold you a man of fortune! Come, old fellow, let's drink a glass of wine to your advancement!"

"For the cause which produced that advancement," began Clarence, "do you not think that I should retire from this gay scene?"

"What a humbug!" exclaimed Gustavus Purvis; "do put off that long face."

"True," said Clarence, relenting, "it will not add a sixpence to the legacy," and they jestingly drank their wine and discussed the heir's future plans.

Nora sent to say that she wished her brother to change his clothes, unless he meant to travel in full dress.

The buggy was at the door, lanterns lit, and the trunk strapped on behind.

Clarence courteously made his adieus and thanks to Mrs. Clarendon, shook hands with the Melbournes, Jenningses, Alicia, Sara, and Grace, embraced Leonora, and bowed to the remaining guests, whose carriages had not yet come up.

"Where is Lily?" he asked—"her majesty, I mean."

"I am here," said Lily, advancing from the library.

"What is the matter, child?" asked Mrs. Clarendon: "your eyes can't stand the light."

"The library door on the lawn is open, and I have been sitting in the dark at it."

"Good-by, my dear Lily."

"Good-by," she answered, gently.

"You will be in town soon—before I sail? Won't you give me a leaf from your crown?"

She bent her head toward him without speaking. He separated a bud from the garland, as he thought successfully, but it caught in the bright long ringlets. She hastily drew back, the fastening of the wreath broke, and it fell in a shower of leaves to the ground.

"Oh, Clarence!" exclaimed the girls.

"I am very sorry."

"It does not matter. You have done mischief, but you did not mean it. My reign is over!" She looked up kindly; her lips trembled; she gave him her hand, and turned away.

"Good-by, Mr. Tracy," said Angel's insinuating voice. "Mr. Clarendon's frisky horse is dancing a pas seul at the door. This is the occasion on which to 'speed the parting guest.'"

A hurried farewell, and Clarence was in the buggy and dashing down the road.

Thus ended the May party.

❀ CHAPTER VII

The next day was chilly, rainy, and gloomy. One of the changes in our variable climate had taken place, and instead of sunshine, warmth, and a soft, caressing air, the clouds were gray and heavy, the grass was soaked with water, the flowers beaten down, and the young people shivered about the house with shawls and worsted "wraps" thrown over their summer dresses.

The dissipation and excitement of the previous day had left them listless and dull. Occasionally Grace would break out in one of her lively sallies, or George would go thundering through the rooms, frolicking with Burleigh, and awaking his mamma's anxiety for the tables and chairs; but, for the most part, the young folks quietly read, or worked diligently at their tapestry-frames.

Angel had another *migraine* (Anglice, she was out of temper), bathed her eyes with rose-water, requested Sara not to tease her with questions, and, retiring to her own apartment, double-locked the door upon all possible intruders.

Nora wondered what kind of voyage Clarence would have. Eight hours at sea in such weather was not pleasant, and that was the stinted space of time in which a boat could manage the trip from Georgetown to Charleston.

Lily was silently busy as usual. Their stay in the country was drawing to a close, and she began to gather up a few books and personalities which she desired to take with her, this wet day affording an entire in-doors morning which might not again occur, for the young ladies were fond of putting on long sun-bonnets, and diving into the dark green woods even during the midday hours.

Ever attentive to her guests nevertheless, she sent for William Jennings, and begged that he would read aloud to the forlorn occupants of the drawing-room; so, while they were listening to some of Dickens's always amusing old "Boz" stories, their young hostess climbed the steps in the library to the uppermost shelves, and possessed herself of several antique volumes which had belonged to her mother.

Seated on the floor so as to dust them before carrying them off, she got absorbed in one of the old-fashioned tales, and read far into the story before she heard her name gently called. Looking up, Angelica stood at the opposite door to that which led into the drawing-room.

"Lily," she said, in an under tone, "I wish to speak to you."

Lily threw the books from her lap, and, wondering, obeyed the summons. There was an unusual air of sadness about Angelica, but, as she was at all times whimsical, this might be only one of the phases of her temper.

The party in the next room were laughing merrily as Angel softly closed the door behind her, and led the way up stairs, through the corridor, and into her own apartment, which was originally Lily's, but which the latter had given up during this visit, as the most comfortable of the single territories, to her cousin.

It was prettily furnished: the walls hung with dozens of water-color sketches and little drawings, the curtains of a bright lively chintz, and the oval glass on the dressing-table reflecting a thousand tiny trifles, such as all girls with feminine tastes attract about them.

"This is yours," said Miss Purvis, beginning the conversation by placing in Lily's hand a morocco case. "You told me I might have the use of that sink-table, and, being a little stupid and uninteresting this morning, I found no better occupation than rummaging in its angular drawers, for which you had give me leave." She paused.

"Yes," acquiesced Lily, gravely astonished; and, touching the spring, she opened the case and reverently displayed her mother's features.

"I know it is Aunt Mary's miniature," said Miss Purvis, "and it is very like her."

"Yes, so they tell me," said Lily, sadly; "do you recollect her at all?"

"Indistinctly, and yet perfectly as far as my memory goes—like the fragments we see in dreams, shapeless and yet impressive. I saw her a week before she died; you were ten days old, a little pink and white ball, wrapped in linen cambric and the finest flannel; Aunt Mary was pale and shadowy, with eyes like yours; her hands were royally beautiful. It was the first time I had ever seen her, for family dissensions had long separated my father and herself. You know Grandmother Purvis did not like Mr. Vere, and wished Aunt Mary to marry that man who has since turned out such a wretch—John Oakes?"

Lily bowed assent.

"I have heard so."

"Aunt Mary was so weak after your birth, and showed so soon that she was not likely to live, that a sort of reconciliation was patched up, and mamma and papa, who had always sided with Grandmother Purvis, determined to go and see their sister. Mamma took me along, I suppose, to cover her embarrassment. All this has been told me, or I have gathered it from vague conversations. My only positive recollection is the pallid, beautiful face, the fine white hand laid upon my head, and the tremulous voice which bade 'God bless me.' When I was twelve years old, they gave me a watch which had been given by papa to Aunt Mary at the same age, and which she had requested should be preserved for his eldest girl till that time. You have seen it—a little enameled trinket, with her initials on the back?"

Lily bowed her head again. These words, spoken with cool gravity, conjured up an image of her mother that filled the blue eyes with moisture.

"I am nervous and weak this morning, Lily. Pray be calm yourself, or one of my ungovernable fits of despondency will come upon me, and I shall be ill and miserable."

"You ill—you miserable, Angel! Impossible!" Miss Purvis looked at her cousin with one of those deep, dark glances, which gave such power to her countenance.

"You think me—" she said: "no matter; I have, ever since the time I saw Aunt Mary, cherished a kind of mysterious reverence for her. It was not a sentiment strong enough to affect my manner toward you, but it was a sort of personal interest between myself and her memory; just the dreamy notion of which I spoke a while ago, and which never included you. You see I am candid." Miss Purvis took the miniature from Lily, and, looking steadily at it, went on.

"This morning, when her face for the second time met my gaze, it was like an electric shock. Again I felt the pressure of her hand; again her almond-shaped eyes looked tenderly at me, and my cold, withered, scornful heart gave one of those throbs which I suppose are experienced (disagreeable things too!) by other young girls. A strong desire seized me to be of service to her child, to show some kindness to her rich, powerful, poor little orphan. I went in search of you. I have brought you here, before this passing emotion should fade from my grasp, and I am going to do you a service, which now you will not appreciate, but which, if you profit by it, years will show its worth. Shall I?"

"You will give me your confidence—your friendship, Angel? is not that it?" asked Lily, timidly.

"My confidence! my friendship!" exclaimed Angelica, bitterly; "no, my innocent Lily, that would not be a favor bestowed. My friendship exists for no one—my confidence! yes, I will give you a small dose of it. You will, perhaps, then understand me a little better. My mother has a sister, the wife of Mr. Oakes's elder brother, and they have a daughter, Margaret Oakes, whom you know. Margaret is four years older than I, but from my earliest infancy I loved her with all the energy, all the devotion of which my selfish nature was capable. Very precocious, never child-like, I have always been her companion. I was 'grown up' and in society at fourteen; vain, conceited, self-satisfied, and exacting, all my claims, nevertheless, were waived at a signal from Margaret or at her approach. She is beautiful, intelligent, accomplished, well-bred, but, though prone to cry down the perfections of other rivals, Margaret's pre-eminence I never disputed and never envied. What Margaret said must be right; what Margaret did could not be wrong. Sara was too young and too heavily silly to occupy me; my time, my thoughts, my wishes centred in Margaret. Every pleasure-party, every offered amusement, must include Margaret, or it was to me a failure. The world recognized our friendship with respect, and where I was most abused for haughtiness, insolence, or impudence, still truth would utter, 'But her unwavering love for her cousin, that is a redeeming point.'"

A tear started to Angelica's proud eye, and her voice was mournfully soft.

"Yes," she said, as if she had forgotten Lily's presence, and spoke more to herself than to her listener, while her clasped hands she slowly raised till her bowed head rested wearily upon them. "Yes, it was the one purely unselfish act and sentiment of my life. Long was I blind! I lavished the best and strongest feelings of my heart upon her. Cold to every one else, haughty as if born a princess, to her I was all warmth, all self-forgetting attachment. I thought her pure and perfect. Religious votaries might lead lives as unsullied, but where could they usurp the credit of Margaret, who, dwelling in the midst of temptations, and pursuing worldly pleasures, still preserved herself unscathed from harm! To me her baptism was a prophecy—she was indeed a pearl!"

Lily crept closer to her cousin, and laid her cheek upon Angel's shoulder.

"Yes, Lily; and what was the result of this? How was my worship, which I believed absolutely reciprocal, requited? Imagine the horror—the stunning shock! to be awakened from the dream that 'as I loved, loved was I,' to the consciousness that she was willing, ready, yes, anxious to cast me off; that on her heart I had no hold; that she was supremely indifferent, and wished to give that indifference full sway. It would be tedious to tell all the circumstances. They were slight, and apparently of no weight. Straws indeed, which marked which way this cold wind blew. It roused me from a sentimental sleep. There was no reason to be given. I asked no explanations; none were offered. What availed reasons as opposed to facts between us two! I was unpopular—offended people by my sarcasm, and by my contempt for frivolous conventionalities. She fancied she would get along better alone. The rope was strong which had long united her graceful bark to the sturdy and more uncompromising boat manned by me, as we floated over 'life's ocean.' Cut it! 'She can drift alone, thump herself into pieces against the jagged rocks and huge billows from which she knows not how to steer clear; my insinuating progress can be carried on better by myself. Some day, if this tie be not destroyed, we will swamp together, whereas now I shall be safe.' It was done. I was eighteen, but an old stager. This storm, of which the palpable breeze could not have ruffled the wings of a humming-bird, passed like a tornado over my sensibility. Margaret Oakes and I are very civil and very amiable cousins. You see us meet—you see us part. Sometimes I sneer, sometimes she retorts. It was a mistake I made, but a mistake which has shriveled up my heart till there is no more vitality in it than exists in this crumpled leaf." She tossed a withered fragment of a rose worn in her bosom on Lily's lap, and gave a deep sigh. "Ah! the bitterest of life's burdens is to learn the treachery of one in whom you trusted. To have thought, all besides may be false—*this* one is true, and to be rudely shaken into the knowledge of—" Angel paused abruptly.

"My heiress-cousin," she continued, in a moment, passing her hand, on which flashed Mr. Langdon's engagement ring, over her broad and haughty brow, "you see that after this trial I would not be likely to engage in a second female friendship. I thank you for the offer of yours, and for the sympathy which glistens in the shape of that dew-drop on your cheek; but I am an unlovable person, born to dazzle and to surprise, not to be loved. With a different training and different experience, I might have made an admirable woman. Such as I am, I suit myself, but satisfy no one else. Mamma has always preferred Sara's unmeaning loveliness to my charms, which owe their power to the mind rather than to feature and coloring. She brought me before the world early, because it was easier to do so than to keep me in; and her pride and interest in me amble an even pace with the admiration that I excite. Papa has grown to—what is the word? love me? yes, that is the comprehensible syllable—love me more after every rich offer for my hand. Mr. Langdon has several hundreds of thousands of dollars. Papa considers me at this time several hundreds of thousands of times superior to his other children; Gustavus, Sara, and Charlie hold me in meek respect, and will not be sorry when, on the first day of June, the bridal wreath and *application de Bruxelles* veil proclaim me Mrs. Archibald Langdon."

"Angel," said Lily, speaking at last, "you are not sincere; you can not think all that you say; and if you do, why encourage such morbid sentiments? You have so many of life's blessings, dear Angel, why not enjoy them without these terrible misgivings and doubts of those around you? Should Margaret's treachery cause you to suspect your nearest and dearest, as well as the world in general? Do you think that all are false? Oh!" she shuddered, casting her eyes upon the dreary landscape without, closed in by the brooding gray clouds, "as well say that this melancholy day is a picture of all the days of the year. There is sunlight, Angel; it must come again."

Angelica shook her head impatiently.

"To business, Lily: you forget, in your desire to comfort me, that I have a favor in store for you. Now listen to me. You love Clarence Tracy!"

Lily blushed painfully, and replied, with evident embarrassment,

"Of course, I like a person who has been my frequent companion, and is the brother of a dear friend like Nora."

"You do not speak with that candor which is your salient charm. You know what I mean, Lily," said Miss Purvis. "You are very young, it is true, but you know enough of life to understand that with your fortune, position, and looks, your hand will soon be sought as a matrimonial prize; and, though I may be mistaken in my supposition, I fancy that Clarence Tracy has imperceptibly taught you to distinguish him from the crowd of George and Willie's schoolmates;" and she looked searchingly in the deeply-suffused face which was resolutely turned away.

But Angelica mistook the cause of Lily's embarrassment. My innocent heroine blushed more for her cousin than for herself. She had been so much interested in Angel's recital, and felt so much moved by her evident sorrow, that she had quite forgotten her own griefs against her; and the recollection of coquetries of which she could not approve was suddenly brought back by the mention of Clarence—the victim, as she fancied him, of unmaidenly arts.

To attempt an attack on him, or to suspect her of a sentimental attachment, aroused her to action.

"Indeed you *are* mistaken, Angelica," she almost *retorted;* "Clarence is to me only a brother, just like Willie or George. Do you suppose that he has ever talked of hearts or love to me? or that he has asked me to exchange rings with him, or, in fact, to do any of the silly things that some girls and boys think about—dancing-school nonsense? I call him Clarence, just as he says

Lily, because I have known him so long. He reads with me, and teaches me. We began German during his last vacation, and there is no master I ever had who is stricter and more exact with my lessons than Clarence."

"Very good, my dear child, and I have no doubt he expects you to prove always as tractable; and, as matters stand upon so prosaic and friendly a footing, it will cause you less pain to hear and to put aside for a life-time consideration these simple but important truths. Clarence Tracy has inordinate vanity—Clarence Tracy is utterly false, hypocritical, and time-serving—Clarence Tracy is cold, hard, calculating—Clarence Tracy will try to marry you, and will be careless if, when that is done, your heart breaks from neglect and his indifference—Clarence Tracy is outwardly refined, delicate, gentle; inwardly, he is sensual, coarse, and violent; unhesitatingly selfish, constitutionally indolent."

Lily sprang up indignantly. How those mild, soft summer eyes lightened their anger!

"Angelica!" she exclaimed, "you are—"

"What?" demanded the young lady, coolly, throwing back her haughty head.

"You are mistaken," said Lily, while the strong feeling which moved her showed in every bursting vein through her pellucid skin. She seemed terrified at her own unaccustomed passion, and with effort kept down the first rising reply.

It was a glorious victory, darling Lily!

"You think, perhaps, that you know this hero better than I do," resumed Miss Purvis; "you don't know him at all. His character is as much ignored by your unsophistication as if he had lived in Timbuctoo, and you in Brazil, till this moment. You will not believe even when I give you proofs of his duplicity. Can you credit me when I tell you that, after his caviling speeches about me two evenings ago—speeches which I recommended him to make—his first thought, his first act last night was to lay his freshly-acquired hundreds, with the addition of his hand and self, at my unworthy feet?"

"Is that true? oh, Angel, is it true?"

"I should say, ask him; but that would be an uncertain method of reaching the truth. Lily, this is the favor I bestow on you; I warn you against Clarence Tracy. He is plausible as Lucifer himself. I don't dislike him. The boy has talent, superficial earnestness, temporary passion, which make him eloquent and dangerous even to those few who understand him; besides, he is not yet *quite* all that he will be. The germ is there, and will develop itself. So surely as the playful and pretty tiger-cub grows, not into a soft, sleek Angora, but into a fierce and bloodthirsty animal, so surely will the latent qualities of his youth swell into full-grown vices. He will find victims—he will find followers—he will find believers in his make-believe virtues, who will, on his assertion, testify that he is all that he would have them think he is; but for you, my little cousin, the only child of my dead aunt, whose sweet face haunts me, be warned, be wise. Who can direct you? Mr. Clarendon is a good, excellent man, an admirable judge of a horse's points, but I should prefer my own discernment about an individual's qualities. Mrs. Clarendon is a capable and worthy woman, so far as regards cutting out negro-clothes and making sausages, but she never saw deeper into her acquaintances than the outer cuticles of their skins. George is a lively, hair-brained boy, and Willie is abroad. There ends the list. Accept me on this occasion, and only for this occasion, as your guide."

Lily had covered her eyes with her left hand, while with the forefinger of her right she drew cabalistic figures upon the dressing-table without interrupting her cousin by word or look. Angelica rose, drummed upon the window-pane, and seemed to be weary now of the conference.

"Lily, are you asleep?" she said, gracefully yawning; then, lifting up her cousin's head, and pushing back the ringlets which fell over her face, she pointed toward the reflection of both countenances in the mirror.

"Do you see, my dear, how sallow I am beside you? how old I look for my years? I can not compare with you in beauty; I have not the fifth of your sweetness, and yet my conquests can be reckoned by scores. The world is before you, Miss Vere. You are fifteen: in three years you will make a great sensation. Do not imagine that life has lost its charm, and that, because one is false, all are. I quote back to you your own consoling words."

Lily had some faults; she certainly possessed a strong infusion of sturdy Scottish obstinacy. Gentle and docile as she was, she had an opinion of her own, and liked to keep it.

"If I remain silent, Angel, you will think that I implicitly agree with you, but I do not. The very things that you tell me, which to you are conclusive, only convince me that Clarence has more impulsive feelings than you give him credit for. That he is sometimes carried away by momentary emotions, and that he is not proof against the charms of those—against those charms —" Lily hesitated and broke down.

Angelica's cold, scornful look lazily rested upon her.

"I do not think that he is perfect," Lily blushingly recommenced, "but he is far from being the odious character that you would make me believe him. I am surprised," here her soft eyes took a sterner shadow, "about his behavior last night. His forgetfulness of what this legacy might do for a sister like Nora, who has been so devoted to him, gave me then most concern. Her aunt's home is not a kind one, and I immediately thought of himself and Nora living together on this little income, and was surprised that he did not instantly think of the same thing. But if his mind flew to you and his footsteps followed, you must allow that he had one excuse for momentarily forgetting Nora."

"Sweet sophistry!" sneered Angelica. "Lily, I have spoken. Here let the matter end. What do you think of this morning-gown? Is it not pretty?" and Miss Purvis spread out the Oriental pattern of her Cashmere robe, and began, learnedly, to discuss its beauties. She replaced the miniature in its drawer, and wondered when the weather would clear.

"Is there time for a nap before the dressing-bell? We have gossiped away the morning."

Lily consulted the great clock in the corridor, and answered affirmatively.

"I am much obliged to you, dear Angel," she said, timidly, holding the door ajar, and preparing to depart; "you have treated me like a woman, and talked openly to me. I shall not forget what you have said; I shall consider it always as a mark of cousinly affection; and your interest in my dear mamma, whom I never saw, will be a pleasing recollection to the last day of my life. Kiss me, and tell me that you believe me."

She ran back, threw her arms around Angelica, and embraced her warmly. Miss Purvis quietly returned the embrace without deranging Lily's collar, took up a book, and began to read.

A marble statue could not have been colder.

❧ CHAPTER VIII

In a week after this, Chicora Hall was shut up. Through its wide corridors echoed the trailing footsteps of an old *maumer*, left in charge of the house, who carefully visited the different rooms from time to time, to see that the wind had not blown open any shutters, and that all was safe.

The overseer would come occasionally to give an eye to the flowers, by Miss Vere's order, and to gather a few roses for his children, to whom she granted that privilege.

Under the "royal oak" the throne still stood, and a withered garland had been left twined about it as a memento of the late event, and "to show how long it would stay there undisturbed," George suggested.

The Queen of May had "resumed her studies," like other young ladies and gentlemen, after the April vacation, and she and Alicia were soberly perfecting themselves in all the knowledge which their different teachers could impart. I forgot to mention that they had not been to school during the whole winter, but took lessons at home from a stern-visaged Englishman, very careful of his *h*'s; a little Frenchwoman, who had *des attaques de nerfs*, a long nose, and an odor of ether; a music-master, who thought himself Listz, Herz, and Baggioli combined; and a minute dancing-master, who looked like a dirty-faced grasshopper.

On the first day of June, Angelica was married with all "the pride, pomp, and circumstance of glorious" wedding. Mr. Purvis did not demur at the expense. He thought of Mr. Langdon's thousands, and permitted his "suffering" wife to enlarge her party list, and to bring as many people into the house as the walls could hold.

The old Purvis mansion, standing in the midst of a beautiful garden, blazed with light. But to those who preferred coolness and a summer evening's breeze to wax candles and damask curtains, there were the tall French windows opening to the floor, through which one passed into the broad piazzas, dimly lighted. Sofas and chairs of bamboo, with linen cushions to lean upon; tables spread beneath the colored lanterns (which swung in the light air, arising in gusts direct from the sea), and on which could be found heaped up crystal baskets icy with frozen fruit; the clean garden-walks, freshly graveled, and leading through a wilderness of hardier sweets to the green-houses beyond; and, above all, the moon shining down with an unusual brightness, as if Miss Purvis had had it rubbed up with chamois, like the family plate.

As the whole house was thrown open, when the guests got tired of the first story, they could mount the noble, winding cedar staircase to the second. There was another range of piazzas; bed-rooms handsomely furnised *en suite,* and all inviting admiration and attention. Mrs. Purvis's apartment looked like a *bric-à-brac* shop, and *a friend* could fancy her badgering her unhappy maid within those painted walls, and occasionally hurling a stray *objet de virtu* at Miranda's Madras-covered head. Mrs. Clarendon rather liked privately, sometimes, to pity Miranda, and she often pitied Mr. Purvis too, while Mrs. Purvis took it out by just as privately pitying Mrs. Clarendon for her lack of style and fashion, and her faded looks. In fact, it was pleasant for a by-stander to listen to these two excellent ladies—to see how each despised the other, and yet how civil they could be. At heart they were both very good women, but Mrs. Purvis was passionate and fretful, and Mrs.

Clarendon liked to pass for a martyr to her "duties," and enjoyed making unnecessary sacrifices.

In the bride's dressing-room were displayed her presents, and here crowds loitered continually; for Angelica had too superlative a taste in dress to wear jewels in June, so her diamonds lay in their morocco receptacles, and all the company could admire Mr. Langdon's magnificent homage, and envy Angel her newly-acquired and sparkling ornaments.

In a white velvet case was an emerald cross. This was Lily's gift—worthy of the donor's fortune, and of the recipient's acceptance. I do not intend to go through the list. It made some young girls think that getting married was a nice way of procuring rings, brooches, and et ceteras, and the diamonds improved Mr. Langdon's appearance in their eyes somewhat.

Not that Mr. Langdon was a frightful man by any means, nor an ungainly one; but he was one of those saturnine, dark, unapproachable kind of people, who do not make agreeable impressions upon first acquaintance. His sister, Cecilia Langdon, a younger brother, and two dry-looking friends, had come on to stand sponsors for him during this important business.

The brother was a perfect specimen of young New York. He was small and thin, slightly knock-kneed, and very carefully dressed. His hair was parted with unwavering regularity; his collars were so stiff that they never yielded a momentary turn-down; his face was pale, his eyes fatigued, his manner nicely divided between indifference and superciliousness, his tone a drawl, and his air rather gentlemanly. He lived on dancing and a little opium. Wine had lost its power to arouse him; so, when he wished to be awake in society, he "brought himself up" with morphine, or red lavender, or ether, like a broken-down actress. He was quite proud of this incapacity to enjoy life. It proved that he had lived "fast," and he used to boast of how many drops or tea-spoonfuls he had taken of such or such stimulants before he was equal to the exertion of entering a ball-room. Being almost as rich as his brother, Edward Langdon had a great terror of falling into some matrimonial net, and his New York life was a succession of attempts upon his liberty, which he labored to ward off—in a faint sort of way. He was a great flirt, liked to dance unlimited attendance upon some *demoiselle à marier*, and then, when he saw the meshes coming over him, dodge, and escape rather frightened, but ready to start again with somebody else.

He had warned Mr. Langdon (who was not at all a man of society, but who had lived entirely for and with his business) that the Purvises were "trying for him" the preceding summer at Newport. Mr. Langdon scorned the advice, and had not the slightest objection to being caught, if any young lady *could* catch him. Angelica did, and he gave in without a struggle. The result was this grand wedding which I am trying to describe.

Cecilia Langdon was, of course, one of the bridemaids, of whom there were four—Sara, Margaret Oakes, Lily, and herself.

Miss Langdon was as admirable a type of her class—New York belles—as her brother Edward of his. She was tall and showy. Nature gave her a straight, slight figure, and art added the "fillings in." Her dress fitted exquisitely, cut very low at the back, but quite modestly in front, the skirts falling with a gradual, graceful slope, of a decided outward tendency from the waist to the feet. Her hair was arranged so as most to become a face neither pretty nor plain, but for which fine eyes and dazzling teeth were expected to do the work of beauty. Not an available point was left uncultivated. Cecilia knew in which position her features looked best. A dimple on the shoulder was cherished like a dear friend, and never forgotten; her very eyebrows were smoothed to a certain shape, and her hand was not seen ungloved unless by mere accident. The effect was worth the care, it must be allowed; for a girl who, "let alone," would not have been otherwise than plain, produced the notion that she was verging on decided good looks. But then every thing she wore was so fresh, so unhandled—every thing matched—nothing predominated; her costume was like a well-mixed salad, where no ingredient strikingly prevails. And, after all, what is a woman without her dress?

To my mind, the Venus, in a shabby, short-waisted gown of tawdry colors, would never be an attractive object; but here I entreat that no reader will lay down this humble volume, and begin to prate about the absurdity of modern fashions at all for the Venus, and talk of French corsets and her untrammeled waist. I know the whole tirade beforehand—who does not?—and I merely mention the Venus to show how a perfectly beautiful woman might look badly dressed, as compared with one of lesser natural attractions, who knows how to put greens and pinks together, and where ribbons and flowers are well chosen and suit her.

Now this aptness of toilet Cecilia Langdon had studied and thoroughly understood. There was no other branch of education in which she could take her degree of M.A. except in dancing; but she was a lively, conversible girl, full of the small phrases of society, who made a little talk wherever she went, looked interested in what was said, never dreaded to compromise her dignity by being seen with so and so, decidedly preferred her "own set," but could chat just as gayly in some one else's; consequently, though surrounded on this occasion by dozens of young women who surpassed her in beauty, and who were her superiors in solid reading and acquirements, she quite overlaid them by her facility of access, and by her power of using the "small change" of fashionable dialogue.

Angelica enjoyed her new relations vastly. Edward's emptiness and self-conceit, and Cecilia's overflowing bustle and superficialness, with their united pretensions, charmed her.

I don't think she ever longed for a confidante more than on that evening, to whom she might slyly indulge in a few remarks about her husband's brother and sister; but, as Margaret was out of the question in that line, Lily would not have enjoyed satirical laughs, and Sara would have needed explanations, Angel quietly kept them to herself, and played her part to admiration. So full of suavity, so dignified, so graceful, she was determined that the last impressions she left of her girlhood should contradict former ideas of insolence and indifference.

Mrs. Purvis was in her glory; and Mr. Purvis nodded his grizzled head, and winked his eyes under his near-sighted spectacles with delight. He rubbed his large nose, and thought how cleverly he had managed to marry off Angelica to so rich a man without paying down a single cent of dowry more than the ten thousand dollars left her by her grandmother Purvis.

Clarence Tracy had returned from New Orleans a few days before the wedding, and was invited for groomsman. He had not seen Angelica since their interview on the night of the May party, and he was longing for some indication that she remembered him.

He had made his congratulations with the others after the ceremony, but no glance, no whisper from the bride betokened that she had him more in her thoughts than any one else. He was restless, uneasy, put out. Lily's manner to him was uncertain. She had not given him her usual, open, girlish, frank reception on his arrival in the city; and this evening she seemed to avoid him, and, though her words were kind as usual, there was a misty coolness, a flickering cloud between them.

Toward the close of the party, just before the supper was announced (for, with us, you can not have a buffet, the positive rule being that every lady rushes home immediately after serving refreshments, and with such precipitation that one might fancy they only came for the meal, except that they eat nothing, so that why people give parties, and why others go to them, has always puzzled me, seeing that their notion appears to be to get to the house as late as possible, and to leave it as quickly as they can)—but, as I said, the supper hour was near at hand, when Clarence, who was listening to Cecilia Langdon, saw Angelica comparatively alone. Mr. Clarendon was speaking to her, and Clarence knew that, being an elderly gentleman, he would beat a hasty retreat so soon as an unmarried youth came near.

"Are you not going to Sharon or Saratoga?" Miss Langdon asked; "no, to Europe? Ah! how delightful! We shall all go next year, Angelica and my brother—probably this autumn, to winter in Rome. Will you go to Rome? I do love Rome and the Roman Catholics. There is something so *entrainant* in their religion. Are you—"

"I beg your pardon," said Clarence, bowing profoundly; "permit me to present to you, Miss Langdon, Mr. Alfred Greville;" and he rapidly seized by the arm a young man who was standing near him, and went through the introduction with marvelous celerity.

Alfred Greville looked amazed, but was quite conformable, and Miss Langdon continued her uninterrupted flow of words as easily to the new-comer as to the previous victim. It made no difference. She had come to Charleston to be civil to the inhabitants, and to tell "our set" when she got home how queerly they dressed, and how little they danced—one man was no worse nor better than another.

Clarence hastened to Angelica. She received him cordially enough, and Mr. Clarendon backed out as expected.

"You have not been kind this evening," Clarence began; "you have not tried to cheer me or to comfort me."

A wide lifting of Mrs. Langdon's eyelids brought him to a sudden stop.

"Did you not promise to consider me always as a friend?" Clarence began, in another key; "and is it not a legitimate source of distress for a friend that you should be on 'the eve of leaving us forever?'"

"Not forever," answered the bride, with one of her gravest smiles. "I am not banished from Carolina, I hope. You are going away as well as myself, and I do not think that any wonderful dejection is perceptible in your looks or manner."

"Piqued, by Jove!" thought Clarence; and the fact is, that absence and a little gay society had enabled this volatile young gentleman to recover bravely from his heart-attack. He had begun to look upon a renounced voyage to Europe as a terrible calamity, and already thanked Angelica for her rejection, although he desired ardently to keep up a little sentiment with her.

"Won't you take my arm?" he said; "let us find a vacant seat more comfortable than this glaring light and heat."

Angelica consented.

On their way out they passed Lily. She was quite surrounded by a group of young men already scenting her thousands, and her prettiness and gentleness aided their admiration. Angelica gave her a kind glance. Lily returned it with one of grave displeasure, and turned away. It was the crisis of her life. Had she not misunderstood her cousin at that moment, probably this story would never have been written.

Angelica's bitter smile aged her face for an instant, and her part was taken.

"Clarence," she said, when they had found one of those cool, comfortable couches in the piazza, "I was a little cross just now; let us make it up;" and she held out her hand, which he warmly pressed.

"You are always sweet," he said; "always more charming than any other woman."

She fixed her dangerous eyes upon him, and played with the end of the "*application de Bruxelles*" veil.

"And Lily?" she asked.

"Oh, Lily is such a mere girl."

The beautiful bust, shaded by folds of transparent lace, heaved with one half-sigh, quite audible and perceptible to her companion.

"It is fate. It can not be avoided, Clarence. You must marry Lily, and before you leave for Europe. When do you go, by the way?"

"Next year—next week—to-morrow—how do I know? I only know that I am talking to you again."

"You will never talk to me again, if you go on in this absurd manner," said Angel, smiling and putting out her red lip with a pout of assumed displeasure. "Before you go to Europe, I say—this very night, if you choose, have a talk with her. You will find her a little impracticable. Shall I tell you why? I was angry with you, angry with myself—nervous and vexed with all the world. I had the blues the day after the May party, and I called up Lily to do—what think you?—to warn her against you, and in a measure I succeeded."

Clarence started, and compressed his thin lips. "Did you tell her—" he asked.

"That you had laid your new fortune at my feet? Yes."

"How did she take it?"

"Not as *I* would have taken the defalcation of a man I loved," and Angelica's dark eyes flashed, and her white hands trembled; "not as I would look if at this moment I could believe—any one—I love—false." It is impossible to render the bewitching softness of her accent as she concluded, as contrasted with the fierce passion of her first words.

"Lily can never experience your depth of feeling," said Clarence, with a sigh.

"I told her that she would never be happy with you; that you were inconstant, cold, and unreliable. Now let it be your part to undeceive her. Tell her of your own accord, without a question from her, that you come a penitent to her feet; that you were led astray by my 'wicked wiles;' and I leave it to your cleverness to shadow forth your own failings as I clearly depicted them, in a manner to convince her that, though you have faults, she can make them virtues. Don't abuse me. Lay the blame of your proposal to me on your own momentary folly, for it is the inconsistency of your words and actions which most grieves her in this business. The little thing loves you, but she scarcely knows it; and her heart speaks very strongly for you. Disarm her criticism by acknowledging your failings, and this step, which I at first intended to be against you, will ultimately end in your favor."

"Why did you say such things of me?" asked Clarence, with reproachful accent.

"That you were hypocritical and false?" answered Angel, laughing; "because it is true, though she need not know it." But, seeing Clarence's brow darken, and an impatient, angered look in his eye, she continued, "I had the blues—I was cross—Heaven knows what. Don't question me too closely, Clarence. Perhaps I envied her the happiness which could never, with prudential considerations, be mine—I was 'dog in the manger'-ish. The bright fruit I could not gather, I did not choose that she should pluck, and I told her the core was decayed."

With an exclamation of joy and gratified vanity, the boy caught the beautiful hand which coquettishly was tearing to pieces her bouquet of snowy flowers, while her heavily-fringed lids were alternately raised toward him or tenderly cast down.

This was a step too far.

"Mr. Tracy!" she exclaimed, with a tone of wounded pride; and as Clarence muttered a "forgive me" in the humblest manner, she gravely proceeded.

"If you wish that the friendship that subsists between us should continue, you must learn to put a little more control upon these boyish outbursts; but I pass this over now, and what I wished to say to you must be quickly said. The prospect before you—the prize within your grasp—is one to be envied. You speak of Lily always as a child. She *is* a child in her worldly notions, her ideas of rectitude, propriety, and so on; but, so far as these are concerned, she will be just such a child always; only, as she grows older, she will get these staid principles more firmly fixed; she will lose her childlike belief that all her acquaintances possess these virtues, to her mind so essential; and soft, yielding, and pliable as you find her now, she will become as adamant to the incursions of those whom she may fancy desirous of throwing down the bulwarks of her character and disposition. We will live to see Lily a strong woman, but strong only in her feminine qualities."

"What a picture!" ejaculated Clarence. 'You either overrate or underrate her. She is sweet-tempered, gentle, dove-like. The only fault I find in Lily is her want of strength."

"There lies your egregious mistake. She will not be an insipid companion. Her intellect is not of a brilliant order. She will never admire your favorite authors, nor adopt your sneering opinions, but she will have the charm of natural simplicity. All that is true, all that is pure, will strike an answering chord in her, and her love of what is right, and her deep religious sentiment, will constantly threaten to sweep away her love of what is 'pleasantly wrong,' and her sentiment of physical and mental admiration as set forth in yourself. Do not fancy that you are likely to fall asleep holding her hand; you will have to keep wide awake in a year or two, during your time of probation, so as to conceal from those earnest blue eyes a few little discrepancies."

Clarence smiled slightly and mused a while.

"I shall be very comfortable, I suppose," he said. "There was a time, and it was not long ago either, that I imagined a life with Lily the very perfection of human bliss. I taught her, and she looked up to me: she was so mild, so entirely unselfish, and admired me with such hearty yet timid fervor. It was flattering and very sweet. Now, it appears to me as if it was too sweet—all sugar and water."

"The time will come again," said Angel, rising, and leaning with graceful abandon upon the balustrade of the piazza, "when she will be to you the type of perfect womanhood. Cautious, scheming, gray-hearted women like myself will be too much of your own stamp to be loved. You will seek us as pleasant companions—charming creatures to trifle with, but it is such beings as Lily that men of mark wish to marry. Adieu, Clarence. We will meet again in some crowd to-morrow, but this is our last 'talk.' Recollect that in marrying Lily you gain wealth, a pretty wife, and cousinship to 'yours most devotedly.'"

Angelica laughed, and bent her flexible waist in a dismissal of regal suavity and smiling farewell.

Her companion would have spoken again, but, passing her fingers lightly over her lips as a sign of silence, she entered into conversation with a gentleman who joined them, and whom her quick and ever-watchful eye had seen approaching.

Clarence Tracy walked slowly away, and thought over Angelica's words. How she puzzled him! She had twisted him around from point to point, till his head was quite bewildered. She liked him, and she didn't care two straws about him. At one moment, to marry Lily would be a sacrifice to mere gold; at another, it was indeed a thing to strive for.

But never, for one second, did this promising youth doubt but that Lily herself would gladly accept the favor of his hand. His only fear was lest he should be giving himself up for too small a return.

After wandering about for a quarter of an hour, he thought he would go and speak to Lily. She was still hemmed in by a little circle of admirers, who were endeavoring to fix her attention. She listened, and smiled, and replied with courteousness, but occasionally her eyes would travel beyond them, and seek some object out of view.

Clarence drew near. Her color varied, and she answered absently, but she did not turn toward him, so presently he moved off, saying to himself,

"I will go to see her to-morrow morning."

The looked-for supper arrived—a most elegant, sumptuous, and well-chosen feast. The ladies were duly plied with bon-bons and tiny drops of Champagne, and the entertainment was over for them.

Mantles and hoods were in requisition; carriages were called; horses, startled out of their stand-up naps, drowsily moved at the summons; their drivers, who had been discoursing each other with eager volubility, and catching pleasing glimpses of the company over the garden walls, tightened their reins; old gentlemen carefully deposited old ladies (their hands full of wedding-cake boxes) into the old coaches, and young gentlemen gallantly and whisperingly escorted young ladies (who went tripping along with modest condescension on the arms of their partners) into the same venerable conveyances; the larger portion of the gentlemen returned to the supper-room for a final glass, and Mrs. Purvis wearily bowed out her last guest.

One great feat of her life was accomplished. Angelica was married! The bringing up of children in the world generally bewilders my reasoning powers as much as the giving of balls, in Charleston particularly. There is an equally strong desire to have them and—to get rid of them.

🧠 CHAPTER IX

Lily was preparing her French lessons the next morning when Clarence entered the dining-room where she sat.

She received him with quiet grace, and asked after Nora.

"You are early and busy to-day, Lily, in spite of the gay doings and late hours last night."

"Yes," she answered; "Alicia is tired out, and has a headache; but I am quite well, and feel fresh as ever."

"You look fresh as a rose-bud," said Clarence, admiringly, as he noticed the fine, transparent texture of lips, cheek, and brow. "You have such a wonderful skin! See your hands! they are like little rolls of white velvet, with a reflection of a new-born carnation thrown on the palm."

Lily laughed, and withdrew her hand. "Will you have some figs?" she said. "I put them there for Mademoiselle Durony, but there are enough for both you and her;" and she offered a plateful of yellow and purple fruit, lusciously tempting.

"No, thank you, Lily. The fact is, I am come this morning to have a little chat with you; are you at leisure? But I need not ask, for I shall not detain you long. Lily, I have been a great fool, and I wish to tell you about it."

"Well," said Lily, simply, and she carefully placed her Grammaire des Grammaires on the top of Du Verger's Phrases, supported it on the one side with "Corinne," and on the other with Bonilly's "Contes à ma fille," piled her exercise-book on the summit, removed them all again, and then replaced the structure with renewed diligence and assiduity while Clarence spoke.

"While we were at Chicora, Lily, I fell in love with your cousin Angelica." He paused. "You don't seem surprised. Did you guess it before this?" He sighed. "I suppose you did. She is very attractive and very dangerous. She flirted with me, and I was taken with her beauty and cleverness. I ought not to say that I was 'in love,' for the sentiment, the fancy, was too evanescent to be dignified with that title; but I was dazzled by her, and it went farther than you will almost believe. When I received the news of Mr. Clarence's legacy, I offered myself to her. You know we had gone roving the previous afternoon, and she let me perceive that she was not happy—that she did not care for Mr. Langdon, and I foolishly came to the conclusion that she might be happier with me. I can scarcely regret this, however, for, though it was a mortification at the time, no sooner had I said the rash words than I repented of them. Before she answered me I had begun to think that I was hasty, and during that drive to Georgetown I felt as if I had made a luckier escape than I deserved. My heart, in the end, was not to suffer from the heedlessness of my fancy."

Lily raised her eyes, and looked for an instant at her friend gravely and silently.

Clarence left his chair, and seated himself on the sofa which she occupied, but a little way off.

"Not that I mean, Lily, to say any thing against Mrs. Langdon, but she is not, to my quieter aspirations, the wife whom I would seek. You smile a little at that magic syllable 'wife,' but recollect that I am nearly twenty. We are getting old. I never wish to keep any secrets of this nature from you, and I feel as if I acted with duplicity in concealing the amount of my admiration for your cousin during my conversations with you; but truly it was only when I was with her that I felt her power. She has that brilliancy which does not permit you to analyze while under its immediate charm, and it is not till you call upon yourself to 'define her position' that you perceive how weak is an influence which passes with the presence of her who speaks. Believe me, she is most dangerous for a life-time devotion, whose gentler qualities increase as you dwell upon them, whose sweet and persuasive excellences act upon you gradually and imperceptibly."

Lily's heart beat rapidly, and Du Verger fell on the floor. Ah! Mrs. Clarendon, instead of being engaged in sunning your pickle-jars, and tying down your blackberry jelly, why are you not assisting at this visit?

"I am of an excitable temperament, Lily: it has cost me hard study to acquire a cold and cautious exterior. Very often I have forced myself to play a part foreign to my feelings, lest I should excite ridicule by my fervency. I suppose it is for this reason that I frequently err on the other side, and say more than is strictly true in an opposite direction, so as to mislead indifferent listeners as to what is moving me, eager to elude detection and sneers. A habit such as this brings on an unnatural state, which many would call hypocritical. Heaven knows there is nothing I so much admire as truth. I should like to pass my days in such a circle, and with such surroundings that perfect purity and childlike candor should be our watchwords and our principles."

Lily smiled her commendation, and made room for Clarence nearer to her.

"I said just now that I did not regret having made an idiot of myself by laying my fortunes at Miss Purvis's feet; it opened my eyes to my folly. I might have gone on forever fancying her perfection whenever we met, if this plunge into rank stupidity had not brought me up like a shower-bath. I am too impulsive, and think *after* action. It was an absurd performance—a boyish freak, and, though it worried me at first, now that I have made you my confession, I feel quite indifferent about it. Scold me, Lily, if you choose, but forgive me for my previous want of confidence."

Lily's look was all pardon.

"I am afraid you *were* foolish, Clarence. I saw how much you were taken with Angel, and I would have liked to speak to you about it, for I did not think that, even if she were disengaged and cared for you, she was just the person to suit your ideas. You know you are strict in your notions of female propriety, and lecture Nora and me dreadfully. Angel thinks differently from you, and is too strong and proud to change her opinions; but when we were alone, and her name was mentioned, you always spoke with the greatest indifference. I understand it now: you thought I would laugh at your desperate passion;" and Lily's small white teeth shone between her fresh rosy lips as she smiled mischievously. "I must be equally candid, though, Clarence; I knew of this offer."

"She told you?"

Lily nodded.

"Did she abuse me, Lily? What did she say about me?"

"That is another affair, Clarence. She did not say that our conversation was private, but I don't think she intended me to repeat it. I shall let her know that, after your confidence, I mentioned my acquaintance with the solitary fact. But one thing I can say, she thinks quite as well of you as you do of her."

Clarence Tracy shook his finger at Lily's sauciness.

"Well, never mind what she says. I dare say she thinks me a very presumptuous youth, and, provided she has not injured me in your opinion, Lily, I would not give a fig—that purple one, for instance (here is an old case in point)—for her decisions. She is very clever, and she is very handsome, and she will be a very splendid New York matron. By-the-way, I will accept your offer now. Peel the fig for me, Lily fair. You will not much longer be able to do me such services."

"When do you go to Europe?" she asked, bending over the plate.

"I leave for New York next week, and just in time to take the Atlantic steamer."

"That is very soon."

"The sooner I go, the sooner I shall return," he said, philosophically.

"Nora will miss you very much," handing him his figs. Her eyes were full of tears.

"Will *you* not miss me?" Clarence said, putting down the fruit untouched. "Lily, you are only fifteen. I hoped to leave this country without saying what my heart longs to say. I love you, Lily. I don't know when I first loved you. Grave, modest, gentle, tender, you have stolen upon me, and filled a great nook in my heart without a recognized wish on my part to secure you there. I never knew how very dear you were to me till I found myself uttering those mad words to Miss Purvis. I thought I loved you as I cherished Nora—with a brother's unimpassioned attachment; but I discovered, with a pang of self-reproach, that Angelica was a fancy—a miserable outbreak of flattered vanity; you were 'the perfect type of budding womanhood' (*he* did not put the quotation marks) that I adored with a purer worship. I do not wish to bind you now by any promise—any vow of constancy. I would scorn to make you look upon it as a duty to remember me. I only beg you to accept *my* vows, without a single promise in return. You are free as air, dearest Lily. If you find that others are more deserving or more pleasing in your eyes, do not hesitate—tell me so—trust me that I shall never advance a claim. I only wish to assure you of my unbounded love—yes, unbounded and unchangeable: a love made up of reverence for your virtues, tenderness for yourself, and a desire for your society. Do you listen to me, Lily?"

At every pore she listened, and her little trembling heart fluttered, and her bright ringlets hid her blushing cheek, as she dipped her hands in and out of a fingerbowl, and tried to seem quiet and controlled. Clarence took one of the wet hands in his own, and pressed it gently.

"Do I wrong you, Lily? or do you believe me, and do you accept my unasking devotion?"

The novice in worldly arts turned her sweet, modest face, with its heavenly eyes and earnest expression, toward her companion. Many an actor (of eminence too) would have paid a high price to secure the recipe for Clarence's eager, impassioned, but respectful air.

"I do believe you, Clarence, if the whole world doubted you. I do not know if I really love you enough to authorize accepting so unselfish an offer, for if I consent to consider you bound to me, I ought to make some promise in return. As you say I am very young, I may meet hereafter with some one who pleases me more. I don't think so," she added, with playful tenderness; "but, any way, I am sure that my uncle would object to such a step, and, of course, you had no idea of keeping it secret?"

"Of course not," said Clarence, with indignant surprise.

"Then let us stay as we are. Both are free to all appearances. We alone will tacitly understand that both are not."

Clarence caught the fluttering hand to his lips. He felt already like a sober married man, for he knew Lily's truth and steadfastness were firm as her life.

"It is not an engagement," Lily pursued; "far from it. We are only going to be better friends than ever, and when you return from Europe, and I shall be a 'young lady—' *Bonjour*, Mademoiselle," rising hastily, as the French teacher, with her nerves and her ether, entered.

Clarence took leave with a smile of open cordiality and affectionate regard. Lily began her lessons. She did not know one word of them, but she was in a happy state of subdued satisfaction, which rendered her oblivious of Mademoiselle Durong's displeasure.

Clarence was true—Clarence had been guilty of only a temporary and fleeting infidelity. He was her friend again, and he had told her, with an eloquence which was music to her prejudiced ears, that he loved her, and had never *loved* but her.

❀ CHAPTER X

I do not intend to follow my heroine minutely through all the remainder of her juvenile days. After this conversation, or explanation with Clarence, and his departure, the time moved on with monstrous calm. It is terribly the fashion nowadays to transport the higher regions of sentimental history, as well as all others, into the bosoms and lives of children. Dickens has a great deal to answer for in inventing Little Nell, for his imitators have since flooded the world with a host of "serious girls," and "prayerful babies," and unnatural infants generally, which will soon induce the readers and admirers of such tales to fancy that, after sixteen years of age, life ends instead of beginning. Little people who can scarcely talk lisp Methodist sermons, and argue with their elders, and show judgment, tact, and energy which invariably throw into contempt the strongest efforts in the same line of all grown men and women.

In fact, their labors are superhuman. They bake, wash, and brew—educate, and care for their fathers, mothers, grandmothers, and grandfathers, to the remotest generation, and *naturally*, after all this, die of extreme old age at fifteen or thereabouts, leaving behind them reputations of unparalleled magnitude. Their conversations are of the deepest theological research, though, for the most part, a little ungrammatical; and, in short, were I capable of portraying such monsters, "which the world ne'er saw," my book would always lack one important reader—myself. I am happy to say that Lily, though a grave, earnest, and, in her way, precocious girl, affords no field for continuous history during the next two years. She studied her lessons and recited them; she kept her things in order; she read improving books, and practiced music and drawing. Clarence wrote to her openly, and told her of his travels, of the places that he visited, and of the people that he knew, with a few *réticences*. In the course of the following autumn he mentioned having met Angelica, who had gone to winter in Rome. She passed through Paris, and he described their dinner at Véry's with Mr. Langdon, Cecilia, and some other Americans. Lily was very proud of his letters, which came once a month. She kept them in a rosewood box inlaid with mother-of-pearl, and lined throughout with rose-colored, scented satin. As a mark of supreme favor, she read them aloud to her favorites, for Clarence behaved with his usual attention to outward observances, and never wrote one line which could not be repeated to her guardian. He understood Lily as far as that went. She would approve of no clandestine nor veiled words. She meant what she had said. It was only to be tacitly an understanding. Both were free; and Lily's true heart needed no reiterated vows, and could not have been brought to comprehend a doubt existing of her future ratification of the present vague position. Truly, she never thought about the future as regarded Clarence except that he was to come home. She lived in the present childlike contentment; and if Mr. or Mrs. Clarendon had questioned her about Clarence, she would simply have answered, "When I am grown up, Clarence and I will be engaged."

Her own letters were frank and girlish. She told him all the news that was likely to be interesting about their juvenile friends; she consulted him about her studies; advised him of her progress in such and such branches, and made her artless comments upon his gay life, and compared it with Willie's.

Willie Clarendon was leading a very quiet existence. After a month or two of amusement, he had settled down at one of the German law universities, and was drinking beer, smoking meerschaums, and enjoying slightly prosy views of domestic felicity among the plump frauleins. Clarence meant to join him after a while, and pursue their legal ambitions together, but he was not ready yet. Paris had so many attractions; he was rapidly acquiring the "true Parisian accent" (the attaining of which is apt to cost so much in more ways than paying French masters), and it would be a thousand pities to leave while on the point of perfecting himself in this useful and agreeable language.

With these letters, and her unvarying contentment and equable temper, the summer would have passed agreeably even without a change of air or scene; but Alicia's health failed, and they went to Sullivan's Island to give her the benefit of sea-bathing.

The girls had not been at this pleasant ocean resort, situated only six miles from the city, at the mouth of the harbor, and open, consequently, to the broad Atlantic, since a few months after the death of Mr. Vere, when Lily's thinness, want of appetite, and visible pining had induced a similar pilgrimage.

Mr. Clarendon indulged in a notion that Charleston was quite as cool and far more agreeable than 'the island,' as Charlestonians familiarly call the patriotic spot made sacred by its palmetto fort and Revolutionary glory. He complained of the sand, the glare, the monotony, as if the city boasted of no evils in comparison; and Mrs. Clarendon was too good a wife to have a contrary opinion from her husband. Even if she had delighted in this calm, peaceful retreat, with the great waves ever breaking in glorious, church-like music upon the shore, and a three-mile stretch of beach, wide, firm, and glittering, she would have deemed it her "duty" to encourage an opposite sentiment, and to feel and to express her preference for the dusty, stifling city, which only grows endurable when the sea-breeze, after giving its first blessing to the Island and its inhabitants, wafts a faint semblance of its precious comfort to the fevered expectants in mouldy wooden houses and built-up streets.

But Lily and Alicia delighted in the Island. Through the closed Venetian blinds all day came sufficient air to make them willing believers in the excellence of the climate. They lived in a house hired, with the furniture, for the season. A long apartment, surrounded on two sides by piazzas (those unfailing appendages to Southern buildings), which were covered by *jalousies,* served as sitting-room and dining-room. At one end, a piano, books, work, and flowers proclaimed the "dress-circle;" at the other, a sideboard and round-table, with a fly-brush of peacock's feathers, spoke of meals served and eaten. The mantle-shelf was broad, and held a range of old volumes, with numerous candlesticks, and the tall glass shades under which the lights are protected from the wind. A pantry, and bedroom for George, on the same floor, completed these primitive and unexpensive arrangements, if you except that in the wide entrance-hall, which opened into the sitting-room with a folding-door never closed, there stood a refrigerator, offering iced water and cool bottles of claret to all comers.

The girls took possession of what they dubbed the "sky parlor," refusing the second floor of bed-rooms, and preferring this attic, which had windows at every point of the compass, and in which apartment they shifted their beds to which ever quarter the wind blew from.

Lily would stand for hours, before going to rest, gazing upon the old surf, the white sands, the huge crested billows, the light-house winking in the distance, the indistinct walls of Fort Moultrie, and across the channel, seated as it were upon the waters, the stately pile of Fort Sumter, not yet completed. Alicia would call out, "Lily, do you never mean to go to sleep?" several times, and then my heroine (who was not in the least heroic) would put out her candle (burning in a lantern, which all candles must do, if they burn at all in this positive breeze), and would go to bed, lulled on her pillow by the sound she loved—the ceaseless roll of the mighty king of oceans.

And how delightful they thought the drives, rides, or strolls upon the beach at low tide! With no bonnets nor "last-style" mantles—no gloves nor necessary parasols, they sauntered out toward sunset, scarfs tied around their waists or hanging from their arms, in case they should feel chilly, and thick boots protecting their feet from the disagreeable effects of the salt water upon clean stockings.

They would meet several young people, bound, like themselves, for a walk upon the beach, and, joining forces, the little regiment of damsels would scamper along, or walk soberly, or run races methodically, just as best pleased them, for "the island" is a spot free from conventional rules, where you are not forced to remember "behavior," nor to conduct yourself with the stiff propriety and full-dress customs of "fashionable watering-places."

The walk over, many of them would adjourn to each other's houses, and spend the remainder of the evening in mirthful though quiet enjoyment, with cards, music, and chat, parting at a reasonable hour with the certainty that a fair sky would enable them to resume the following evening the like entertainments.

How sweet to recall those thoughtless, early days! I have spent many, many summers upon this calm old island, which has a rooted, settled look like a place which existed before the surrounding country was made. I suppose it is owing to the weather-beaten, antique appearance of the houses, which no paint can do more than temporarily freshen. There are few attempts at gardens or vegetation; but here and there, around some residences, a green patch is cultivated, a pride-of-India gives its sickly, fragrant blossoms to the breeze, or an oleander rises to a superb height in this salt atmosphere, which promotes its growth. Geraniums of the hardier sort flourish in profusion. Within the walls of Fort Moultrie thick hedges of the rose-geranium are seen, and it was a great pleasure for Lily and Alicia at high tide to visit the fort instead of the beach; to walk upon the broad grass-grown ramparts, and to carry home with them afterward whole branches of green, perfumed leaves, to dress their hair and the flower-pots.

It was during one of these martial rambles that I first met and knew Lily Vere. I was then young enough to believe in perfection, and to my eyes Lily was perfect. The matured dignity of her manner, and the entire simplicity and unsophistication of her feelings and conversation, struck me as something quite wonderful and very lovable.

We became sociable and mutually pleased. I received an impression of her beautiful character which has never left me, and this is the reason why I have undertaken to write her little story. A good many of the details which I have already narrated I listened to from her own lips, but the most part I have sought out and learned from others, for I saw Lily Vere but seldom after this summer, which we spent together so joyously and so free from care on Sullivan's Island. My pathway through life has been very obscure, and we were not likely to meet in the brilliant, sunny, well-beaten high road which was her track.

She was very fond of talking to me of her father (when we grew well acquainted), and of her mother dying when she was born, and which sad event had certainly impaired her father's health. She seemed never to think of her acres, her bank stock, her houses, and her general independence, except as a means by which she could always keep her friends together.

"There are the Jenningses," she would say; "when I am twenty-one, or if I marry before that"—and I did not then understand the little blush and the momentary droop of the well-opened but modest blue eye—"if I marry before that, I will not hear of their teaching and wearying themselves with governess work, leaving us all for distant homes. I know that I am rich, and where is the use of riches if it does not enable you to surround yourself with those whom you love. What is there that money will buy or can procure to equal the pleasure of assisting those whom you have known and cared for all your days?"

There was no ostentation in this; it was too sincere; and having discovered that, by family reverses, these early companions were to be sent upon the world as teachers, she had taken the resolution to assist them, never mentioning it to her guardian, lest he should oppose it; but I learned afterward that he accidentally discovered her plans that very year, and carried them at once into effect. An annuity was settled upon both Ella and Kate, which they enjoy until this day.

To return to the girls: they bathed daily in the sea, and Alicia recovered her color and appetite, so that Mr. Clarendon began to respect the Island, if he did not love it as an abiding-place.

At the eastern end, where but half a dozen houses are built, there stand tall sand-hills, the most glorious spots for romps. A little creeping vine, with dusky purple flowers, covers the miniature valleys between these hills like a stiff carpet of prim pattern, and here and there spring up little branches like vegetable coral, with hard sprays of a brilliant red, and minute white blossoms. On the summits grow the wild oats and wild fern, which wave their yellow ears, and contrast with the dark masses of the wild myrtle clustering in the depths beyond; but among these last it is not very safe to enter after nightfall. They are unhealthy, damp, and give unfailing promise of fever and chills, arising from the malaria of the "back creek."

No such cautions are necessary a few yards in front, amid the hills and facing the ocean. Here Lily and her companions would amuse themselves with games of all sorts, shut out from observation by the intervening heights of glistening sand. The boys of the party, commanded by George Clarendon, would bring from the carriages in waiting jugs of lemonade, and baskets of ice and cakes. They would spread their pastoral refreshment upon those hard, unlife-like vines, and laugh, and joke, and enjoy their youth and liberty with a blue sky above them, richer than satin flutings, and streaks of vermilion shooting up from the western horizon, bidding them "good-night" in the sun's name.

Then Mr. Clarendon would ride up on his famous bay mare, "Lady Bessy," and inspect the company; sometimes Burleigh would be with him (having been forgotten at home, or left purposely), and he would show his indignation for the neglect by refusing, at first, to notice any of them, standing close at "Lady Bessy's" heels, and turning away superbly from confectionary offers; but, relenting presently, he would suffer Lily to pat him and to feed him, expressing his disapprobation of her cruelty or carelessness by one of those grave, concentrated nods which had won him his name.

Again I exclaim, happy, thoughtless days!

In October the Clarendons moved to the city, and the winter was spent in uninterrupted calm, but the following spring brought a great change. Instead of going into the country for the month of April, they were to sail for New York early in June, and Mrs. Clarendon could not sanely contemplate additional packings-up; besides, for a five months' absence, she had a world of preparations to make. It was years since she had gone farther north than the Santee River Plantation, and it is a wonder that the good lady did not break out into open rebellion; but Mr. Clarendon had been pestered with questions as to the wisdom of allowing his daughter and his ward to grow up without fashionable accomplishments from better masters than Charleston afforded. "Was it right," some officious individuals suggested, "that such an heiress as Miss Vere should not have advantages as great as the daughters of other Southern gentlemen enjoyed?"

Mr. Clarendon thought it over, and decided that the girls should go to a Northern boarding-school for a year or two, but it was not so easy to fix upon the precise school. Each young lady who had been "finished" beyond Mason and Dixon's line had her especial scholastic bower, which she cried up as a very fount of learning and propriety; so Mr. Clarendon determined that he would go and judge for himself, place them wherever his choice fell, and reside in their vicinity afterward for a little while, to watch the system, and to see if it answered.

Mrs. Clarendon groaned and labored, put a double quantity of pepper and camphor into carpets and woolen clothes, as if she knew that the moths would be tempted to extra ravages during her absence, and kept the family on a short allowance of spoons and forks for a week before her departure, because every article of plate was sent betimes to the safest bank.

At length they were ready, and the luggage was something overpowering to behold. The dear lady suffered under the idea that she could procure nothing so good in Yankee-land as what was purchasable in Charleston, so that one huge trunk held medicines, old linen in case of fractures, superfine tea, some best brandy, a "trifle" of old Port wine, ditto of Madeira, and a general collection of odds and ends, which, had she been going to Europe instead of to New York, would have caused the party much detention and suspicion at the custom house, or "duane," as bearers of unaccountably strange articles.

Mr. Clarendon, as was his wont, laughed, and asked "my dear" if she would not carry some more boxes; and, in fact, "as the transportation of boxes was more convenient than the handing about of young ladies, would she object to putting up Lily and Alicia in long French trunks, with iron bands and a few air-holes?"

🕮 CHAPTER XI

New York was a great surprise and a terrible trial to "the daughter of Carolina," with her fixed ideas and her objection to novelties.

The noise, bustle, and confusion only amused and excited the girls, who, finding Mrs. Clarendon positively averse to venturing out, but resigned that they should go, with George as their chaperon, shopping and sightseeing, would walk off daily to Stewart's and Beck's, and buy loads of "pretty things."

It must be confessed that their tastes were not strictly correct, and Angelica would have held up her hands in just indignation had she seen them laying in their supplies. Fortunately, it was not the season for worsteds, or, with the unfailing mistake of Charleston habits, they would certainly have paid high prices for "full-dress" gowns of bright-patterned mousselines, only suitable for robes de chambre.

I remember once feeling my cheeks quite in a glow while standing by

Stewart's counter, waiting until my unobtrusive appearance should awaken the attention of a dashing clerk. A lady, who was purchasing a silk of the richest lustre, turned over a pile of gaudy mousselines, rather fine in texture, at my elbow.

"Pray," said she, tossing her little nose contemptuously, "*who* buys all these stuffs?"

"South Carolina ladies, madam," announced the clerk, bowing; "they prefer this style for walking and visiting;" and he grinned.

I recalled the streets of my native place, and felt the truth of the announcement.

This reminds me of Mrs. Clarendon's adventure in shopping. Growing tired, at last, of the little chamber, eight feet by ten, in which she was drearily knitting away her time, she bethought herself that she would purchase a new breakfast set of china, and that was the commencement of her New York walks.

The young ladies, grown familiar with Broadway, undertook to conduct her safely, and safely she was deposited in one of the great China emporiums, dazzled by the brilliancy, and very fearful of being cheated.

"Some breakfast sets—tea and coffee cups?" she inquired.

Half a dozen cups were rattled down before her, and the active salesman was preparing to bring others, when she hurriedly said, "Never mind to get any more; just let me know the price of these first; I am only looking about before buying." But the shopman continued to pile up plates, to name prices, to dive after others, to draw forward slop-bowls, and to worry his customer dreadfully. He was so polite.

"Never mind," she repeated; "I can see them up there. I may not buy these, after all. I hate to give you so much trouble, for I am not sure that I shall buy."

The "young man" turned around and looked lazily at her. He laid aside his springy, cat-like motions, and said, with calm dignity,

"I am put here, ma'am, to show these goods. It does not make the least difference to me whether you buy or not. I receive my salary, just the same, if not a purchaser comes into this store during the entire day;" and then resuming his "store" manner, the accomplished and philosophical salesman placed a new stock of porcelain under the good lady's nose, who flurriedly sounded it with her knuckles, while Lily and Alicia retired a few steps, and were convulsed with laughter.

Mr. Clarendon inquired about schools; had a preference for Madame Chegaray, discussed Madame Binsse, thought of Madame Canda, and, while making up his mind, discovered that it was so warm it would be better to go to Saratoga; then Newport offered inducements; but Niagara and Canada carried the day.

They traveled in every direction, enjoyed themselves very much (even Mrs. Clarendon grew a little reconciled), and, meeting some friends now settled in Philadelphia, they came to the conclusion that the city of straight streets and very clean bricks was the favored spot for female education.

It must not be supposed, meanwhile, that Miss Vere and Miss Clarendon, though very pretty young girls, created, like all heroines of novels every where, and like all other young Charleston beauties who travel North, an immense and surprising sensation. The fact is, that among the curious and incomprehensible circumstances which make up that hash "common gossip," nothing knocks one over with more unerring amazement than the belleship of my ordinary acquaintances.

A flock of creditable enough girls sail for New York to pass a summer, no one suspecting (unless they judge from foregone conclusions in other cases) that they are going to take the land by force of—fascination, but the very first advices after their departure speak of their "stunning" effect upon the hitherto benighted inhabitants. They are overwhelmed with attentions; they walk the streets with a tail of followers like a Highland chief, and they come home pursued by rumors—I must say seldom by the causes of these rumors.

These stupendous reputations for agreeability and corresponding charms, which yet, to our eyes, bring them back not different from when they left, always call to my mind an anecdote of a little lady who was describing a visit she had paid in a distant part of the country.

"Oh!" she wound up, "I was such a belle!"

"My dear," said her attentive listener, "why did you ever come back?"

Lily was often admired in a quiet way, and, had she kept her ears open to every sound, she would have heard her own praises not unfrequently. Alicia's pretty, innocent look, and her dark-brown eyes, likewise attracted attention, but there was no rush made to know them, and they passed many evenings seated side by side in various ball-rooms, at various hotels and watering-places, enjoying the sight, without any partners to take them on the floor, unless they had danced alternately with George.

In fact, Mr. Clarendon was much to blame; he ought to have held his head higher, sniffed the air with disgust, refused every thing on the public tables, talked a great deal of "South Carolina," and given the world to understand that he "was a man, sir, not used to associating with common people, and of a fortune which enabled him to command the best, and to scorn even the second best."

On the contrary, Mr. Clarendon kept very dark about himself and his family; was open to advances from respectable-looking persons; avoided snobs; uttered no boasts of his pretensions, and didn't seem to despise any body. They made a few new acquaintances; and, though the novelty of the thing pleased them, the girls were sure that this was not the very most delightful summer they could spend, and that "traveling at the North" in a humdrum way, and associating principally with Charlestonians, would not make a lively trip, after you had once performed it; and that they must be singularly devoid of capabilities for pleasing strangers, since their career had not in the least corresponded with the triumphal march which Jane Griffiths, and Susan Fuller, and other young ladies had made through the Northern watering-places.

In Philadelphia they came to a decided halt, and the 1st of September found them inmates of an admirable Pensionnat de Demoiselles, where, after Mr. and Mrs. Clarendon had, from a neighboring boarding-house, kept watch over them during six weeks, they were installed positively for a year at least.

The "rules and regulations" for their comfort and instruction were based on liberal and enlightened views. They were not forced to rise before daylight; they did not perform their ablutions in tin basins, twenty at a time, with their dresses "hooked up," and their shoes and stockings already drawn on, trusting to a Saturday or Friday night's general wash to bring them up, for Sunday only, all clean; they were not starved at any meal, nor served with ill-made dishes; in a word, they were treated like creatures who a few months later were to appear as modest and refined women; and, surely, a régime such as I have hinted at could never, by itself, produce this result.

I do not think that I am exaggerating when I give this picture of what some schools for young ladies were ten years ago, but it is to be hoped that the march of civilization has destroyed such singular methods of cultivating feminine instincts; for it was never *necessary*, in educating young girls, to consider their physical condition as a matter of little consequence, while their mental culture was taxed to the utmost.

At this rare and model school the youthful Charlestonians made much progress, and profited by their advantages.

They did not become miracles of accomplishments, but they improved in every respect; wrote home that they were quite happy, and did not pine unnecessarily for the arrival of Alicia's seventeenth birth-day, which, arriving in the following autumn, was to be the signal of their release from school thralldom, and their entrance into a state of young ladyhood. Lily was seventeen in April, and her cousin Angelica, who returned soon after from abroad, sent her a birth-day gift, and a polite invitation to both to spend their summer vacation with her—partly at her beautiful country-seat on the Hudson, and partly at Saratoga, where she was going to exhibit her Paris finery while fresh from its enticing-looking and every-thing-promising white cartons.

They actually declined the tempting offer, though Alicia was sorely inclined to forget her promise to her father, who had urged that they should remain quietly at school, and continue their lessons, if possible, during their vacation; but Lily was firm, and studied diligently.

Three hours a day her fresh, young voice, or her pretty, graceful touch was heard at her piano. She was no great musician, but she had taste, if not execution; sang with sweetness and correctness, though her notes were few, and was, in short, one of those unpretending performers to whom one can listen without an hour's praying and prelude.

Alicia did not sing, but she played brilliantly, and read music fluently; was rather indifferent about it, and lacked that love of the art which, though restricted from want of *genius*, gave interest to Lily's playing.

"I know why you plod over your music in that untiring way," Alicia said, one warm afternoon toward the close of the vacations, when the two sat together in the back parlor at Madame —'s, Lily patiently deciphering a difficult passage in Thalberg, and Alicia lolling back in the easiest chair she could find, fanning continuously with a lazy motion, and too enervated to look into the Italian book she held in her other hand.

"Why?" asked Lily, pausing, and turning round for a second, with her finger raised over the next note.

"Because Clarence Tracy has chosen to go mad at Heidelberg over the trombone, or ophicleide, or Jew's-harp, or Heaven knows what, and you intend to perfect yourself so as to perform duets with him."

"Nonsense!" said Lily, bringing down the rose-leaf finger upon the un-offending key with sudden force; "instead of talking such folly, help me read this, Alice, dear."

"It is so very warm!" said Alicia, yawning; "and if it had not been for you, we should have gone to Angelica, and been comfortable at Arcadia, or gay at Saratoga now. Papa would never have refused, and mamma never cares what we do, if only we keep well."

"But, my dear, we should have lost so much time! Next summer we can accept Angel's offer, and, after a winter's campaign at home, we shall be better able to enjoy very gay society. Think how much we can study during the next few weeks!"

"What is the use of study?" asked Alicia. "Somehow every one marries so early, and then you give up music and every thing. Look at all the women we know at home. They are taught French, music, drawing, 'geography and the use of the globe,' and as soon as they marry, they shut the piano, never open a French book, give their paints away, and might a great deal better have had all the money spent on these accomplishments put in the Savings' Bank instead. It is a great waste of time and dollars to study."

"Oh, Alicia!" exclaimed Lily; then she added, "Do you intend to marry?"

"I don't intend to be an old maid," said Alicia, bluntly.

"Why not?"

"Why not?" said Alicia, imitating Lily's soft voice; "because there is a prejudice in favor of marriage. There is no one I intend at this present moment to honor with my hand, but I have no doubt there is somebody waiting somewhere who is destined to impress me favorably, and to whom I shall one day say, 'Ask papa.'"

"Well, I can not understand," said Lily, musingly, "that one should marry any body except a person whom you have known a long while; and marriage in the abstract—just to think that you will probably marry, no one in particular occurring to you—seems so queer."

"Pshaw!" ejaculated Alicia, "you have the most extraordinary notions. I am sure I don't care to marry. It must be a dull business—almost as dull as these wearisome days, which appear to grow longer instead of shorter. Let us—" She stopped suddenly. A peculiar low whistle sounded beneath the window of the front parlor, and came faintly to her ear.

She sprang up, and was about to enter the next room, which was darker than the one in which they sat, but, changing her mind, she came toward the piano, and, pushing Lily gently aside, said,

"If you *will* practice forever, let me help you with this, and then we can go and take a walk afterward, if Madame will allow us."

She struck a few bars rapidly.

"Why, Lily, what a fuss about nothing! I declare it is as easy as this;" and she played "Fly not yet—'tis just the hour," and then broke into "Whistle and I'll come to you, my lad," touching the keys with a skillful hand.

As she paused again, again the low whistle sounded, and this time Lily heard it too.

"Oh stop, Alicia! Some passer-by is attracted by your brilliant performance, and is presuming to answer it. Keep to my piece."

"I tell you what, my love," answered Alicia, striking a few notes at random, "if you will leave this tiresome old music till to-morrow morning, and go to walk with me now, I will teach you every line of it then. The sun is nearly down; I wish some things at Hauel's, and, if you will ask Madame's permission, and promise in my name that I will be as 'sage' as yourself, she will allow us to go out together."

Lily was not very loth, so they proceeded to make the request, which Madame granted, adding to Miss Clarendon,

"Je te conseille, ma fille, de suivre l'exemple de ma chère Lily. Promenez-toi en demoiselle bien élevée, et ne regardez point les flaneurs."

Oh, Madame!" exclaimed her pupil, casting down her pretty brown eyes, and speaking in French good enough to please and to mollify her instructress, "what makes you think that I look at people in the street?"

Madame nodded her head sagaciously. "My eyes see every thing, though I do wear spectacles, chère enfant. And where are those same lunettes?" she added, turning round in all directions, while Lily suggested "her pocket," which, after due search, did produce the articles in question, though Madame persisted that they were not there, and had overturned every book and paper on the table beside her before she would consent to follow Lily's advice. "Les voilà!" she exclaimed, placing them on her well-defined nose, and fixing her penetrating, handsome, coffee-colored eyes on Alicia, while she patted the young lady's smooth-braided hair. "You like to see who is looking at you, ma chère Alice. I do not need my spectacles to find that out;" and her mind reverting to her recent hunt, she ejaculated, "Que Dieu vous préserve la vûe, mes enfants," and dismissed them with a kiss apiece.

The girls occupied a room together, and thither they now flew to make their toilets. Alicia ran first to the window, and peeped over the blinds into the street. Apparently what she saw pleased her, for a smile was dancing all over her face as she selected her prettiest dress, and laid out her most becoming bonnet and mantle.

"Pray, Lily, make haste," she said several times, and at last they were both ready.

"Why are you so impatient?" inquired Lily.

"It is late," answered Miss Clarendon. "I wish to buy several things, and Madame does not let us go out alone so often that we need waste the few hours that we have."

"And if she thinks that you look at young gentlemen," remarked Lily, smiling mischievously, "adieu to future walks, unless we go with the whole troop of our schoolmates when *les classes* are again in full operation." They opened the street door as Lily said this, and Alicia, after one quick glance in the opposite direction, called her companion's attention to the block of houses facing them.

"Did you know," she inquired, "that formerly these houses were called 'Carolina Row?' such numbers of our country people occupied and owned them."

Talking of home and home concerns, they pursued their way and entered Chestnut Street, Lily's unsuspicious mind never imagining that the sauntering walk of a tall, handsome man, who was loftily progressing on the other side of the street, had any connection with *their* promenade.

Alicia was very demure and very proper. She spoke in a low tone, kept her eyes in their legitimate direction, and behaved in a way to have perfectly reassured Madame's fears.

At the perfumer's they stopped, and Alicia produced a list a quarter of a yard in length. She wanted pomade, eau lustrale, hair-pins, perfumes, soaps—you would have supposed that both fire and water had aided to sweep away and destroy the whole contents of her dressing-box with one storm.

The pretty little Frenchified shopwoman, with graceful empressement, produced samples of the first article, and Alicia commenced her selection.

Every pot of pomade was turned, twisted, examined, smelt. Alicia's dainty kid glove first approached the surface of the smooth, perfumed *moell de bœuf,* then she drew off the delicate *gant de Paris,* and with the ends of her small taper fingers felt the grain of the blessed unctuous compound destined to assist in the shining structure of her dark tresses.

At this instant a manly step sounded beside them, and a deep grave voice said,

"Some pomade?"

Lily turned almost involuntarily, and was struck with the beauty and stature of the new-comer; but Alicia called upon her to decide "which jar was prettiest, since all were equally good."

She had not looked at the stranger, who now was obliged to join them at the same counter, and who was objecting to the strong fragrance of the article which another and still prettier grisette offered him.

"Give me some *à la vanille blanche,*" he said; "such violent perfumes are so vulgar!"

The well-bred Frenchwoman glanced hastily at the elegant young lady who had just laid aside a cut-glass jar of the condemned "*fleur d'orange*," and, as if accidentally, the gentleman looked in the same direction.

With a faint exclamation of surprise, he removed his hat, and bowing profoundly, a movement which he executed with peculiar grace and extraordinary respect, said,

"Miss Clarendon, I believe?"

Alicia returned his bow with a momentary expression of uncertainty, and then smiling as if a gleam of recollection had darted through her mind,

"I beg your pardon; I did not at first recognize you."

Lily looked and felt surprise. She touched Alicia's arm with a warning pressure.

"Are you alone?" asked the gentleman.

"No," answered Alicia; "my friend, I may almost say, my sister, Miss Vere, is with me. Lily," turning round, "allow me to introduce Mr. Barclay."

Once more the hat was removed from the stately brow, and short, black, wavy hair, and the tall, haughty figure bent itself in grave courtesy.

He was very handsome—what is called "a splendid-looking man"—large and powerfully made, with well-proportioned hands and feet; his eyes were dark and expressive, but the general expression was one which those men whom he eclipsed, and those women whom he neglected, pronounced "disagreeable." On the contrary, those ladies whom he "adored" considered the eyes irresistible, and would allow them no rival but his mouth, which was of a beautiful but voluptuous cut. His teeth were not of a dead white, but had that slight, unbroken sallow tinge, which, like certain skins and colors, lights up at night to a dazzling whiteness; while his mustache looked like floss silk dipped in India ink, admirably suiting the bronzed shade of his smooth cheek.

The peculiarity of his appearance was a certain nameless dégagé, don't-care-a-straw carriage, which seemed to be the foundation on which he had built the loftiest, most dignified, and yet most insolent manner. Looking at him, you were at a loss to decide whether the first or the last were his natural self—whether he was born and educated for a handsome rowdy, and overlaid it with this assumption of haughtiness, or whether he had chosen on his stately basis to graft these opposite qualities.

In a word, if you liked him, you could find a thousand charms in his appearance, and if you chanced to dislike him, you could turn every beauty into disparagement.

Before her acquaintance had fully accomplished his elaborately respectful bow, which was far from being a mocking one, but which really seemed the expression of his deep consideration for "the sex," and his personal conviction of the effect that he was making by showing this respect, Alicia had found time to whisper to Lily, "I'll tell you about him presently."

But Harry Barclay had no idea of allowing those earnest blue eyes to wonder any more, or to permit that calm reasoning power which he (a good judge of character from countenance) saw lay under her feminine exterior to decide for itself about this meeting; so he remarked to Lily,

"I have not had this happiness before, Miss Vere. I met Miss Clarendon last June at a small tea-drinking, given, I think, to both of you, but from which indisposition prevented your assisting."

"Don't you remember Mrs. Elliott's invitation, dear?" put in Alicia; "such a nice party!"

"Yes, perfectly," said Lily, smiling; "but I think you told me then that it was rather dull."

"Oh! things improve as you look back upon them," said Harry Barclay. "I trust that I do not interfere with your shopping," he added, with sudden recollection; "but, if I might be permitted to join you in your walk, and see you safely home afterward, I should feel very proud of the honor. I do not know if Madame — allows such attentions, but Mrs. Elliott will be answerable to her for my good behavior and my trustworthy qualities."

"Mrs. Elliott is not in town," said Lily, gravely disapproving.

"I beg your pardon; she returned from Saratoga a week ago. I had the pleasure of meeting her in New York, and we reached Philadelphia in company."

"Oh yes, Lily," said Alicia, coaxingly, in a low tone; "where *is* the harm?"

Lily could not exactly say where, but she yielded against her better judgment, remarking gently,

"It is getting late."

"Help me, then," said Alicia, tearing off the half of her paper list, and thrusting it into Miss Vere's hand; "choose those for me while I am getting these." And her next purchase required a move to the opposite counter, leaving Lily where she was.

"So you have come back at last!" were Miss Alicia's first words, in a reproachful tone, to her tall "acquaintance," who strode leisurely after her, and stood looking down *du haut de sa grandeur* upon the pretty, pettish little girl, whose small and graceful figure did not reach his elbow.

"At last!" echoed Mr. Barclay; "have you wished to see me sooner?"

A tender look from the *pensionnaire*, whom Madame had suspected of such accomplishments, was her only answer. Then she said,

"I staid here all summer, thinking that you would soon return from Virginia with your health quite restored, otherwise I should never have consented to give up Mrs. Langdon's invitation—I don't like this soap: let me see some more—Matilda Browne gave me your message yesterday, and by your whistle under the window and presence now, I suppose she gave you my note in return?"

"She did, and cross enough it was too. What a little vixen you are! But the winding up was better."

"Did you destroy it?" asked Alicia, eagerly, hoping to hear "No."

"Certainly; I tore it up, and threw the scraps into one of those horrid American inventions for a people who use tobacco in all shapes."

Every fibre in Alicia's lady-like organization revolted against such a receptacle for the ashes of an *almost* billet-doux, and Master Harry Barclay was never nearer the loss of a conquest than at that moment; but jealousy saved him.

"What a lovely creature Miss Vere is!" he went on, noticing Alicia's darkening brow. "She looks so sweet-tempered!"

"Have you come here to talk about Lily's beauty?"

"No, I have come to admire anew Alicia's beauty," said Mr. Barclay, imitating her defiant, spoiled-child tone. "What are you angry about? You are the most difficult creature to please! Here I have occupied two hours of this warm afternoon, first waiting under the windows of Madame —'s select *pensionnat de demoiselles*, running the risk of losing my character, and passing for a dissipated youth, who flirts with budding school-girls; then sitting in the apothecary's shop at the corner, drinking minute glasses of soda-water (which might well have served as 'minute guns' of distress from a ship fast sinking in despair), while uncertain whether to go or stay—whether you were making a toilet of unexampled freshness, or whether Madame was inexorable, and you never meant to come at all! After all this, you receive me with a frown that makes a great ridge down your forehead, and frightens that poor shop-woman into fits."

Alicia smiled relentingly, and, seeing Lily approaching, began diligently to select her purchases, while Harry stooped to examine some trinket within the counter, and murmured close in the small, curved ear, tucked away in her white chip bonnet, "This is so like you! We meet for half an hour, and you take twenty-five minutes to get through your first scold."

"Come, Alicia," said Lily, her hands full of small packages; and in a short time the whole list was gone through, the address given, and the party left Hauel's, Mademoiselle Céleste saying to Mademoiselle Alphonsine as they went out,

"Voilà M. Barclay lancé une autre fois! Elle est jolie cette petite dernière."

Lily felt very uncomfortable. She knew that Madame's rules were strict, and yet how could she make up her mind to tell this stalwart, lazy, haughty, handsome gentleman, who walked beside them, that he must go, and thereby deeply anger Alicia, who set no bounds upon her wrath when thwarted?

Mr. Barclay proposed a *sorbet* at Parkinson's, but Lily steadily refused.

"Then I shall go alone, Lily," said Alicia, decidedly. "We are not babies. This is vacation too. You know that if we were not under Madame's care, we could go and eat as many ices as we chose, with a regiment of young dragoons to escort us. Although we are still at school, we are old enough to know what is in itself right and proper, and to guide our actions accordingly. Do you think that ice cream is a sin?"

The result was, that Lily found herself at Parkinson's, and very silently swallowed her *sorbet;* but Mr. Barclay was so perfectly well-bred, so much at his ease, so respectful, so deferential, and, at the same time, so agreeable, that she found herself enjoying his society, and forgetting the reproofs awaiting them at home.

At the corner of the street next to Madame's establishment, Miss Clarendon paused and dismissed their escort, who bowed and withdrew, though Lily longed to catch him by the skirts of his coat, and to insist upon his taking them to the door. This clandestine parting augured badly for a full confession to Madame, and, sure enough, Alicia began, so soon as they resumed their walk,

"Now, my dearest Lily, you do not intend to mention Harry Barclay to Madame?"

"Indeed I do."

"You are, without exception," exclaimed Alicia, coloring violently, "the most strait-laced, tiresome girl! Pray tell me, did we not, in Charleston, and during our travels last summer, walk constantly with young men? and did we not, two years ago, on Sullivan's Island, run races, and stroll about forever with dozens of youths? That was not thought wrong, why should this be?"

"It was not forbidden by those in authority over us," said Lily, gently. "We never concealed it, which proved that there was nothing hurtful in so doing. Depend upon it, my dear Alicia, our own feelings guide us more unerringly in all cases than the reiterated commands and injunctions of our protectors and guardians—our parents, if we have any. From childhood up, we can almost always be sure that those of our actions which we would hide from the knowledge of our elders are tinctured in a more or less degree with impropriety. Sometimes we perform a good deed of which we do not boast, but we would not fear to have it known."

"Do join the Quakers, and 'let the Spirit move you' frequently to exhort," said Miss Clarendon, contemptuously. "How you do prose!"

"Dearest Alice!" exclaimed Lily, using her pet name for her guardian's daughter, and throwing her arms about her, for they had now reached home and were safe in their own little apartment, "dearest Alice, listen to me. I am not suspicious, I trust, but I am not utterly blind and foolish. At first I thought this afternoon that this meeting was accidental, but too great an intimacy exists between this gentleman and yourself for me to believe that you have only seen him once before, and that at a formal evening party. Your whispers at the opposite counter, the significant smiles exchanged between those two Frenchwomen, and a certain air on both sides, convince me that you have entered into a foolish flirtation, in which you can but gain much discredit. Who is this Mr. Harry Barclay? and where have you seen and learned to know him?"

Alicia pouted, shook off Lily's embrace, and trotted her foot angrily.

"I do not wish to force your confidence, my darling, nor bribe you into being candid with me; but if you will explain this affair, we may consult about it, and probably we can decide to bring it to a more respectable conclusion, without waking Madame's ire."

Still the little Spanishly perfect foot wearied itself, and the proud owner remained obstinately silent. Alicia Clarendon was inclined to sulkiness, and a fit of this most unendurable temperament was upon her. But not Annot Lyle's magic instrument had greater power over the moody Highland chief, or that more ancient harpist, David, over the fretted soul of his king and predecessor, than Lily Vere's sweet and soothing accents over those who listened. There was such a spirit of truth, gentleness, suavity, persuasion in her low, heart-seeking voice.

Her words were like those of an old ballad, sung to an old melody, remembered since the day you lay upon your mother's knees. Simple words— not eloquent, not poetic, but stirring your inward nature, and awakening your best and least earthly sentiments.

"You would not quarrel with me for a stranger, dear Alice, and you do not fancy that I wish to be unkind or tyrannical. I am the elder, you know, and ought to assist you to think. It is thoughtlessness and girlish vanity which has led you on. Tell me about it or not, as you choose. I shall say no more; and, unless you were to repeat this walk, I shall never mention it. If uncle were to discover that you had been talked about for a Mr. Barclay, he would surely decide that I had ill repaid him for his kindness to myself. Not that I consider my own feelings, except as regards you. I could not bear that my darling Alice should lose her own self-respect, which she *would* do by permitting these clandestine attentions. In a little while you will be a 'young lady,' and ready to receive the open and undisguised homage of twenty Mr. Barclays. Now it is over, and we are friends again, querida mia."

The loving, tender arms stole once more around Alicia's averted neck, and Lily's pure, innocent lips kissed her friend on cheek and brow. Alicia was subdued. She played a second with the ribbons of her bonnet, and then, hastily untying them, and tossing the airy perfection upon her bed, she caught Lily's hand, who had moved away, and said, "Come here, snow-bird, and I will tell you all about it."

Miss Vere gladly obeyed; and Alicia, slowly rolling and unrolling one of Lily's long ringlets about her fore-finger as she spoke, continued:

"You know Mrs. Elliott, remembering mamma's kindness to her at Niagara last year, asked us to tea in June, just before she went away, and you could not go. You had a headache, and I accepted alone. It was rather dull work at first, just as I told you. The parlors were so dark you could scarcely see your hand; for, after the tea-table was removed, they turned down the gas to a little red bead, so that the rooms might be the cooler for it, and one groped about in a gloomy kind of twilight, with no music, nor cards, nor any thing. The rest of the company did not seem to find it stupid, however, for every body knew every body, and they sat about in corners, or strolled into the garden, and laughed and talked as merrily as possible, while the fans fluttered as if it were a Tertullia of West Indian beauties. Mrs. Elliott talked to me about the school and the girls, and bored me to death, as if I had not enough of them at home. At last she was called off, and I sat quite forlorn till Miss Elliott came to do a little propriety too, and she asked me about the school and the girls all over again, precisely as her mother had done. What makes people who invite unhappy tenants of *pensionnats* always drive at them about their 'studies' and their 'schoolmates?'"

"What other topic can they choose?" suggested Lily, smiling.

"Very true. Well, when Miss Elliott got upon music-teachers, you may imagine how weary I was of the business from my eagerly launching out into praise of Rhinehart, and actually consenting to show what proficiency I had made rather than continue in this agreeable Inquisition-victim chair. So I sat down to the piano, and performed a series of things, and, getting sentimental, I played a few of your languishing favorites, feeling emboldened by the 'darkness visible' around me. When I stopped, Mrs. Elliott brought up a freshly-arrived gentleman and introduced him. I could only distinguish a great, tall creature, who bowed profoundly, and took a place beside me."

Alicia gave a tug at the golden curl, and Lily, quietly disengaging her *belle chevelure*, said,

"Mr. Harry Barclay?"

"Just so. He knew Matilda Browne, and she had mentioned me to him. He began a very flirty conversation, though he does not pay compliments except by his manner and look. I suppose I encouraged him, for he kept his seat during the remainder of the evening, except when we took a turn in the garden, where he managed, by the moonbeams, to find out that I was not ill-looking, and where I discovered that *he* was very handsome. He is handsome, isn't he, Lily?"

"Y-e-s," answered Lily, musingly and doubtfully.

"Oh! I know he has not sharp eyes, and a sallow skin, with thin lips; nor is he slight and slender," said Alicia, laughing, for that was Clarence Tracy's *signalement*. Lily shook her head, and Alicia went on.

"Several times Mrs. Elliott looked as if she wished to break up the conference, but I had no idea of 'resuming my studies' again, and Mr. Barclay stood firm, and the evening would come to an end, and the carriage brought me home. The next Monday (this was on Friday evening) Matilda handed me a rose, with some foolish message from Mr. Barclay, who had been paying a visit to her sister; and after that, when I got leave once to walk with her, and on the two occasions when I dined at the Brownes, Mr. Barclay was there. You know you do not like Matilda, and you always refused their invitations; and, I must confess—"

"That you never pressed me to accept them."

Alicia laughed.

"Some body must have told Madame about him, for she is so watchful and strict, she will not let me dine any more with Matilda, and looked so narrowly at her yesterday when she came to see me. Now that is all, Lily."

"A bad business, my dear;" and Lily looked grave. "I fear Mr. Harry Barclay is a fortune-hunter, and these underbred Brownes his aiders and abettors. He takes advantage of your youth and inexperience; and, if he finds that you have wealth to match your beauty, he will try to secure his prize. If not, it is only a school-girl flirtation."

Alicia was scornfully indignant.

"No, indeed. He may be a flirt, but he is not a fortune-hunter."

"Very well, darling, as you will," said wise Lily, pressing the matter no farther, but determined to be very careful of Alicia for the future. "Let us go and show ourselves to Madame, tell her that we have eaten an ice, consequently do not mind losing our tea, and have been at home half an hour."

But Madame, with her usual kind thoughtfulness, had kept their evening meal spread for them in the dining-room, apologizing to herself, as she always did for extra spoiling, that it was holiday-time, never considering that, had it been during any other portion of the year, she would have acted in the like manner, urging that well-worked school-girls should be plentifully fed. For, strict and positive as she was, never did there beat a kinder or a more judicious heart than in the bosom of Madame —.

While drinking her cup of milk, cooled with a huge lump of ice, Alicia washed down any pangs of self-reproach which lingered about her at her shortened and partial confession. Not one word had she said of her note, of the signal beneath the window, of the *nearly* lover-like terms on which they stood.

Many persons will doubt the existence of such consummate hypocrisy and finished coquetry in one so young, brought up so quietly; a few will decide at once upon the cause—"boarding-schools! those curses, those pests! those terrible abiding-places of iniquity!"

Patience, my friends—if not, justice! Alicia Clarendon was born a flirt—born with an especial turn for sentimental intrigue. When she was five years old, she cut off a strand of her ebon braid to bestow upon Charley Murray, a youth of eight, and never till she was married did she reveal the secret. At eleven she received and wrote childish love-letters in a big, sprawling hand, and at fourteen she considered herself "engaged" to Bill Jennings, whom she smiled upon simply to draw him away from Sara Purvis, whose devoted boy-attendant he had long been. All these little affairs, and many intermediate ones, she never told, but delighted to know and keep to herself.

Meanwhile, Mrs. Clarendon, good soul! saw that her daughter's health was excellent, her dresses clean, her face smiling, and, busied with her pantry, her poultry, and her preserves, she asked and looked no farther. While Alicia was an infant, and while, consequently, a good and trustworthy nurse was her principal want, Mrs. Clarendon could not be torn from the child's cradle; and even a little later, every step must be guarded by the mother alone. The physical education was perfect, but the mental—ah me! Who can import for us some mothers to watch over the intellect, the budding wishes, thoughts, aspirations, and evil tendencies of giddy, grave, clever, dull young maidens?

Difficult, dangerous, but necessary task!

🌰 CHAPTER XII

Alicia's behavior was so circumspect during the next few weeks that Lily had great hopes about her, and was finally convinced that Mr. Harry Barclay's reign was over, and this foolish, imprudent affair at an end.

The time for Mr. Clarendon's arrival was drawing near, the school duties were in full force, and Madame was alternately urging and encouraging her two favorite pupils (if favorites she had) to waste no moments that were now so precious.

It was Saturday, and Lily was suffering from a headache, which made her prefer her own darkened room to any scheme of pleasure (such innocent pleasure as the half holiday brings to bread and butter misses), when Miss Clarendon entered their mutual apartment on tiptoe.

"Are you asleep, dear?" she said, bending over Lily. "Here is an invitation from Mrs. Elliott, who wishes us to dine and spend the evening with her. Madame consents, and the carriage, her servant says, will come for us at two o'clock."

"I shall be obliged to decline again," said Lily, drowsily, and yet noticing through her half-shut eyes a tremulous, eager, mischievous smile, which hovered about Alicia's face. "Make my excuses, Alicia. I am glad you have so pleasant an invitation offered, and I really regret that my only headaches should occur whenever Mrs. Elliott thinks of us."

Scarcely expressing her own regret, Miss Clarendon flew off to give the answer, and on her return, Lily heard her dancing down the corridor, humming in the most joyous key, and making amends by the excellence of her time for the harshness of her voice.

She moved noiselessly about the floor during the progress of her toilet, and said nothing, except an occasional "Poor dear!" as she would pass Lily in her journeyings to and fro; but Lily was still a little surprised to perceive, when her face was visible, that it was yet dimpling over with the brightest smiles.

"You do not seem to dread Mrs. and Miss Elliott's questions about the school?"

"Not much. I shall insist upon their talking of Saratoga."

"They have not given very long notice in their invitation?"

"Not very. It is nearly two o'clock now. I suppose they have just remembered that this is Saturday."

"You seem to anticipate a pleasant day?"

"Your head must be worse," *riposté'd* Alicia, turning round, and giving a hasty roll to her luxuriant black hair. "I never knew you put so many unnecessary questions before."

Lily was silenced, and presently Alicia went on:

"Any thing is better than passing the whole afternoon in this stupid place. Every one is gone or going out; you are indisposed; so that even the Elliotts are a relief."

"How pretty your new silk is!" said Lily; "and you look so high-bred in it. Come nearer, darling. How well it fits you! My uncle will be very proud when he comes. And he will have nothing to hear but praises of you, Alice. That only little folly! you have quite abandoned it?"

Alice stooped and kissed Miss Vere without answering, except by a smile and a tap on Lily's cheek.

"Adieu, 'airy, fairy Lilian!' Be quite well when I return, for I hear the carriage rattling to the door, and I must be off." Waving another kiss to her friend, Miss Clarendon caught up her gloves and handkerchief, and disappeared.

Imagine Lily's consternation when, some few hours after, the maid who answered the street bell knocked for admittance, and handed her a card.

"The lady asks for you, miss. She says she knows as Miss Clarendon is not here."

The card bore on its grayish, fashionable, unpolished surface,

"MRS. I. CARLETON ELLIOTT."

"Here? down stairs? alone?" gasped Lily, hurriedly rising, and drawing the strings of her dressing-gown, while her trembling hands next attempted to arrange her collar and smooth her scattered curls.

In a second she was in the drawing-room, and holding out her arms imploringly,

"What is the matter with Alicia?" she said. "My dear Mrs. Elliott, tell me."

A broad and puzzled stare was Mrs. Elliott's first unmistakable reply. She glanced in amazement at Lily's costume, and said,

"Indeed, there is nothing the matter, unless it has happened during the last ten minutes, which can have seriously affected Miss Clarendon. I think just that time has elapsed since I saw her walking in Chestnut Street, and as you were not with her, I concluded that you must be at home, so I came to offer a drive. Will you go? What made you fancy, my dear Miss Vere, that some accident had occurred, or that I knew of it?"

Lily strove to regain her composure.

"I beg your pardon," she said. "I was almost asleep, having suffered during the whole morning from a tedious headache. The servant told me that you knew of Alicia's absence, and wished only me. I fancied—being aware—thinking— Who is with Alicia?" she abruptly wound up.

"The eldest Miss Browne—one of the Brownes, of Walnut Street—those dashing 'men's beauties.' Did you not know that your friend was with them?" and Mrs. Elliott's curiosity overcame her good-breeding, for she narrowly watched Lily's face.

A hot blush overspread the young girl's brow as she stammeringly answered,

"I have been stupidly ill to-day, and I have misunderstood what Alicia said. Pray excuse my extraordinary behavior and costume," she added, wrapping her dressing-gown more closely. "It makes me anxious indeed to dream even for a moment, and with my eyes open, that Alicia is in danger of any sort."

"Ahem!" coughed Mrs. Elliott, with a little significant sound.

"I am not so much older than Alicia in reality, but I feel the weight of years and responsibility more than she," Lily continued, forcing a smile; "consequently, while we are here alone, I have a sort of motherly watchfulness and anxiety about her."

Mrs. Elliott thought so lovely a young creature had never lived as Lily looked at this instant, her large, light curls hanging in transparent masses about her shoulders, a pink flush, deepening to scarlet, in the centre of her cheek and on her lips, and a feverish light glittering in her blue eyes.

"You will drive with me, I hope? I have a visit to make in the neighborhood which will just occupy me while you dress; consequently, without excuses, *à tantôt.*"

No sooner were they in the carriage than Mrs. Elliott said, with a little hesitation,

"I may be taking a liberty, my dear, but will you allow me to ask you a question? How old is Miss Clarendon?"

"Not quite seventeen—six months my junior," answered Lily, frankly.

"Can I put another question? Do you know any thing of Mr. Harry Barclay?"

"My kind Mrs. Elliott," said Lily, grasping her hand, "if you will be good enough to tell me something about him, I shall be very much obliged to you, and if you will guide me a little— This is scarcely an answer to your question; but I can guess at what you mean, my own mind being quite occupied with this very subject. I am, perhaps, too candid with an almost stranger, but there is no one here to whom I can apply for advice, and to write to my uncle Clarendon and arouse his suspicions would put an eternal source of disagreeable feelings between my dear Alicia and me. You have either noticed for yourself or heard of his attentions to Alicia; if he is worthy of her, and will wait a few weeks until she leaves school, then he can renew his devotions without their exciting the animadversions of the world. Her father is a man never likely to thwart his only daughter's wishes, if she will but make a respectable and prudent choice." A slight smile played around Mrs. Elliott's starched lips, and she looked a moment out of the carriage windows before she replied, not wishing to distress her companion by showing her own amusement while Miss Vere's agitation was so evident.

"You have answered my question very plainly, my dear, by speaking of Harry Barclay in the light of a marrying man. It is evident you know nothing of him. He is a young gentleman who has passed through a series of flirtations and 'desperate love-affairs' that have sufficed to give him the character of a downright 'heart-breaker.' He has enough money to live upon comfortably as a 'young man about town,' and has proved in so many instances that he prefers his liberty to no matter what high matrimonial prizes, that it would be a losing bet to stake a sixpence upon any young lady's serious captivation of him. He is a terrible flirt, and yet takes no trouble about it. There are so many silly women and girls ready to run after him, 'tame enough to perch so soon as he holds out his finger,' that he walks along, gathering a string of victims, like a saunterer through an orchard, with the ripe peaches and pears falling about his feet. He will let Miss Clarendon receive his lazy homage, and accept her attentions in return, until some newer beauty arises, or until she worries him with fault-findings; then he will take off his hat with profound courtesy, and take likewise his leave."

Lily colored indignantly.

"What a detestable man!" she cried, with honest disgust.

"Not so, my dear," resumed Mrs. Elliott, warming to her subject and doing it justice, for she was really a clever woman, and a kind-hearted, though a little cold and patronizing; "not so, my dear. Harry Barclay is not naturally conceited nor very indifferent; that is, not more so than most men with a quarter of his personal and mental advantages; he is only spoiled and selfish. Your little cousin—excuse me—is just as great a flirt as Harry Barclay, and will be, I think, quite as unscru—quite as—in short," slurring over the sentence, "she took to him at once, on first seeing him, and was quite ready to flirt too, on his own terms. I am speaking very plainly, but it would be as well to stop this business. Miss Clarendon was so attentive to me during Mary's illness at Niagara, and hailing, as we both do, from dear old Carolina, I feel as if I might venture to warn you. The Club has taken up the story, and every window on Walnut Street has some lounger who "knows all about it."

Lily was in despair.

"But, after all," she pleaded, trying to put down the unsparing criticism of Mrs. Elliott, "there is still no positive harm in this. She has walked with him occasionally—"

Mrs. Elliott gave her little cough again, and passed her thin, neatly-gloved hand over her upper lip.

"Mr. Barclay's reputation is not such that I should like a daughter of mine to receive the 'cachet' of his admiration. If you were older, my dear Miss Vere, I might tell you of a few of his escapades with married women. But, however," she interrupted herself, "I have said quite enough. I trust you do not mistake my motive."

"What would you advise?" asked poor Lily, quite subdued, while the beating of her temples seemed to her almost audible.

"Since you prefer not applying to your uncle about your cousin—"

"One moment," interrupted Lily. "Mr. Clarendon is not my uncle; he is more to me than that. I owe him more than a mere blood relationship would demand. He is my guardian, and has taken care of me since I was an orphan six years old."

"Better still," continued Mrs. Elliott: "you then feel disposed to serve him and his family. Now, from what I have seen of you, your propriety and dignity of manner, your persuasive voice, and earnest tone, I have a plan of my own. I saw you one day at Niagara reduce a set of staring men to modest glances by the mere power of your calm look and womanly bearing, girl as you are. *You* must speak to Harry Barclay."

"I! good Heaven!" exclaimed Lily, starting up, to the detriment of the pretty bonnet (a match to Alicia's) which she had hastily thrown on for her drive.

"Yes, you," repeated Mrs. Elliott, calmly. "I will invite Mr. Barclay to tea to-morrow evening, and you will do me the favor to come with Miss Clarendon. I shall give you an opportunity of speaking to him, and I do not doubt that, in spite of your 'school-girl' position, you will impress him."

Lily ran over in her mind the pros and cons. Madame was out, and had not seen her driving with Mrs. Elliott. She had merely asked leave of a *sous-maîtresse*, which was readily granted. She would frighten Alicia by telling of her discovery, and by dealing gently with her it would perhaps induce the wayward girl to listen once more to reason. She could give Madame some explanation for the second visit, in such rapid succession, to Mrs. Elliott— the true one, in fact, a person to be met, whose presence had not been possible on Saturday. It would be a dreadful thing to talk with propriety while facing Mr. Barclay—to bring him to task—to call him to account, and to ask his forbearance for the future. But Alicia's name was at stake. It was evident that no one else meant to "do the deed."

"Thank you, Mrs. Elliott, for your kind intentions, and I accept gratefully such a mark of interest and consideration for us," Lily at last warmly said.

Mrs. Elliott winced a little, for her conscience slightly murmured that kindness was less the motive power than her predominant passion for dipping her fingers into other people's pies; however, her conscience was rather tough on that score, and in this instance, although she really pleased herself by having a little "neighbor's business" to manage, still the action was commendable, and destined, she hoped, to be of use, and eventually to be crowned with success.

If Lily had been terrified and confounded by the announcement of Mrs. Elliott's visit at six o'clock, her amazement scarcely equaled Alicia's when, on that young lady's return home at ten in the evening, Miss Vere quietly gave her the invitation for the next day, without one syllable of explanation.

"Mrs. Elliott begs that we will take tea with her to-morrow."

Miss Clarendon opened her eyes until the long lashes of the upper lid threatened to invade her arched black eyebrows; and the smile which was, on her entrance, irradiating her pretty face, faded and lengthened into unconcealed wonder. In a moment she burst into a merry laugh, and said audaciously,

"So I am found out!"

"You have been with the Brownes?"

"Yes."

"You deceived Madame and me?"

"Yes," repeated Alicia, defyingly. "I am no longer a child, and both you and Madame wish to keep me in leading-strings!" And this sentence was a text from which she preached a long sermon against tyranny, caprice, prejudice, and a few other "lesser crimes," which she proved, to her own satisfaction, had been practiced upon her by Lily and by Madame.

"My dear Alicia," Miss Vere said, when the charming vixen had gone through her grievances, ending with a tear or two, provoked by her severe trials, "my dear love, I do not pretend to control you; and unless Madame should discover this business through some other source and question me, she will never get a word from my lips. I have accepted the invitation for both of us; good-night;" and Lily's milky eyelids closed over her violet eyes like a snowflake settling upon a cluster of blush roses, which simile, introducing in two lines animal, vegetable, atmospheric, and floral beauties, simply means that she went to sleep.

The next morning Madame was informed of the new engagement, and offered no objections. Alicia remained sulky, but did not refuse to go, and they went.

Mrs. Elliott's drawing-rooms were well stored with albums, and *étagères* of costly knick-knacks; so, while Lily was listening to the prosy details of mother and daughter (who had not precisely that gift which lies in investing trifles with charms), Miss Clarendon wandered from shelf to shelf, or pored over sketches of the Rhine and costumes of Europe, which alternately filled the pages of a richly-gilded and papier-maché-bound volume.

She was comparing this evening with her last, and inwardly yawning at the contrast; for, of course, it is needless to say that Mr. Barclay had joined Laura Browne and herself in their afternoon walk, and had accompanied them home. His image only was before her eyes, though in reality they rested upon the grim features of a Cossack chief, when, as if in answer to her thoughts, Harry Barclay himself entered!

"What a clever creature!" she exclaimed within herself. "How did he guess that I was here?" and a radiant flush gathered upon her cheek as she bowed without looking up.

The conversation was general and dull enough.

"Is this the company I am invited to meet?" thought Harry Barclay. "I never suspected that Mamma Elliott would so amiably consult my tastes," and he gave a side-glance at the dark little fairy, so demure and so proper.

In a few moments one of those unexceptionable young men—one of those safe youths, who might be trusted *almost* with the flirt dearest to you—I say almost, for you must not reckon without her part in the game—was announced.

He was mild and slim, with straight, light hair, looking always as if it had just been submitted to the most thorough inroads of a "patent, self-cleaning, fine-tooth comb," and a large nose, which, big as it was, failed to give character to his face.

Immediately after him followed a quick, jerking, not ill-looking and very busy gentleman, whose eyes roamed around as if in search of some hidden object, while his hands rapidly arranged the flossy curls given him by Nature, or drew down and smoothed off the waistcoat, cravat, or coat, for which he was indebted to his tailor, but which seemed equally parts of himself.

He spoke very quickly, bowing incessantly, and flourishing his handkerchief now and then; giving you the minutest account of where he had been, and where he was going, and where he would like to go.

During the bustle occasioned by their entrance, Mr. Barclay caught a look from Alicia, and moved toward her, seating himself in a huge chair next her low *causeuse*, and gazing down upon her prettiness and coaxing ways, as you might suppose a great Newfoundland dog would amuse himself with watching the graceful beauty of a coquettish little Blenheim.

Not long did Alicia enjoy her *tête-à-tête;* for as to whether Harry Barclay enjoyed it there is no saying. He took every thing so indifferently, that, although he did not show anxiety to exchange her company for any body else's, yet he seemed to find only a lazy satisfaction in it, which apparently partook more of endurance than of delight. Be that as it may, Mrs. Elliott interrupted the conversation by bringing up the second gentleman, whom she presented as Mr. Greene, and who, dropping into a place beside Miss Clarendon, despite the frown that lowered upon him, began a voluble detail of the expected brilliancy of the following winter season, and of the past glory of the preceding Saratoga gayety.

Meanwhile Mrs. Elliott stood up, talking to Mr. Barclay, who, hat in hand, listened with profound attention, and gave as many deep, respectful glances to her parchment skin, and light, inexpressive eyes, as he had bestowed languidly admiring ones upon the youthful loveliness of his previous companion. The hostess was blind to the angry curl of the young lady's lip, who would from time to time seek an answering look of encouragement from the tall creature far above her head, but who could not snub off the persevering Mr. Greene.

"You know how anxious I was about my box from Italy, Mr. Barclay? It has arrived, and the cameos are arranged in the cabinet. Let me show them to you."

Alicia almost cried as she saw Mrs. Elliott thus sweep Harry away, while the intolerable Greene flirted his handkerchief, and launched out into praises of somebody's horses or somebody's houses, she did not care nor hear which.

She *did* hear Mrs. Elliott invite Lily to look at the cameos too, and the trio disappeared behind the folding-doors (partially open) of the inner drawing-room.

No sooner were Miss Vere and Mr. Barclay busily engaged in admiring the cabinet, than the accomplished Mrs. Elliott was called out through a side "exit," unseen by those in the other room.

Poor Lily! how she trembled at the very idea of beginning. Her hands nervously drummed upon the inlaid sides of the buhl cabinet, and Mr. Barclay admired at his leisure her exquisite fairness, the abundant beauty of her hair, the pure outline of her oval face, and the candid modesty that seemed to perfume her very presence, and to be enthroned upon her smooth, gentle brow.

"I may as well speak," thought Lily; and, arming herself with a recollection of the importance of her duty, she commenced, in the lowest tone,

"I have seen you but once before, Mr. Barclay—"

"I beg your pardon?" said the gentleman, bending his ear to catch the sound.

Lily cleared her throat, and said, more distinctly,

"I have seen you only once before, but I think I have not judged too hastily in taking you for a person who has a—whose natural kindness of heart and whose gentlemanly feeling will authorize this step—who will willingly agree to my views."

Harry bowed, and, much amazed, felt like muttering to himself, according to De Balzac's hero, "Quoi! cette futeresse aussi!" but in a second he smiled at his own coxcombry.

"My guardian's daughter—my dearest friend—is too giddy for her years," pursued Lily; "she is not aware yet of the difference between childish attentions from boys who have grown up with her, and a flirtation with a gentleman—like Mr. Barclay. Will you not aid me to set her right? She is not conscious that walking with you, being seen with you, while she is still a school-girl, exposes her to unkind remarks. In a very little while we shall return home, and then—" Lily raised her eyes; no lover-like ardor was perceptible in Alicia's admirer, but, on the contrary, his brilliant teeth shone below his black mustache in a faint smile of amusement, which vanished when he caught Lily's look.

"I do not care to mention this subject to Madame, nor to write of it to my guardian. All that is necessary is that you should deprive yourself of the pleasure of seeing Alicia, and that you should not encourage any opportunities of bringing you together. You will not think me bold or interfering, but you will do justice to the feeling which has decided me to trust you?"

"A few words under some circumstances, Miss Vere," replied Harry Barclay, with real admiration, "show us the true beauties or defects of a character better than months will often bring them to light. It *is* but the second time that we have met, and yet, nevertheless, I feel as if I could draw your inner self with an unerring pencil. You are right—you must always be right—and I promise to act according to your wishes."

"Yes; but Alicia?" inquired Lily. "You must explain to her that you think it most proper to await her father's arrival before renewing—"

She had made a false step. She had taken for granted that Mr. Barclay wished to marry Alicia, and a surprised look from him showed her mistake, and proved that she had compromised Miss Clarendon. Mrs. Elliott said truly, Harry Barclay was not a marrying man, and Lily hated him for an instant as he executed his well-feigned stare for explanation.

Tears filled her eyes, and she turned her head away sadly. Her pride was wounded through and for Alicia.

With a manly tenderness which well became him, and which he rarely displayed, Harry undertook to console her.

"You are annoyed," he said. "Let me deal as frankly with you as I would with my sister—if I had one. You are displeased that there should be nothing serious in my attentions to Miss Clarendon, and think that I have been trifling with her. Excuse me; we are to speak candidly, and I wish to correct your mistake. There is no stronger feeling on her side than on mine, take my word for it. I met her by accident in this very house, and recognized her as a young lady who had already attracted my attention in the street, as much for her beauty as because she was walking with a young girl not 'in society,' and whose flirting habits I know."

"Matilda Browne? People whom we met traveling a year ago, and whose manners I always disliked. They insisted upon knowing us."

"Miss Clarendon is very bright, very pretty, and, conscious of her powers, she lays siege to every heart. Finding no one else at hand, she honored me with her smiles; but I am not sufficiently vain to construe her lively sallies and her occasional girlish preference of my society into a 'belle passion' for me. Any one would have answered just as well to stand the brunt of her whims and her little playful confidences."

"Do you really believe that?" asked Lily, fairly in for it. "She has never confided in me so far as you are concerned."

Again the saucy smile brought out a feminine dimple on Mr. Barclay's brown, rounded cheek.

"Indeed I do," he answered, with emphasis upon the "deed."

"Why do people call you conceited and spoiled?" asked Lily, naïvely.

Harry threw back his head and laughed heartily, whereat Miss Vere blushed, and was shocked at herself.

"We all have enemies," Harry said presently, recovering his gravity. "I am better than my reputation; and from your remark I conclude you have heard me spoken of as a desperate 'lady-killer,' going about with my hands full of trophies, and breakfasting daily on broiled hearts. I have been fortunate enough, from time to time, to attract the notice of some little girls, who, instead of minding their crochet-work, have looked at me because I chanced to be taller than most men—that is all. Upon my word, I am *not* dangerously fascinating."

"You will not let Alicia hear of this conversation?" Lily said, smiling faintly in return, as the gentleman concluded his speech with a bow, and the prettiest air of mock modesty. "She would rebel at my assumed authority, and the whole business would deeply wound her sensibility."

"You may trust me. I shall not give myself any longer the selfish pleasure of cultivating the friendship of even so charming a person as Miss Clarendon, since it excites remark. However unfounded I know these remarks to be, I shall unfalteringly respect your wishes, and am even pleased to think that by depriving myself of such happiness I insure your good opinion. Should this little business ever come to Miss Clarendon's ears, I trust you will do me justice with her; for the present, I shall be very circumspect; later, she may again enroll me among the humblest of her slaves."

Lily timidly extended her hand and thanked him.

"Bravo, Harry!" thought Mr. Barclay. "What a dear little thing it is! so courageous and yet so shy. You can see how much this effort has cost her. But, by Jove! how mad Alicia will be!"

CHAPTER XIII

LETTER FROM CLARENCE TRACY TO
MRS. ARCHIBALD LANGDON.

"Heidelberg, Sept. 4th.

"Geneviève! I have been reading Pynnshurst, the book you liked so much, and told me months ago that I should find so congenial. It is a gem! No longer 'let your name be called' Angelica, but Geneviève; 'Angel' less well suits you. How delightful is the dialogue throughout, and with what delicacy is the strongest passion painted! Every nerve thrills as you bend over the true, unaffected detail; you feel the mighty throb of Pynnshurst's noble heart, the intensity of his love; you bathe yourself in the lustrous light of Geneviève's dark eyes, and you softly press her small, trembling hand as he does, and listen silently to the inward whispers of your full happiness. For those who love, it is a beautiful book, but the *dénouement* is stupid. Do you know a man who, in Pynnshurst's situation, would have contented himself with tumbling down on a gravel walk? He was quite right to go away, but a very simpleton to go alone; didn't you think so? And then Geneviève, why need she turn idiot all of a sudden? Didn't she know that she had a husband who must come to light some day? It would have been far more satisfactory to my feelings had they gone to the magnolia-bowered cottage in the South. But, romance apart, although it sounds very pretty and nice, how long, think you, could two lovers exist by themselves on a plantation at the South as it is?

"Alice is a poke. She was just fit to make a decent end of herself by marrying some other man; not to live single and bore poor Pynn, nor to die and leave him with remorse on his conscience for having been too agreeable unintentionally to his little cousin whom he had brought up.

"Well, well, it is all over now. No doubt Pynnshurst is in reality a stout, respectable man, with a buxom wife, and Geneviève is a scraggy French-woman, with *café-au-lait* eyes and a nascent mustache.

"I would rather think of *my* Geneviève—not Pynnshurst's. But why should I, pray? She is utterly heartless, and cruelly refused to believe in my sincere attachment. I verily think it would cost me less pain now to put an end to a friendship where the most perfect devotion on the one side meets so little return from the other. But alas! how truly does that famous Frenchman say, 'The influence of mere personal charms is limited; curiosity forms the great ingredient of this kind of love; but add the fascination of intellect to those attractions which habit and familiarity will diminish each day, and you will find them multiplied tenfold. If, besides intellect and beauty, you discover in your adored one caprice, irregularity and inequality of temper, close your eyes and seek no farther. You are snared for life!'

"Apply this as you choose, Madame. Perhaps I love my Geneviève also, because she writes such charming letters, and in so pretty a hand. I admire excessively a pretty handwriting in a woman; it is probably because my own scrawl is so frightful, so boyish, with great, irregular letters, and very uncertain capitals, like the temper and character of the destined-to-be-loved-ones.

"Apropos, your last epistle was received by me with heart-stirring joy, only I was tormented by your account of the Saratoga boy-lover with whom you strayed along those 'green and flowery paths.' Who is he? Let me pursue him to the uttermost parts of the earth! But perhaps you snub him, and then, poor fellow! I sympathize with and pity him.

"Why do you drive me frantic, likewise, by telling me how your European breadth of shoulders causes such bursts of admiration? Don't I know every dimple in them? Can I ever forget that night, last winter, when you dropped a Parma violet from your bouquet? You stooped to raise it; I stooped to prevent you, and my presumptuous lips grazed the dazzling slope of that very right shoulder which you have sometimes turned coldly upon me! As Corinne says, 'Les plus heureux moments de la vie sont encore ceux qu'un *hasard* bienfaisant nous accorde.'

"But I am really delighted that you have had a pleasant, endurable summer. Have you left the Springs? Will you be in New York in October?

"That is the eventful month which is to witness our restoration to our native land. William Clarendon and I will make superhuman exertions to leave Heidelberg by the 1st of October; sooner, if possible, so as to pass a day or two in Paris.

"There is nothing to keep us here. We are so crammed with law and learning now that we are eager to get to Charleston, lest spontaneous combustion should entirely destroy this work of years before it finds an outlet.

"There is, besides, a fat and languishing widowed fräu, our opposite neighbor, who makes such desperate attempts upon Clarendon's heart that I tremble sometimes for the result. So far she has failed to impress him. He is impregnable; more's the folly. I do not understand the philosophy of refusing the gifts the gods provide; however, I have known a duel fought because one man helped another, clumsily, to a very nice dish, and I suppose Willie doesn't like things thrust at him, even if they are *farcis aux truffes.*

"Good-by! My chief happiness is to think of you, and to imagine, when the shades of evening come on, that I hear in the sighing of this German autumn air your low voice murmur,   CLARENCE.

"P.S.—Have you seen Lily Vere? She and Alicia Clarendon will be 'finished off' about the same time as ourselves. How will old Charleston stand such a galaxy at one blaze? Happily, Miss Sara prepared it by slipping off her chrysalis last winter. How do *her* wings unfold, upon the whole?"

ANSWER TO THE ABOVE.

"New York, October 1st.

"MY DEAR CLARENCE,—You have a fever—I am sure you have. Let me feel your pulse. Yes; how it beats! Pray consult a physician at once; several, if your purse will stand it, for I consider you alarmingly ill, and—absurd. I direct this to Paris, *poste restante,* for I have learned through Lily, whose advices from you are better than mine, that you will not sail for America till the 25th; consequently, go to Cazot, or what is the man's name, and let him prescribe for a common and rather incurable disease, which in *this* country, you, I am sure, will never be able to conquer. Your malady is too much good luck, producing a chronic case of tremendous conceit and flippancy, and an intermittent fever of complete self-satisfaction and entire belief in your own powers.

"Your letter was very amusing, I grant you, but rather less respectful than my dignity demands. 'My sponsors in baptism' gave me the name of Angelica; after that I was addressed as Miss Purvis; now 'I come when I am called' Mrs. Langdon. I am neither Coleridge's, Pynnshurst's, nor your Geneviève. A truce to reproof, however, and I will tell you a little about ourselves.

"Lily is here with me. Alicia and herself were to have remained in Philadelphia a little longer, storing their minds, like the busy bee, with the honey of fashionable education (having declined my invitation for the summer), and Mr. Clarendon was to have taken them home direct from their 'Miss Pinkerton's'; but, from what I can gather in careful cross-questioning, I fancy that Alicia has begun to practice a profession in which she will very soon rank as Bacheloress of Arts—coquetry.

"There is some story which she hinted at, looking daggers meanwhile at Lily, about a certain Mr. Harry Barclay, whom I know pretty well, and if our youthful *compatriote* has taken her first degree from him, she has well begun in her especial line. Lily, of course, frowns (as frowningly as Lily *can* frown) upon such proceedings, and wrote to ask permission that they might leave school at once and come to me, thus killing two birds with one stone— separating Alicia from her admirer, and giving her a chance, amid the gayeties of New York, to forget that she missed him.

"For the first, Philadelphia is very near New York, and Harry may pop in any day; but for the last, there is some hope of success. My demoiselles *font fureur.* I shall describe them, and, beginning with Alicia, my pen will have accustomed itself to a theme of beauty before I take up Lily.

"Alicia is small, round, dimpled, indolent, brown, graceful, and extremely wide awake. She has those same large eyes which you recollect, but how Mrs. Clarendon's daughter got their expression of subdued fun, passion, languor, and *diablerie,* I never shall understand. Her nose is piquant and slightly *retroussé,* just a very little; it seems anxious to catch a glimpse for itself of those handsome eyes and their deeply-marked black brows. She has pale, plump cheeks, and very bright lips, with a shade upon the upper one, which you sneer at in Geneviève-grown-older, but which really adds a great and peculiar charm to Alicia's face, for the moment, while it is so slight, and she so fresh and unsunned. Her forehead is low, very low, and her cormorant's-wing hair crimples naturally, independent of nightly plaitings, and needing little trouble to arrange in bandeaux of *la dernière* mode.

"You will recognize in the picture, perhaps, the little 'girl you left behind,' and who, from fourteen to seventeen, has progressed as I try to show you. I need not amplify this *narrative* by giving you her character and temper as I see them. If you can not divine her, as I did, on first view, you are dull indeed, and philosophic pages would not enlighten you.

"Lily Vere is so different from this pen-and-ink sketch, that I could almost draw her by contraries. Lily is tall, gentle, fair, soft, kind, steady, tractable. Her figure is beautiful; not stiff, though classically regular and perfect. It is like the figure of an angel. Fully developed—yet 'diaphanous' is the word you feel best describes it. Her waist sways and bends like a flower on its stalk, and her lovely head is set upon her shoulders with one of those long, transparent, downy throats, with the hair springing from the *nuque* in three points, evenly divided, and never straying down in ragged ends. (This is a rare beauty, let me tell you, and one that neither bandoline nor *crême d'amande* will with certainty produce.) This hair is of the same golden luxuriance as ever, but she has been taught to dress it more carefully, and her abundant ringlets are trained to fall so as not entirely to hide the turn of her cheek, which is peculiarly oval and graceful. Her eyebrows and lashes are darker than they were, her eyes unchanged. I never saw such eyes. What the mischief ails the girl? They are so blue, so deep, so confiding, and so unsparing! Not a freckle, not a spot mars the purity of her skin. On her temples, below her eyes, around her mouth, there is the pellucid transparency you might look to see only in a very young child. Her tastes are simple; her dress corresponds to her tastes. While Alicia covers herself with trinkets, and playfully shakes her little fist at you, shining with rings, most of them gifts from Lily, the heiress herself, 'draped' in grayish silks or pure white, allows her statuesque arms no ornament but fine lace ruffles. Lace is her only extravagance. Owing to this difference of costume, and Alicia's curiously evident likeness to me, we are often taken for cousins, and Miss Clarendon for the heiress. But Alicia is too well satisfied with herself to desire that sort of homage which would reach her through her fancied possession of Lily's gold, and she carefully un-deceives every body.

"You see them now, do you not? these young creatures, just stepping into life's struggles? From my pedestal as a married woman, and my five years' seniority, I contemplate them calmly. I like the sensation they make. I am proud of Lily. They don't interfere with me. They attract their own circle, and don't infringe on mine. Alicia is amusing—full of *espiègleri* and little ways. Lily is grave, smiles at Alicia's follies, spoils her when she thinks she may venture to do so, and floats about the house like a visitant spirit. If it were not for her fortune, she would not be nearly so popular with young men as that naughty Alicia. She is so circumspect, so dignified, and so intolerant of double-entendres, fulsome compliments, and free and easy manners.

"I have scribbled pages, never stopping to consider the length of this effusion, but I have a double motive. I wished to prepare you to meet your old friends, and I was dying to talk openly about them. Of course, my hostess-ship commands that I should speak of them with equal praise, and it would never answer to tell Charley Williams or Percy Patterson just what I have told you. Praise of one's cousin, and disparagement of one's guest, is very ill breeding.

"You ask about Sara. She is certainly handsome—but your anxiety can wait till you see her in Charleston. Mamma and herself went to Virginia this summer, after a flying visit to me in New York in June. Sara fancied that her complexion was *out of tone,* and mamma's nerves were shaky; so they have been drinking White Sulphur water, and Sara writes me one of her interesting letters of a page and a half, to say that they are perfectly restored.

"In passing through Philadelphia on their way to the Springs (having come here per steamer), they behaved with such characteristic affection to papa's niece! They paused for the next train of cars, and drove round to Madame —'s. Lily was out walking. They left their cards and compliments, and went on.

"I shall not say adieu; wind and water permitting, we shall meet so soon. Think about that fever, and be sure to consult the most energetic physician.

"Still yours confidentially,   A. P. L."

This was written upon several sheets of note-paper of a tea-green, last-fashion hue; it smelt faintly of *Maréchale;* the initials, in dead gold and in anagram, headed each first page; the envelope was long and narrow; the writing neat, lady-like, and flowing. It was sealed with wax of a darker shade than the paper, and the impression was given by an emerald seal-ring, worn on Mrs. Langdon's fourth finger, and bearing two words—"*Je veux.*"

After an unprecedented short run, the finest steamer of the Collins line was moored at its New York wharf, and among the first passengers who stepped on shore, valises in hand, were two young men. They were both young, and one was strikingly good-looking. He was dark, tall, well-made, and gentlemanly, with a pleasant, musical voice, and a laugh which, though not frequent, was joyous and hearty.

The other was smaller, slighter, and owed what personal beauty he possessed more to expression and cultivation of feature than to positive natural gifts. Though still in his "sea-clothes," they were of a Paris "build," and the rough material showed an artist's hand in their make. His eyes were flashing, hazel-black, and capable of deep concentration; his forehead high and broad, and the hair grew well around it and parted easily. His mouth was too sarcastic, but a mustache of a dark chestnut color sufficiently veiled its defects, while very white teeth constantly showed themselves in a smile more sneering than gay.

They got possession of one trunk apiece by superhuman exertions, some coaxing, and a little flattery, and leaving the rest of their luggage in the hands of those most intolerable harpies, the New York custom-house officers (who, in parenthesis be it said, are nuisances of the greatest impertinence, and who truly, harpy-like, ruin every thing which they touch), William Clarendon and Clarence Tracy drove to their hotel.

It was late in the evening—dinner just over; so they ordered a few scraps to be gathered together, and then, after refreshing baths and fresh toilettes, took their way to No. — Fifth Avenue, losing as little time as possible.

"The ladies all out," was the unsatisfactory reply of Mrs. Langdon's footman, who had a smack of un-American livery on his legs and on his back.

"Dining out?"

"Yes, sir."

"Do you know where?"

"No, sir. The coachman is laid up. Mrs. Langdon had a carriage from the stables, and I didn't hear the orders as Mr. Langdon gave the driver. Mrs. Langdon sent me in the house on a message jist as I was a shutting the carriage-door."

"We may as well give it up," said William Clarendon. "We can come early to-morrow."

"If you would like, sir, I'll call Mrs. Langdon's maid, Miss Rosylee. She mought know."

"Thank you."

Miss *Rosylee* came smiling down, and gave a little shriek of recognition when she saw Clarence, sinking for a moment into one of the moyenage chairs which solemnly adorned the marbled walls and tesselated floor of the entrance-hall.

"M. Tracy! how surprise will be Madame! She did not expec you and M. *le frère* of Meess *Al*ice until two days more. *Donnez vous la peine* to walk in."

Clarence was always full of little absurd gallantries for this class of people. Waiting damsels and shopwomen quite adored him. He used to talk any quantity of highflown nonsense to them, which, as he never carried it farther, only delighted his listeners.

He complimented Rosalie on her improved looks, on her tasteful cap (which Angelica insisted that she should wear—on it, indeed, her wages rested), and on the grace of her manner.

Rosalie courtesied and smiled, and, led on by Willie's evident amusement, Clarence's French tongue rattled away most untiringly, till he was recalled to their principal business by Clarendon's remark,

"I do not think we yet know where we may be likely to find the ladies."

"Oh, *ces dames!*" cried Rosalie; "Monsieur must wait till de morning. Dey dine with Mrs. Antony Hardcastle, and will not be back dese tree, four hours."

"Very well; then we are off. Rosalie, New York agrees better with you than Paris, where I last saw you, trying to persuade Madame, while you were dressing her hair, that *les Etats-Unis* was a *vilain pays*, unfit for Christians and persons of taste. By the way, how is Marquise?"

"Oh, *la petite chérie!* she barks at every one still. *Elle déteste* Monsieur, and snap at his heel as always. Madame *en raffole*."

"Clarence, you are a curious specimen!" exclaimed William Clarendon, as they left the gorgeously-subdued hall and superbly-furnished drawing-room behind them, and walked down the broad, white marble steps into the street again. "I never knew a man more particular, more nicely discriminating in his choice of a woman to talk to in society. Many a pleasant enough girl, with some slight inaccuracy of language, and many a handsome woman of doubt-ful manners, whom other men would find interesting for an hour or so, you scorn with uncompromising rejection; but place you any where with a humbly-born and under-bred person of the softer sex, old or young, pretty or ugly, and you win her heart instantly with ridiculous speeches and bows like a willow-tree blown by the wind; whereas I, who can manage to get on very well with women who are nominally, at least, on the same footing as myself, however deficient in positive refinement, find an absolute lack of something polite to present in an agreeable way to this sort, unless I were to make love to them."

"I think it is very simple," said Tracy. "A *lady* must, to my mind, be a real lady. Betty or Molly, whether she wear a calico gown and scrubs the steps, or a *robe de percale,* like Rosalie, or waits behind a counter like the little grisette of whom I ordered my last supply of cravats, or brings me my handkerchief like the stewardess of our late steam home, I treat with regard merely to her womanship. I expect nothing from her. I amuse myself and please her with a little frolicsome *badinage,* or, if she be an 'elderly,' with a little sympathy, until the humor passes; then I break up the conference, and there is the end of it. But for an individual passing as my equal, the currency must be pure, the metal ring clearly; and the coin, no matter how dull outwardly, must be sound within. Fast women—under-bred women in silks and satins, who expect you at least to leave cards upon them, I avoid with cowardly terror."

"And yet I have seen you doing a deal of grave tenderness to a woman who was certainly not a lady, and as certainly, I think, not one of the naughty ones of the earth."

"Where and when?" asked Clarence, wheeling round abruptly, and eying his companion with a fierce spark beneath his dark brows.

"My dear fellow," said Willie, laughing, "I met you in the Bois de Boulogne. The 'object' was very humbly dressed, and yet your air and manner were deeply respectful. She had your arm, and her veiled face was turned from you. You were gesticulating with energy. She gradually listened with fast-returning confidence and head, when suddenly a winding in the *allée* swept you both out of sight. Upon my honor I was not watching you. Accident gave me this scene, and that is my whole story. I did not catch a glimpse of her ensnaring beauty."

Clarence's brow relaxed, and he laughed out also; but a short, quick breath showed his relief.

"Yes, that is a poser, Willie. What is the use of going straight to the hotel?" he went on, without farther explanation. "Here is a play-bill which says that Miss Julia Dean will favor the world in general, *moyennant* seventy-five cents per head, with her reading of 'Adrienne,' at the Broadway Theatre. Let us join them. I saw Rachel in 'Adrienne' the very last time that I witnessed that grand creature's performance. It will be amusing to compare this Western girl's acting with the world-renowned tragedienne's."

"Thank you," said Willie, yawning; "I shall go to bed. It will be a real comfort to sleep in a real bed once more, which is what all people say if they have been at sea two days or two months."

"Good-night, then;" and, nodding to Mr. Clarendon, Clarence threw away the cigar which he had lit on leaving Mr. Langdon's, hailed an omnibus, and sprang in. He watched Willie for a second, the gas-lamps and his still burning Havanna pointing him out, while the omnibus rumbled lazily along, jolting at every turn of the wheel.

"He did not see her, I am pretty sure of that," Clarence muttered; "and, besides, Lorenza never leaves the house. He will be a sharp man who can find her gadding."

On paying for his ticket at the box-office, a mysterious door-keeper suggested that the only seat he could get was one on the first bench, immediately next a private box.

"But you must wait a minute or two. There is a gent as is sitting there who is mighty drunk; he has snored out twice a'ready, and hung his feet once over the railing. When he does that agin, I'll have him out, and you can take his place."

Clarence asked if there was no hope but this inebriated one.

"I reckon the house is chock full," replied the man. So Clarence waited, and, sure enough, presently there was a scramble, a scuffle, a cry of "Turn him out," and in plunged the door-keeper, collared his victim, and winked at Tracy, who, obeying the signal, made his way to the front bench and struggled into the vacant seat.

Adrienne was on the stage, and, although Rachel was in his mind, he soon felt that the "Western girl" deserved that he should forget unkind comparisons with her great original, and, taking her only on her merits, commend so praiseworthy an actress. So he listened and looked, as much as possible, without *arrières pensées*.

Presently his attention was distracted. He sat close beside the private box, leaning his head against the pillar of the partition, and a woman's hand suddenly fell on the cushioned front of this box, just beneath his eyes.

I do not mean a hand severed from the arm, and lying all bloody and terrible, but a living hand, whose owner was concealed behind the curtain.

It was ungloved, and white as a magnolia leaf, except just upon the outer edge of the palm, where a rosy tinge appeared, deepening to a henna-like pink as it reached the ends of the fingers, and lying beneath the almond-shaped nails like carnation leaves covered over with the inner lip of a sea-shell. It was not a "tiny" hand, nor a "little" hand, nor a "fairy" hand, where proportion is sacrificed to smallness; it was like the hand of an antique statue, and, as it rested calmly and *silently* upon the cushion, the fourth finger naturally divided itself from its sisters with a "line of beauty" which was indescribably graceful. A wrist of delicate shape, needing no bracelet to give it a borrowed roundness of outline, joined this beautiful hand to the arm which swelled above it.

Clarence watched the exquisite thing as it lay so pure and so still before him. He dreamily tracked a blue vein which presently struck his gaze, rising like a little stream from a bed of snow, and slowly he followed its course till it buried itself in the white arm. He almost leaned forward to look after its progress behind the curtain; but the hand moved, and, slightly turning up its roseate palm, with its fingers gathered together like the petals of an opening flower, gave him a new phase of perfection to admire.

At length a thought crossed him. The hand seemed familiar. He listened to catch the voice of its mistress, but, except once, when a deep-drawn sigh either proclaimed her attention to the business of the stage or her weariness, no sound but the confused murmuring of the other members of the party reached him.

The third act was over, and, if I remember aright, it closed with the mournful discovery to Adrienne that the Count de Saxe had left her to meet a rival whom she herself generously protects.

There was that rustling and settling of skirts which always follows the dropping of the curtain; men scattered out on all sides, as if they had been intensely annoyed, and now thankfully escaped; and Clarence wondered whether he should run the risk of losing his seat by going to the opposite side of the house, and there facing the lady of the hand, or stay where he was, and trust to chance and her exit.

Suddenly a voice he knew as well as his own spoke in the box, and a sparkling fan touched the hand gently.

"Why so pensive, dear?"

"When is the Liverpool steamer due?" said the hand's mistress, withdrawing it.

It was Lily.

Clarence Tracy sprang over the benches and tapped at the door.

The box was filled, but his entrée was most effective, and very gratifying to his vanity.

Angelica, Alicia, Lily, an elderly lady very much dressed and excessively red in the face, Mr. Langdon, and some "young men about town," formed the party.

He was at liberty now to fold the hand in both of his own, and to gaze unreproved upon the lovely, stately, blushing, shrinking creature, with her "grayish silk" dress, and knots of silver ribbon, partially draped in a huge, soft white shawl, which trailed from her fair shoulders as she rose to greet him— to greet him with tears swimming in her blue eyes, alternate gusts of color or pallor lighting or blanching her cheek, and not a word of welcome on her lips. Joy spoke loudly enough when she looked her happiness.

Clarence bent his eyes *into* hers, and a stranger would have sworn that their emotion was equal. The trembling eagerness of his grasp, the *effort* to tear himself away, the sudden change of manner as he turned with cordiality to Alicia, who was next Lily, was quite a study to witness. It reminded one of the attempts (often successful) of actors, who storm through a line or two, frightfully ranting, and then, reducing their voices to a summer softness, leisurely lisp out the next sentence.

Angelica enjoyed it. She passed her handkerchief over her mouth, and while her large eyes seemed full of tender sympathy for this happy meeting, a smile was dancing in every dimple.

"What a consummate hypocrite!" was her muttered comment as she next raised her lorgnette, and looked over the gaping crowd in the parquette, waiting for her turn.

A flash of amusement showed her appreciation of the scene as she shook hands with Clarence, who was stolidly unconscious, and made no answering signal.

He was presented to Mrs. Hardcastle, the stout lady in permanent crimson, who had as great "an eye for men" as good Queen Bess, and who seemed only moderately satisfied with Clarence's spare proportions; then he and Mr. Langdon exchanged remarks, and the young men were duly named and bowed at.

"But where is Willie? where is my brother?" asked Alicia.

"Alas! poor Willie! how little he dreams, as he now lies asleep at the hotel, what pleasure I am enjoying! We hurried to your house," inclining his head toward *Mr.* Langdon, "hoping to find you all, and, being disappointed, Clarendon went home to bed, and I strolled accidentally to this theatre. Chance placed me in the very next box, where soon I heard familiar voices, having first been attracted by . . . . That reminds me, however, Rosalie informed me that you were dining out."

"Yes," said Angelica; "our visit here is impromptu. We dined with Mrs. Hardcastle *en petit comité*, and some one proposed encouraging 'native talent;' so, despite our evening dresses, we ventured, trusting to these high partitions to conceal our 'grandes toilettes' and bare heads from the hoi polloi. But leave ourselves, and tell us about Mr. Clarendon and you."

Till the curtain rose again, Clarence talked with few interruptions. His style was easy, full of amusing detail, and interesting. Though he took the whole conversation upon himself, still his egotism appeared more a desire to please his listeners than to show off his own powers.

When the play recommenced, he turned his whole attention to Lily, whispering close to her ear, and yet not with undue familiarity. She was very silent; her bosom heaved now and then with a happy sigh, and her eyes would sometimes meet his own; but, for the most part, she fixed her absent look upon the stage, with changing color and a subdued beatitude of expression.

Angelica saw them unmoved. She exchanged remarks about Adrienne's costume with Mrs. Hardcastle, who was an uncompromising dresser, and occasionally she would cast a word at the youth who leaned over her chair, drinking deep draughts from her intoxicating eyes, and whom Clarence, without looking at him, decided to be "the Saratoga boy-lover." Adrienne draws off her gloves, and, smarting with bitter and unavenged insult, recites her rôle from "Phèdre," while her hostess sneeringly suggests that she should give them "the deserted Ariadne."

> "I am not of those sinful ones
> Who feel in crime naught but a tranquil joy,
> And bear a brow insensible to shame!"

Glowing with honest indignation, she peals forth these lines, and pointing with scornful finger at the "sinful one," typified by the princess, who receives unflinchingly the well-aimed rebuke, while confusion prevails in the courtly circle met to applaud the supposed unmeaning recitations of the great actress.

"Serves her right!" exclaimed Mrs. Hardcastle, alluding to the princess; "what business has a married woman to interfere with other people's lovers?"

Here a discussion ensued, which was learnedly taken up, Angelica insisting that for her part she objected to such interference simply because it was "such trouble." "When a woman had a husband to manage, why under heaven should she undertake to battle with other women for the direction and care of their property? Men were only useful and agreeable as whetstones on whom one sharpened one's legitimate powers of control. No reasonable creature could seriously think that there was any comfort to be gained in exchanging one man for another. They were all alike; their envelopes only differed. You were as likely to find contentment, or rather strife, in one man's society as another's. Therefore satisfy yourself, if a married woman, with the man whom the law gave you an unlimited right to govern and to lead. Everything else was a humbug."

"You appear to forget the morality of the thing altogether, Angelica. Has that no weight?" asked Mr. Langdon, from the background.

"Did you speak?" inquired Angel, with an impertinent drawl, scarcely turning her head.

Her husband repeated his remark.

"Oh!" she answered, shrugging her shoulders scornfully, "I did not know that any one was entering into the *haute morale* of the business. If this is to be a heavy discussion, as I presume from your taking part in it, I shall withdraw. You will crush my butterfly wings beneath the Juggernaut car of your criticism."

Clarence had paused to listen to Angel's flippant retort, and he inwardly muttered,

"Handsome, diabolical creature! Is that first speech a taunt at me and a final warning off the premises?"

While Dick Everett, little conversant with the outward appearance of angels, and proud of his French, whispered to her, stirring as he did so the great diamond *solitaire* which adorned her little, close-curled ear, "*Démon, cousue dans une peau d'ange!*"

Alicia was busy with two or three admirers, smiling, coaxing, commanding, glancing, like a canary-bird of lazy habits, with several lumps of sugar to dispose of at once. She pecked here, and flew off there; now bestowed her whole attention upon one tempting morsel, and then, turning her back upon it, chirped her admiration for another heretofore neglected.

The last scene of Adrienne's sad life drew near.

She took from the box, sent her, as she fancied, by the count, her own faded bouquet, when she had fondly hoped that its contents would offer her a token of his renewed affection. She presses the poisoned leaves to her lips—to her heart; she inhales her speedy death through its fatal agency, and already the work is begun, when Maurice himself appears, and she sees him once more her devoted lover.

All is forgiven—all is forgotten. She thinks no more of the withered flowers, whose rejection had been her doom, when suddenly the sharp pang of the insidious perfume recalls her from realms of future bliss as Maurice's bride to the stern present.

"The flowers!" he cries. The horrible certainty is guessed. They come from the jealous, fierce hands of the princess, and Adrienne's fate is sealed.

With his arms around her, soothing her last agonies with his love, his touching misery calling upon Heaven to spare her young life, she dies.

"Better so—better so," murmured Lily, her low voice drowned in tears; "better to have died believing him entirely true, leaving with him the sweet recollections of her sorrowful fate, her beauty untouched by care or time, dying through his unconscious means, than live to have him again desert her for the flattering smiles of unworthy women."

"But do you think he would have done so, Lily?" whispered Clarence, humoring her grave way of witnessing a mimic passion.

"I fear it," said Lily, hastily wiping her eyes. "He would always have found an excuse for encouraging or responding to flatteries. He was a vain man; *they* are weaker than vain women."

The party was on the move.

Little Everett was folding Angel's shawl around her, and looking as if he worshiped and envied the happy Cashmere. She was languidly "sipping the delights" of his ingenuous adoration. Mrs. Hardcastle, with the air of a critic, was saying,

"Julia Dean was better in those two last acts—much better. Her dresses were really pretty, whereas in that first scene she was hideous. I never saw such a machine as she wore on her head."

Alicia was "making up her book" of polkas and waltzes for a party the next evening, so nobody listened to the poor old lady, for Mr. Langdon had gone to see after the carriage; consequently Clarence, with his usual far-seeing policy and never-failing vision, read "good dinners" to come in Mrs. Hardcastle's punchy figure, and dissatisfaction at the general neglect in her scowl.

Turning from Lily, he remarked, with an insinuating smile,

"Don't you think she did well? It was extremely effective, that drooping of the chin and the half-closed eyes."

"Pretty well—indeed I may say very well," replied the lady; "she got her train admirably from under the count's feet. I have an evening reception every Friday, Mr. Tracy, and I shall be happy to see you at dinner next Wednesday. Mr. Hardcastle will leave his card to-morrow on you and on Mr. Clarendon."

"Thank you. Should we stay until that time, we should be most happy. I shall do myself the honor of calling, and answering more positively. Prosy old women must be looked after, Lily," he added, in an under tone, as he offered his arm, Mr. Langdon having returned to take charge of Mrs. Hardcastle, and to report the carriage "driven up."

"Come early to-morrow, Clarence," said Lily from the coach window, kissing her hand.

"And oh!" cried Alicia, dismissing her covey of beaux, "give my love to Willie, and tell him I am dying to see him."

"Don't forget my invitation," mumbled Madame Hardcastle, grinning her favor.

The carriage drove off.

"Not a word, not a look from Angel!" thought Clarence. "To the last moment she was whispering nonsense to that conceited boy with his curls and his airs, who planted himself in the street mud so as to be as near her as possible till they drove off. She is deuced cool; but she will find her match!"

🌺 CHAPTER XV

Probably there are some people who will be tempted to exclaim, "False, false—false to human nature, that a man so young as Clarence Tracy should deliberately seek to win the heart and hand of a little girl merely with an eye to her money; that he should be encouraged in this deed by her own cousin, at the same time flirting with this very cousin, who, a married woman (pile up the horror!), listens to his speeches, plays him fast and loose, and, in a word, acts like a real unprincipled demon leagued with a brother spirit of iniquity. If they were older—but so young—it is unnatural, and, consequently, devoid of interest."

I can only answer, it may be so, but, for all that, it is true.

Let me take your objections backward, and first reply to the charge of Clarence's youth. He was certainly but a little over nineteen when I first presented him, but, besides a born talent for deception, he fell into the hands of a woman who never had been young. Do you deny such a proposition? Angelica Purvis reasoned selfishly when she was five years old; planned, plotted, and carried out her plots with a calm reserve which ripened each day.

She had never had a thought in which Angelica Purvis did not figure largely, save in the case of Margaret Oakes, and, meeting a heart colder than her own in that instance, she applauded her previous sagacity, and only determined that not one exception should exist to the broad, unfailing rule, "Every one for himself."

Her family she despised—not openly, not with cross words and abuse (she was too well-bred for that), but with inward sneers and outward indifference.

Mrs. Purvis was not likely to command the respect of her gifted daughter, she was so frivolous, so foolish, so fretful. She felt this, and never interfered with nor tried to govern Angelica, who grew up from cold childhood to reserved girlhood, whence she imperceptibly glided into haughty, self-concentrated womanhood.

She was more at home with men than with women. She liked to excite their interest by occasional details of her fancied sufferings—sufferings invented for the moment, which filled the eyes and hearts of her listeners, induced them to waste most wholesome and excellent sympathy upon the distresses of this syren, whose luxurious home was a wilderness, and made them feel as if they longed to do battle for her, and to die happy if her fine white hand waved them on to slaughter.

These desperate admirers were the very young ones, of course; for those of an older growth she had half-uttered sighs over a wasted life, regrets that she had not been born where genius alone reigns supreme, and dark glances through her moist lashes which were even more effective than her words.

Not one could boast of peculiar favor from Angelica Purvis. Her flirtations, strange as it may seem, were strictly *proper*. She was too clever by far to permit a familiarity, which, however much it may momentarily increase the admiration of the other sex, eventually leads to their indifference—perchance disgust.

Her beautiful figure was dressed always so as best to display its perfection; her little foot did not unkindly hide itself beneath her flowing skirts; her hand and arm often gesticulated with ensnaring grace beneath the very lips of her listener, and her wondrous eyes meltingly sought their meed of praise.

But woe to the man who fancied such theatrical performances were to be applauded nearer than you give your "hand" to a fascinating "Fotheringay" upon the stage. For such a breach of decorum Angelica was inexorable.

Admire her, sigh for her, die for her—devour her with your eyes, worship her footprints, but keep your distance in word and in action.

"*La vertu basée sur le calcul est invincible.*" Angelica, whether as Miss Purvis or as Mrs. Langdon, was invincible. She would flirt to the very borders of positive encouragement, and then retreat with as much ease as a court beauty from the presence of her sovereign. You did not even see her kick her train from beneath her heels.

Angelica never cared for the quality or duration of the admiration she excited. Numbers, facts, and figures were her rule, principle, and wish; something new to dazzle was always preferable to something old to fix.

Besides, she had seen enough, and read enough, and knew enough to be aware, when she was fourteen years old, that an object in view, a prize to be striven for, is more valued than an object grasped, a prize won.

She liked to keep a train of "adorers" always on hand, and at the same point; to make them whirl for her pleasure as a juggler spins his plates; with one touch to set them off, watch their revolutions, give a twirl of her finger to bring up an expiring waltzer, retire a step or two to admire the effect, and then again apply the slight impetus where it was needed.

She took charge of Clarence Tracy because at Chicora he was useful to practice upon, and, moreover, he was clever enough and well enough looking to amuse her. Gradually he interested her. Instead of dropping him on her return to the city, and when her approaching marriage would afford ample occupation, she thought he might be worth keeping for life. She studied him, looked into him with her discriminating eyes, and recognized a spirit congenial to her own. Soon she perceived his boyish influence over Lily, and her girlish preference for him; a preference that threatened to grow into a passion, and which he would willingly return with all the love of which he was capable.

Angelica had an inordinate swallow. She was a true "daughter of the horse-leech," and her cry was always "for more" conquests. She was intolerant of other women's charms, and if any woman attracted any man, it was, she fancied, because she, Angelica Purvis, permitted it without interference.

She was willing that Lily should marry Clarence, and was indeed anxious that Clarence should enjoy Lily's wealth; but, at the same time, it was necessary that Clarence should feel her power, and that her nets should display their accustomed prowess.

A few hours sufficed to turn the boy's vain head, and to make him fancy that he had a heart, and that Angelica filled it. Lily was a pretty, sweet, endearing child. Angelica was a haughty, grave, matured woman, whose attentions were the most witching flattery. She never told him that he was a charming youth; she only gave him a glance or two from her *repertoire* of looks, and a phrase or two from her vocabulary of insinuating speeches. She meant no harm either to Lily or to himself. She was amusing *herself*, and passing the time. Then came the boy's sudden accession of fortune, and his surprising offer. Angelica did not wound his self-love (his strongest sentiment) by a scornful rejection. No; she secured her future power by a half-uttered regret, and a magnanimous withdrawal in favor of Lily—to benefit him.

She drew her meshes tighter, and did not leave the hem of her dress in the entangled skeins.

By this time, though, with all her real liking for his brilliant parts, she thoroughly understood his faults, his glaring defects. They did not interfere with her own fancy, since she meant to rule him merely at a distance, but they were sad qualities for a husband to one like Lily.

Her heart (?) melted one day; a ray of sunlight thawed the thick slab of ice; the memory of her aunt came over her, and she spoke. Instead of being grateful, Lily opposed and refuted facts. Quickly as it came, the tiny ray disappeared, and Angelica wondered at her own folly in seeking to do good.

"After all," she reasoned, "why should I wish to prevent this match? I happen to know Clarence Tracy, and to understand his weakness, his instability, his hypocrisy. No doubt there are other men quite as bad as he, and worse, who would marry Lily, spend her money, be indifferent to her, and not do it in half so gentlemanly a way as Clarence. She likes him. She is bound to be the prey of fortune-hunters, and if he don't marry her some one else will, who, as I have suggested, won't consult appearances as strictly. Why should I desire to make little Lily unhappy for nothing? whereas, if I keep Clarence under my own hand, I can stop him, *dieu merci,* when he goes too fast, and can always prevent his distressing her by running after other bright eyes; for, so sure as there are bright eyes, Clarence Tracy will pursue them."

This train of thought, which I have put into regular phrases, visited Angelica pretty often. It occupied her mind on her wedding-night; and it was this feeling, mixed with a sort of feminine revenge, to convince Lily in the future of how truly she judged, that induced that conversation in the piazza. A double motive—a treble motive—to assist Clarence in his wooing, to attach him to herself, and to let Lily perceive, some half dozen years after, that "Angel was right."

On the Continent she met Clarence twice; they resumed the old manner, talked in the old way; she riveted her chains instead of loosening them, and continued her half-playful, half-serious correspondence with him.

But when she received his last letter, there was such a tone of mock admiration that she quickly felt the change, and let him enjoy a touch of cool dignity and matronly indifference, to teach him a lesson; moreover, Lily had really charmed her. It was genuine admiration that Angel now felt for her cousin. Their styles were so different, they could never clash; she had the love for her that she might feel for a beautiful flower, an exquisite statue, a rare painting. She liked to look at her, and to have people acknowledge that a "Southern cousin" was a "joy forever." Angel would have given up any thing to Lily except—her admirers.

She poured out her praise of Lily to Clarence with all the nonchalance for the effect it might produce on his feelings *for Mrs. Langdon* that she would have felt had she described to him a heroine in a novel.

But when he arrived, and, on their first meeting, not content with giving his first look to Lily, he continued to treat her as his first object, Angel inwardly vowed to resume her sway, and to prove herself a match for her fickle adorer. In speaking of Angelica I give you a clew to Clarence, for they were so alike in many points that the only surprising thing was that they never knew it.

From a child, Clarence Tracy had marked out his line of life; to keep his own counsel, to rise on the backs of his friends, to flirt with little girls, to make a great parade of sincerity, and to bear in mind that there was only one creature living who needed, merited, and demanded his sole care and atten-tion—Clarence Tracy! His sister Nora idolized him. From the time that she could first thread a needle, her idea was to hem handkerchiefs and make shirts for Clarence. Later, when she knew Lily, Clarence must enjoy the same privilege; and when it was whispered about among the girls that Lily Vere, with all her quiet looks, was a great heiress, Nora's head formed her first and last scheme, which she scarcely acknowledged to herself.

Clarence liked Lily very much. Her gravity, her modest ways, her submis-sion to those she thought wiser, quite impressed him. He was yet very young. As Angel said to Lily, "It was only the germ." But soon he learned to feel his power over Lily, and to give her, in place of an anxious wish to please her, a grand bashaw attention, and he looked down upon her sweet ignorance with superior eyes. Then she made rapid progress under his tuition, and he came to regard her as a possession of his own, and to treat her accordingly. She was almost as deferential to him as Nora, except when he did what she thought wrong, but that was so infrequent.

He was too sure of her friendship and devotion. It did not excite him. He began to think her insensible; she was so still; and with that delicious boy-tyranny which so early betrays itself, he liked to show his command over her, and the more she yielded, the less impression her yielding made, and the less he valued it. But still he was tender of her and kind to her; his behavior was not displeasing to her eyes, for she considered his reproofs as marks of his interest, such as he showed Nora.

On his final return from college, he was more struck than formerly with Lily's prettiness and gentle ways; he had learned the full weight of "plenty of money;" and though even to himself he did not say "I'll marry Lily Vere for her plantations," still his boyish mind took in the idea, and with greater deference he made his advances to his sister's friend.

He was the oldest of a group of boys at Chicora that spring. Angelica singled him out; he was flattered beyond measure. She made him read to her, she talked nonsense to him, and enjoyed his nonsense in return. *She* scarcely understood then her own influence; for, though he was by no means the first youth whom she had captivated, she was the first woman (I do not count college belles) who had made his pulses beat.

Skillfully she twined her chains about him, and, with all his cleverness, all his knowledge of her cold calculations which instinct gave him, he could not throw off her tightened and tightening clasp.

He forgot Lily, and became a mere puppet in Angel's hands. She pulled the wires; he fancied that he was a free agent, whereas he only followed out her plans. He thought she admired, whereas she commanded; and, happy in her languishing looks, he moved hither and thither with a vague idea that she must love him, or why should she trouble herself about him. At any rate, she herself said, "Marry Lily!" so he would; and as for the future—"oh, hang the future!"

When he was at Heidelberg, away from home, and one of Lily's pretty letters would come sliding in with its fresh, innocent tone, he would think that he really loved the writer, and that she was indeed a treasure. But then a long, narrow envelope, with its uncompromising seal, "*Je veux*," would fall into his hands, redolent of *maréchale,* recalling by its lingering perfume the very aspect of Angel, and it would be so *spirituelle* or so sarcastic, with only a word here and there which meant "something," that he would muse over it, and try to divine a hidden thought, and begin to dream about "those eyes," till Lily's little letter would fade in the distance, and be quite forgotten.

I might prose on for pages, when two lines would amply give the word of this enigma.

Lily was the speculation ventured, pocketed, and laid aside for future use. Angel was the speculation yet to be decided, which kept the gambler on the alert, and warmed and cooled him with alternate fits of hope and doubt.

But there was about Lily, as she dawned upon him in her pure loveliness, rising from her chair in that dingy box, a certain halo of almost forgotten boyish dreams, a certain reminiscence of German romance, which was in very truth a foundation for his ardent welcome; and when Angel met him with her amused smile, the recollection of her last letter, and the desire to pique her, aided fully in producing a devotion and singleness of purpose, which caused a like indifference on the side of the really indifferent one, so that Clarence went home to bed dwelling on Lily's beauty, and wondering whether Angel was absolutely as careless as she looked.

I do not pretend to write "thrilling romances," with sudden surprises, mysterious secrets, and dark horrors, nor even multitudinous accidents which bring the strangest things to light. Mine is simply a little tale which seeks neither to dazzle nor to terrify. I try to write of human nature as it passes daily beneath our windows, or throbs beside our own hearts. Many will call me "tame," and others will cry "unnatural." It may possibly be both. I only do my best, and write according to my knowledge and convictions.

I once had the honor of being in company with the greatest living novelist—of course, I allude to Mr. Thackeray—and a lady, celebrated for her wit and beauty, said to him, "I detest your books, they are so false. Why should you always make vice flourish and virtue go to the wall? If one reads you believingly, one would doubt that there exists upon this earth a really good man or woman, unless he or she chances to be an utter simpleton or poke. I close your books always with a dreary feeling. Every thing is hollow, hypocritical, selfish. The world is bad enough, truly; why make it worse?"

"My dear madam," answered Mr. Thackeray, spreading out his hands, which some Washington belle had told him "looked so nice and English, with their clean nails," "my dear madam, I write as my eyes see. If I were to *invent* human nature, depend upon it I should make even stranger pictures. It is not my fault if life appears to me as I show it. I have no imagination—I only copy."

From my corner I listened to the great man, drank in his words, and added my humble approbation and conviction.

It seems quite an act of temerity to mention this world-known name, and to call the attention of a reader to possible comparisons between the author of Vanity Fair and the author of the Busy Moments of an Idle Woman. But my admiration for him is so unqualified, so sincere, that I feel as if his name might add a dignity without instituting a comparison; and no one, I trust, will accuse me of conceit or imitation when I suggest that, following at great distance the example of this discriminating writer, I endeavor not "to invent a new human nature," but to paint the thing itself—to sink a shaft in the breast of my neighbor, and to draw thence a living stream—to eschew portraits, but to make "fancy sketches" life-like enough to induce people to say, "Ah! that is meant for so and so."

I take no interest in those delightful books which are composed of alternate layers of devils and angels, like the hands of boys and girls laid upon a table for the game of "head and cheese"—now angel, now devil has the best of it, and the "upper hand rules." I do not believe in sudden reformations, where the "devil" of the piece is made instantly good by the death of the "angel," or by his marriage with her, and turns as quickly as you turn the leaf into an excellent and virtuous character, just as if excellence was a coat or gown, and virtue a cap or bonnet, which you purchase or have presented to you, and wear comfortably ever after.

I believe that every living creature is susceptible of some kind impulse, and liable to some wicked thought or action. Opportunity is more a leading spirit than even education. We must all pray against temptation, dread the workings of selfishness, and try to do our best. If we undertake to write novels, bear this in mind, that heroes and heroines of the present day must act like men and women of the present day, or else they are mere *Marionnettes*, and show their rags and wood-work instead of their flesh and blood.

Angelica seems wicked almost without a reason, but she had never checked her desire for indiscriminate conquest, and for power over those within her immediate circle. She was not positively unkind; after acknowledging her supremacy, you might be as happy as you could. Clarence was vain, but doubtful; ambitious, but indolent; clever, but vacillating; eager for men's praise, but fonder of women's smiles; bent upon conquering them, but always ending in being by them conquered. With decided talent, he frittered it away; always intended to do something, but never did. And, to sum up his character, he was as uncertain as a coquettish woman, for the thing he held was less valuable in his eyes than that which he could not reach.

I have prosed enough. Let us return to my sweet Lily, who has no shield to oppose to scheming heads and hoary hearts but her good sense, the atom of Scottish shrewdness that she inherited from her father, and an instinct which oftentimes rightly guided the glance of her blue eyes.

CHAPTER XVI

"And when do you go home?" inquired William Clarendon, smoothing down Alicia's already smooth hair, and looking admiringly in her face.

It was the morning after their arrival, and they were all sitting in Angelica's "sulkery," which barely held the party. It was the tiniest place imaginable, hung with a thick striped silk of pink and fawn color, the ceiling stuffed and *bombée* to look like a tent, with a pointed drapery below the cornice around the walls. A long divan and cushions filled one side opposite the windows, across which and the solitary door there ran, on rings, fluted curtains, so that, when drawn at night, there appeared neither entrance nor exit. The carved white mantle-piece was held up by dancing Floras, who balanced on the tips of their slender fingers the low, broad shelf, covered with deep pink velvet, on which stood two exquisite statuettes—one of Siluria, the other of Bacchus and Ino. Between them, in an elaborately gilded and jeweled frame, arrayed like an easel, was one of David's finest miniatures, a half-length of Angelica herself, looking like an empress in love, with a bouquet lying in her lap, and from the hand which languidly hung over the *console* beside her drooped a half-opened letter, while her eyes gazed dreamily ahead.

She seemed to reign supremely if indolently, and to be the ruling genius of her dominions. Two huge China vases, enameled with birds, flowers, and Cupids, occupied either side of the chimney. Through the pierced holes in the bottom of one came the hot air which warmed the room; into the other, Angelica threw the invitations, *billets d'occasion,* and et ceteras which daily beset her path.

In each of the corners *encoignures* mounted from the floor to the ceiling, and on the tapering shelves of two of them beautiful *Sèvres* flower-pots held fragrant exotics, which were renewed whenever the close and perfumed atmosphere caused them to fade; on the other two were piled such profuse treasures of rococo *trifles* that Alicia declared she had not yet been able to see and admire them all.

Each chair was a "possession," from the originality and costliness of its design and build; and now seated in the most luxurious of them, a perfect lounge, covered with satin and needle-work, was Angelica, folded in her dressing-gown, and wearing a cap, collar, sleeves, and petticoat of fabulously fine *broderie-Anglaise.*

There were but three other chairs: one, of polished satin-wood inlaid with *nacre,* like an old-fashioned work-box, with a pale blue velvet lining, Lily occupied, looking in her white Cashmere morning-dress like a pearl in its shell.

Another, of fine scarlet morocco stamped in gold, showed off as a rich background the sunny beauty of Alicia, while the last, of heavily-carved ivory, cushioned with amber-colored damask, was claimed by Clarence, and the whole sofa and its countless pillows was given up to Willie, who had drawn Alicia's chair near him.

"And when do you go home, darling?"

"That depended upon papa's coming; but now I fancy he will shirk the trouble, and trust us with you."

"Don't speak of going home," said Angelica. "Where is the use of it? Charleston is the dearest place to love at a distance."

"Oh, Angel!" cried Lily, "it is a place to live and to die in. I like to visit other cities, but for a home, give me Charleston."

Angelica slightly applauded with a gentle beating together of her hands.

"Bravo, Lily! your color fairly mounts. I agree warmly with one portion of your praise. It is indeed a place to die in, for I know no other which one could leave with fewer regrets."

Alicia and the young men laughed, while Lily shook her head.

"Don't you really like your native place?"

"Its bricks and mortar, its trees and stones, and, more than all, its wood-work? y-e-s, after a fashion; but its people? no. They are better abroad than they are at home. I recollect often being struck by the agreeability of my townsmen and women when once you get them over that impracticable bar of our harbor. Whether it be that the shallowness of the channel reacts upon their feelings, but they never unbend till they have cleared it. Then, judging them by an ordinary standard, they are sociable, conversible, human. You say reproachfully, 'The so and so's are really nice people; I must cultivate this pleasant acquaintance.' You return home; that hateful bar dips again, and you find your charming *foreign* friends ossified again."

"But one thing is certain, Mrs. Langdon," said Clarence, withdrawing his eyes from Lily's face; "they are unlike most stiff people in one respect: they are as eager to claim their *concitoyens* out of the city as they are shy in it. I asked a forlorn party once in Paris, whom I met dolefully sight-seeing, if they were enjoying their trip. 'Oh no,' they said; 'there is not a Charlestonian at an hotel.' Again, I put the same question to another party. 'Indeed, yes,' was answered with alacrity; 'there are at least twenty Charlestonians in our house.' Now I knew that at home neither of these families cared to see twenty people more than twice in a year, and on both these occasions they must be twenty selected and select individuals."

"Yes, they are deliciously inconsistent. They fold you to their hearts in New York, and scarcely bow in Charleston."

"But," pursued Clarence, who enjoyed differing a little from the last speaker, "they are high-toned, chivalric—"

"Mercy! mercy!" cried Angel, "spare me! I agree. I grant them every thing, and they may take the rest. They don't boast, they don't parade—"

"Oh, Angel!" that was Lily, of course.

"The women are not old-fashioned, dowdy, nor contracted in mind and body—"

"Treason!" exclaimed Willie; "they would not appreciate this pretty room, perhaps?"

"Indeed they should," said Angel, yawning after her graceful vehemence, and sending back her chair to a lower angle by a touch upon a secret spring. "Indeed they should, for M. de Trévillier says, alluding to its only door, that, after all, '*Ce ne peut être qu'un boudoir Americain.*'"

"Apropos of American productions: there was such a funny little scene this morning in the hotel parlor, while Clarendon was swearing up stairs at a tight pair of boots. A prim little woman was being evidently bored by a tall, deaf old fellow, who was asking questions without number. She unrolled a package of slippers, and began looking over them. 'Are those Europee-*an?*' he asked. 'No, sir, *Ammery-can,*' she answered, without a smile, though she saw me laugh out. Lily, I have brought you a pair of slippers: by the way, here they are; they were at the top of one of my trunks, and actually we got our luggage this morning."

"I believe Clarence made up that slipper story," said Willie, "to introduce his gift with becoming nonchalance. They are Orien*tal,* Lily; and here is my offering, which I ought to have prefaced with some anecdote about a fair girl dying of a broken heart."

Lily received with a bright blush the fairy slippers, which were worked with white lilies in seed pearl, and extended her hand for a little box which Willie gave her.

"Try the slippers first," said Willie; "let us set to work leisurely."

"I fear they are too small," said Lily, putting up her foot.

They were tight.

"I must give them to Angel," said Lily, sorrowfully, "unless I can keep them without wearing them."

Angel sat up and took the slipper, which slid on like the *soulier vert* upon Cinderella.

"You were too complimentary to my foot, Clarence. You forgot that I am only half a Purvis. You must have been thinking of Angel."

"She has never shown you her foot, then," said Willie, laughing, while Mrs. Langdon's satirical smile played around her lips as she turned the dainty slipper from side to side. "You can never step into Angel's shoes, Lily, though she may into yours."

Lily shuddered involuntarily, and Clarence knelt to remove the slipper. As he did so, Angel said,

"Have you never acknowledged the supremacy of the Pope?" and she thrust toward him, with a playful gesture, the high-arched instep, with its lofty curve, as if born to plant itself triumphantly.

"I am willing to do homage to the emblem of purity, the immaculate Lily," said Clarence, gravely, and he touched with his lips the embroidery of the slipper.

"Pshaw!" said Angel, dropping the pretty thing from her foot; "I have stretched it now, dear; you can wear it. There is very little difference in the size of your foot and mine; one shoe would do for either of us."

Sure enough, it was comfortable now, and Lily looked at her new property with delighted eyes.

"Let us see the contents of Willie's box," said Alicia, with a slight inflection of pique; and at that instant a footman brought in a package, which he said had come from the hotel, directed to Mr. Tracy.

"It was time," exclaimed Willie, "for I think Lily's presents were not giving satisfaction to all the company—*eh, puss!*"

Lily produced a garnet heart, through which was thrust a golden arrow, and a Venetian chain studded with garnets fastened it around the throat or upon the arm.

"How very pretty!" exclaimed Alicia; and, although she was presented with a bracelet, and a set of pink coral by her brother, and a fan was offered by Clarence, with any number of *bergers* and *bergères* in hoops and powdered hair, still she looked wistfully at Lily's trinket.

"I have lots of flowers and furbelows for you, *petite sœur,* in the depths of some great boxes," said Willie, who noticed that Alicia was not satisfied.

Presently Lily perceived it, and guessed rightly.

"This heart is too bloodthirsty for me, Willie. What should I do playing off tricks with 'daggered hearts?' Alice, would you like to exchange if Willie permits it?"

Alicia's eyes sparkled.

"If you wish it. It is all the same. Willie's memory and kindness will be just as well treasured. Take my bracelet;" and she drew her chair forward, turning the back of it upon Clarence and Angel, while she and Lily called upon Willie to agree, and to help them decide.

While they were clasping the turquoise bracelet on Lily's arm, where it looked so pretty that Alicia's grasping propensity caused her almost to regret the exchange, Clarence had unfolded another parcel, and brought to light a paper-cutter, which he passed over to Angel, bending upon her one of his most concentrated glances.

It was of ivory, and the centre of the blade was painted delicately in water-colors, representing a moonlit river, with a boat gliding upon its waters, containing, of course, a sentimental couple. The handle was formed of a woman's hand grasping a tiny globe.

Angel smiled, and Clarence begged her acceptance of it. She expressed her thanks, and, without a word more, placed it upon the table.

"I fancy a likeness existing—"

"To me, in that blue-gowned female?" said Angel, without affectation. "*Merci du compliment!*"

"More in the allegorical hand," said Clarence. "Small as it is, it holds the whole world in check."

"My hand deals little in checks," said Mrs. Langdon. "Lily's will soon be more in that line."

"You have learned to pun."

"So feebly."

"With true French principle, it is the hand of a *femme mariée* which is symbolized. It is a left hand, and a wedding ring is faintly marked upon the third finger."

"Yes," said Angel, indifferently. "Mr. Clarendon told me, or Lily, or perhaps it was Alicia, that you sing, Mr. Tracy. Young ladies, can not we persuade Mr. Tracy to sing for us?" and she leaned forward and over the back of Alicia's chair with such an evident determination to encourage no *tête-à-têtes,* that Clarence bit his lips, while the girls eagerly seconded the request.

Clarence yielded, and, turning to a small cabinet piano which was niched into the wall, he struck a few bars, saying,

"I have no voice for operatic music. I do not distress even myself with such attempts. Here is a little ballad which may please you;" and he began a rather monotonous air, to which were set these words, written by I know not whom.

> "Thou hast, left me to my sorrow,
>   And withdrawn thy love from me;
> Yet my memory still must borrow
>   All its dearest thoughts from thee.
> Though I know that I am fading
>   'Neath a cold world's bitter blast,
> And they tell me 'tis degrading,
>   Yet I love thee to the last.
>
> "Where thy false vows first were plighted
>   'Twere needless now to tell;
> How this constant heart was slighted,
>   Thou canst still remember well.

But I mean not to upbraid thee—
　　May'st *thou* never feel the smart
When some loved one has bereft thee
　　Of thy foolish, doting heart.

"On thy path of pleasure hieing,
　　When joy brightens in thine eye,
May no thought of him now dying
　　Wake thy bosom's faintest sigh.
But should sorrow e'er o'ertake thee,
　　And thy dreams of pleasure flee—
When at night thy griefs awake thee,
　　Think of those thou gav'st to me."

The spirit of vanity was stirred up within his breast, and, forgetful of Lily, he pursued recklessly for the moment the sneering Angel. His whole character revealed itself in that instant—a worthless object, which resisted him, outvalued the richest prize which was truly his own. His voice was not powerful nor very sweet, but he sang with expression and feeling—too much feeling; for, as he deeply murmured,

　　"When at night thy griefs awake thee,
　　Think of those thou gav'st to me,"

the utter abandonment of his reason to his sorrow (seemingly), and the glance he gave Angel, aroused Lily.

She turned pale, and looked from the one to the other with a quick, searching gleam; then her lids fell over her eyes, and a shadow darkened her brow.

There was a pause as Tracy finished, and Alicia was the first to thank him, and to compliment him on his performance.

Angel played with her paper-knife, and assented to Alicia's remarks.

"And you, Lily?" he said, turning toward her.

"I am but an indifferent musician," she answered, coldly. "Alicia's praise is far more important than mine;" and she rose and leaned her elbow upon the mantle-piece, gazing down into the tiny, sparkling little wood-fire.

"No one has seen my present," said Angel.

Alicia admired it, and touching with its sharp point Lily's hand which hung beside her,

"Look, Lil," she said.

It was not calculated to allay Lily's fears. She instantly recognized the intended allusion, and, to Clarence's surprise, who had so completely satisfied himself of her want of perception that he almost fancied her blind, she said, with quivering lips,

"This is a memento of the May-party. Where are the Hatton roses that you brought home that evening after your moonlight row?"

"Is that the intention? What a pretty compliment to my *beaux jours de jeunesse,* Mr. Tracy," said Angel, carelessly. "It is a dear little toy. The hand is like yours, Lily."

"By the way, Lily, I knew your hand last night before I knew you," said Clarence, approaching her with his most insinuating countenance: "*it* has changed very little."

"Lily's hand is perfect," remarked Mrs. Langdon. "I am rather proud of my own," holding out a soft, perfumed, dainty cluster of taper fingers, "but I yield to her."

Thence ensued a discussion on hands—the true proportions, the relative merits, the requisite beauties, which was kept up by Angel, Alicia, and Mr. Tracy, while Lily was silent, and Willie occasionally put in.

At length the latter said,

"But, after all, Clarence, there is one hand you prefer to all others—a hand at cards."

Lily turned quickly and fixed her eyes intently upon Clarence's face, where the blood was rapidly mounting.

"Oh! that was long ago," he said; "now I care very little for cards, except in a friendly game."

"Was that a friendly game on board ship?" began Willie, laughing mischievously.

"What a tell-tale!" exclaimed Angel, coming to the rescue. "We shall all be afraid of you, Mr. Clarendon."

"Mr. Clarendon!" repeated Willie; "this is the second time you have called me so formally. I used always to be 'Willie' for Miss Angel Purvis. I have a great fancy for hearing that soft dissyllable from you."

"Willie, then, will you be kind enough to tell me the hour of this bright day?" she said, with her sweetest intonation. "That valuable time-piece in the drawing-room is sufficiently trustworthy for my purposes, but should you have 'a man of business' to meet in Wall Street, or a note in bank to pay up, don't risk your credit upon it."

It was nearly two o'clock, so Angel lazily pronounced herself in great haste.

"You two gentlemen will of course dine with us. I heard Mr. Langdon naming six o'clock to you as our dinner hour. Just ourselves, of course—perhaps with the addition of poor Cecilia, of whom I am now going in search."

"By the way, how is she?" inquired Clarence, who seemed anxious to break his own awkward silence.

"Did she not marry abroad?" asked Willie.

"She did; and a miserable business she made of it. This Count Ravel de Montanvert is a little insignificant creature, with red eyes and a red beard, not to speak of a red nose—every thing, in fact—"

"But read-y money?"

"Just so; but Cecilia had a rage for titles, like all her countrywomen—had dreams of a coronet and countess-ship, and, being of mature age, in spite of her brother's advice she married this Comte—de la Bohême, and wrote herself comtesse, after getting up a trousseau fit for a princess. We left her in Paris, looking as if the gilt had been a little washed from her spouse's coronet, and she very soon was obliged to sell out stock to pay his gambling debts. He had told her that he owned silver mines in Peru, diamond drippings in Brazil, and, I suppose, malachite diggings in the Ural Mountains, but somehow the supplies from these rich store-houses never came to hand, and, rather weary of him, she wandered back home a month ago with a feeble little baby, as red-eyed as its aristocratic papa, and who, I fear, will never be wiser than its clever mamma."

"Poor thing!"

"I have no patience with her. She might have married very well, or, marrying badly, she might have made the best of it; but she allowed this little animal to involve her fortune, and to ill use her, and then she spends her time pining or else boasting. She has herself comtessed to distraction, but abuses the comte as a rascal of the first magnitude—for his size. But what could she expect from a gambler?"

Lily sighed heavily.

"I have promised to take her to my dress-maker this morning. My dear girls, you will walk, you said;" and, bowing with her own especial grace, Angel swept away with her magnificent "action" and her voluminous skirts.

"Trojan women trailing their long shawls," repeated Willie, following her with admiring looks. "See here, Alicia, doesn't she do a little of this?" and he touched his cheek as if painting it.

"For shame!" ejaculated his sister; "wait till you see Cecilia de Montanvert, and then you will know what rouge is laid upon bare bones."

"Mrs. Langdon is handsomer than ever; there is no doubt about that. But you are all improved. Even you, puss, are very nearly a beauty," and he passed his arm affectionately around her as they left the boudoir.

Meanwhile, Clarence was determined to spring the mine or to take the castle.

"Lily," he said, softly, when Angel left the room, "you are angry."

"Not angry, but mortified and fearful."

"Great heaven! about what? I did play cards on board ship; but, unless I had wished to make myself conspicuous and priggish, I could not have done otherwise. Would you really desire that I should give up an occasional game of whist because I lost a couple of hundred dollars six months ago at cards? Whatever you wish seriously, Lily, I would promise to do."

"You promised me then, when by a strange accident I heard of this thing, never to play for money. I felt as if it had been providential that you inclosed carelessly within the envelope of my letter the note you had written to send your creditor. It runs in your family, Clarence. Horse-racing, betting, card-playing *in a gentlemanly way,* have, through succeeding generations, helped to dissipate the originally fine fortune of the Tracys. I did not ask a promise, but I thought you implied one."

Clarence's face assumed a mournful look, but within him a kind of suppressed anger seemed to whisper,

"My canny Scottish *fiancée* trembles for her father's hoards. Lily," he said, aloud, "this is a sad business—but you must not think that I allude to my gambling propensities" (with a bitter smile); "I mean that we should so soon fall out. I am not given to cards or bets. I can not with safety promise to give them up entirely, but I shall only repeat that you may trust me. Your wish would be always stronger than any oath made in my own name. Do you doubt me, Lily? By heaven! if you knew—if you could guess the immense power you have over me, you would be tempted to act the tyrant; for slaves make tyrants, and I am the slave, dearest, of your lightest thought. Wield your influence with care, my own sweet Lily!"

He took her hand, and poured out his eloquent vindication. The time had come which Angelica had predicted: it was no longer the timid, blushing girl who accepted his decisions. He divined the kindly, resolute young woman, who steadily watched him, and sought to read him before she gave up her point. A word now was not sufficient to convince her. She was not a child except in her child-like innocence. Give her a clew, and she was capable of following it. This was a prize to strive for. He might chafe under the unwavering gaze, but he could not despise the loving dupe she once was. He petted, but it was an occasion for him "to air his vocabulary," and to bring the machinery of his stage-tricks to the foot-lights, and there conceal wires and trap-doors.

It was troublesome, but exciting; for, abandoning presently her first attack, Lily calmly spoke of the evident understanding between Angel and himself—spoke calmly, gravely, without tears, without reproaches, without iterations or repetitions.

He respected her; he admired her; he began to love her.

She was as firm as if she had been cold, though her hands trembled, and her white cheeks sometimes flushed, and her voice faltered once.

"This is not a sudden notion, Clarence; I have had it before. Madame de Montanvert hinted one day before me at Angel, and I fancied her words then the peevish innuendoes of a foolish woman; afterward little circumstances almost forgotten rose up; but this morning a light seemed to break in upon me. You love me as a sister: take a sister's advice."

"As a sister!" cried Clarence, and he hastily brushed his handkerchief across his eyes; "never."

They talked long and earnestly, and fierce were the protestations of the gentleman as gradually the girl's own heart helped to plead his cause.

Of course, she forgave him; but her suspicions were aroused, and, as they finally rejoined Willie in the farthest drawing-room, where Alicia, with her usual tact, had dragged him off, he said to himself, deep in his own breast, and wonderingly,

"Take care! I may yet lose her."

But still, with minute observance of outward honorable punctilio, Clarence did not seek to bind her by any promise yet. He must wait till she was beneath her guardian's roof, and under his immediate protection. The world should never say that he had gained the heiress's hand by a clandestine engagement, unsuspected by Mr. Clarendon. He knew that she applauded his delicacy, and that she delighted in attention to points of etiquette such as this.

He was charmed with her. Long and intimately as he had known her, this was a new and startling phase of character. It might grow very troublesome; but he felt all the delight of a game to play—a race to run—and it was with a feeling of excited interest that he had never experienced before in her society that Clarence left that house, after they had all decided that it was too late for their intended walk.

✿ CHAPTER XVII

How grand Mrs. Langdon looked at the head of her dinner-table!

Owing to the party at which they were to appear that evening, all the ladies were in full dress, and around the sumptuously-served board, and beneath the blaze of the chandelier, whose light was tempered by shades of thick ground glass, they formed a charming group.

Angelica had assumed for this occasion her most dignified and stately aspect. In a dress of orange-colored moire antique, with a pattern of great roses and cactuses tied together with a loop of gold ribbon running over it, and made with the square front and half-high corsage of our grandmothers, she looked as if she had just stepped from some old picture, particularly as the sleeves and neck were ornamented with lace of wonderful richness, and around her throat was tightly clasped a single row of rubies matching the drops in her ears.

Nothing could be finer than the mode in which Angelica's head was placed upon her shoulders. She and Lily equally possessed this distinctive and rare charm. It gives a character to the plainest features, and elevates the commonest figure; but whereas in Lily it was only graceful and high-bred, in Angel it was predominating and imposing. It blended in Lily's *tout ensemble;* it was perfectly distinguishable in Angel's carriage, and immediately called your attention. She had a way of throwing back her head, and toying with the drooping ornaments that usually adorned her coiffure, which was both easy and haughty; or else, while speaking, she would fix her eyes upon her companion, and smooth over and over the lustrous blackness of her bandeaux, as if through careless thought, while in reality she was considering how pretty must be her white fingers threading these dark masses. Today, long lappets of lace fell from her braids upon her shoulders, and as she would twine the gossamer costliness about her hand, the jeweled butterfly, which, mounted on great pins, fastened her head-dress, shook, and trembled, and fluttered like a living thing. I do not know if there was truth in William Clarendon's conjecture, but certainly the sallowness of her cheek had given place to a faint color, which was infinitely becoming, while, though she could not compare in fairness with Lily, there was nothing disagreeable in the dead whiteness which alone remained of her once yellow tinge.

There was a mixture of stateliness and languor about Angelica, a softness in her eyes, and a haughtiness around her mouth, which constituted her charm. Every chair or seat which she occupied became a throne for an enamored Eastern princess.

She looked passion, and commanded obedience. Compare her now with Lily, and see how possible it was for a man to hesitate in outward admiration between them. The one seemed made up of light and purity, while the other was dark, designing, distracting.

Both were calm, and had great repose of manner. Both were grave, both smiled more than they laughed, and neither of them were "talking women." And yet, with these points of resemblance, with a cast of features singularly alike, they were as different as night and morning. So much does mind influence matter.

Clarence Tracy sat on the right of his hostess, and Lily beside him; opposite to them was the Countess de Montanvert, who had got herself up with tremendous trouble.

Poor Cecilia! her bones were bared till you could count the vertebrae in her back, *que c'était une douleur à voir.* Dark lines were under her eyes which rouge could not conceal; the lids were stenciled, pearl-powder glistened on the forehead, the eyebrows were carefully penciled, and countless yards of curviline swathed her lower limbs.

She was fidgety, rattling, full of *minauderies,* imbibed quantities of Champagne *frappé,* made eyes at William Clarendon, and sported a handkerchief with *"application"* a quarter of a yard deep around it, and a two-inch-square centre, just large enough to hold the coronet and the initials. Somehow the coronet corner always was uppermost.

Presently, however, she deserted William, and directed her fire toward Clarence. As it had often happened before, Willie's beauty stood no chance against Clarence's fascinating manner.

Tracy was so overflowing with kindness to all woman-kind that he never suffered any of the softer sex to be uncognizant of his claims upon their attention. He never wished them to lose the opportunity of appreciating him, provided *he* considered them worthy of the privilege; and by a few adroit remarks about Paris, and a certain air as of free-masonry existing between them, touching society of *la haute voleé,* he won Madame de Montanvert's delighted acquiescence and support.

She leaned eagerly across the table, shrugging her poor, thin shoulders, and flashing her black eyes, talking rapidly with an accent and tongue becoming more French at every sentence.

"You know Egbert de Montmartre? *Quelle joie! et cette chère petite* Madame de Havrecourt? It is a *liaison qui dure depuis des années. Sont-ils heureux!* Why do we never see such things in this country?"

"Cecilia!" cried her brother, "how can you talk so foolishly? You don't think of what you are saying. Pray, my dear, speak both English and sense."

"Archibald is really '*moyen-age*' in his notions," said Madame de Montanvert, laughing affectedly; "and yet *il sent son Etats-Unis d'une liene.*"

Mr. Langdon chose to take the "moyen-age" literally, and answered with some asperity,

"Let us say nothing about ages, Cecilia. You are only five years behind me."

"Years!" repeated Clarence, coming to the rescue; "who talks now of years? Alphonse Karr has decided, with all the force of his wit, that 'years'—a certain number of months and days elapsed—go for nothing. Looks and actions alone proclaim youth or age. A woman of twenty, faded and dull, must always be older than one of forty *bien conservée* and charming. So, ladies, what a chance for all of you who look toward forty as a bourne beyond counting; and yet at forty you will still plead youth to your budding neighbor if she has not the genius to *faire valoir* her scanty but withering summers."

"Did you ever see Alphonse Karr abroad?" asked Mr. Langdon.

"I never did; but I did see de Balzac, and Dumas, and Eugène Sue."

"I desired very much to meet M. de Balzac," Angel went on; "and I actually invited Mr. Langdon to procure that pleasure for me, but he seemed to think I might as well request him to move heaven and earth for no purpose but to introduce into our lodgings a wild hyena."

"Much more like a very tame elephant was the deceased lion. M. de Balzac was the most ungainly, huge mass! The advocate and defamer of pretty women was not a dangerous man in his latter years, even to the grateful hearts of *des 'femmes de trente ans.'*"

"How did you manage to get on so well in French society too?" inquired Madame de Montanvert; "they are so exclusive."

"I was fortunate enough to render a service to a *cadet* of a noble family at Baden-Baden," answered Clarence, with an uneasy blush, "and when I went to Paris last winter for six weeks, after you left," turning toward Mrs. Langdon, "he found me out, and overwhelmed me with civilities, invitations, and kindness."

"Where was I then?" asked Cecilia. "Oh yes, I was in all the horrors—*faisant mes couches.* As some woman says in some novel, it is indeed *un chien de métier.*"

Mr. Langdon groaned at this new demonstration of his sister's foreign manners, and William Clarendon said,

"How did you get over Dumas's kinky head?"

"I contented myself with thinking that I was not in Carolina. Béranger is a fine old fellow. I succeeded in seeing him by accident and a little strategy."

"Ah! if you have recently seen Béranger, I shall introduce you to-night to a gentleman who, on learning this, will, I am sure, take you to his arms *en plein salon*," remarked Angel. "He has but one French passion, but that absorbs his being. He passes his time translating Béranger, and, while he *affiches* the fiercest morality and prudery, no author is so simple, so whole, so perfect in his eyes as the laudator of Lisette. He will bore you to death with abuse of French men, French women, French nature, French poetry, French morals, French manners. The men are disgusting, the women *devergondées*. He has no patience with them—no admiration for them. They are coarse, they are heartless, they are unbearable. But Béranger! he is strong, he is pure, he is honest; and my discriminating acquaintance labors over his stanzas with a zeal, an energy, a love which he might as well bestow elsewhere."

"Where?" asked Mr. Langdon, who only spoke to ask questions or to reprove.

"Eh? any where," answered Angel, rising, with a half smile, and stepping back with nonchalant dignity, to make way for her lady-guests as they left the room together.

Tracy was close upon their skirts, and coffee was served as they entered the drawing-room. Madame de Montanvert helped herself to six lumps of sugar, which caused her tiny Sèvres cup to overflow, and began feeding Marquise with these impromptu Mocha-drops, discoursing most voluble nonsense.

"Where did you get your cook, Angel? I have given up in despair. These terrible *Irlandaises* are utterly incapable. One was recommended to me as a first-rate cook, and I ordered the first day *des petits canetons canaris aux jeunes légumes glacées*, with a *Bavaroise mousseuse à l'Anana*, and she made me repeat the order three times, and then flounced off, telling me she had not come there 'to be made game of.' I assured her that *canetons* were not game; they were the tame ducks hatched by geese, only very small; but she would not stay to listen. Now your *cailles bardées aux feuilles de vigne* and your *grenadins de veau aux petits pois* were delicious. I can't say quite as much for your *petits biscuits soufflés à la crème*. I am sure Marquise would not have touched them. *N'est-ce pas une belle aux yeux dorés?* Angel, why don't you send Marquise to see Zora? Zora is so lonely; she had a great deal of society in Paris; but here I am afraid of permitting her to visit, the dogs are all so common. Mr. Tracy, do tell me if Marquise's eyes are not like Madame de Chateauper's?"

Clarence was talking to Lily, and he obeyed the summons with rather an ill grace, which, however, soon subsided into his usual suavity and gallantry of manner, and Cecilia immediately pinned him for a "chatter."

"Such eyes! Zora has beautiful eyes too, and sometimes she fixes them on me with so deep an expression, that, if she were not Zora, I might fancy that, in the transmigration of souls, the heart of some impassioned prince was beating beneath her long curls. But I suppose male souls always inhabit male bodies. Is it not so? I should like to think that Zora has a man's heart."

"How can you, Cecilia, be so exceedingly absurd?" asked Angel.

Willie Clarendon, who enjoyed fun beyond every other sensation, was charmed with the comtesse.

He did not like to make her exhibit before his host; but Mr. Langdon having remained in the dining-room for a smoke, Clarendon proceeded to draw her out.

In vain Lily shook her head disapprovingly; but Angel, lazily amused, listened with a glitter in her eye, and Alicia rather encouraged him.

It would be wearisome to detail poor Cecilia's torrent of folly. She hopped from subject to subject, with shrugs, and flutters, and glances, and smiles, fancying herself intensely *Parisienne*, while she was only lamentably foolish.

Once she made three of the party wince, however; for, not satisfied with Willie, she continued her hold upon Clarence by addressing him, no matter how abruptly, if he attempted to rise from beside her. Either she began some story about herself, or about some fancied Paris friend of his, whose recollections he might have escaped had he chosen to disavow their, his, or her acquaintance; but, with his usual vanity, Tracy was satisfied to be bored if he could produce an effect, and liked to be thought an *habitué* of many French houses where he had really been only a chance visitor.

He saw Lily watching him, and tried to glide away under cover of some outrageous compliment paid by William; but Cecilia broke out,

"As for compliments, it is my pleasure to make them, not to receive them. Mr. Tracy, I made you a very pretty compliment at Rome once. A lady—that Venetian Countess Balsacor—asked me one night who was the young gentleman in constant attendance upon Madame Langdon. *'Apparemment c'est le porte-queue de la chére belle-sœur.' 'Vous prononcez mal, belle comtesse,'* I replied; *'c'est le porte-cœur.'* Pretty, wasn't it?"

With an impatient exclamation, Tracy got up and approached Lily, who abruptly left the room, closing the door quietly in his face.

"It is time to start, for our soirée is an early one," said Angelica. "Lily has already gone to smooth her ringlets. Can I offer you my mirror and Rosalie's services, Cecilia?"

Madame de Montanvert hesitated; but Clarence had moodily picked up a book, with an evident intention to say, and listen to, nothing farther; and that day's post had brought a letter for Miss Clarendon from home, whose contents she and Willie were now discussing, as it had to be answered by the morning's mail; consequently Cecilia, quite unaware of the mischief her "pretty compliment" had caused, thought she might as well examine into the state of the enameling on her features, and accepted the offer.

❀ CHAPTER XVIII

Mrs. George Beresford had determined to introduce a "new style" of parties. She had enjoyed "new style" dresses, and followed the lead in "new style" bonnets, but she would set a fashion of her own now, and have "conversation balls," that could incontestably be considered "new style;" so that when her rooms were full, and the rumor went around that there would not be a leg in motion except to walk about, a chorus of vituperations was raised by the dancers of "our set," and Alicia Clarendon was among the pouters.

"No music?"

"Conversation."

"Who'll make it?"

"What a take in!"

But the hostess glided about in a brocade so stiff that her tiny figure seemed lost in its ponderous plaits, and her spirituelle head rose above the triple ranges of ribbon, lace, and silk which composed her corsage like a brilliant blossom from the midst of a huge bed of verdure.

Her diamonds sparkled in their wheat-ear setting, and her wickedly bright blue eyes followed suit, while from the somewhat thin but very red lips flowed a stream of saucy sayings, which her admirers caught up and repeated with delight to those on the outside of her immediate circle.

Tremendous flirtations became the order of the night. Couples lounged in the conservatory—you "flushed" a "pair" in every nook—and really there ensued a low, murmuring hum of "conversation" that was quite marvelous. Mrs. Beresford labored assiduously. She gave the "ball" a roll whenever it flagged on its course; the *buffet* was stored with the choicest dainties; the big punch-bowl continued full, and all went merrily and most successfully.

It was not an easy thing. Constantly a dull silence would reign in one corner, and youthful heroes, *teetering* on their polka legs, found no words to express their want of ideas to their equally embarrassed partners. Quick as lightning, Mrs. Beresford would dispatch one of her satallites with a newly-invented scandal to rouse them and set their tongues in motion; or she would sail up herself with a jaunty, spirited air, which served to clear the heavy atmosphere like sheet lightning on a summer's evening.

There were some very hard novices whom she almost despaired of; but, arming herself with courage, and her memory with recollections, she broke in upon one body of silent, bored, and boring guests, and, aided by two or three choice spirits, began to talk most perseveringly, peremptorily, and persuasively.

Leaving the dear little soul *aux prises* with these unamusable creatures, I must tell you what became of our party.

At the door, on entering, of course little Dick Everett was waiting to meet his stately idol, who smiled on him from the depths of her luxurious eyes, and after making her compliments to Mrs. Beresford, she took the boy's arm, dismissed Mr. Langdon, and bewildered Dick by a few of her prettiest and dreamiest phrases.

Alicia gave a half start on being addressed by a well-known voice, and Harry Barclay appeared, to be warmly welcomed by Angel and herself, and timidly by Lily.

Presently, however, they all changed their positions: Mr. Barclay, with his quiet manœuvring, took possession of Miss Vere; Clarence sidled little Everett out of the way (who frowned his displeasure till Angel gave her fiat in Mr. Tracy's favor, and then he submitted); Alicia was flirting with a New York admirer; and the only two who retained their first belongings were William Clarendon and Madame de Montanvert.

"At last!" ejaculated Clarence, seating himself by Mrs. Langdon.

"At last!" echoed Angel, with a mocking smile.

"I began to despair of speaking three words to you. Why have you avoided me? Why do you wish to prevent me from pouring out to you, my confidant, my benefactress, my *friend*, the happy result of all your teachings? I wish to tell you—to assure you, even before I speak to her, of how deeply I venerate—I adore Lily. She is the sweetest, purest bud that ever bloomed for man's delight. What a companion! What a gentle hand to guide the helm of a wayward being's career! Is she not a tender glory? With all her feminine graces, her dove-like virtues, her speaking silence! Who would not trust those loving, meek, and innocent eyes? Ah! dearest Mrs. Langdon, let me thank you over and again for your far-seeing kindness. You bade me watch and wait for this treasure. She is a woman full of every womanly charm. No spark of deceit or cunning lurks in the blue lustre of her starry glance. A man might with unasking confidence place his honor, his life, his hopes in such keeping as hers."

Deeply from under the royal lids, with their long, searching, sneering glance, Angel listened.

"Yes? You think all that of Lily? How very nice!"

It was like a bucket of cold water suddenly dashed on an excited head.

With some difficulty Clarence proceeded:

"I do indeed. She has ripened into a most lovely, most lovable woman."

He paused, and Angel played with the lace lappets, and the jeweled butterfly danced among the shining folds of her black hair, while she now looked haughtily and indifferently over the crowd.

"I fear I am not worthy of so precious a care."

No answer but a slight smile.

"Has she not many admirers here? Does she not, do you think, regret her humble choice?"

"Clarence," said Angel, sitting up, which was a sign with her that she meant to speak to the purpose, "it is quite needless to talk to me in this exaggerated, melodramatic style. Lily is very charming, but you will never persuade me that you understand or feel her real charm. You are laboring violently to produce a dreary, famished soft of admiration, which does not in the least impress me. Be natural. Tell me that you find her wonderfully improved, that you thank Heaven for your good fortune, and that you will endeavor to make her happy. Happy," she repeated, with a deep-drawn sigh—"happy, because she is unselfish, true, devoted, and less anxious for personal preeminence than any creature I ever saw. She has listened to her heart; she means to give her hand where that heart has led the way; and, come what *will* of this act, she may live some blissful hours yet. She will never love any but you, and, struggling against her convictions, will continue to invest you with a whole catalogue of virtues—happy for that very reason, just as a vivid fancy enables its possessor to enjoy real pleasures more than a matter-of-fact one can attain under the same circumstances. Don't waste your time embroidering Lily for my benefit. All I ardently desire is that you should seriously appreciate her innocent, unworldly qualities. I am so hard, so old, so worn, I live in Lily's freshness as the flies do in amber. I let it envelop me, and lie dead and withered within its pure transparency." She smiled her bitterest smile: "We never show to greater advantage than side by side."

"Each the other reflecting," said Clarence, with one of his stereotyped phrases and bows.

Angel sighed, her eyes drooped, and a shade of pain contracted her lofty, languid brow. She placed her hand quickly upon her side, and then withdrew it as quickly.

"Are you ill?" asked Clarence, anxiously.

"A mere trifle; a spasm of that curious article, the heart. I should not know I had one, I suppose, unless these little twitches came occasionally. Velpeau says one great start some day will end my busy life. I don't mind them much. They rouse me, and set my blood stirring, and my brain thinking."

"It is very sad. Can nothing be done?" inquired Clarence, quite moved.

"Nothing. Don't you hear me say I enjoy them?" said Angel, impatiently. "Good-evening, gentlemen," she went on, with her accustomed insolent grace, as two men paused before her chair. "You are fortunate, Mr. Tracy: not only can I make you acquainted with Mr. Oldmeath, the unfailing translator of Béranger, whom I promised, but see! he comes doubly welcome, for he brings my poet, my poetical proser, whose name is fame."

"Unkind, ungrateful Mrs. Langdon!" exclaimed the last gentleman, while Mr. Oldmeath was executing his most Englishly awkward of awkwardly English bows. "I have been from the distance adoring you in your grand-dame trappings, longing for powder in your blackest hair, to complete the picture, and come now by easy stages to tell you what an appreciative audience you have this evening, and you receive me in this way!"

"Have done with your 'appreciative audiences,'" said Mrs. Langdon; "in your paper it always means a *very* small crowd, of whom you can say nothing farther. Mr. Tracy, know Mr. Parker, and be happy in that knowledge."

Mr. Parker was tall, florid, light-haired, with an English expression (partly based on a *nez retroussé*), which he cultivated to the highest degree. His eyes were haggard and worked, and his dress fantastic and dandified. Of himself you saw no more, for his beard, curling in minute ringlets, covered his face. His manner was deferential, soft, and considerate. He made every woman to whom he spoke fancy that she, by herself, could govern a king-dom, so complete was her power over him, and if over him—why, the rest of the world was easily managed.

Mr. Oldmeath was not possessed of more grace than falls to the lot of most of his countrymen from the white cliffs of Albion. You could never doubt but that he was a gentleman, with all the natural reserve which is their time-honored privilege. He had the bluest eyes, with the merriest twinkle in them—the whitest teeth—the squarest nose. Prim, particular; neat, rectangular, he *professed* a taste for the society of the strictest matrons, and somehow managed always to be found *courtisant les plus belles,* without the slightest reference to the hugely moral nature of their pretensions and principles.

He worshiped Béranger, he loved himself, and he honored the queen.

A lively chat ensued.

"I saw one of your most desperate admirers last night, Miss Langdon, the poet T—," said Mr. Parker.

"*I* never saw him in my life," said Angel, quietly.

"Impossible! you can't keep the list. They jostle one another, and you let them drop aside, fall, and wither like leaves from your bouquet. You must have known him. He described a certain drop of your eyelid—a bluish shade (nearly a vein) which tracks it—too closely for a street-gazer."

"Bear one thing in mind, Mr. Tracy," said Angel, "Mr. Parker speaks always for print and pay, either in ready money or in ready smiles, from his listeners. He does not expect me to believe him. I am very happy in the friendship of these two gentlemen. Mr. Oldmeath is so rigid in his translations, even of his thoughts, that he never tells me any thing which could not be proved by the original on the other page; whereas Mr. Parker—" and she paused, with one of her lustrous, upward glances—"no matter; I call them 'Fact and Fancy.'"

"That is not so good, my dear Mrs. Langdon," said Mr. Oldmeath, "as your speech to Parker that night at supper, when you were seated between the *millionaire,* old Carr, and himself. 'Behold me,' you said, 'between Mammon and Gammon.'"

"For a memory so apropos, and which brings to light forgotten witticisms, becoming, alas! fewer each day, you deserve, Mr. Oldmeath, a reward. Mr. Tracy (my townsman) is fresh from Paris; embrace him (mentally, I pray you) as one who has lately looked upon your idol, Bé—"

"For pity's sake," interrupted Mr. Oldmeath, raising his hands imploringly, "let my follies be! I have never bored you with my taste—"

"With your want of taste, frequently," retorted Angel, laughing one of her rare laughs.

"We shall not mind Mrs. Langdon's sneers," said Clarence, with his sympathizing smile, as he drew Mr. Oldmeath aside in deference to Angelica's "Pray talk him over," in a whisper.

But scarcely had Mr. Parker commenced one of his pretty fairy tales about a princess, whose name was Mrs. Some-one-or-other, and whose magic castle was built of bricks and mortar in Brooklyn, or in some such prosaic field, when Mr. Oldmeath called out,

"But, indeed, Mrs. Langdon, listen to this; acknowledge its graceful turn, its kind and honest impulse. Recite them again, pray, Mr. Tracy, and we will convert Mrs. Langdon."

"What is it?" asked Angelica, as Clarence hesitated.

"I was simply repeating to Mr. Oldmeath a couple of stanzas which were given to me in Paris as *'des vers inédits'* of Lamartine and Béranger. I do not vouch for them as being entirely unpublished, but they were so called, and appear new, even to one of Béranger's most trustworthy admirers," with a bow to Mr. Oldmeath.

"Let us have them," said Angel, languidly.

"Lamartine wrote in some lady's album,

> " 'Dans ce cimetière de gloire
> Vous voulez ma cendre! à quoi bon?
> Tandis que j'inscrits ma mémoire
> Le temps pulvérise mon nom.'
> —LAMARTINE.

"Upon seeing which, Béranger gallantly added,

> " 'Si le temps, pour montrer jusqu'où va son empire,
> Pulvérise en effet le beau nom que voilà,
> Puisse-t-il sur les vers que j'ose encore écrire,
> Jeter un peu de cette poudre-là.' ' "

"Is it not charming?" exclaimed Mr. Oldmeath, in an ecstasy.

"*De*-li-ci-ous," drawled Angel, with provoking coolness. "I am too impulsive to listen with proper calmness to such bursts of genius. Don't recite any more, Clarence—although your accent is very good."

"Why don't you take up the literary line, Mrs. Langdon? You are so difficult to please. Might you not give us something worthy our admiration?"

"On the contrary, it is you who find only one author—no, two," she added, with a significant look, and what, in a less haughty face, would have been superlative sauciness. "I would not dare to write even a magazine story. Mr. Oldmeath would praise me too little, and Mr. Parker too much. My reputation would be unmeaningly tepid between the two. Besides, I have no imagination. How could I cope with those budding, nursling vestals at the shrine of Poetry and Prose, who incessantly do pour out their sweet and sentimental phrases, and are cried up as 'graceful and interesting writers;' stain my fingers with even violet ink to be placed 'a little lower than these angels,' well 'got up' in Yankee-English, and very strong in the manners and customs of fourth-rate fashionables! I should as soon attempt to quash Mrs. Harriet Beecher Stowe with one of those interminable, tiresome replies to 'Uncle Tom's Cabin,' or enter the lists against the Bowery wit and refinement of Fanny Fern."

"Do not you admire Fanny Fern?" said Mr. Parker, turning uneasily.

"Admire her! what a misplaced sentiment! I may be surprised at her—wonder at her for being so heartily coarse—"

"Oh, Mrs. Langdon! she is so earnest—she feels so strongly—"

"Saul among the prophets! What business had you, my sentimental friend, with Fanny Fern? In what does she resemble your Nell Noodles and Poll Poodles, the eternal Rosa Matildas of your weekly journal? And, by the way, I heard some one complaining recently of the worn-out state of your sugar-sifter. You sprinkle the sweet too thickly over your critical notices, and induce this fault-finding subscriber to purchase such cart-loads of trash that he fervently hopes the secret will be soon discovered of making printed paper serve twice. He will gladly dispose of your cried-up volumes at less than the price of 'old rags per pound.'"

A smile made the white teeth of Mr. Oldmeath visible while Mr. Parker was receiving this reproof, given out in Angel's laziest manner, with a languid fatigue of gesture contrasting curiously with the vivacity of her words.

"There is something in the misfortunes of our best friends," &c.; but he was not destined to escape the feather-tipped lash of the scornful lady.

"And you, my dear sir, since I am in a candid vein, conduct your literary notices (with a difference) very much in the style in which Byron said the great English nation treats improprieties: every seven years it wakes up to a huge sense of virtue, and somebody must be punished, after which it falls asleep again, and nods and winks over far more culpable actions. In the reverse of this, you carry the war into every body's leaves, hitting right and left during at least seven weeks; then, with an amiable feeling ripe within you, or the moment at hand for the necessary layer of 'sweetening,' you light gently upon some new work, no better nor worse than its predecessors, and talk of it so kindly, and quote it so discreetly, that one might almost think—you had written it yourself."

Certainly both these unhappy gentlemen would have fled before this devouring sword; but what mattered these sarcastic sentences, when the scarlet lips that uttered them were so fresh and dewy, and the great eyes swept through their haughty lashes looks of the most bewildering insolence?

Mr. Parker only took a mental portrait of his tormentor, to be dressed up as a "Belle of our Days," and Mr. Oldmeath only thought her handsomer than any American woman he had ever seen.

How beauty drags all other gifts in its train! Without those eyes, and without her thousand charms, natural, acquired, and modified, Mrs. Langdon would have passed and been passed over as a rude, disagreeable, snappish woman.

So, my young reader, if you have no positive proof of your attractions, cultivate a winning grace of manner; but if you are only silly enough not to venture beyond the weather and ordinary beau topics, you are safe. Does any man know any thing more delightful than a real fool? a fool pretty to look at and sweetly affectionate? They are feminine—they are lovable—they are earth's blessings. Amen.

Clarence Tracy listened with amazement to Angel. He had no idea that she assumed so uncompromising a stand with every one, and he wondered to see two men, who were both in their way celebrities, bowing delightedly beneath her blows.

He rushed into the breach, and disputed Mrs. Langdon's position with a playful fervor that gained him two friends at once. But, even united, they were no match for the Saracenic blade, that cut as far as it intended, never going deeper than the wielder of it calculated; if there was a "graze," healing the wound with a smile so radiant that you would almost have preferred to be "hit again" for the pleasure of the cure, and in all her fiercest attacks never varying from a graceful languor, which made you sometimes fancy that she only spoke, after all, to please you, for the effort was more a bore to her than otherwise.

"I am quite hoarse," she said at length; "no doubt my friend, Mrs. Beresford, has provided unlimited supplies of soothing liquids for her guests. She must know that their unaccustomed throats will tingle after their first essay at conversation."

"What shall I get for you?" each gentleman eagerly asked.

"Nothing. I have a fancy for personal exploration of the *buffet*. Mr. Tracy is a stranger; he must be taken about and shown the people;" and with a softly-bending motion she arose, her heavy train swelled out behind her, she passed her fair, full arm through Clarence's, lifted her lofty head, the gemmed butterfly trembled and shone, she put back her impeding skirts with the air of a queen mounting the first steps of her throne, and with a backward glance smiled over her shoulder, and was lost in the crowd.

"Magnificent—is she not?" said Mr. Parker; "the turn of her shoulders is as natural and sweeping as that of her conversation. Do you know, Oldmeath, there is nothing so much neglected, so foolishly unthought of, as a woman's back. We go into phrensies about a beautiful face, while we never consider her back. There are lines about a handsome woman's spine which are constantly uncelebrated. I can not forgive Mrs. Langdon for that dress which covers those delicate traceries. A hand does not so surely define the character as a woman's back."

"And what of her face?"

"Never attempt to read a woman in her face. They are fitted with alabaster masks so soon as they can run alone, and time never washes off a layer of the composition. He wrinkles it and fades it, makes spots upon it, and worthlessly defaces it with additions, but he can not separate the clinging disguise from the real countenance beneath."

Mr. Oldmeath shrugged his own shoulders dissentingly.

"I am still young enough to believe in the innocence of the female character," he said, "and in the possibility of deciphering that innocence in the countenance. Nothing can be more detestable than a creature who places a perpetual guard upon her features. Let me see a woman whose sweet thoughts you can follow in the workings of her ingenuous face."

"Such a one as Mrs. Langdon, for instance," suggested Mr. Parker, slyly, being perfectly aware of Mr. Oldmeath's weakness in that quarter. The latter reddened slightly, and with an uneasy laugh began to talk of the last European news.

"You recognize those two gentlemen," Angelica said, as she left them, to Clarence. "I often wonder what unites them in a sort of hesitating intimacy—the one so sentimental, the other so matter-of-fact—except that the one practices what the other preaches. Mr. Parker always talks of the influence of women, and never yields to it. Mr. Oldmeath professes to despise it, and always falls under it."

"Perhaps their similar business," said Clarence; "they are both newspaper editors."

"Not at all," replied Angelica, answering his first proposition. "Mr. Oldmeath has taken up his editorship without interest in it; abominates the whole concern, and considers himself a martyr to printer's ink and proofsheets, while, on the other hand, Mr. Parker really enjoys his weekly gossip with a circle of ten thousand silent listeners. You and Mr. Oldmeath ought to be good friends, Clarence. I have often noticed points of resemblance in you."

"Which, may I ask?"

She looked quietly at him.

"I am too tired to talk now. I shall listen a while to my own praises, murmured by little Dick Everett, who is only waiting, like a pretty Persian fire-worshiper, for one glance from his Sun to fall down and adore it. You had better see after Lily."

Clarence started. The name recalled him.

"What is there about you," he asked, musingly, "which makes all the women seem insipid? When with you, I forget that there is another being of feminine nature who exists. You are—"

He paused.

"Oh, Mrs. Langdon, wield your power gently. You abuse it. What are you?"

"I am original sin," said Angel, with a soft glance; "no one can quite resist me nor cast me aside." Then beckoning Dick Everett with a quick motion of her fan, which he instantly obeyed, she left it optional with Mr. Tracy to remain by her or to undertake a solitary survey of the company.

CHAPTER XIX

Meanwhile Lily, much to her amazement, found herself in close conversation with Harry Barclay.

Instead of talking to Alicia, he had singled out Miss Vere, and Alicia seemed quite indifferent about it. The fact is, this young lady was always bent upon the last object, and as more than a month had elapsed since she parted from Mr. Barclay, his place had been filled over and over again by "eternal" new conquests. She was glad enough to see him, but not very enthusiastic, and her present fancy was for fair men, with light curls and blue eyes, as typified by Charley Newton, who was a genuine specimen of young New York—blasé at twenty, and lazily amused by the sprightly sallies of the bright little Southerner.

He actually thought her more agreeable than all Seracco's girls, and she "went the reverse step so nicely."

Harry Barclay had found himself several times thinking of Lily Vere. At the Walnut Street Club, lounging in his own especial chair at his own especial window, he had frequently neglected to notice a passing pair of ankles, because an image of girlish purity, with golden ringlets, filled his mind's eye.

It had not been his lot to meet many young girls whom he considered worthy of a serious thought; and as for marriage—a vision of a wife and domestic felicity—he would have deemed the penitentiary or a lunatic asylum the fitting spot for the honey-moon after such a rascally or mad proceeding. But there was something in his recollection of Lily which made him a little pensive and a little doubtful. He had found out that she was a great heiress: "perhaps, after all—what! marry?" He saw a white hair glistening in one of his crow-black curls—he saw Lily's smile. There was nothing definite in his ideas, but he packed up his trunks and was off for New York.

See them standing now, she with her ingenuous brow, and Harry with his most captivating expression. Mrs. Beresford was an old flame of his: she tossed him a flower as she passed, and a kiss from her finger-tips.

It was a beautiful and rare exotic—the gem of Louisa Beresford's bouquet. He played with it for a second or two while going through the first greetings, and then offered it to Lily.

She was so abstracted, and thinking so little of Mr. Barclay, that, with a slight bow, her white glove closed upon the "declaration," and she placed it in her belt-ribbon, where its beautiful petals and deep green leaves glowed upon the snowy ground, and were left to strike her hostess's eye in the most conspicuous and unconscious manner.

"You like New York, of course?" said Harry.

"I am not very sure that I do. It is too restless for me. I can not follow the tide with such quick turnings and sharp angles. I never can remember who are 'the very best people,' and who are 'not in society;' and it does not amuse me at all to know that Mrs. So-and-so bought four yards of *point d'Alençon* this morning, and Miss So-and-so has ordered six bonnets from Paris."

"You are severe," said Harry, smiling.

"Am I? I don't intend it. I think such gossip very tiresome, but it is better than slander about people's tempers and habits."

"You prefer intellectual society?"

"You wish to laugh at me now, Mr. Barclay. I am a very commonplace young lady, and very 'slow'—is not that the word? This perpetual motion—this constant stirring, depresses me. I can not roll the ball forever, even up mole-hills, and I long for quiet—the quiet of my dear, drowsy Charleston."

And she sighed.

"Your cousin and your friend both prefer New York."

"Yes. Angel and Alicia are fitted to adorn wide fields. They enjoy a crowd—a bustle."

"Very differently, however: Mrs. Langdon likes a commotion because it serves to throw out artistically her dignified repose, while Miss Clarendon mingles with the flood and joins herself to it."

"You read characters well," said Lily, feeling that she must speak, but with a hopeless, dreary headache that made her long for the absolute quiet that she was lauding.

"It is my misfortune to do so," replied Mr. Barclay. "I read people so easily that I can never deceive myself in them. I can never take them for what they are not; consequently, I find little to admire in my fellow-creatures."

"Since you find the rule universal, then," said Lily, gently, "why not decide that you only see human nature—that you must bear with it as God has created it; and, never dwelling on their ordinary short-comings, reserve your particular dislike for those things which are peculiarly bad?"

"What a dear little Methodist it is!" ejaculated Harry, inwardly; but these grave words which Lily's saddened feelings had brought forth, and which, from some old woman, would have disgusted and bored him, came with another effect from the bright lips and earnest eyes of the sweet mentor.

"I did not say that I found the 'rule universal,'" he continued, aloud; "on the contrary, I appreciate, with more intensity than another could do, real excellence—when I find it."

He did not bow, but he sufficiently marked his meaning.

"The world is all wrong, Miss Vere. Goodness is too dull—vice too pleasant: an idea by no means novel; but it would be an original invention if we could discover a remedy for this evil. How rarely can we find a woman who is both pleasant and proper—who interests and who instructs! Once, perhaps, in a man's life, he meets with a creature who at the same time delights his mind, and his eyes, and his better nature." This time a momentary bend of Mr. Barclay's stately head attested his intention, but Lily did not heed nor understand.

She still thought him Alicia's admirer.

"But," he went on, "ten to one he ignores his good luck, and passes her over for some vain, selfish, unstable, designing woman, who has more head than heart, and who, as Madame de Genlis said of Madame Agnes de Bouffon, *'N'a rien de bien que ce qui est beau.'*"

A deep flush deepened Lily's color.

"Was her new acquaintance talking at her? Did he allude—"

At this very moment Angel's name was pronounced near them.

"Mrs. Langdon will see it."

"Oh no; she is busy with a fashionable-looking man, whom she has in her train this evening. Show it to us, *dearest* Mrs. Beresford."

"Come, Lou, produce it."

The voices belonged to that whilom silent party whom Mrs. Beresford had been endeavoring to amuse. They were approaching a small cabinet placed beneath a mirror, which filled up the space between two windows.

Behind the curtains of one of these windows stood Miss Vere and Mr. Barclay. Unless she had stepped decidedly forward, she could not be seen by her hostess, as Mrs. Beresford's back was turned toward them. To the rest of the party Lily was a stranger, whose connection with Angel was not at that moment uppermost in their minds.

Louisa, laughing heartily, drew from a portfolio a square of Bristol-board.

"Now, honor bright," she said, "this is between ourselves."

"'The Lionne and the Lamb,'" read out an affected, faded, skinny woman, with a hooked nose and a very gay dress. "Is it not like? See the large Angelica, with her languishing looks, and little Dick, with his lambkin face."

"I wish to have it daguerreotyped; may I not have it for a day or two, Mrs. Beresford?" said another voice.

"Oh no; impossible. I show it to you as a great favor."

"Well, I keep it—as a great favor to all the world," the second speaker went on, who was a man with a very disagreeable face, not from its ugliness, but from its sneering superciliousness, and whom Lily recognized as a pet aversion of Angel's.

Only the week before Mrs. Langdon had said, in answer to an inquiry at the Opera, "Do they let in all sorts of low newspaper reporters to the dress circle?" "Only Frank Sherwood;" and he had heard her, too.

Mrs. Beresford playfully refused to give up her picture, but with so little determination, that Mr. Sherwood was about triumphantly to pocket the object in question, when Lily came quietly forth from her curtained retreat, and drew the sketch from his astonished hand. At the same moment Mr. Barclay gave him a significant nod, and a profound silence fell upon the group.

Lily glanced hastily at the picture. It was very cleverly executed in water-colors—had caught all Angel's peculiarities made offensively glaring, and represented her, with leonine-ish outline, caressing a lamb, who bore just as striking a resemblance to little Everett.

Lily's beautiful figure rose and dilated with honest contempt as she fixed her eyes upon Mrs. Beresford.

"I do not ask your permission, madam, to destroy this picture; I do it at once." She tore it into fragments. "Beneath your own roof a guest should have been sacred. These ladies will excuse my interference;" and as her blue eyes rested upon each in turn, there seemed an electric light in them, which flashed a momentary shame into their callous souls.

Mrs. Beresford recovered herself the soonest.

"I had no idea, Miss Vere, that you were near us; but I must say that this saucy piece of caricature would amuse your cousin as much as it has amused us."

"Perhaps so, madam; you may let her judge for yourself, if you choose; I shall not. I can not regret, however, that I was near enough to prevent the farther spread of so—" She paused, and at that moment Louisa espied her flower gracing the corsage of this repining little miss, who stood so loftily before them.

Piqued, she cast an angry glance upon Mr. Barclay.

"I am not surprised," she said, "to see you appropriating other pieces of my property, Miss Vere;" and her spirited eyes, with their mocking sparkle, took in gentleman and flower.

Lily, with a wondering stare, was drawn off from the original topic, and might have lost her self-possession had not Angel herself arrived upon the scene of action, with great amazement depicted in her face.

"What is it, Lily?" she whispered, looking around upon the embarrassed circle.

"Nothing," said Lily, throwing the torn bits she still held into a pastille-burner on the cabinet, whose dragon's mouth opened wide enough for the purpose.

"*I* will tell you about it, Angelica," exclaimed Mrs. Beresford, boldly, determined to take the "bull by the horns," and she entered into a playful account of the business, slurring it over with her usual tact.

Mrs. Langdon listened with a smile, while her indignation rose.

"You should have shown it first to me, Lou. You know how much I admire your genius in this line. Could you not make a second? My cousin Lily is so provincial that she can not understand the warmth and depth of our city friendships, where we are willing to sacrifice ourselves in every way to *faire valoir* the talents of those we like. She can not understand that I would be perfectly willing to have myself made entirely ridiculous and disgusting, if, by so doing, your cleverness as a sketcher were bruited abroad."

How dignified, how commanding Angel was now, as she spoke these words in her melodious accent!

Lou Beresford was no match for her, which the little woman painfully felt as she shrugged her shoulders and shook her head deprecatingly at her offended guest, whose smile had not faded for a moment.

"Come," said Angel, taking Mrs. Beresford's hand, "I wish you to present me to that prosy old woman you wot of, who invites me all the time to her dull dinners, which I never accept. Lily, darling, there is a gentleman looking for you;" and, as Clarence approached, Angel called to Harry Barclay, who was obliged to join her, and Lily was left with the person whose society could, whether wearied or worried, best console her. She was agitated. The excitement gone, she trembled, and turned first red, then pale, and then red again.

"What is it?" Clarence urged; and finally Lily told him.

"Why, Lily, what a heroine you are! Face that party of strangers, and actually tear a paper from a man's hand! But," he added, his own color rising, "this is an impertinence which should be looked into."

"Not by you, Clarence. I fancy Angel thinks differently. She has gone off arm in arm with Mrs. Beresford, and, I have no doubt, wishes the whole thing considered as a jest. It would be awkward to take it up seriously. She had her revenge in the sheepish looks of both men and women. I don't think they will say much about it. Let us talk about something else. When are you going home? Has Willie decided? I wish so much to be at home!"

"So do I, dear Lily. At home. How pleasant it sounds!"

"And to see Nora again," said Lily, with her old childish manner, "and the Jenningses, and the Melbournes. Julia Melbourne is thought to be engaged, Clarence; is not that absurd? And oh, Clarence, Burleigh still growls affectionately when George says 'Lily sends her love, Bur;' he has not forgotten me. And the orange-trees, uncle writes, are grown amazingly at Chicora. Beautiful Chicora! Will it not be delightful to get among these things once more? to see a little of one's childhood's life? And, Clarence, did Nora ever tell you of your Aunt Sarah's offer? That dried-up Dr. Talbot wished her to marry him!"

Clarence laughed out; and the two having started a chapter of this nature, they talked on, forgetting the place, the circumstances, the surroundings. Lily's sweet face was radiant. Passers-by were struck with her tender beauty; and many a man in that gay assemblage paused a moment to envy the dark-browed, grave-aired stranger, with his distinguished carriage, who was listening so attentively to the constant prattle of the usually silent and reserved Southern belle.

There was peace between them, and it was long since Lily had felt so perfectly happy as she did that night, when, after she had retired, Angel came to her bedside, and, kissing her warmly, said,

"Thank you, dearest Lily. I do admire you and love you sincerely. You are worthy to be your mother's daughter. May God bless you, Lily," and a tear—a real tear, fell from Angel's haughty eyes on the upturned forehead of her cousin.

A tear from Angel! Lily's heart overflowed. She caught Mrs. Langdon's hand.

"Oh, Angel—"

Angelica placed her soft fingers, heavy with diamonds, upon Lily's lips, and, kissing her again, she swept from the room with her stately, languid, luxurious grace.

❧ CHAPTER XX

A week more, and the trunks were packed ready for their homeward journey.

Mr. and Mrs. Clarendon were naturally anxious to embrace their son, from whom they had so long been separated, and William himself had a strong wish to be again under the paternal roof. Angelica pressed them kindly to prolong their stay. Madame de Montanvert was wretched at her departure, and Edward Langdon, who had been all this time shooting over on Long Island, condescended to express, in his weariest accent, his distress that the ladies should leave just as he returned to town.

But this fact rather hastened their start, for Mr. Edward Langdon had filled up the vacuum in his vapid head with an idea of matrimony, and had chosen as its opposite and apposite object Miss Vere, whose fortune, as our French neighbors say, "smiled to him." This was more than the lady herself did; for if Lily had a positive dislike, it was for her new *soupirant*. His utter inanity she would have borne unflinchingly, but his conceit, his selfishness, his hardness almost angered her; and for such a creature to break in upon her conferences with Clarence, and to join her daily in Broadway, was a continual irritation to her gentle spirit.

However, she only made matters worse for herself in the end, and thus it was:

Pestered by Edward Langdon, she gratefully turned for relief to Mr. Barclay, who, flattered by her growing attentions, really began in earnest to recommend himself to his unconscious listener. There was something very taking to a worn-out man of fashion in the freshness and perfect simplicity of Lily. She was so natural, so honestly unsophisticated, he liked to listen to her opinions and sentiments shyly uttered with her sweet voice and her stately manner. The mixture of girlishness and maturity about her was new and singularly attractive. He found himself hanging around her with all the devotion he had ever given to the most dashing woman, but he soon discovered that instinct prompted him not to pay devotion of precisely the same character.

He never embarrassed her with looks and words; he was calmly attentive and respectful, and Lily fancied him still desirous of recommending his pretensions to Alicia through her.

Clarence did not interfere. His confidence in Lily was entire. It was the best trait of his character; he believed in her; whether it arose from belief in himself or not, there was at least that firm conviction.

He watched her a good deal, and was puzzled about Angelica.

This last week in New York has ever been a pleasing recollection to Mrs. Langdon. The tear that fell on Lily's brow did its work. She made a vow with it, and kept it. For once in her life she acted without a selfish motive, and showed herself what she might have been—perhaps.

There was no more sublime coquetry, no feigned indifference, no feigned interest.

She was true, frank, honest; and if, in her present gay and brilliant career, when magnificence and dissipation hide the hollow, wearied satiety, she wishes to dwell upon some green oasis in the arid desert of her past life, the haughty Mrs. Langdon, the superb Mrs. Langdon, with her jewels, her Cashmeres, her court, and her dignity, looks back with sad satisfaction to those short seven days, when her gentle cousin said to her at their conclusion,

"Dear Angel, we understand each other now. You have made me very happy."

For very shame, Clarence could not have renewed his shuffling attentions. He did not attempt it; and there lies Angel's praise, for the fact of his withdrawal was the incentive for her to proceed.

A coquette may abandon her prey, while she still leaves him sighing for her; but it is very rare to see one sheathe her eyes, and put her pretensions in rest, when the victim appears willing to retreat.

Alicia was the busiest of all. She had hundreds of dollars to spend in finery, and an untold number of admirers to dispose of. The last evening came. It was Opera night, and Mrs. Langdon's box was hemmed in by a double row of gentlemen. It was the *point de mire* of the whole house, for New York seldom boasts of three such beauties united, and so attended.

I should be sorry were I obliged to set down all the platitudes uttered on this occasion.

There was the usual wonder how Miss Vere and Miss Clarendon could consent to bury themselves in Charleston, anticipations of pleasant meetings the following summer at Newport and Saratoga, and general expressions of regret that they should leave New York.

Alicia most mourned the balls, Lily the Opera; and the latter begged to be allowed to listen tranquilly to the entrancing notes of "Favorita," since it might be many months before she again enjoyed such a privilege.

She leaned back in her chair with a rapt countenance, and Mr. Barclay promised that no one should molest her. But at the fall of the curtain he claimed his reward. She must listen to him.

Under cover of the incessant tattle around them, undismayed by the threatening looks which lightened from the brilliant eyes of Mrs. Beresford, who was watching him from her own box, Harry Barclay made his first proposal of marriage.

It was open, manly, straightforward, like his real self before women's flatteries and guilty opportunities had contributed to spoil a naturally fine disposition.

His heart beat more rapidly than it had done since he was sixteen, and he could have recommended himself to ten of the handsomest matrons in that Opera house with less embarrassment than it cost him to say, "I love you" to this young girl, with her gentlest manner and subdued tone. So much for habit.

It was a painful surprise to Lily. No one could know Harry Barclay well without liking him. Through that foppish exterior, under that indifferent air, disguised by that insolently-carried head, there lurked the germ, the promise, the foundation of a noble character, and which, like the single grain of perfume hidden in the mass of deadening cotton, retains its power, and can be guessed at when you come near enough to seek the latent cause of your involuntary approach.

Clarence Tracy did not possess half the real worth of this dissipated votary of fashion, but a different education had in the two men worked different results. Clarence had never run the gauntlet of vanity and coxcombry which had been the existence of Harry; he had never had his admiring female circle; he was brought up in a strict school, and had taught himself to assume opinions and phrases which were foreign to his thoughts, and yet nature and natural instinct remained strong within him. He talked very finely, but his actions did not keep pace with his words; whereas Harry Barclay, his own master since his boyhood, reverenced inwardly the things at which he sneered outwardly. But, after all, this might only prove that education can not correct nature, so that I had best leave the discussion. I am not wise enough to sift the business. I can only tell the result. I sometimes think that pigs are but the type of people. If you wish to produce a movement toward the right, pull toward the left. If you wish Master Johnny to be a parson, you must rather encourage him to gambel and frolic; if you wish Miss Lucy to be staid and sober, you must early train her to dissipation and beaux.

How else can we account for the children of pious parents so often proving great rascals, while excellent, God-fearing children take their rise from the household of the most careless thinkers and actors?

To the eyes of the world Clarence Tracy was a moral and respectable, though fashionable youth, while Harry Barclay was cited as a dangerous and abandoned young gentleman, conversant with every vice. A father would simply have demurred about Clarence's want of fortune, should he have asked for a daughter's hand, while Mr. Barclay would have been peremptorily dismissed from any family circle as a firebrand with black eyes and hair to match. Yet the latter possessed the material from which one could extract a tender and honest husband, whereas Clarence Tracy, with his sentiments, his prudery, and his fine feeling, was but an unpriggish Joseph Surface, after all.

Lily's kind heart suffered. She was really grieved to be forced to say "I can not promise any thing. Don't look to the future, and fancy that I shall change."

"I do not pretend to be ignorant of your great wealth, Miss Vere; it is the least of your claims upon my sincere admiration; but since I heard that you were an heiress, it seemed to me as if Fate could not provide for mortal man a more perfect future than you could insure him. I am lazy—I am very worthless, I suppose. I have enough to live upon alone, and it would be a difficult matter for me to undertake life in a cottage at my age. I looked at you, and sighed and mourned over my wasted hours. Never had I seen the woman before whom I should have gloried in marrying. You see that I am frank—too candid, perhaps. I heard accidentally that you were rich and independent. It appeared to open a sudden vista of hope and happiness. You will not, perhaps, comprehend my feeling. I never imagined for one moment that I could be accused of mercenary motives in seeking you; my consciousness of your attractions was too deep to fear a reproach of that nature. If you can love me, if you can accept my love, the study of my life shall be to show my gratitude."

"It can not be," said Lily, again, while her heart taught her that these words were true and positively earnest—a consciousness that softened still more her soft voice.

"I do not wish to weary you or to annoy you," Harry went on; "I never wanted to marry any body before this—I never offered myself, as it is called—so that probably I do not say the right things. Consider before you answer me, dearest Miss Vere. I do not think I shall poison myself, nor try drowning at the dock, but I feel—" here his voice faltered, and the slight levity which he had assumed to cover its previous tremblings failed him—"I feel that I stand upon the precipice of my Fate. Your hand will draw me with its lightest touch to wisdom and to safety; without it, I shall renew my old course, no doubt, and be ever—what I have been."

No longer with daring eyes and with cynical smile, but with a pleading, honest lustre in the one, and a scarce perceptible quiver of painful anticipation about his lips, Harry awaited her reply.

"I will not trifle with you, Mr. Barclay, nor put you off with unmeaning sentences. I believe in you—I think you better than you care to show yourself to all the world. You say that I may consider your words out of order; what I am going to say may be just as irregular." She blushed till the crimson flood even darkened her white shoulders. "I have loved the person whom I hope to marry since I was a mere child. I am very young still, but circumstances have hastened my years. I like you very much," she continued, raising her blue eyes ingenuously to his deep gaze; "I appreciate the compliment of your belief in my power, and you will not think me wanting in maidenly delicacy if I beg you to accept three words of counsel from so young and so inexperienced a girl as myself."

"Any words from you," answered Harry, gravely bowing, "I must always receive at their proper and highest valuation."

"Do not waste your time and thoughts on me," said Lily, still blushing; "but pray, if you do care for me, think better of women for my sake. It hurts me so much to hear you speak slightingly of the whole sex."

In her mind she meant Alicia, and was grieving over this proof of the effect produced by Miss Clarendon's faulty manner.

"I admit the reproof," said Mr. Barclay; "it *is* bad taste to praise one person by running down others, but—" He paused. "This, then, is final. You can leave no hope?"

"None," she said, gently.

He sighed.

"You are a singular being, Miss Vere. I wonder if you affect every one as you do me. While speaking to you I seem to put off my individuality. I am years younger. I believe in virtue, goodness, piety, excellence. I can not speak to you as one speaks to other young ladies. There is about you a halo of almost unearthly purity, without a shade of prudery or moroseness. You smile with as much joyousness, you enter into passing events with as much playful grace as your neighbors, but you seem, after all, only to *lend* yourself. You are out of the world. If you were nervous or affected, I should fear to say what I am going to do. It seems to me as if you will die young. Heaven will never permit so perfect a whole to crumble away beneath the friction of years."

A startled expression crossed Lily's brow. She shuddered.

"Don't say that. I am not nervous, but life is bright to me. I do not wish to die."

"Forgive me. Of course, I speak, I can not say jestingly, but with a kind of romantic thoughtlessness. You will not utterly forget me, Miss Vere? In your own sunny home, surrounded by all those mementoes which you so much love"—he would not distress her by alluding to her confidence a moment before—"you will sometimes remember, will you not? that one 'hardened wretch' bears you in his mind as a type of what woman can be?"

Harry's hand shook as he took up his lorgnette and began to arrange its focus. He was very calm, and had spoken very quietly, but he felt as if he had had a great blow coming from an unknown source: it was overwhelming and unaccountable.

Lily was silent and uncomfortable. The curtain rose, the hum of conversation ceased, and Clarence Tracy, who had gone off to speak to a foreign acquaintance whom he recognized in the parquette, guessed, as he passed her on his return, that the supercilious-looking Philadelphian had met with a rebuff. Human nature is so curiously constituted that Tracy admired Lily the more at that moment because somebody else did too, and he exchanged a familiar look with her, so reliably affectionate and confiding that Mr. Barclay immediately divined his rival.

He scanned that dark, grave, distinguished face with discerning eye. During the whole of the act he furtively watched its expression. The result of his study was not satisfactory.

"Hard and selfish!" he muttered. "God help this tender creature."

But is a man just refused by a young lady capable of giving an unbiased opinion upon the merits of another man whom he has reason to suppose the favored hero?

❧ CHAPTER XXI

"We are over the bar, Alice, darling. Rouse up. Here is our dear old Charleston in sight."

Lily was animated far beyond her usual state. Her eyes sparkled, her little feet almost danced upon the cabin floor of the steamer as she pulled at Alicia, who lay helplessly in her berth, disgusted with every thing.

"Well, suppose we are in sight of Charleston, I need not be in a hurry to look at it. We shall see enough of it, I dare say, before we see any thing else again."

"But look at the Island! Fort Moultrie! and all those new houses upon the beach! Fort Sumter is at least six feet higher from the water's level."

"I smell the marsh mud," said matter-of-fact and cross Alicia, struggling into her sea-gown of dark merino; "and how hot it is! Have we been six months making the voyage from New York, and is this June? What a horribly monotonous climate! and where will be the use, pray, of my beautiful ermine muff and cape in this eternal summer?"

Lily at last got her on deck, where Willie quizzed her unlustrous hair and forlorn looks, and even the "courtly Clarence" could not deny that three days of sea-sickness had considerably wasted her beauty.

Excitement had done the work of rouge, kohl, and pearl-powder laid on by nature for Lily. She drank in the balmy air, she opened wide her lovely eyes, as if to absorb the surrounding view, and she sometimes stretched out her arms, as if to clasp it to her beating heart. Her voice was full of sweetest melody. In every intonation spoke the love of her native soil. The young men watched her with admiration, and Alicia yawningly said,

"Has Lily all her life been bottling up her enthusiasm for this patriotic burst? Subside, my dear, or you will startle our gentle *compatriotes*. Fancy Sara presently a victim to your want of equanimity. By the way, I trust she will keep that aristocratic nose of hers out of the house until to-morrow. If she sees me in this pitiable plight, she will spread an account of my appearance that weeks will not undo."

"By Jove! I am hungry," cried her brother. "When you mention Sara, it always makes me think of eating. How that voracious child used to pitch into the victuals and drink, to be sure! She always chose for her sweetheart at dancing-school the boy who had the most pocket-money, and the most liberal disposition for candies and tart. Won't mamma have a great dinner for us to-day! and the governor will bring out his oldest Madeira."

"Is this the season for okra soup? I should like okra soup," said Alicia, languidly.

"Alice," exclaimed Lily, turning round with a merry smile, "you know that okra soup is in season in the midst of summer. You remind me of that girl who had always lived in the country until she went to pay a visit in Savannah. She staid six weeks, and when she came back, on taking her first walk through an old lane, she suddenly stopped and screamed, 'What is that? oh! what is that?' 'Betty,' cried her sister, 'are you foolish? Don't you know a cow, Betty?' "

"Thank you, Lily, for a miracle worked in my favor," said Alicia, with mock anger, when they had stopped laughing at her: "Miss Vere relating personal anecdotes of an absurd tendency, calculated to throw ridicule upon her friends.

The steamer now neared the wharf, and the dusky outline of Charleston, with its weather-beaten aspect and its dingy coloring, changed from indistinctness to hard reality.

There it lay, "with all its faults upon its head." It is not picturesque; it is not imposing. It neither makes you wonder at its commercial grandeur, nor admire its pleasing beauty; but there *is* something attractive in its irregular and peculiar construction. Each house is built by itself and for itself. Each man's domicil is indeed his own especial castle, fronting whichever point of the compass suits his taste, and displaying any style of architecture which suits his pocket and plan. The predominating air is respectability. There is nothing flashy, nothing daring, nothing ostentatious. If a *parvenu* (and there are "a few" now in Charleston) erects a mansion of pretension—bold, staring, and glittering—six months of this atmosphere tones it down to a harmonious shade, which cavilers might call dusty.

Gardens are numerous—blocks of houses rare. The streets are moderately wide; the pavements irrationally narrow. There is no hurry, no throng any where. Business men walk almost as leisurely as *les flaneurs.* They keep early hours in Charleston—still hold to three o'clock dinners; and the "last bell," which rings at nine o'clock on winter evenings, and at ten during the summer, to warn the negroes to their homes, is the signal for the simultaneous closing of shutters, and barring of doors up and down the streets—the notification of bedtime to this virtuous city.

There were few passengers besides the Clarendon party on board of the steamer, so that but a limited audience assisted at the growing delight of Lily as one familiar object after another met her gaze, as they slowly swept into their moorings.

What an eager assemblage welcomed the travelers home! Mr. Clarendon and George leaped upon the deck as the boat touched the wharf, and the honest old gentleman knew not which first to embrace. The girls, of course, claimed that right for themselves, and so he simplified the business by folding his arms around both at once, and extending his hands behind their backs to his eldest boy, grown in five years from youth to manhood. George had to satisfy his feelings with Clarence, who felt a little forlorn, with no relation to meet him, till he espied Nora making frantic efforts to dislodge herself from a distant carriage, and waving her arms imploringly to him.

He ran to her rescue, and helped her down the steps of one of those antique coaches, now seen, I believe, nowhere but in Charleston, which are mounted on C springs, in shape like large squashes, and in discomfort indescribable.

It is presumed that their owners cling to these vehicles with a kind of aristocratic pride, saying within themselves at every jolt, "At least people can see that *our* carriage was not set up yesterday," and healing their bruises with this salve. Miss Sarah Tracy would not have exchanged her "family pumpkin" for the "thousand dollar" coach which took the prize at the last State Fair.

"How handsome you are, Clarence!" cried his admiring sister, releasing him for a second from her clasp, "and oh! what a time you have been away!"

But her attention was now diverted to Lily, and how those girls did kiss each other, to be sure!

Mutual compliments were exchanged.

"How tall you are, Lily!"

"How little and nice you are, Nora! not bigger than Alicia."

Alicia protested that she would not be looked at, and, drawing down all her veils, made a rush for the carriage, and here a surprise awaited them. Beside the comfortable, well-known Clarendon turn-out, which was not of the very oldest type (such as Miss Tracy's), there stood an elegant coupé, drawn by two fine bay horses, and the reins held by one of Lily's own servants, whose shining black face was fairly oiled with happiness.

"Why, Plato!" exclaimed his mistress, as she shook hands with him—not daintily, like one dreading contamination, but a hearty, good shake—"what carriage is this?"

"'Tis youu'n, my n'young missus," quoth radiant Plato, "and I'm coachman; and dat is leetle Sambo, what you 'member—big Betsey's oldest chile, what Mass Clarendon tek in de house now for go wid your carriage." And "leetle Sambo" stood grinning, and scraping his foot, splendid in his new clothes, and eager for notice.

It was pretty to see the fair, patrician-looking girl bending her kind glance upon these "persecuted slaves," giving to each her white hand and her cordial greeting—not only those subject to her own "lash," but likewise to her guardian's helpless victims—inquiring after their relations and their health, and understanding their talk and their habits like one who had from childhood lived familiarly among them. It was not only Lily whose good nature and sweetness prompted this behavior, but Willie, and Alicia, and Clarence were cognizant of the claims of these "miserable Africans," who crowded up to "shake hands" and "bless God" that he had restored the wanderers to their homes.

"Mamma will be impatient," suggested Mr. Clarendon, when Lily turned to inquire from him, as he emerged from the steamer, how that coupé was called hers. "Yes, dear, it is my gift to you—my Christmas present, anticipating the 25th of December. I did not send you a check for finery, as I did to Alicia, but put it in that shape. Get in, darling; and you, Sambo, leave off staring at your missus. She is not going off again."

"It shall be for both of us," said Lily. "The boys may go in the carriage, but Alice must come with me." So Alicia, not very loth, was transferred to the well-appointed vehicle; nods, smiles, and "We'll see you soon's" were exchanged; and while the coupé dashed triumphantly past the cotton-bales on the wharf, and took its rapid way home, the last view Clarence caught of it showed Lily's face still turned toward him. They passed through King Street, the fashionable walk containing the fashionable shops.

"How pleasant it all looks!" said Lily.

"How dull it all looks!" said Alicia; "ah! how different from Broadway! and such bonnets I never did see."

"Yes you have, often," retorted Lily, with her quiet smile. "I think that they are the same we left behind us two years ago. But they seem so like old friends!"

"You are incorrigible, Miss Vere," ejaculated Alicia. "I believe you love this dust, because it rises from the earth of Charleston."

"Of course I do. But here we are, and there is aunt."

Yes, there was the dear old house, with its wide garden, not bare and empty, but filled with shrubs and evergreens. The genial warmth of the Southern December sun had brought out here and there a flower or two, and great pots of geraniums and hyacinths bordered the stone steps, on which, crowned with her sunbonnet, stood excellent Mrs. Clarendon.

A mother's welcome she gave to both. It was now twelve years since little Elizabeth Vere, the orphan heiress, had been conveyed from her father's grave to those hospitable arms, and it warmed the good woman's heart to think that she had done "her best" as well for Lily as for her own girl.

If there were faults in "her best," she did not know it, for, with all her unostentatious qualities, Mrs. Clarendon had no mean opinion of herself; and the fact is, I have seen among the dowdiest, primmest, and most home-staying of our matrons as much perfect self-satisfaction as ever sat enthroned upon the brow or in the secret soul of the most consequential beauty.

"Come in—come in, children. Your maumer is dying to see you, Lily; and here come all the servants, and there is my Willie."

Such a crowd poured into the entrance hall! old and young, men and women, so that while Mrs. Clarendon was feasting her eyes upon Willie, straining him again and again to her bosom, and holding him at arm's length to admire him, the girls were surrounded.

There was Lily's maumer, a dignified colored woman, with an immense head-handkerchief, who laid her withered hands upon the light tresses of "her child," and patted her cheek, while tears of joy silently rolled down her face.

There was Alicia's maid, a smart, smiling black girl, who claimed the right to stand closest to her "young mistis," and to keep off intruders.

The girls had a joke and a remembrance for each one. None of the elderlies were quite well: "Only so-and-so," "I day" (*Anglice,* I am here), were the best accounts; "ain't so bad now, bless the Lord," were the most favorable reports. It is a wonderful circumstance that you can not persuade negroes to acknowledge themselves perfectly in health. No inquiries could reach the root of the disease, nor even graze its surface, but it is a point of honor or of elegance to be ailing. With all their natural gayety, they dote on funerals; with all their love for high colors, they delight to put themselves into mourning.

No jesting can move their equanimity on these subjects; they let all your strictures and pleasantries roll innocuous, like rain on a goose's back.

I might make out quite an interesting chapter by detailing at length the first conversations held between the young ladies and these "slaves," who were brimfull of the adventures of the past eighteen months, and who were anxious to call for "Miss Lily and Miss 'Licia's" sympathy or good wishes; but there have been so many dreary attempts to depict the manners and customs of these "unhappy descendants of the aborigines of that delightful and interesting country—Africa" (as I once heard a distinguished senator say), my "maumer tongue" has been so profaned by those who undertake to transcribe it, that I renounce the task.

I should only be stigmatized as a follower in their halting footsteps, and I have neither the ambition to fill up their ruts nor to bury myself in them. I may say in passing, however, that the generally-received idea as to the dialect of our Southern negroes is about as correct as the French manage to convey when they relate that their English neighbors write on the tombstones of their wives, "Farewell—adieu; adieu—farewell;" and that the lady-killing Lord Edward Poggins, on being introduced to the daughter of his friend, "Sirr Thompson," says, "Good-morning, Mees."

"It is three o'clock! Dinner—dinner," sings out Master George. "I must be off to the counting-house;" for be it known that George had determined to make himself a merchant, and he was in training "on the Bay" (which is the commercial part of the city) as a clerk, which humble position is no longer scorned by the most aristocratic scions of the most aristocratic houses.

How tastefully and prettily were the rooms furnished which awaited our young beauties! opening into each other, so that their occupants might be together as much as they chose, and looking upon the back garden, with its thickets of gardenia and hedges of box.

But Alicia had no time to examine or to admire. She had a vision of Sara Purvis driving round that afternoon; so she wished her trunks unpacked, her dressing-case opened, her bath prepared, and herself to be "under arms" for the approaching scrutiny.

However industriously given, there was no counting-house for George any more that day. It was not till five o'clock that Alicia declared herself "ready," and they sat down to dinner.

"This *is* comfortable, by Jove!" exclaimed Willie, with his old-fashioned and favorite *juron*. "There is nothing like home, is there, sir?"

And Mr. Clarendon gave a delighted assent. With what beaming looks did this honest gentleman survey his family circle!

There was not a care in his heart nor on his face. His pretty Alicia, with her beautiful toilet, her saucy smile, her merry words, her indolent attitude, and her good appetite; Willie, with his handsome face, and manly figure, and hearty laugh; and George, with all the amusing consequentialness of his recent advancement to a place of business constantly breaking through the under-current of his boyish frivolity and fun, made a group of his own possessions which had not yet declared its independence, nor given him one moment's serious uneasiness. Then, to complete the picture, there sat the child of his adoption, whom to look upon was to love, so irresistible was her gentle charm. It was indeed a happy dinner. The servants found it difficult to keep their gravity while waiting, for their state of excitement contributed to make every jest or good story overwhelming; and the "boy" of the establishment, who is always the recognized butt in every house, was on this "auspicious occasion" threatened with so many wondrous punishments by "Mass George" if he should venture to laugh out again, that Bob was fain to retire to the entry, and there explode into a perfect fusilade of guffaws, until cuffed into silence by the majestic "Daddy Jacob," Mrs. Clarendon's right-hand man.

Nowhere in this country, save in one of those cellars such as that of which Mr. Clarendon kept the key, could you find a bottle of Madeira like the one that Jacob placed, when the cloth was removed, before his master.

Bright-tinted, oily, sparkling with subdued paly lustre, decanted into cut-glass of the old diamond pattern, and drunk in thin, bell-shaped glasses with straw-thick shanks, and little stars sprinkled upon the delicate surface, it slid down the throat indeed like

"Neat bottled velvet tipped over one's lips."

"This is glorious!" cried Willie. "None of this on the Continent, sir."

The Purvises were announced—the ladies only.

"Show them into the drawing-room," said Mrs. Clarendon.

"And, Lily, tell Sara," cried the eldest hope of the Clarendons, "that I am prepared to fall desperately in love with her, and I shall come presently to do so."

I can not possibly introduce Miss Purvis at the close of a chapter, so I shall pass over in silence the meeting between the relatives, only mentioning that Alicia was quite satisfied with the effect *she* produced. Her costume evidently astonished and dazzled both Mrs. Purvis and her daughter.

✿ CHAPTER XXII

"Mr. Tracy would like to see you, sir."

"Who, Jacob?"

"Mass Clarence," explained Jacob.

"Oh, show him in here," said Mr. Clarendon, putting down his newspaper and taking off his spectacles. "What does Clarence want, I wonder?"

Great was the consternation of the good gentleman when Clarence explained his want. He wanted the sanction of Miss Vere's guardian to his
engagement with that young lady.

"Good God! my dear boy, this is very sudden. When has this happened?"
and Mr. Clarendon got up and paced the dining-room with uneasy strides.
"Lily! why she is a mere child. Have you her consent?"

"I would not have presumed otherwise to ask yours, sir. I am well aware
that Miss Vere's fortune, and even more, her great attractions, make an offer
to her a presumption of no ordinary nature. You can not wonder at such a
gift falling to my lot more than I do. Should it meet with your approbation, I
shall indeed stand in a position to make me the envy of the world."

"You may well say so—you may well say so. The prettiest girl and the
sweetest temper in all Carolina, not excepting my own daughter, and a clear
income of—more thousands than you need spend. But how has this come
about? In these two days since she returned? Upon my word, you have
improved your time, young gentleman."

"We had an understanding before I went abroad—"

"The devil you did! I wish I had understood it too."

"I regret, Mr. Clarendon, that you should show such annoyance," said
Clarence, coldly, and somewhat haughtily. "I know that my own fortune is
not sufficient to enable me to consider myself on *that* level with your ward,
but it is scarcely necessary to tell my father's oldest friend that in birth and in
position I might aspire to Miss Vere's hand, and I trust that my character is
sufficiently unimpeachable to warrant the same act of temerity. Lily and I
have both acknowledged a preference since we were children; and although,
as a lad of twenty, I told the girl of fifteen that I loved her, still I scrupulously
would not bind *her* by any promise, and in not one of my European letters is
there a word which could not have been written to my sister. I found her free
on my return, save that she still held to her *unworthy* regard for me; but I
awaited the moment when she should be restored to your paternal care
before I renewed, or, I may say, before I ventured to offer her those vows
which it shall be the duty and happiness of my life to keep holy, sacred, and
faithful."

"Very good—very good, Clarence. That was right—that was honorable.
But an heiress like Lily must not be married off in this hurried way; it is a
great responsibility. By heavens! my dear fellow, I would rather you had
asked me for Alicia. I could have found out whether she loved you; you
might have lived here in this house all your days, and that would have ended
the matter. But Lily—it is a great responsibility."

"I grant you, sir, that you may find, at any time, a better *parti* for your ward. There is her cousin, Gustavus Purvis, or your son William—"

"None of your confounded foreign stuff! your *partees*, Clarence," cried Hugh Clarendon, fairly stung. "No, by George, sir! I don't mean Lily for my son. Who put that notion into your head? I may once or twice," he added, with an honesty that forced him to speak, "I may once or twice have had such an idea, if the young people fancied each other; and it is true, in sending Will abroad, I thought, in a vague way, that he would come back fresh and new to her; but—Well, well, Andrew Vere would have liked it, I think. Where is Lily?" he asked, abruptly.

"I will send her to you, sir."

A light step, a soft rustle of a silken shirt, a faint rose perfume, and Lily stood blushingly beside her guardian.

"So, my dear, you sent that young gentleman to me?"

"I did, uncle."

"This is a great surprise, Lily; but your father gave me no right to control you. Do you love Clarence Tracy well enough to be sure you wish to marry him?"

The blue eyes were hidden by their white lids and dark lashes, the head was partly turned away.

"Yes."

"Then I suppose it is all right." A half sigh raised Mr. Clarence's broad chest; with it departed his momentary chagrin. He would have been ashamed to cherish a second longer the innocent plans that, almost unconsciously, his heart had framed during many years. He almost thought himself mercenary, and, wounded by Clarence's chance shaft, he considered it necessary to further this marriage sooner than be accused of inveigling his ward for his son.

He folded his arms around Lily with his usual fatherly tenderness.

"God bless you, my child. Clarence!" he called out. Clarence entered from the adjoining room.

"Make her happy, Clarence; you have drawn a prize."

And so Lily was betrothed formally; and so are many young girls given in marriage, without an inquiry made into the habits, the principles, the morals, the antecedents of the man to whom she becomes the veritable legal slave. A young girl, brought up with every care, educated in every refinement, tutored by nature and by association in delicacy of sentiment and taste, becomes the victim of a possible brute, without her family or friends troubling themselves farther than to know that he has a roof to shelter her—often that but a temporary one.

He may have debts, he may have mistresses, he may have associates that will ever after cloud her future. Who knows it? who asks about it? His companions know it—his enemies guess it; but it is not surely their place to step forward and turn informer. I knew a girl once who, at an age scarcely beyond childhood, married a man whom her parents thought "an admirable match," *i.e.*, he had a plantation and some negroes; it turned out that, besides these advantages, he had a broken-down constitution, a taste for drink, a number of debts, and a vile temper.

"*We* all knew it," said his comrades.

"Why did you not tell her parents?" demanded some pitying souls.

"Did they inquire into his belongings? Was it our business to enlighten them unasked?" was the natural retort.

And so was this young creature sacrificed, and so are many young creatures sacrificed here and every where. "Marriage is a defective institution," cries out a wicked French novelist, and some virtuous people agree to it too; but though the world has been saying this these centuries past, *I* see no reform— do you? In France, a young aspirant for matrimonial honors is thoroughly sifted, it is true, and they search every *recoin* of his past history; but these are called "marriages of convenience," and the bride sees her bridegroom only as a bridegroom; it is their first acquaintance, and if those little defects of character which make up humanity don't fit and tally, so as to enable them to rough it through life side by side, why, they part amicably to different quarters of the house, and if they make their peace with Heaven as easily after that as they do with the world, so much the better for them. Consequently, to my mind, neither are "marriages of convenience" just the right thing.

After all, I don't pretend to be a sage; and, like many who preach "improvement," I can't tell how one should set to work to bring about the said improvement; only of one thing am I certain: had I a daughter, and a suitor came "a-wooing," I should not look only to his houses and land, and satisfy myself of that superficially, but I should like to know a little of the private life, the inner existence of him who was anxious to rob me of that which I should love beyond "jewels, gold, or fine linen"—the treasure committed to me by God, and for which to him am I answerable.

I can swear to my philanthropic northern brethren that we sell a "slave" with more hesitation to a new owner than we give our girls in marriage.

Mr. Clarendon made no inquiries—instituted no researches; his first feeling of disappointment past, he soon grew reconciled to the engagement, and Clarence became a greater favorite than ever. Tracy was so respectful, so attentive, understood every thing so well; he never looked weary when Mr. Clarendon prosed about the "state of the country," or demurred when Mr. Clarendon assured him that without the South the North would go to the dogs—two things which William sometimes did.

Tracy was the firmest adherent, he thought, of the glory, rights, and power of Carolina. Tracy firmly swore to those opinions which that great man C——n put out for other people to believe, and to the truth of which Mr. Clarendon subscribed with as much fervency as he did to his Bible—consulting them, I am sorry to acknowledge, more frequently than he did the latter—and Tracy was as good a judge of horseflesh as Colonel W——H——himself.

Mrs. Clarendon was satisfied because Mr. Clarendon was; and at that particular moment her thoughts were bent on sausages. She, however, at once undertook to superintend all Lily's *trousseau* in the linen line, and immediately took two extra girls into the house, to be drilled in button-hole stitch, felling, and seaming, in readiness for the moment when their services should be needed.

Alicia rather turned up her nose, more than it was naturally, at Lily's choice. She was prepared for it, but scarcely approved.

"With Lily's fortune, *I* should aspire to a baronet's eldest son at least."

"Pooh! puss, you are a little simpleton," her father said. "A Carolina gentleman is equal to a nobleman."

The Purvises were very angry. They blamed the Clarendons—they vilified the Tracys—they wished to cut Nora—and called upon Angel to help abuse the whole business. "Such a shock to poor Gustavus!" wrote Sara to her sister; "we believe that Mr. Clarendon is involved, and that Clarence Tracy is to buy off his consent. It is a real case of *bribery and coruption*."

"Lily had no more idea of marrying Gustavus," said Mrs. Langdon, in her reply, "than of waiting for my demise to espouse Mr. Langdon. Don't be foolishly angry, my dear Sara (to please papa, isn't it? How many new ball-dresses does he give you?), and pray don't write corruption with one r."

Lily was happily indifferent to all these lamentations. By the time that these letters had been exchanged, they were in the country—not at Chicora, but on Mr. Clarendon's Santee estate—riding, driving, strolling, boating. Clarence and Nora were both of the party, and how merrily sped the days!

A Carolina Christmas is generally a beautiful season. The balmy, bracing, delicious atmosphere, cold enough, morning and evening, for fires, egg-nogg, and dancing, warm enough during the middle of the day to discard heavy wraps, and to wander about in the shady woods, with the long moss hanging in huge graceful pendents from the great trees, the red Christmas berries shining like rubies or coral in their green-leaved setting, and above one's head a blue sky so clear, so bright, so pure, so brilliant, that one almost longs to see a cloud to save one's dazzled eyes.

The crunching of the dead leaves beneath your feet sounds pleasant and cheerful. You can not associate autumn, dreary fancies, with this air, which answers to Lamartine's description, *"tiède et parfumé,"* and every distant report of a hunter's gun seems a *feu de joie* to celebrate Nature's festival.

December is almost as gay and joyous an out-door month as April.

Alicia and Nora did not interfere with the lovers. Sometimes they would go "briding" with William and George, or they would stay at home and practice duets, or they would walk out together, and Alicia would give little Nora (who was the merest mite of a young woman) such accounts of her feats of strength and endurance as a *polkense* that Nora would lift her hands and eyes, and rise on the ends of her toes with amazement.

It was at Sunny Hill that the time of Lily's wedding was decided. She would be eighteen in April, and Clarence urged that she should fix on that month. Why wait? So it was settled they should be married on the 3d of April, spend the honeymoon at Chicora, and sail for a European tour in May. Nora was to go abroad with them, Lily was bent upon that.

"And may we not take Alicia, dear uncle?" Lily urged, when first the plan was spoken of. Alicia's eyes sparkled, and they all pleaded so earnestly that objections were overcome, reasons talked down, and never did a more prosperous, contented, and merry family party eat their Christmas turkey, and, a week after, drive into Charleston—hearty, healthy, happy—dreading no duns, independent of the world, at peace with all mankind.

Lily paused on the steps to say good-by to her betrothed, while Nora waited for him in the carriage at the door of Mr. Clarendon's house.

The servants were jostling and tumbling over each other, unloading the second carriage, answering a dozen different calls, receiving a dozen different orders.

"Please, Miss Lily, to take care," said old Jacob, as he stopped Bill and a basket from carelessly upsetting her. "These young niggers, now a days, hab no sort o' respec."

Clarence drew her out of the turmoil. They stood beside a luxuriant rose-bush, as full and fragrant as if December frost was a myth.

"This has been a happy month, dearest," he whispered.

Beneath her bonnet, among her curls, were some clusters of flowers, now faded, which George had stuck there.

"Do you recollect giving me a bud from your wreath on May-day, when I was leaving for New Orleans? We had then spent just this length of time together, and were to separate for different roofs. My rough hand destroyed your garland then, and we all thought it a bad omen. Has it proved so? I took that flower with a half-formed wish. I have it still. Give me, my own Lily, another blossom to-day which your bright ringlets have adorned."

"Not a faded rose," she said, shaking her head, and tossing George's tokens to the ground; "but here, I give you this"—and she plucked a just opened bud. "I wish this *very* flower to be the centre ornament of the bouquet which custom ordains you to present to me on the 3d of April."

CHAPTER XXIII

Race-week is the only one of the fifty-two during which Charlestonians appear to give themselves up to amusement. Of course this does not include the whole population, nor even the half of it; for in many families the races are looked upon with extreme disfavor, and some churches distribute among their congregations about this period astounding tracts, headed "Horse-racing and Christian duties incompatible;" but, for the gayer (?) portion of the community, the first Wednesday in February is an exciting and often longed-for day.

The most inert of our fashionables

"Give themselves a rousing shake,

and do very truly

"Just at twelve awake,"

ready to imbibe a sufficient quantity of dissipation to last them for the ensuing year.

But the week is always ushered in the evening previous by a ball, which surely demands a eulogium at the hands of those who have danced in St. Andrew's Hall.

The St. Cecilia Society can look back to its birth and foundation with justifiable pride. Few societies at all, and none of this character, can so well challenge attention to its age, and to its uninterrupted course and prosperity.

The date on forks and spoons belonging to this power shows that, some eighty years since, the gentlemen of Charleston first organized a series of concerts, to be given for the amusement of the ladies, and to restrict its members to the *élite* of the city.

Thus arose its name. Dedicated to the saint of song, for many winters our grandmothers, after their afternoon drive and their cheering cup of tea, would flock, in brocades and powder, to listen to the sweet strains provided to beguile their weariness by the gallant gentlemen in velvet coats and queues. The hours were very early—they went at seven, and were at home by ten.

Presently there arose an innovation. St. Cecilia was not permitted to remain sole patroness of these entertainments. A heathen divinity, Terpsichore by name, divided the honors with the Christian maiden. After the concert, dancing was introduced, and minuets and country reels enlivened the scene.

Years passed, and, alas! Terpsichore shoved St. Cecilia into the background—out of the establishment. They treated her like a married woman, poor thing! They went to parties given in her name, in which she took no part. These assemblies have never been discontinued, nor have they ever fallen into disrepute. The managers have usually been young men of family and fashion; the subscribers to the society are voted for or blackballed by the members at their yearly meeting, and the invited ladies are those entitled to a place in any ball-room.

They have rules and regulations which are implicitly followed. Strangers (on their first visit), and officers of the army and navy, are always guests. They have the best music to be produced, and the very worst suppers. I am sorry to say this, but truth is my idol.

It must be allowed that if the St. Cecilia balls are still respectable and properly conducted, they can not boast as uncompromising an attention to the social position of its members as it once did. Almack's has long fallen; its glory lies only in recollection, and in that charming novel which has always furnished me a hero—(Lord George Fitzallen, with his gilded spurs, was my very first love); but so long as it was a force, a body, it kept up its aristocratic flavor. But it died out. Unlike many aristocratic houses of old England, it refused to prop its failing fortunes by the admixture of plebeian interests, and so the thing came to an end, and no one hears of Almack's now. Across the wide ocean, our little Almack's learned wisdom by others' experience—wise little St. Cecilia Almack's!—and there are *habitués* of its boards whom, some time since—well, well. The balls (there are three each winter) are very pleasant balls; but, for my part, I return to the suppers. I should like fewer attempts at "woodcock for the million," and a positive success at scalloped oysters.

Mrs. Clarendon kept her word. Not to her mind was it necessary to follow her girls to a ball-room; she saw them dressed, admired their toilettes, and when Mrs. Purvis's carriage stopped *en passant,* watched them enter the Clarendon coach with Willie, and then went to bed and to sleep.

Through a crowd of young gentlemen loitering in the entrance-hall, our cloaked up beauties hurriedly passed to the dressing-room. The attendant handmaidens relieved them of their wraps, and Sara put out her small feet to be disencumbered of her overshoes, while she scanned the looks of her companions.

But, first, I may as well describe Miss Purvis herself. I have been putting off this duty too long.

Sara Purvis was decidedly a fine-looking, high-bred girl. She was tall, and a little too thin, but so good were her proportions, that one excused her want of plumpness in consideration of the absence of sharp angles. Her skin was like white wax which has taken a straw-colored tint, quite transparent, smooth, and unblushing. She had handsome eyes, if one is not fastidious about a variety of expression, or any especial purpose in them, and her hair was beautifully black and glossy, like her sister's. She was particularly proud of her mouth, which she fancied to be of a *coupe aristocratique,* and carried her nose, which her anteadmirers called enormous, with a very lofty air. She dressed with taste and style, laughed a good deal where she wished to pass for good-natured (with young men of fortune), and was unutterably empty-headed, vain, and frivolous. Had she been clever, she would have been a dangerous woman; but, devoid of talent, she was only disagreeably malicious.

From her earliest childhood she had disliked Lily, but she was afraid of Alicia, who never hesitated to snap at her, if she gave occasion for it.

To-night every body was in good humor. That martyr, Mrs. Purvis, had every reason to be satisfied with the youthful becomingness of her gown and other "fixtures," and Sara knew very well that she was looking her prettiest in a Frenchified costume trimmed with autumn leaves frosted with dew, and mingled with crimson ribbons and gold pendents.

But how do justice to Lily? In white, of course—such a snow-wreath of a dress, all soft and vapory, like the clouds that drift across a blue sky on a bright day, with large *bouffantes* that fell with irregular grace around her skirt, and were looped up with fringes of white bugles and feathery sprays.

She was simple, exquisite, spirit-like, and might have sat for the portrait of *la Feé aux Perles*. Alicia sparkled in a yellow silk, with red velvet cactuses drooping on either side of her broad, shining *bandeaux*.

"All right," said Mrs. Purvis, nodding her head approvingly; "very nice, upon my word. I have been so ill all day I scarcely thought that I should come to-night; but, really, I am called upon to make sacrifices of my health which would kill any other woman. Dr. Jobbers says it is my nerve and spirits that keep me up—nothing else. I have eaten nothing this day."

"Except a hearty breakfast and a very hearty dinner," muttered Sara. "Come, mamma," she faintly continued, "shall we spend the night in the cloak-room?"

"No, indeed, my beauty. I am ready."

How many beating hearts, fluttering in the bosoms of *débutantes*, have trembled up that staircaise!

That hall is the first battle-field of our young Amazons who go forth to conquer the male sex. Their success or failure is determined within those walls. She is predestined to rule who finds herself engaged at least "six deep" before she smooths out her skirts for her first quadrille, and she is a wall-flower for life who passes her evening on one of those very hard chairs planted around the room.

Sully's portrait of Victoria dominates the crowd at the upper end of the hall; a string of likenesses, representing the series of Presidents of the St. Andrew's Society (to whom the hall belongs), line the walls, and a carpet upon the floor gives a drawing-room look to this festive spot.

I went to one of these balls once. Alas! the seats are very uncomfortable, and I had no other experience. My chaperon was very kind, and not satisfied with the small effect that I produced. She varied my position as much as she could, so as to bring out my best points. Sometimes she engaged me in conversation, to exhibit my intellectual expression; then she encouraged a pensive, down-cast seriousness, to show my eyelashes, which are rather long: it was all in vain. No young man flew to secure my hand for the "mazy dance."

"Stand up, my dear," she said, presently.

I timidly obeyed.

"Sit down again," she added, after a while, and sighed hopelessly. It was of no use.

Then she signaled a manager and whispered a few words. I felt my cheeks tingle, for I guessed what was coming.

The manager bowed and hurried off. I could see him earnestly appeal to a dandified youth, who looked at me through an eye-glass, and evidently bade his managerial friend "to go (playfully) to the ——."

Then the gentleman in office collared a grave young man in spectacles, with frizzly hair, and lugged him along. My destined partner was too polite to struggle. He had large, projecting knees, and helpless hands.

"Miss ——, Dr. Larned."

"Allow me the pleasure of dancing with you," he said, sepulchrally.

"No, I thank you," I answered, hurriedly. He was so unprepared for my reply that he held out his arm, and my chaperon nudged me.

"I'd rather not. Do, please, let him go," I said, imploringly, in a low voice.

The manager released his victim, and with another bow the large knees returned to their former position in the door-way.

That was my first and last ball.

I am not courageous and not over patient. From the beginning of that entertainment I wondered who was to take us to supper. The result showed me that a manager took my chaperon on one arm and me on the other. I could not hope for this luck at every ball, and, as I said before, the chairs are not cushioned, so I have never been to a second "St. Cecilia," and the truth is, my kind friend, Mrs. ——, has never urged me to do so.

However, I meant to tell about Lily's ball, not about mine, which had preceded hers by some years.

"There is Miss Vere! How beautiful she is!" murmured some voices, enthusiastically, as they entered.

Then Alicia's eyes flashed from under her black brows a few side glances, and Sara put up her head with the craning motion peculiar to her, and leveled her *lorgnon* here and there with a disdainful haughtiness she copied from Angel, and the crowd wavered in their first allegiance, and chorused forth their admiration for the two other beauties.

They were the belles of the room. Lily's engagement was, as yet, scarcely believed in; it was not so certain, so positive, at any rate, as her thousands, and she was surrounded.

But, I say it with pride, I believe there are few cities in the world where mere fortune so slightly influences ball-room attractions and belleship, or even solid courtship. It is not the young lady with the wealthiest papa who receives most declarations and is most attended to. Heiresses have often been left to *faire tapisserie,* while girls in plain white muslins have danced into the hearts of the flower of chivalry and Charleston.

It used to be said, "in the days when I was young," that never "had there been known in our city an heiress who was a belle, nor a belle who was an heiress."

They tell me this is changed now, and that "money" rules here as elsewhere. Gold whitens dark faces and brightens dull eyes. "Papa's plantations" send mademoiselle home danced to death, while pretty Clara, in her cheap tarlatane, has had no chance to cope with her plain neighbor.

It may be that the "rich girl" was just as agreeable as Clara, and it would be equally hard that her papa's purse should render her ineligible as a belle: would it not?

A word to a stranger, though, on this topic. Let not the "cheap tarlatane," if joined, too, to a pretty face, deceive you. Don't pass the wearer over as a "losing business." Many of our "finest people," with the longest credit at their factors' and bankers', dress like dowdies, and wear gowns which fadedly proclaim the worthy endurance of the original stuff. Their income is so well known—they are so thoroughly respectable, that "outward show" is not necessary.

Let doubtful credit display glistening freshness—established position can spare the expense. They call it "sparing the trouble," and dye their old dresses.

Clarence Tracy was a great favorite in his own circle. Out of his own circle he was called a tuft-hunter sometimes, and before he went abroad a few young men used to be very satirical about his boyish preferences; for he had mixed a good deal in society at an early age, and that last winter of Angel's girlhood he had first learned to admire her stateliness in ballrooms, before he met her at Chicora.

Clarence maintained that he had a right to give his attentions where it suited him to do so, and now, on his re-entrance into the same atmosphere, he again singled out his former fancies.

Margaret Oakes was one of them. He admired her cold, collected manner, and the unsoftening indifference of her tone. She took no pains, like Angel, to make conquests; she was not popular; she had few favorites, and Clarence liked the distinction of being one of them.

After dancing with Lily, he sought Miss Oakes, who welcomed him with a smile, and made room beside her for him to sit down.

"Tell me about Angelica," she said; "are you good friends still?"

"Very. I admire her, as ever."

"You look foreign, do you know? I don't like your style much. You have a Frenchy look."

"I am very sorry, for I have a young Frenchman on my hands who arrived this morning, and for whom I must do the honors of our city. He will be here presently, and I wished to present him to one of our fairest ornaments; but if you dislike a 'Frenchy look,' you will frown down my vicomte. What shall I do for him?"

"Who is he?"

"Le Vicomte Marc d'Ambermesnil."

"Come to marry a fortune? Introduce him to Lily Vere."

"Thank you; I'd rather not."

"Then your engagement is positive?"

Clarence bowed. Margaret's eyebrows contracted.

"She is very sweet-looking—clever, is she not?"

"Not what people usually call clever. She has not a brilliant mind, but a great deal of good sense."

"Oh, of course she is clever enough for her condition. You are fortunate, Mr. Tracy. You do not like hard work—you are a little lazy; what a pleasant thing to find such a ready-made income, with only the trouble of asking for it."

Clarence winced. This was but the beginning of his experience in marrying an heiress. He thought Margaret Oakes looked old; he was sure she said disagreeable things, but he was too much a man of the world to resent them or to show his pique.

"There comes my vicomte. Let me introduce him to Miss Clarendon, and then may I return and dance with you?"

Margaret agreed, and thought within herself, "I shall say something more before I have done with you."

She did not even mentally add the reason, which was, that, since Mr. Henry Clarendon's legacy, she had contemplated keeping his godson for herself.

During his introduction of the stranger, who was rather an agreeable-looking man, to the willing Alicia, Margaret said a few words to Sara, who moved with her partner toward the end of the room where the presentation had taken place.

"Is it a real vicomte, Mr. Tracy?" whispered Sara, insinuatingly.

"Real, fresh, lively, and just landed. *Mon cher*," added Clarence, in French, "permit that I increase your happiness by naming you to Miss Purvis."

Sara's tongue, outside of her own vernacular, was somewhat limited, but she struggled through a phrase or two, and after promising a polka to the vicomte, she left him to Alicia and went off.

Lily's evening was placid and pleasant. She was enjoying the ball in her own way, when Sara sauntered up and said, in a nonchalant tone,

"Has Mr. Tracy introduced his Frenchman to you?"

"No."

"That is singular. They are very intimate. They used to live together at Baden-Baden, the vicomte tells me."

Lily, who never forgot what she had heard fall from Clarence, immediately conjectured that this must be the gentleman who sealed their acquaintance by afterward launching Clarence in Paris; but Baden recalled play-debts and saddened her face.

"Maggie Oakes looks very handsome to-night. Clarence is quite devoted. He has danced twice with her."

Two thrusts. Lily knew very well what jealousy is. Sara had spoiled her pleasure. Why did not Clarence introduce his friend? Was he afraid of a Frenchman's indiscreet talk? And why need he hang so earnestly over Miss Oakes?

But at supper-time Clarence was punctually at his post, spoke carelessly and naturally of Margaret, and when Lily asked him about his foreign friend, said that he was a good, empty-headed sort of a fellow, who would in no wise interest her. He did very well for Alicia to make eyes at.

And did not Alicia make eyes at her new conquest? This was the moment when Mrs. Clarendon should have been at hand, with her maternal energies brought to bear upon her daughter's actions and engagements.

Who was there to direct, to warn, to counsel, or to ward off? Mrs. Purvis had enough to do to take an occasional inventory of Sara's *tablette de bal.* She sat in the scanty line of dowagers (of whom there are about three to every thirty young ladies), and gossiped, and bemoaned herself, and boasted of Angel's New York house, and thought how immeasurably superior her appearance was to her co-mates. For it is amazing to see how economically the chaperons get themselves up. In fact, I have often thought, from what I have heard, and what I have witnessed at *my ball,* that there ought to be a "theatrical wardrobe" kept in the cloak-rooms, in which the chaperons might be invested each evening. There are so few of them, and their business is such a regular one, that subscriptions ought to be taken up among the damsels whom they convoy to dress these ladies properly for their "parts." It injures the look of the thing to see, scattered about the walls, a worthy matron or so in shawls and caps of such strict simplicity.

Willie Clarendon was too busy with his own partners. He saw other young ladies going about with "no mammas," and he supposed it "was all right."

Lily dared not interfere with Alicia, and, besides, it was impossible to answer all the demands upon her own time. She was very much liked, very much sought after. Clarence made it a point, and told himself and her that it was a sacrifice, not to hang about his *fiancée* in society. He had a large number of sentimental friendships—Margaret Oakes headed the band—and he was always deep in talk with one or other of these young ladies. Lily had an uneasy feeling about it, but she would have scorned to be jealous, exacting, or suspicious. The soft eyes followed her lover hither and thither, and she put down the rising thought that she was not necessary to *his* amusement with irritation at her own unworthiness. It was instinct working within her, and she considered it an ungenerous and unfeminine emotion.

Strange, is it not? that so often in this world we see this unaccountable fact! It is not the woman most worthy to be loved who is the most loved. I have seen treasures of affection lavished, wasted upon a flirt—a heartless recipient—while a tender, loving creature, fair as her neighbor, and giving her own pure and entire devotion to the chosen one, is looked upon with lukewarm regard. I have seen wives whose past existence has been one series of well-performed duties—and duties, too, which were not only all duty: they have been misunderstood, disregarded, neglected by men who, perhaps, when they bury these uncared-for companions, love, marry, and cherish others, who could in no wise compare with their predecessors.

Lily, with all her gifts, failed to inspire a love equal to that which she gave. Why was it? I can not tell. Her beauty, her freshness, her sweetness, her gentleness were indisputable. Clarence acknowledged their undoubted existence; he fancied himself desperately in love; he would have fought the man who questioned his affection; he would have been plunged in grief had a quarrel arisen between Lily and himself; but he did not feel for her that yearning, insatiable, unsatisfying sentiment that makes up a love which is worth inspiring.

And what is more, I say candidly I do not believe that any man would have loved Lily as she ought to have been loved. Let novelists write about the passion called forth by ingenuous, unsophisticated, unworldly beings: it is mere curiosity—a desire to rifle the bud of its untouched bloom. Men marry these girls or these women—for innocence is not a mere matter of age or circumstance, and a grandmother may be more truly innocent, the innocence of the heart, than a maiden of fifteen—men marry these, and have immense respect for them, and "think highly of them," and honor them as the mothers of their children; but, if they are gay and "fast" men, they soon return to their old, merry, wicked loves—some haughty, worthless coquette, some dashing, daring jilt, or some sighing, sentimental sylph; if they are staid and proper men, with principles and a sense of justice, they try to banish recollections of other eyes and other hands, and they conceal from "Madame" (who is often happily unconscious) that there are nooks in their hearts where lurk buried sighs and hopes, and niches where stand statues that have foreign names upon their base. I take the liberty to lay it down as an axiom that no woman is heartily loved unless she has a spice of the devil in her. Dispute it—you can't refute it.

I know that some men will say contemptuously, "it is a different sort of love." I am aware of the fact, but the most virtuous of her sex prefers "a different sort of love" to the love which she often receives in return for her whole love.

Lily was one of these women. She had every virtue, every charm; she was destined to be regarded with holy admiration; but Angelica would bind a man to her with chains of iron and clasps of steel, while Lily's power was no stronger than the circlet formed by her two white arms.

I am wandering from the ball-room, and prosing unmercifully.

The last waltz was over; Alicia stood in the entrance-hall, her arch face peeping from beneath her pink *nubie* as she gave her fan and bouquet to the Vicomte Marc to hold while she crossed the swan's down of her Opera cloak over her dimpled shoulders.

"I may offer mes homages to-morrow to Mademoiselle?" said M. D'Ambermesnil, interrogatively.

"On the race-course," assented Alicia, smilingly. "Our bets will be decided there before we can meet elsewhere."

"Ah, yes! I had forgotten. In some company one forgets every thing."

Mrs. Purvis bustled along, swathed like Gliddon's mummy, and calling vociferously for her charges.

"*Elle est riche, cette charmante jeune personne? n'est ce pas, Tracy?*"

Clarence was thinking of Lily, who had asked where he got the vinaigrette whose odor she perceived as he put her in the carriage.

"*Immensement, mon cher,*" he answered.

"*Voilà mon affaire,*" muttered the viscount, as he lit his cigar.

A dark green landau, with servants in bright olive livery, with gold bands, and containing three ladies, followed by a light *coupé,* in which sat two other ladies, took the road for the race-ground.

What beautiful, cheery weather! Very little dust, a clear sky, an unclouded sun, and no wind.

Such days are rare, and ought to be remembered with delight, besides being enjoyed at the time. The road was full of horsemen, carriages, buggies, and carts. Omnibuses rumbled along, foot-passengers strode bravely forward, and the negroes were, as usual, the loudest and most conspicuous partakers in the pleasures of the day.

Plato and Sambo, on the box, made bets as they drove along, and the little ragged darkies hurraed the finest vehicles, and "chaffed" the comical with as much unconcern as if they had a "paid" part in the procession.

Under the oaks skirting Loundes's Grove (one of the prettiest little scraps of a drive in the neighborhood), and through the gate labeled conspicuously "Entrance for Members' Carriages," drove the landau and the *coupé.* The coachmen showed their tickets, and, with a dash, bowled up under the covered doorway of the ladies' stand.

Members of the club, with the red ribbon fluttering at their button-hole, and strangers with a white ribbon, marking their position, sauntered about, or talked eagerly, or looked anxious, and bowed to their fair partners of the previous evening with smiles which they hoped hid the tremors they suffered lest Pretty Poppet should be beaten by Colonel ——'s filly.

Mr. Clarendon sported a red and white cockade as one of the stewards.

"Take care how you bet, puss," he said to Alicia, as she sprang last from the landau, after Mrs. Purvis and Sara. "You will ruin me with your glove-bill if you trust to Pretty Poppett's clean legs. She isn't strong in the pasterns," he whispered. "Take Colonel ——'s filly against the field. Where is Lily?"

"Here, sir. Grace Meredith is with me," said Lily from the *coupé,* as Sambo hastily opened the door, eager to have them out, and to be off himself to secure a good "stand" for the race.

Our old friend Grace was as lively and frolicsome as she had been at the May party. Lily and she had just met for the first time since they had each leaped from girlhood to young womanhood. Grace had arrived late on Tuesday evening from the country—too late for the ball, which she regretted with great fervor, but not too late to unpack a box of New York finery awaiting her at home, and to make her appearance this morning in "a love of a bonnet," which Lily had chosen for her, with the assistance of Angel's taste.

"Who is that wonderful dandy, looking like a dyspeptic peacock?" she whispered to Lily as they stepped out of the carriage.

"A Frenchman—le Vicomte d'Ambermesnil."

"I don't like his looks. And who is that supercilious, black-browed—"

"Why, Grace!"

"Heavens! it is Clarence Tracy!"

She glanced merrily at Lily, and shook hands with Clarence.

William Clarendon she received with unqualified approbation.

He offered her his arm as they all went up the staircase.

"You have not grown much, Miss Grace, in the five years that I have been away," he said.

"If I could borrow the ends of your mustache for the top of my head, I should be tall enough," answered Grace, saucily.

"You are all such fairies of ladies! There is Alicia, she is not more than four feet high, and Nora Tracy, and you. I keep on looking at you, and wondering when you will grow up."

"Your mind's eye is filled with stalwart German vröws and big Englishwo-men, I suppose. But there is Lily. She is tall enough to insure your admira-tion. Why don't you make her your model."

"Oh! Lily is an exception to all rules," said William, gravely. "I would sooner say my prayers to Lily than fall in love with her. She is lovely, but too spiritual for me."

"Lovely is the word, indeed, that best suits her," said Grace, enthusi-astically. "Do you know, Mr. Clarendon, I can't understand her engagement? Is Clarence Tracy worthy of such a prize?"

"She thinks so," answered Willie, evasively. "But I could not give an impartial opinion, Miss Grace. Clarence has cut me out with my father's ward."

Grace turned her mutable Irish face toward him.

"Truly?"

"No, indeed. I do but jest. Lily was always, in spite of her fewer years, my senior in gravity and wisdom. When I came home the other day, I was dazzled by her peculiar beauty; but, besides seeing at once that she and Clarence were on the eve of an engagement, I was, indeed, only dazzled. She looks to me like a snowbank with the sun upon it. There is a deal of warmth in the earth below, but too much unbroken calm above."

"Not to my mind. She is like a bank of violets on a spring day—cool, green, modest, refreshing, and giving the perfume of her presence and her kindness to every comer. But we are getting wretchedly poetic and prosaic. Let me do the honors of the ladies' stand, built since you left. How do you like it?"

This was not Grace's first winter in society; she had come out the preceding year, and William thought her a very agreeable girl as they strolled up and down the long hall, which opens with many doors upon the covered platform whence the ladies enjoy the race.

"The horses are saddling!" some one cries; and numerous flirtations, carried on behind parasols in the doorways, or upon the settees scattered in the hall, are hastily suspended for the moment.

It is a charming sight, these rows upon rows of fresh young faces. With little exclamations at the glare of sunlight, they venture out upon the platform to look at the horses (which, enveloped in their blankets, "wonderfully resemble burnoused Bedouins on all fours," Grace Meredith said), and consult their cards, and risk bonbons and gloves, and change their minds, and "hedge" shamefully, as it is a woman's privilege to do.

Then they consult some knowing old steward, who answers at random and hurries off, being seen presently, whip in hand and hands in pocket, earnestly discoursing turfy-looking individuals on "the ground" below.

There are a great many children scampering about, who are stuffed with unwholesome tarts, and threaten to precipitate themselves out of the clutch of "mamma" in the stand upon the head of "papa" on the turf.

The red flag waves from the judges' "perch;" there is a rush to the members' stand, which is next the ladies', and in which congregate those sheepish gentlemen who "avoid society" and frequent dinners; a great deal of confusion, a loud voice dominating the crowd,

"Keep back! stand back! clear the way, there!"

The horses are off—and I shall not attempt to describe a race.

"Is it not exciting?" cries Alicia, clapping her little lemon-colored kids; "*mais vous ne regardez point les chevaux*, Monsieur?"

Le Vicomte Marc's stake is not on the running horses. He is playing for higher game, and fixes his eyes upon the fancied heiress, and not upon the slender legs of Pretty Poppet.

"Have you bet much, Clarence?" asks Lily, hesitatingly.

"A mere trifle."

'Tis the first heat—here they come. Pretty Poppet wins; the young ones who are against her are in despair, but the older hands know the effect of four miles repeated, and are quite sure still.

The gentle little Southerners are aroused. Their pale cheeks flush, and they chatter like magpies.

Every body walks in the long hall, and sweetly unconscious of her superiority Sara tries to look as she is attended by three gentlemen, while Alicia only has her Frenchman's arm.

But put the title in the scale, and Sara kicks the beam!

The second heat is at hand, and the same performances are re-enacted, only there is a little more bustle in the members' stand, for many "stiffish drinks" have been swallowed, and there seem to be more legs and arms in the crowd than there were before.

Two of the horses are withdrawn, three remain—the contest is over, Pretty Poppet comes in victorious, the knowing ones are "bit," and Mr. Clarendon wants to be savage, but can't manage it very well, when Alicia says to him, with charming archness,

"And how about her pasterns, papa?"

"Ain't you sorry it is not a broken heat, Miss Clarendon?" yawns Alfred Greville, who is very *blasé* about races, having joined the club the day before; "we consider this a dead failure. A man can't get up an excitement on so little staple. Going to stay for the next race?"

"It depends on Mrs. Purvis."

"Better stay—aw—I drove up with Gustavus. How mad he is about Tracy! says Miss Vere might as well have married some confounded beggarly Frenchman like that man Tracy—"

"Mr. Purvis had better choose more discreet confidants," said Alicia, glancing toward her companion; and Mr. Greville, discovering his mistake, blushed furiously and backed out.

The drive into town is never so pleasant as the drive out. Every body is tired, and some people have lost money, but it is very gay and bright nevertheless; and with an occasional threat from Mrs. Purvis that she would probably faint from exhaustion (which she did not do), the party got safely home.

CHAPTER XXV

It could not possibly interest you, my dear reader, for me to procure the minute, uninterrupted detail of this winter's campaign.

The young ladies danced at balls, Lily received two formal declarations, and Alicia flirted incessantly with the vicomte.

One of these declarations was from her cousin Gustavus. This young gentleman was considered by his family "the first match in the state." We have all of us seen a good many such "first matches," and they seemed to think that Lily could not have thoroughly understood that she might have Gustavus, or she would never have accepted Clarence.

Gustavus was a weakly, well-disposed youth, with a gentlemanly carriage and pretty features. He made great use of an eye-glass, and very little of his tongue. Lily listened to him with much amazement when he declared himself.

"But, Gustavus," she said, with calm honesty, "you know that I am engaged?"

"Yes; but mother said I had better try."

Lily could not help smiling.

"And, my dear Lily," Gustavus went on, "I do not feel quite at liberty to explain, but in your present choice you have been hasty. Mr. Tracy is—"

"It is very unbecoming your position at this moment to attempt to speak against a gentleman of whom you can *know* nothing, which would be injurious to him," interrupted Lily, warmly.

"I am one of your nearest relations, Lily," said Gustavus, who had been strongly "crammed" by Mrs. Purvis and Sara, "which is my excuse. I renounce all hope of recommending my love to you, but I should advise you to make a few inquiries as to how many gambling debts Tracy owes, and where—"

Lily rose abruptly.

"Not one word more."

"What is the bond between this French adventurer and himself? He encourages his attentions to Alicia Clarendon because he is afraid to thwart him—"

"Gustavus, you are my mother's nephew; you have been put up to this; you would never have imagined such insults yourself. Our near relationship, which you make an excuse for uncalled-for interference, is my reason for forgiving it. But this conversation ends here, and any attempt at renewal will force me to decline your acquaintance, and to inform my uncle and Mr. Tracy of the cause." She bowed with dignity, and an angered loftiness most foreign to her sweet face, and joined Alicia, who was lounging on an ottoman near, in the ball-room, which was the scene of Gustavus's defeat.

Alicia was whispering and coquetting with the vicomte, and seemed not over-delighted at Lily's advent; but as another gentleman soon came up to ask Miss Vere for a promised dance, Alicia forgot all about her, and continued her flirty dialogue.

Lily was silent and *distraite,* worried and ill at ease. The new-comer was fortunately a great talker, so she assumed a listening attitude, and put in a word or two at random.

"It is now at the close of the season; the weather is growing warm, and the parties few, Miss Vere; have you enjoyed your winter?"

"Very much."

"I believe every body has. And we have had so many new beauties this year!"

"Oh! I am afraid, when it comes to the last," said Alicia, in a very low voice, and in French. "Papa is very indulgent; his consent would not be difficult."

"There is Miss Purvis; but she came out last year. By the way—"

Lily was listening again to Alicia; she could not hear M. D'Ambermesnil.

"Why not wait? Even if he refuses at first, I am young enough not to marry so soon, and can bring him round in time."

Lily's heart almost stopped beating. It was not honorable to overhear Alicia, but for worlds she could not have desisted.

"How lively Miss Meredith is, too!" said the valuable dealer in commonplaces. "She does rattle so!"

"Ah, monsieur! ah, Marc!" Alicia murmured, "do not doubt me. Well, I promise. To-morrow, then."

"Ange!" exclaimed her companion, as the first notes of a waltz sounded, and he arose to offer her his arm. Her skirt was beneath Lily's foot; she disengaged it without looking up, and went off.

Lily's partner prosed on, and Lily felt so ill, so helpless, that at last Mr. Morton's eyes were opened to her pallid cheeks.

"You feel badly; you are fatigued. Shall I get you any thing?"

"Only a glass of water; and will you call Mr. William Clarendon for me?"

Clarence came up.

"You look ill, darling."

"I am not ill, but bored," said Lily, smiling faintly.

"It must be a bad case, if you acknowledge it."

"Clarence, do you owe any money to that Vicomte d'Ambermesnil? Has he any hold upon you of any sort?"

"None whatever," said Clarence, coldly and decidedly. "You begin your interrogations early."

"Forgive me, my love," Lily said, with disarming sweetness; "why will the world invent scandals against the innocent?"

"And why will the most innocent of all women believe scandals? Had you asked me about Ambermesnil more particularly than you did, I could have added to my previous information, that he is of undoubted good family and position, the fact that he is also too fond of card-playing and dissipation to suit your rigid notions."

"And you have allowed him to tie himself to Alicia's sleeve?"

"My dear Lily, Alicia tied him there herself. I did not warn her about him, but I told Mr. Clarendon that he was not a saint—that he was a gay, good-for-nothing dandy of high family. Willie knows all about him. Sara Purvis has made Gustavus pick his brains of every thing she could get hold of, and Alicia has chosen to dance with him, and to walk with him, and to philander with him, and none of them have interfered. It is the custom in this country for young ladies to make their own associates: it was not my place to snub off from Alicia a man who had been personally kind to me in Paris. Well, Willie, what is it?"

"I obey Miss Vere's orders. Speak, queen of this night. Morton says you are the most agreeable young lady in the room, with the finest mind, and sent for me. Was it to enjoy your fine mind that you wished me?"

"I want to get home. Do see if Alicia is ready."

As Clarence told her good-night, Lily whispered,

"How delightful it is to think that whenever I begin to fancy you have done something wrong, you can always reassure me, and never fail to show that I only am always wrong when I doubt you."

Clarence pressed the soft hand which lay so tenderly in his.

"She is as good as she is beautiful, as beautiful as she is lovable, as lovable as any one woman can be," thought Clarence, as he buttoned his overcoat; "I was born under a lucky star. Ha, Marc! où vas-tu? Combattre le tigre?" translating our American slang.

"Non, mon cher; comme vous, je me range."

"Mais, moi, je me marie."

"Eh bien!" answered the vicomte, shrugging his shoulders; "perhaps I do as much. Bon soir."

"What the devil does he mean?" muttered Clarence.

🌸 CHAPTER XXVI

The clock of St. Michael's church, which regulates Charleston time, had chimed three quarters past three when Lily opened the door communicating between her room and Alicia's.

Alicia's head was suddenly raised from her pillow, and she called out,

"Is that you, Lily? What is the matter?"

Lily's hand trembled as she put down her candlestick upon the toilet-table, and then approached the bed.

"What is it?" asked Alicia, peevishly. "If you wish to play ghost or Somnambula, my dear, pray do not choose a ball-night, when I have danced my feet tired and myself sleepy."

"I am going to play, I fear, a very thankless part. Dear, thoughtless, reckless Alice, what is the meaning of that 'to-morrow' which I heard you utter as a promise to M. D'Ambermesnil?"

The blood rushed impetuously into Alicia's face, as she angrily exclaimed,

"Upon my honor, Lily, you seem to watch me very closely. Is this to be a Harry Barclay business over again? Is it your 'mission,' think you, to dog my footsteps and to pry into my concerns? Your interference annoys me—your questions bore me; have the goodness to let me alone. I presume I may make engagements for a walk without telling you of it. Where are you going now? What is the matter with you?"

She caught Miss Vere's hand.

"I shall consult your mother in the morning. I am no tale-bearer, my love, but circumstances force me to interfere where I could not conscientiously avoid it."

"Stop. The fact is—oh Lily!" and Alicia burst into tears.

With Lily's kind arms around her, with Lily's white cheek pressed to hers, as it always had been in Alicia's childish troubles, so it was now. Her petulance was over, and she confessed the folly she was on the eve of committing. She had promised this Frenchman to elope with him the following day.

"We were to be married; he had engaged a clergyman to perform the ceremony, and I should have come back to ask papa's and mamma's pardon."

"Did you think it romantic to do so disgraceful a thing, Alice?"

"I did not think at all."

"Are you in love with him?"

"Well, I don't know. He is very agreeable, and then I should like to be a vicomtesse; and he is certainly handsome, and it would be very nice to live in Europe."

"Like Cecilia Langdon; you know she is the Comtesse de Montanvert. She has a happy ménage."

Alicia flouted.

"I don't think any man would have a chance of neglecting me, or the wish either," she added, with a pretty grimace.

"Why did not this gentleman ask my uncle's consent? why must your marriage be secret?"

"Marc says his family have other views for him, and would never agree to his marrying an American. Papa will require letters and recognition from them, which he is sure they will demure about giving. He thought it much better to have the business over, and then, when it was done, why it was done, and both sides would be obliged to be reconciled to it. Papa would never hold out against me, and his papa would never have an objection when once he looked into the lovely face of his new daughter-in-law."

"Those were his reasons?"

"Yes, and very sufficient ones."

"Not to my mind. Trust me with this business. If you and M. D'Ambermesnil are seriously attached, a little opposition will not destroy your affection. If he is worthy of you, he will be willing to suffer a little for your sake. Think for a moment, dear Alicia. You were going to wound, in the unkindest and most careless manner, parents who have delighted throughout your whole life to make you happy. Imagine the mortification to them. In a momentary caprice, you behave with the most cruel want of confidence. Tell M. D'Ambermesnil that it is impossible. If he hopes to gain you, he must strive for you."

"I don't think papa will like him."

"I don't think he will give papa a chance. There are rumors concerning the vicomte—I do not wish to hurt you, Alice—but I doubt if he will ever come boldly forward to claim you."

"Lily, you are absurd!"

"Alicia, you are thoughtless beyond belief. Life is to you the veriest child's game. To one who did not know you as I do, your conduct would appear utterly impossible. A vision of Paris, the jingle of a title, the flattery of a well-looking young man, have caused you to forget that this stranger is indeed a stranger; that this step is a step for life. You have not engaged yourself for a dance, for a drive, but for a sacred and ever-enduring tie. You enter into it as lightly as you would put on your ball-dress. When will you learn, dear, that this world and its emotions and actions are solemn things?"

"You are a solemn thing."

"I am. I think I feel deeply. I hope I do. I love you deeply. Oh, listen to me, dear one, here, with your head upon my shoulder. Did you say your prayers to-night, Alice? Did you pray for the man you were about to marry? Did his name arise with your thoughts to God? Always mistrust those important events which you do not connect with God's blessing. It is a simple test. Do not weep so bitterly, my little one. It is only an imprudence now, and we shall set it all right again."

"You are so good—I am so naughty," murmured penitent Alicia. "Brought up together, with the same care, the same attention, you always go right and I always go wrong. I must be very wicked."

"Not so *very* wicked, dear. We have not the same temptations. Our characters and tastes are different. I have no leaning for the things which please you. I am not obliged to conquer fancies and to put down thoughts which arise in you. I am not brilliant; I don't shine in society. My mind is indolent, and it would give me no pleasure to dazzle people as you do. I deserve no credit for being a little prudent and discreet, because I am naturally quiet."

"You are very good," repeated Alicia.

"I have been very fortunate in some things," said Lily, with her gentle smile. "God deprived me of both my parents, but he gave me a kind friend in your father, and he early opened my eyes to my own faults. When I was a little girl I was inclined to be very conceited. You were always in scrapes, and I was always praised for my goodness. I began to think myself quite a model; but one day, when you were kept in at school for some freak, and I came home with a ticket of good behavior, my uncle noticed my self-satisfied smile, and he said to me, 'Don't imagine, Lily, that you deserve a great deal more credit than poor Alicia. She is too lively, and you are very demure. If you had the same wish to be frisky, you would have found it a hard matter to get that ticket.' It was an unusual thing for my uncle to make such a reproof. I thought of it a long time, and the longer I live the truer I find it. We see people with different natures, different positions, under different circumstances, and we measure them all by the same rule, giving praise to the results without looking into the causes."

Lily smoothed Alicia's glossy hair and kissed her on the eyelids.

"So it is, dearest, that I blame you less than I would another. You have impulses stronger than principles. I am very sure that, after consenting to this mad step, you felt to-night very much inclined to withdraw."

"Indeed I did; and I feel so much happier now, I longed to tell you. If mamma had the habit of looking after us—"

Lily laid her hand on the daughter's lips.

"We measure all by the same rule. My aunt must not be blamed for us, dear. Will you write three lines to the vicomte now? One of the servants will take the note to him in the morning."

"What shall I write?"

"Simply, 'If M. D'Ambermesnil will call on Miss Clarendon at one o'clock, she will explain why she has broken her engagement.'"

"I don't care much to see him."

"Alicia!" cried Lily; "and yet—"

"You see, dear Lily, it was the romance and the mystery of the thing—"

"I see, dear Alice, that you are a child who is utterly unfit to use the woman's privileges with which you are intrusted. Ah! if your heart could really be touched—if you could meet with one for whom a perfect esteem would be the basis of your love, and whom you could with pride present to your parents, then I should have no fears for you. Let this be a warning. See how dangerous it is to be led on step by step in the foolish path of flirtation. Scorn such hackneyed means of being admired, and live for higher aims than ball-room triumphs."

Lily's soft eyes glowed, her voice faltered; she was thinking of Clarence. She saw herself his honored and beloved wife, cheering him in worldly trials, comforting him when Heaven's blows should fall, aiding him in their mutual path of duty, and supported by him in all and through all.

A knock resounded upon the ceiling from the bedroom above.

"Girls," came Mrs. Clarendon's voice, faintly, "go to sleep!"

The note was written and given to Lily; then the thoughtless Alicia turned over for a sound nap, the last thought in her mind being,

"What will Marc do? Will he really ask papa, or is it as Lily says?"

Seeing the light through her closed shutters, Burleigh, who slept outside Lily's door, in the garden, scratched upon the panel. She unlocked the door and spoke to him. He sprang upon her with demonstrative joy, and the gray dawn lighted up the picturesque scene: the lovely girl, with her flowing curls, standing upon the threshold; the great dog, with his paws embracing her; the pretty chamber as a background, and the garden stretching out from the steps below.

"Always watchful, always alert, and loving me as much now as you did before I deserted you for my *education*," said Lily, playfully, to her pet. "So it is with true affection, Burleigh; absence will not weaken a bond which has a foundation worth having. I would not buy that long-eared Blenheim. You shall have no rival, old fellow. There; down, sir! that's enough now."

The Vicomte Marc D'Ambermesnil left cards of adieu upon all his acquaintances, and Charleston was reft of his presence. So true it is that things are never found out unless people tell on themselves—there was not a gossip who knew the reason of this sudden departure.

Some inquiring minds, who like to indulge in a liberal and undiscriminating curiosity, asked a few questions and suggested a few hints, but the general idea was that he had been rejected by Miss Clarendon, and had consequently retired in disgust.

Now the fact is, on receiving Alicia's note, the vicomte, after sundry invectives on woman's caprice, went to his friend Clarence Tracy, and began, with little prelude, to inquire into the fortune and prospects of *la jolie petite* Clarendon.

Mr. Tracy objected to having the young lady spoken of in that light fashion, and his Southern blood was up at the idea of the vicomte's insinuating that she could be had for his asking.

Very soon it appeared, however, that she was not the *héritière,* but that the simply-dressed girl to whom Mr. Tracy was betrothed was the prize in the matrimonial market.

Mr. Clarendon, Clarence reluctantly replied, was a rich man, but could not, of course, divide his property now among his children. The vicomte came to the conclusion that, far from this being a case where he should enter upon lies by wholesale to invent a tangible income, and to offer what he considered would be a positive requisition—a clean bill of previous good behavior—he might congratulate himself on having escaped a great imprudence.

He was spared the danger of having brought to light sundry ugly card-stories, and he might, with the passport of currency in Charleston drawing-rooms, seek a real heiress elsewhere.

He had an interview with Alicia, reproached her with her want of confidence in him, and, with a mutual feeling of relief, they parted.

Alicia was heartily ashamed, and very pensive and quiet for a week or so. She had liked Marc more than she at first thought, and was inclined to retract her dismissal, and to put him on trial as to whether his attachment was sincere; but he accepted her first words of doubt, looked melancholy, was shocked at her coldness, and took an eternal farewell with a gloomy bow.

She was young enough to believe in this claptrap until Lily had a conversation with Clarence, in which, without betraying Alicia's confidence, the former soon discovered the mistake made by the heiress-hunter, and she managed delicately to convey to the indignant Alicia the reason of M. D'Ambermesnil's hurried retreat before difficulties.

"So my taste for splendor deceived him, and he was in love with my diamond cross," said Alicia, with flashing eyes. "What an escape I have made! When I look back, I wonder how I could have gone so far and so foolishly. Depend upon it, Lily, many marriages are made with as little thought, and which turn out as complete mistakes as this would have been. But every one has not a Lily near her. I shall never marry now. I shall live a spinster, and raise a monument to you, dear: 'Sacred to a living Lily, "who toils not, neither does she spin," and who performs more good deeds in her generation than the ugliest and worthiest of her species.'"

Alicia was very good for fully ten days; and then, on the afternoon of the tenth day, she put on her bonnet, took a sentimental stroll with Alfred Greville, and when she came home told Lily he was by no means so stupid, and had very handsome eyes.

And all this went on with an unconsciousness on the part of Mrs. Clarendon, which would be incredible had I not seen it enacted a dozen times.

The third of April was drawing near. Three huge cases had arrived for "Miss Vere" per New York steamer; the trousseau contained in them, and chosen by Mrs. Langdon, was worthy of the bride, and a certain agreeable bustle pervaded the Clarendon mansion.

Since Gustavus's curious "bold stroke for a wife," there had been an increased coolness on the Purvises' side; nevertheless, Sara accepted the invitation to be bridemaid, and Lily secured all her old friends.

There were the Jenningses, the Melbournes, Grace Meredith, Nora Tracy, of course, and Alicia.

Lily was very busy and very happy. Some people may expect to find her weeping, and be disappointed that I do not describe her in some such maidenly act.

But I write the truth. There was not a tear in her heart nor on her cheek.

Why should she weep? I distrust weeping brides as much as I do giggling ones.

A sweet seriousness, a gentle gravity, thoughtfulness but not sadness, should be the natural expression of a young bride's face. There are cases— when a marriage is to be followed by an instant separation from friends and family—where tears are not unsuitable beneath a bridal veil. A woman should love the man she is about to marry, but it is not reasonable to suppose that she loses all other love; it is not desirable that she should seem to do so; but, on the other hand, if her bridal vows do not set her beyond the reach of her girlhood's surroundings—if no recent calamity has made tears familiar to her eyes, I feel them rise to my own when I see the large drops rolling down, or brushed away with passionate energy from a bride's pale cheek. All is not right there. God help that drooping heart—God still that wild and speechless agony—God keep pure that feeble, helpless, suffering creature!

Lily was very busy and very happy. Clarence's manner to her was perfect. I believe he loved her at that time more than he had ever done before or ever could again. It almost surprised himself.

The moment had come. "She was the type of perfect womanhood."

Her consideration for every one, her liberality, her nobleness of mind, the total absence of petty feelings, her large sensibility, her constant thoughtfulness; and, above all, like the white wings of an angel, which appear to brood over and are the motive power of every charm and action, was her love for him.

Yet, in the midst of these incessant demands upon her attention, it was Lily who first discovered a change in her guardian. It was her watchful eye which saw that something had gone wrong. He was a little fretful and a little cross, seemed restless and anxious. The wife of his bosom thought he was worried at the confusion in the house, and his children did not notice it.

His ward waited only for a favorable moment to offer her sympathy in some trouble.

"Those settlements are ready for you, dear," said Mr. Clarendon, as they arose from the breakfast-table one morning.

She followed him to the library and closed the door.

"You must read that paper carefully, Lily; it settles by your wish $5000 annually upon Clarence, independently of you, and to be first paid by the estate before any claim of yours. You can not sign it until you are married on this day week. Your father's will puts you in possession the instant after that ceremony; unless, my dear, you die before then, you make Clarence able to live handsomely apart from you, if he chooses to run away."

"I am quite willing, sir."

"He had better be very careful of you until this deed is signed. Should you suddenly go off in a fit, or fall out of a balloon before you are Mrs. Tracy, adieu to Clarence's $5000 per annum. Do you know who would have it all, Lily?"

"Of course I do, dear uncle; the one who has most right to an estate which he has nursed, and cherished, and improved till he has made me an enormous heiress—yourself."

"God bless you, dear child. Long may you have health to enjoy your wealth."

"Uncle," said Lily, looking with earnest affection in Mr. Clarendon's eyes, "is there any thing in which I can help you? There is something worrying you—what is it? If it is any thing that I can know, pray tell it to me. I am young, but you have often told me that I have sense for my years. Is it any thing about money? That is the root of all evil—"

"Nothing is the matter, Lily."

"I have watched you for several days—you must forgive it. You used to be very confidential with my dear papa; if he were alive, you would tell him. May I not hear it? It must be some money matter, for," she cried, a sudden light breaking in upon her, "in Angel's last letter to me, she says, 'I presume the Clarendons will scarcely choose, at this time, to make a great wedding parade.' I thought she alluded to—to—something else she might have heard; but Mrs. Langdon knows all about 'failures' and 'tightness in the market,' and all that dreary business; it is something of this sort, uncle, and you must tell me."

"I will, Lily, but on one condition: you will let me act as I previously intended; keep this a secret until you hear it from others. It is a very simple story. I have, with blamable folly, endorsed for a man who has left the country heavily involved. The payments must be met at once. I must sell Sunny Hill, or this house. It is a painful alternative. I might struggle on, but I have a horror of borrowing from Peter to pay Paul. I would rather clear myself at once, and be a free man, though a poor one. I have seen too much of this mortgaging, borrowing, shuffling business. Now, not one word, my dear. I see what you are going to say, but it is useless to say it. I hoped to have you in Europe before the affair was blown, for never shall I permit the world to think that Hugh Clarendon took advantage of his ward's generous offers to cover his own culpable act."

"But, my dear uncle—"

"But, my dear Lily, you should never have known this had it not been for your allusion to Angelica Langdon. I perceive the Purvises have scented the game, and I guessed at once that you would seek and get the information from them. But now I rely on your honor. Had you not been my ward, had your father left his child in other hands, I might more readily have accepted favors from Andrew Vere's daughter; but I would rather die in the poor-house than nurse an estate, and then help myself to it."

He got up and strode about the room, as was the good gentleman's wont when excited.

"See here, child! much as I love you, and would have gloried in having you Willie's wife, I am glad now that you and Fate decided otherwise. What the devil—No, my dear Lily, you must not press me in this matter."

She waited until he talked himself out.

"Will you listen to me, sir? What are your liabilities? Fifty thousand?"

"No, no," he said, shaking his head, "don't be absurd, Lily."

"Forty thousand? thirty? twenty-five? Suppose it twenty-five thousand. You have told me that I have in bank stock and in good bonds nearly seventy thousand dollars of easy-to-be-got-at property. If my father were alive, you would apply to him; if he had left me in other hands, you would probably have applied to me. Here I am, the child of your adoption, the orphan to whom you gave a happy home, the little girl who was placed in your arms on that sad night—I remember it well—the only representative of your nearest friend, and for a mere honorable quibble you refuse to take that assistance which is yours by right. What luxury do I lose by your accepting thirty thousand dollars from me? I shall not buy one gown less, nor eat one poorer dinner for it. Sell this house or sell Sunny Hill, lest the world should say you robbed your ward! Oh, dear uncle, when shall the wisest among us learn that we should only dread the world's reproof when conscience has given the first sting? And, for the matter of that, how do you suppose *I* can stand the world's saying, 'Miss Vere is too miserly even to aid her guardian. A fig for her gratitude; had she wished it, she could have forced him to accept a few of her loose thousands.' "

She paused, smiling, and Mr. Clarendon silently kissed her upturned brow.

"My cup of happiness is full," she went on, with that low, enchanting, persuasive voice; "if I needed but one thing more to convince me how wise I am in marrying early, it would be this. According to what you have told me, I might have wished ever so much to make you the handsomest presents, and I could not have done it for three years unless I were married. But it is all right now."

"By the way, and Clarence—a wife's duty is to consult her husband—how will he like this?"

"He would never be my husband," Lily blushingly answered, "if I supposed that in this case we could differ. I shall bring him to you presently, when he comes, and then you must see about this other deed, uncle. But, apropos, do find out, uncle, if Clarence prefers this regular income to having the Waccamaw place given him instead. Whichever will make him less feel that it comes from me."

"But this deed is drawn—"

"Draw and pay for six deeds, sir, rather than let my proud Clarence fancy that he is dependent upon me. Thank you for yielding to my wishes; thank you for your acceptance."

She wound her arms around his neck.

"This is like a scene in a play, Lily. I have been routed and defeated (to my own advantage) by a slip of a girl. The Purvises would swear that I had arranged the whole business."

"Hush, sir, hush! let us leave them alone. I can not find fault with any one to-day."

"Few people part with so much money, and look gay under it. I verily believe, though, that you rejoice in depriving yourself of your possessions. Would not you like to give away Chicora?"

"Not Chicora—no; that is my own. I mean to be buried under the royal oak, where I was crowned queen, so that I may always have a portion of that dear place to myself."

A bright color glowed on her cheek.

"Good-by, sir; I hear Clarence's voice quarreling with Alicia. I must separate the combatants."

CHAPTER XXVIII

On the evening of this day, a woman sat in a neatly-furnished room, diligently sewing by the light of a brightly-burning lamp. The street was a quiet and respectable one in a distant quarter of the city; there was no sound to be heard but the quick jerk of her thread, and an occasional sigh, as she looked at the hour marked by a watch which lay on the table before her. Beside the watch a slip of paper was unfolded from its envelope, and the woman's eyes incessantly reverted to these lines:

"Expect me, dearest L—, at 9 o'clock. C."

She was very handsome—of a passionate, luxurious beauty. There was intellect written on her brow, but it was overpowered by the stronger character of her voluptuous mouth and chin. Her black hair was more abundant than fine; she had a deep shadow beneath her great eyes; and between her thin, nervous nose, and her full, trembling, red upper lip, there was a slight dark penciling, which was more positive than a peach-like down.

Her simply-made dress of sombre colors fitted closely to an admirably-built form, elastic and powerful, with slender hands, and of a majestic carriage.

She was not a Spaniard, for her hair had a crisp tendency unseen in Andalusian or Catalonian beauty, and her complexion was neither olive nor fair. In a word, those to whom this race is familiar would immediately have detected her African blood, shaded through many generations, and almost now defying conviction.

The hands of the watch marked half past nine, and a quick step darted up the stairs, and there was a knock upon the door outside.

A hasty color mounted to the woman's forehead; a smile of delight parted her lips, disclosing the whitest possible teeth, and, removing some lines of care from her face, showed her age to be not more than twenty.

Her arms were folded about the new-comer as the door opened. She murmured in the lowest voice some energetic expressions of joy, and led him to a large chair near the fire, which a chilly spring evening made agreeable.

He removed his hat, and she seated herself on a low stool at his feet.

It was Clarence Tracy!

"You are later than your word," she said, tenderly.

"Oh, Lorenza, you may be glad I am not still later. I am harassed to death. Pray smile, child, for I am miserable, and want consolation. No, keep your smiles; you will need them all yourself presently."

"What is the matter? Tell me at once. You know I can not stand suspense. I would rather dare the greatest danger than wait patiently for the arrival of a lesser which is to come. Are you ill? Have you lost any friend? My own love, my life, what is it?"

"If you speak yourself, how can I? I am in no danger of life or limb, but an event is close at hand which I prefer you should learn from me. I am not rich, Lorenza, and I long for power. What is power? Money. To wait for fat cases, for large fees, is a very slow and uncertain method of getting money. There is but one course open to me. You can guess what that is, dear; can you not, Lorenza mia?"

She shook his hand impatiently from her shoulder, and with whitening lips, and a growing fire in her eye, said,

"To rob—to steal, I suppose."

"No, my pretty one, not that exactly. I wish it were no worse. There is only one safe method of stepping into thousands which are not your own—to marry an heiress."

Lorenza sprang from her seat.

"I guessed it," she cried, "I guessed it. I feared it long since; not from any diminution in your tenderness, for never have you appeared to love me more than while you were plotting this treachery; but in the house from which I procure work, among the sewing-girls I caught your name mentioned one day as the betrothed lover of one of their customers. I scorn to speak to them, but I asked you that evening if you knew her, and you spoke of her as a child whom you had known from earliest childhood, and whom you looked upon as a sister. Oh base, cruel, deceitful! Was it for this that you brought me back to this hateful city, where at every turn I feel the degradation in which I was born? You found me happy, respectable, and pure in Paris. My mother had repented of her early errors, and had taught me, since we left this place, that I might become an honored woman—that there were no barriers on that continent to a virtuous life for me. She died, but I found a friend. I was on the eve of marriage—that good German, the excellent, the worthy man who was to give me his home, and hand, and protection—I left him desolate for you. You met me in the street. You recognized the little girl whom you used to see years before playing at her mother's door-step in front of your aunt's house. I had forgotten those days; I had forgotten that there was slave blood in my veins; I was free—I was contented. Your vile flatteries, your miserable devotion, awakened a love in my breast which overthrew all the virtuous precepts my mother had learned to practice and had taught to me. I deserted my destined husband—I believed in you. Happy in your smile, in your arms, I consented to return here. I knew you could not marry me—you swore never to abandon me—"

"And I will not, Lorenza. I never said that I would abandon you."

"Silence!" she cried. "Who asked you to speak? Do you mean to add insult to insult? Would you insinuate that I should remain a pensioner—a—"

"Remain as you have been, pretty vixen—my much-loved and beautiful mistress. I shall be absent six months or a year, but I shall not forget you. No, Lorenza; in spite of your temper—of your foolish reproaches now, I have no wish nor intention to desert you. Here is a check for your yearly income. I regret to hear you speak of work that you procure. I had no idea that the roughness I sometimes see on this model of a finger was produced by labor of this sort."

She withdrew her hand, and threw back the disheveled dark hair from her fevered cheek.

"Touch me not. And for your money, this is the treatment I give it." She tossed the paper upon the coals, where it blackened, and shriveled, and died out. "So ends my love. Ah me!"

A shower of tears and deep sobs shook her frame.

Clarence watched her with calm eyes.

"You will get over this first burst, Lorenza. Every woman in your position must come to this, sooner or later. Many highly-born ladies see their lovers marry, and must swallow their tears. They often see them depart without the excuse of marriage. You are not hardly treated. Dry up those glorious eyes. Have I said that I love you less? You will reconcile yourself to an inevitable step; and believe me when I say that you are as dear to me now as when I first told you that that face and figure were worthy of a better destiny than to serve in a perfumer's shop as dame du comptoir."

Lorenza made no reply.

Presently, with an impatient gesture, she wiped away her tears, and looked full into her lover's eyes.

"Since when did you intend to marry?"

"Strictly speaking, child, I was partly engaged before I went to Europe."

"And it is to this man, just God! that they will give a young and innocent girl! I almost find it in my heart to pity her. But no; she will believe in him, she will love him, she will be happy, while I—Give me air—give me air—I suffocate—"

She tore open her dress from her struggling bosom, and paced the room distractedly.

"Lorenza, *tu donnes dans le melodrame.* Calm yourself. Your father, you have told me, died mad."

"Do you reproach me with that?" she exclaimed, fiercely. "Leave me! 'tis you that drive me mad."

"I will leave you now. To-morrow, when I return, I trust to find you more reasonable. Why will you, dearest, be so unnecessarily furious? There is nothing changed—there is nothing to change between us. I shall not see you quite so often as I have done, and for the rest of this year I shall be absent. If, in the course of time, you weary of the monotonous existence you lead in these rooms, and if you sigh for Paris and its gardens, *I* shall never oppose your pleasure. I love you too much to thwart you. To-morrow, *ma mie,* I shall bring back another check, since you have seen fit to destroy this one."

She was quieter now, and, with knitted brow and firmly-set lips, stared at him.

"But recollect, Lorenza, that I abominate ill-temper and scolds. You are handsome enough to excuse a great deal, but let this be the first and last storm. It is all over now, is it not?"

"It *is* all over. Farewell."

He nodded, and closed the door behind him.

"Handsome, but the temper of the devil," he muttered. "Never mind; she loves me too much to break with me, and I have not lost my ground by giving way. She will yield to necessity, as her betters have done before her."

CHAPTER XXIX

Among the ceremonies of the Episcopal Church, none is more impressive, without a gloomy tendency, than the rite of confirmation.

It is beautiful to see that band of thoughtful faces thus dedicating themselves to a virtuous life, fulfilling the vows made for them in baptism, and preparing themselves for a yet holier festival which should follow closely after. I like the white, emblematical veils, the snowy dresses. I like to have the sunshine fall upon the bowed heads. I like to note that the confirmed ones are young, and seem penetrated by this "outward form," which is an entrance to a "spiritual grace," and I always trust and pray that there is more than form in this voluntary acknowledgment that they are God's creatures, and destined for his service.

On Wednesday, the 28th of March, Lily was confirmed.

The venerable bishop who had baptized her, who had always felt a lively interest in her well-doing, and whose counsels she had recently sought with filial reverence, seemed to linger fondly in his blessing as his withered hands rested upon her brow.

She was indeed beautiful with a spiritual beauty as she rose from her knees and returned to her seat.

There were many who pretended afterward to have noticed that day an unearthly loveliness in her look and manner; but, on the other hand, many condemned, at the time, the glance with which she sought out Clarence Tracy, and seemed desirous to associate him in her mind with the feelings that imbued her countenance with its holy rapture.

He was in the next pew to hers; and during the sermon, she would sometimes turn without affectation, fixing her eyes for a second on his dark face, as if to assure herself that he was listening.

On Sunday she communed, and the Tuesday following was her wedding day.

Brightly, without an April shower, without a cloud upon its blue surface, shone the sky on Monday morning.

There was a busy hum through the house, and every one wore an important look. Mrs. Clarendon's voice sounded from every quarter—the wedding breakfast was upon her mind—and drawing-rooms which were to be inspected by daylight needed extra dusting and cleaning to satisfy her scrupulous demands.

Alicia had given up her apartment as a dressing-room for the bride. It was now fairly littered with costly feminine adornments, with bridal gifts, and with the bonnets and shawls of the bridemaids, who had come to "see the things" and to chatter.

How they rattled! Grace Meredith was seated on a table, swinging her little feet like pendulums, and talking at the top of her voice.

"What a glorious privilege to be an heiress!" she cried. "Oh, Nora, let's see that love of a mantilla! Point d'Alençon, I vow, as I am a Christian! Don't you wish you were an heiress, Sara?"

"No; I am quite contented to be as I am."

"Listen to her!" ejaculated Grace. "A stranger would suppose that sentiment emanated from a humbly tranquil spirit, but we know that it springs from perfect self-satisfaction. Well spoken, Sara. Now I honestly confess that I should like to change places with Lily."

"What a compliment to Mr. Tracy!" sneered Sara.

"Oh! I forgot the drawback. Excuse my candor, Leonora the Little; but were I a young lady of independent fortune, I should not be in such haste to divest myself of my *libre arbitre*. Not even the dignified devotion of a courtly Clarence should induce me to become a worthy wife. Commend me to Queen Elizabeth's policy. Reign like a man, and be singly powerful and powerfully single. How many hundreds of thousands per annum have you, Lily?" and "giddy Grace," as her companions called her, in allusion to her own fancy for alliteration, caught Miss Vere's skirt as she passed, and drew her caressingly toward her own perch.

"What a chatter-box!" said Lily; "and is this the way you mean to assist me? Choose me some pairs of dark gloves for country wear from that pile; and recollect that I don't receive those unlimited thousands until I marry."

"By the way, I did hear that if you should die before you are twenty-one, or before you marry, Mr. Clarendon is your heir. Is it true?"

"It is."

"And yet Mr. Clarendon consents to your early espousals. Virtuous, exemplary man!"

Lily laughed.

"And what is more," she said, "I believe my aunt rejoices in it. When I was quite a little girl, I used every now and then to hear her talk about the terrible responsibility. Do you recollect, Alicia, the summer after I came here—our first summer on Sullivan's Island—when I was seized one day with a desire to watch the fishermen drawing the seine? In my sun-bonnet I ran down to the beach, and, eager for their success, followed them in their course up the island. They were all very good to me, and let me watch the fish, and pick out a string of them for myself. They were negroes, so I was not afraid, and trudged along, talking to them about sharks, and porpoises, and stingarees. I had two hours of great enjoyment, and was brought home with a huge string of whiting by old Daddy Peter, to whom I had attached myself from the beginning, recognizing him as Maumer's husband. I found the household in great alarm. My uncle alternately kissed and scolded me, and my aunt would not look at the fish I offered her, but repeated very often, 'If Elizabeth had been drowned, people would have said we did it.' I could not understand this, but I never played truant again."

"Why, that is quite an adventure," said Grace.

"And one that greatly interests that seamstress," whispered Marguerite Melbourne.

In the corner of the room, partly concealed by the white drapery of the window, sat a young girl. On a low chair beside her was spread out the wedding dress, which was undergoing some trifling alteration. She had dropped the waist from her hands, and, with suspended thread and attentive attitude, had listened to Lily's little narrative. On perceiving the eyes of the group directed toward her, she resumed her sewing with a deep blush, which burned under her dark cheek.

"Who is that girl?" asked Grace, in a low voice.

"Betsey Ballou sent her to me this morning. I desired her to dispatch some careful hand from her workroom to rearrange the lace on the corsage of that dress."

"She is very pretty."

"For that color," said Sara, contemptuously.

"Hush!" Lily said, gently; "she will hear you."

"She is too pretty for a dressmaker," Grace pursued. "Don't let Mr. Tracy see her. He admires Spanish beauty, and she is very Spanish."

Sara's lip curled, and Lily said—but, low as her tone was, it reached the girl's ear—

"Clarence does not admire low-born beauty. I doubt if I could make him acknowledge that she is good-looking."

Then, crossing the room, she spoke kindly to the workwoman, who answered in a husky voice, and without raising her eyes to the fair and gentle being before her.

Gradually the young ladies took their leave, with many laughing exhortations to Lily not to be late on the following morning.

"And, above all, Lily, don't cry," pleaded Grace, who was the last to depart; "I am so prone to follow bad examples, that if you whimper I shall sob."

"I promise," said Lily; and, throwing her arms around Grace's neck, "Dear Grace," she continued, "if ever the time comes when I shall assist at a like ceremony for you, may your light but true heart be able to say with the sincerity that mine does, 'I love, and I honor my love. I am happy.'"

Tears sparkled in Grace's softened eyes.

"God bless you, dearest Lily."

The bride was left alone except the presence of the sewing-girl, who remained like a statue endowed with certain movements beneath the shadow of the muslin draperies.

Lily came and went between the inner and the outer room. She examined the contents of different drawers, opened an old desk, burned some letters in the empty grate, and remained long in contemplation before a miniature which the workwoman saw was the portrait of Clarence Tracy.

A balmy afternoon succeeded the early dinner which best suits our spring and summer weather.

I was driving into the city. A note from Lily Vere had brought me to town, to be present at her wedding, for the care of an invalid relative confined me at this time entirely to the country during the winter. With difficulty I procured permission to absent myself for a couple of days, and joyfully I flew to embrace the dear girl, whom I had not seen for more than two years.

I was thinking of her, and picturing to myself how she would look on the morrow in that costume which lends beauty often to those who do not own it, and whose graceful appointments are doubly charming when the wearer is young and lovely.

I examined the bouquet of orange blossoms which, destined for her, was carefully stored away in a corner of the carriage, and their perfume, aided by the delicious odor of the yellow jessamine which lined the hedges, combined to wrap me in a sort of Mohammedan paradise.

The horses jogged along, and I dreamed pleasant day-dreams, when I perceived, on the opposite side of the plank road, two equestrians, a lady and a gentleman.

He had just gathered for her, without dismounting, a cluster of jessamine. She placed them in the bosom of her riding-habit. Surely I know those long, abundant, silky, and most beautiful ringlets. A ray of sunlight shot athwart their shining meshes, and kissed the soft, bright cheek about which they played and sparkled. Yes, it was Lily.

"Lily!" I cried.

In a moment she recognized me. One bound of her horse, and she was at the carriage window.

"Dear Molly, is it indeed you? Let me come in."

Her companion lifted her from the saddle, and stood holding her reins and his, while she embraced me with fond delight. How warmly I returned her eager welcome! "Lily, pardon me, but you are beautiful."

"You are saucy," she said, blushing. "Clarence will not permit such flatteries—will you, Clarence? But you do not know him—how thoughtless of me! Clarence, I present you to my dear old friend, Miss Mary —, whom I take the liberty of calling Molly."

I gazed earnestly at the grave, haughty, well-dressed, dark gentleman who was playing groom to my darling, and who bowed to me with perfect grace. He was handsome in a severe style, with dignity enough to fill a throne, and a smile which he could render *suave* enough to ensnare a heart. I did not like his expression. His eye was not frank, his lips were too thin and too compressed.

Lily watched me, and I read in her face a desire to know my opinion. I meant to wait a little before I gave it.

"I have braved a good deal of displeasure to come to you, Lily; I am repaid in this welcome. How fortunate that we should meet on the road! for I scarcely hoped to see you except to-morrow. It would have been indiscreet to break in on Mrs. Clarendon this evening."

"By no means. Come to-night, Molly, and we shall have a long talk."

"Do not hesitate, Miss —," said Mr. Tracy. "*I* am forbidden the house. It will gratify my philanthropic spirit to know that if an unfortunate man is sent to Coventry, at least so agreeable a person as yourself will profit by my absence."

The friendly smile, the genial tone, the kind intention, made me ashamed of my first impression.

"Then I must not detain you now. Finish your ride; and after I have washed away the dust of travel, you will see me at Mr. Clarendon's."

Clarence Tracy placed her once more in the saddle; she kissed her hand to me with her sweet face turned over her shoulder; he raised his hat with courteous bend, and I watched them far, far in the distance, riding close together, the yellow jessamines showering about them, the oaks casting their lengthening shadows over them, and sunlight and brightness seeming to mark ahead the future pathway of Fortune's favorite children. Alas!

Twilight was deepening into night when Lily returned from her ride.

Beneath the overhanging balustrade, wreathed with vines, the lovers lingered and said good-by.

There was no moon, and Clarence urged that she might give him a farewell kiss.

"For shame!" said Lily; "here in the street?"

"Then at your own door—your garden door. It will be twelve mortal hours before I see you again. You might at least say good-by."

Lily protested, but, still protesting, moved round to the side entrance of the house, where the low flight of steps led to her apartments.

A figure, watching from the window, shrank back as the two approached.

"Good-night, my beloved."

"Good-night, my own love."

"This is our last parting."

"Yes."

"Lily, I begin to feel to-night that I have been too fortunate. What has that 'fickle jade' in store for me to counterbalance her gifts?"

"'We praise Thee, O God, we acknowledge Thee to be the Lord,'" chanted Lily, in a low, solemn voice. "Look above; carry your gratitude there, dearest."

"*Petite dévote*," said Clarence, affectionately; "you are a saint, and I expect you to convert me."

A servant came whistling past, and Lily hastily withdrew her hand from her lover's shoulder. He pressed the little palm to his lips, and with a low-murmured blessing left her.

She followed him with her calm, loving gaze till the closing clang of the iron gate, as it swung behind him, and the measured tread of his boot down the street announced his departure.

The light of a single candle upon her toilet showed her the sewing-girl seated upon the floor when she passed into her room.

The girl's head was buried in her hands.

"Are you ill?" asked Lily.

She raised her head.

"No; I believe I was asleep."

Her eyes flickered in the light.

"You were waiting to be paid for your work; I am sorry to have kept you so late."

"I do not mind it."

Lily searched for her purse, thinking, meanwhile, that it was imprudent of her maid to have left this stranger alone with so much of value.

The girl walked uneasily from the door to the dressing-table. Her fine, flexible figure and restless movements struck Lily's attention. She thought she looked unhappy, and her kind heart was ready with its sympathy.

"What is your name?" she inquired.

"Lorenza."

"Do you live alone?"

"Yes."

"You have friends?"

"I *had* one. He has left me."

"Ah!" said Lily, slightly coloring, and guessing the relationship of that friend, "I am sorry for you; but perhaps it is best in the end that this sorrow should come to you now."

Lorenza frowned, and turned aside her face, which worked convulsively.

"Will you give me a glass of water from the table yonder?"

While the girl went in search of it, Lily added a gold eagle to the sum due for her day's work, and wrapped the whole in a stray envelope.

There was a jingle of glasses, as if touched by a trembling hand, and some delay.

"Can you not find it?"

"Here it is."

Lorenza gave the tumbler into Lily's hand. Her dark eyes dilated, and fixed themselves with a strange, wild look upon Miss Vere. Twice she half extended her own hand to take back the fatal glass.

"Where is that perfume of almonds?" said Lily, carelessly. "Thank you;" and she drank off the water, for her ride had made her thirsty.

A shiver passed over her frame; a wild thought crossed her mind; she grasped vaguely in the air.

"Help! Clarence!" and Lily Vere fell dead upon the floor.

❧ CONCLUSION

My pen almost refuses to add one more line to this sad and simple story. How can I describe—why need I describe—the effects of this bitter blow?

Can you not see the crazed Lorenza flying from her victim, repenting of her crime, or, reckless and desperate, hurrying to her own death? Escape was easy. She passed through the garden unarrested; the Ashley River ran rippling near; one plunge—and her earthly troubles gave place to God's judgment.

We can only conjecture the interview, or believe in the imperfect testimony of Lily's maid, who listened a moment at the door before entering from the corridor.

She saw Lorenza dart wildly through the garden, and, shocked and alarmed at her mistress's fall, first sought to raise her, and then cried out for assistance.

They believed her in a swoon. Applications were made—remedies used—physicians consulted. Then came the fatal decision, pronounced with scientific certainty, "Poisoned by prussic acid."

Great God! the horror of that moment! Never shall my brain cease to picture the blank despair which followed those frightful words.

Dead! Lily, who but ten minutes previous stood, full of life and hope, in our midst!

A crowd gathered. They could not be kept out.

There, in that bridal chamber, with its pretty maidenly decorations, surrounded by all the thousand costly preparations for the approaching ceremony, wandered, wondered, suggested, rough men and careless speakers.

Glances were cast at Mr. Clarendon—whispers reached his ear.

He could not give himself up to his sorrow. "Justice"—"legal examination"—"black business," were murmured around.

Faces grew dark, and threats were uttered.

Suddenly a voice, loud, deep, dominant, filled the room.

"I command that these strangers withdraw," said Clarence Tracy.

Way was made for him; voices were hushed; the room was cleared.

"Justice shall be done," he continued; "look to me for it."

Not till this mob had been dismissed did he approach his bride. Not before them would he show his agony—agony not yet complete.

There she lay, white and beautiful, his faded jessamines still perfuming her modest breast, her blue eyes closed, her snowy hands drooping at either side.

What a groan escaped him as, on his knees, he took one of those nerveless hands, and pressed it wildly, convulsively to his lips, his heart, his brow!

Mr. Clarendon, whose honest face writhed with mental pain, grasped his shoulder kindly.

"Unhand me!" cried Clarence, fiercely. "By whom has this foul deed been done?"

"Do *you* suspect me, Tracy?"

"What enemy had she—so young, so kind, so true? Who would have injured her but the man who profits by her early death?"

William Clarendon seized Clarence.

"Were it not for her who lies there in her sweet purity, and whose fond heart beat only for you, I should force your villainous words down your own cowardly throat."

"William—my son—respect a sorrow which equals our own. Clarence, I forgive you. I did but wish to show you this paper, to prove to you that her last thoughts were with you. We found this at her feet. Lily—my darling!"

Clarence Tracy took the paper; he glanced at it; an unspeakable horror glazed his eyes; he trembled, and clutched my dress as I stood beside him.

"Just God!" burst from his parched lips.

The paper fluttered and fell. I raised it.

"Expect me, dearest L., at nine o'clock. C."

He turned and staggered toward the door.

This slip of paper gave the clew to the dark history.

Let me do justice to a man whose very name I abhor, but whose sins were heavily punished.

Clarence Tracy spared no pains to exonerate Mr. Clarendon. That very night, much as the effort must have cost him, he revealed the truth. He did not seek to palliate his own course. He knew he had a partisan in every man who thinks that a mistress is an amiable peccadillo.

The body of Lorenza was found and identified. Whether the unhappy creature bought the poison at first for herself, and afterward was tempted to destroy an innocent life whose last act was one of kindness to her, or whether, in proposing to work for Miss Vere, she did but wish to examine at her leisure the beauty of her unconscious rival, who can tell?

A heavy gloom overspread the city. The sound of tolling bells, the shocked and grave faces, the universal sadness, seemed to betoken no common calamity.

A silent and respectful crowd thronged the gate and street of that late joyous house.

Many asked permission to look once more at the beautiful girl whose gentle dignity and kind demeanor had made her appearance familiar to half the town.

Softly reposing on her last pillow, as if Death had respected such mournful loveliness, she remained beautiful till she was borne to her grave.

I can not describe the desolation of her adopted family, nor the overwhelming grief of those gay girls who were to have accompanied her to the altar.

Even Sara Purvis, who had not loved her cousin, remained in mute sorrow at Lily's side, the large tears rolling unchecked down her pale cheek, and her frame convulsed with inward emotion. She had always heretofore despised my insignificance; this day she turned to me, and her white lips murmured,

"May she pray for us. She was an angel before God took her away."

The glorious sunshine streamed down upon the nodding plumes of the hearse, and lit up the silver plate which bore the name and age of Elizabeth Vere. As we passed from her apartment, Clarence Tracy suddenly appeared and placed himself authoritatively at the head of her coffin.

The six unmarried men who supported this sad shell made room for him.

He was so haggard, so worn, so aged in a single day that no one could refuse him the privilege.

We laid her beside her father and mother, and as the clergyman sprinkled the earth upon her coffin, I let drop upon it, bedewed with tears, her bridal bouquet.

The gardener had sent it, ignorant of the tragedy, and there, in the midst of its fresh and tender blossoms, was the withered bud which, in a moment of playful coquetry, she had desired should form its central ornament.

What an emblem of the truth!

Mrs. Clarendon had waved it aside with horror, but I preserved it.

"She shall have it," I said; "let her every wish be fulfilled."

Oh the start, the mighty thrill which shook her bridegroom as these flowers fell upon that resounding coffin!

I told you that this was no spirit-stirring tale; you may close the volume and be weary; it is but a monument raised, a pillar dedicated to one who was too perfect for this earth.

I do not mourn for her now; I say, in her own words, singularly prophetic,

"Better so—better so; better to have died believing him entirely true, leaving with him the sweet recollections of her sorrowful fate, her beauty untouched by care or time, dying through his unconscious means, than live to have him again desert her for the flattering smiles of unworthy women."

Clarence Tracy left Charleston. He was restless here, and the world looked coldly on him. I think they would have warmed up had they known that Mr. Clarendon insisted upon his receiving the fortune settled upon him by Lily. He refused it, and went back to Europe a miserable if not a repentant man.

Mr. Clarendon wrote kindly to him. "I can not forget," he said to his wife, "that Lily's heart was bound up in him. I dream constantly of her. Her face is reproachful if I seem to blame him. He suffers; we, who are her representatives, must console him for her sake, however much I desire never to be thrown with him again."

Will you be surprised to hear that, not long since, the Purvises went to Italy for Sara's health, and that we saw in the papers the marriage at Florence of Henry Clarence Tracy to Sara, second daughter of George Purvis, Esq.?

Nothing amazes me nowadays. They have a fine hotel in Paris. Mrs. Tracy has her Opera-box, and Mr. Tracy his horses. Of course, you will understand that Mr. Clarendon had forced him to receive his *rightful* portion of Andrew Vere's estate.

Alicia is not yet married. She is very much courted, and will probably be long in making her choice. William is the husband of Grace Meredith.

Mrs. Archibald Langdon is still the proud and extravagant beauty who rules supreme in her own circle. I have heard that her attacks of the heart become more frequent and dangerous, but she disregards them, and dislikes to hear them spoken of.

A month ago I assisted at an interesting and most touching ceremony.

We were at Chicora Hall. The grass was green and dewy, the flowers grew in such profuse luxuriance that the osier baskets could scarce contain them, the mocking-birds kept up an incessant concert, the old oaks, stately and venerable, stretched out their gray-draped arms, and nothing in nature seemed to say,

"Let us be sad."

But a mournful procession moved with regular tread from the very door whence issued the May-party, across the lawn to the Royal Oak.

The throne was displaced, and a marble statue now occupies the site.

It is very like. The sculptor has almost satisfied us. She stands with upward gaze, and with her hands folded upon her bosom, the attitude of hope and resignation. The graceful sweep of her robes and the perfect simplicity of the whole render it a master-piece. At her feet lies a broken lily;

the stem is firm and the flower unwithered, but a serpent has stricken it down, and now escapes with hissing tongue, crouching near her skirts.

On the tablet you read,

LILY,

Aged seventeen years, eleven months, and
twenty-eight days.
Spotless, innocent, and beautiful, she died too soon
for those she leaves behind; but in our
hearts she lives always.

The rough workmen stood aside to let us draw near. We laid wreaths upon the pedestal, and prayers went up from every sorrowful breast.

I thank you for your patience, for your sympathy, if you have followed me through these many pages.

I lay down my pen, and wish you farewell.

THE END

Gerald Gray's Wife

BY SUSAN PETIGRU KING

A tall, pale, thin woman; she is not very ugly, and she is by no means pretty. Her eyes are large and dark, with thick, long, black lashes, and the shape of her mouth is graceful and classic. These are her only beauties. Even these are only perceived when you study her closely, for the eyes are so stony in their usual expression, so cold, so self-concentrated apparently, so defiant, and so distrustful, and the lips have a way of setting themselves firmly together, from which they rarely relax into the smile which can diffuse a charm over the plain, rigid face. She asks and takes nothing from her dress to redeem her lack of good looks. Her father requires that she should wear rich stuffs, fine laces, handsome jewels. She chooses that she should be a parade for his wealth, just as his houses, and equipages, and plate, and hot-houses are constantly displayed; so to-day on this wild, sandy beach, she wears a costly muslin gown, each flounce heavy with rare mechlin, and about her thin, sun-burnt wrists are great gold bracelets, and in her ears two pearls are hung, with diamonds encircling them, of which, when her father tossed them in her lap, on her last birthday, he said:

"Here, my girl; these cost a cool three thousand."

But the rich muslin is carelessly put on, and the shawl she has wrapped about her (for the evening grows chilly,) is a worn old tarltan plaid thrown over her head, and gathered up about her throat in dowdy folds, and she has shoved the bracelets out of sight, far up her arms, and the pure, lustrous pearls, which would have been so beautiful touching a snowy throat, I wot of, only make her's browner. So, to see her pacing along this strip of ocean-beaten land, with low dark clouds veiling the setting sun, the white sea-birds skimming the water crests of the angry waves, and a sullen wind murmuring hoarsely of the storm to come, you might have thought this solitary, sallow, stern woman was some desolate wayfarer, some miserable waif, and stray on Life's ocean, and not Ruth Desborough, the richest and most courted heiress in the whole State.

Ruth Desborough's mother died when she was still a child. She was a gentle, feeble woman, who always seemed to stand in awe of all the luxury which her husband heaped about her. She wore her jewels as if she were afraid of them; Ruth put on hers as if she were ashamed of them. Mrs. Desborough thought wealth a great and glorious thing—something too grand for her to enjoy—she, who had begun life as a nursery governess, and been wooed and won by the stout, jolly, purse-proud Jacob Desborough, long before he made his tremendous speculations, passed for a madman, lowered on the brink of ruin, and then set down his large feet firmly as a *millionaire.*

Of course, Jacob Desborough loved his only child. He saw she was not handsome nor stylish, but she was dutiful to him and proud to all the world. He liked the way she carried herself to the "a-*ris*-tocrats" as he called his neighbors. He rubbed his huge, red hands, and chuckled when she looked over the heads of the Misses Seymours, and Cecil, and Clare—her companions and *friends,* as such acquaintances are called—and when saucy, smiling, sneering Mrs. Berners asked one day at dinner if the two pictures over the plate-laden sideboard were "family portraits"—they were dame and cavalier in silk and satin, rouge and powder—Ruth fixed her unquailing eyes on the pretty questioner and said calmly:

"Scarcely. Papa is an orphan house boy, and my mother's parents kept a little corner shop. Those portraits were bought for a song, at an auction lately. Their owner was a gambler and a swindler, came to grief, and had to sell his own father and mother. His name was Cressingham."

Mrs. Berners dropped her eye glass, and colored scarlet. It was but three years since she used to write herself "Rosaline Cressingham." She had not recognized her own grand parents, disposed of by her own uncle.

"Why, you are a Cressingham," said another guest, as obtuse as some people can be, while the rest of the party were aghast.

"I beg your pardon for my allusion," said Ruth, with stately courtesy, and changed the conversation.

Ruth was now twenty-six years of age. She had had many offers of marriage—but, although more than one of her suitors would have readily been accepted for her by her father, she had never wavered for one moment.

I often have thought the man bold who dared to address Ruth Desborough. I have often wondered how they went about it. I think all the declarations must have been written ones. I cannot imagine a person of ordinary courage and daring to sit or stand before that steel-faced woman and make pretty speeches—speeches that, spoken, or on paper, always meant to her mind—"you are very rich, and I want your money, so I'll take you."

That, of course, was the curse of her life; there was the secret source of bitter waters that, from earliest childhood, had sprung up within her, and forcing its way into every vein, had mingled each throb of her heart with its acrid tide. From infancy her ears had been made familiar with the idea. Her father, in the kindly coarseness of his nature, constantly said:

"You mayn't be as pretty nor as smart as some girls, but I'll be hanged if you can't buy as good a husband as the best of them."

Her husband was to be bought! As a child the idea amused and pleased her. Her dolls were bought for her. French dolls, with painted cheeks and elaborately dressed hair, tiny corsets, and whole suits of clothes; English dolls, just like real babies, with their fat dimpled necks and infant heads turned on one side, their soft rings of flaxen hair, (not wigs,) and their long robes and caps; then when she grew up, instead of dolls, her papa would buy her a husband—a "true-for-true" husband—yes he would. So she confidentially said one day to one of her playmates, and this girl, barely ten years of age, answered scornfully:

"Buy a husband, indeed! I would not have a bought husband."

"Why?"

"Because I heard my mamma say that love can't be bought; and when I grow up and get married I want to be loved," and the little precocious wife tossed her little nose in the air.

Ruth thought over this remark, and soon she went gravely to her father and repeated it.

Mr. Desborough laughed heartily, and patted her head, and told the story after dinner to his two guests, and they laughed, and Ruth, who was eating grapes at her papa's side, grew angry and sullen, and lifted her large dark eyes from her plate, and looked seriously at both of her father's old comrades, and walked out of the room.

From that day the word "husband" never escaped the child's lips. When Mr. Desborough jested, as he had always done on the subject, she kept a sort of wounded silence; and when she was eighteen, and a ball of great magnificence proclaimed the fact that she was now about to enter the market to buy, and not to be bought, her resolution was taken.

She would live and die Ruth Desborough. No purchased love for her.

Since even her own father deemed her unworthy to inspire a passion, she would endure no sweet words, to be paid for in dollars and cents; no lover's vows looking for return in bank stock; no soft glances to match her diamonds.

And the canker of this thought did not extend alone to her views of a wooer's motives. All mankind gradually came under the same leprosy.

She did not reject attentions from men or women, but she decided, with unflinching severity, that every word or action was given to the heiress, not the woman. And what she took she paid back scrupulously. To society she extended an unbounded hospitality. She spared no pains that money could bring about to entertain those who entertained her.

On her more familiar acquaintances—friends, she had none—she lavished gifts, seeking carefully to choose what was pleasantest to receive; not as her father would have done, with loud voiced disclosure of his reasons for offering, letting himself be guided by the cost in proportion to the intention. No; but with an inborn delicacy of thought and manner, which often won for her affection and respect—unuttered half the time—for few cared to speak of affection, or respect, or interest, to the cold, reserved, repellent Miss Desborough.

Such were her antecedents. Such was the morbid, unhealthy condition of her mind. No wonder she daily grew less and less sociable to herself and to the world. No wonder that on this evening, when she was restlessly yet earnestly watching the sea and sky, she felt that a dreary scene like this better suited her than the gay party she had left.

Ruth walked on and on. Fate seemed to lead her, and she was following it blindly. The few houses, scattered at unequal distances along the beach, were all far behind her. The low sand hills were getting higher and higher, and although she did not heed it, the tide was rising rapidly.

Suddenly she paused; a boat was making its way through the breakers, crossing from an opposite island. The occupants were evidently trying to land just in front of her. Curiosity caused her to stay and watch it, it looked to be in such danger. Two negroes were laboring at the oars; at the stern a young man held the rudder. The spray dashed over them again and again; now they were on the top of the highest wave—it would surely beach them; but as it receded it carried back the boat, to be tossed to and fro, and to rise again as before.

At length the work was accomplished, and the little bark lay almost "high and dry." The helmsman leaped on shore, gun in hand, and gave his directions in a low, clear, rapid voice to his servants. They were short.

"Drag up the boat beyond high water mark, and get home before the storm if you can. Take my gun, one of you."

Then he turned and lifted his hat to Ruth.

"Excuse the liberty I take, madam, but it is a wild night for a lady to be abroad; can I offer my escort to your house? My name is Gerald Gray."

"Thank you," Ruth said, drawing back with surprise, and in her measured, haughty, unmoved tone, "I am not far from my home, and it is not yet night."

"Then," said the stranger, smiling, "you must live with the surf-skimmers in the sand, because there is no habitable roof nearer than a mile and a half, to my certain knowledge. There is a regular equinoctial gale coming on, with every dangerous accessory, the moon rises in an hour, but two days past its full, and this is a springtide. Jack! Jim!" he continued, calling to his boatmen, "come on and keep near us. This lady may need your care as well as mine presently."

"You wish to frighten me," said Ruth, "but now I see that I am further from home than I thought. I do not know how I have managed to wander so far without knowing it."

"Nothing easier when there are no especial landmarks to strike your attention. I have been after birds on Crane Island, intending to return through the back creek to take the last boat to the city, but I wounded a magnificent white crane, it got off, we followed, lost it after all, and a great deal of time with it, so I thought it best to cross over here and trust to my legs. I don't like water in a storm. Any strip of land is better, and a man who has just traversed half Europe on foot must not be daunted by a mile or two of sea beach."

Miss Desborough made no answer. She thought her self-imposed companion was too free and easy. Who was he? She had never heard of Gerald Gray. In this dim light his outline of feature was graceful and gentlemanly, but might not his offers of service, and his persistence in keeping by her side, be more the pushing forwardness of some low bred adventurer, than the genuine politeness and kindness of some well born stranger, who would protect her in spite of herself?

She had no *fear*. In the region where she lived such a crime as robbing her or insulting her would have been, is almost unheard of. But she was not disposed to encourage these attentions, and she bit her lips with worried indignation at her own folly in walking so far and in stopping to watch the boat, which had brought on her this acquaintance.

"Do you see that cloud?" Mr. Gray said, abruptly. "It travels faster than we can. When it bursts—*gare!* The wind is rising every moment. If you were under shelter I should enjoy this. By Jove! see that wave."

He caught her in his arms just in time. The huge billow broke a second later over the point of her last footsteps. The wind was wildly tossing about her shawl, and as he set her down again he drew the cords of the plaid together.

"Have you a pin?" he enquired, as naturally and familiarly as if they were on the best terms.

Ruth shook her head; she was getting frightened; she tried to help herself, and dragged the shawl hastily from him. The strong Northeast wind seized it as if it had been a feather, whirled it from her hands, and, a moment more, the old tarltan would have been careering over the sea. Gerald caught it.

"Look at that; let me arrange it. It will be a shark's blanket before long if you don't take care."

Tenderly and gently he folded the shawl about her head and shoulders. "Give me your brooch; that will do to fasten it."

Ruth silently gave him her brooch; he glanced at the pin to see if it was firm, stuck it in, and then resolutely drew her arm through his.

"We are losing time, and time is precious. I am sorry to hurry you so, but indeed we *must* make haste. This *breeze* will take you off your feet if it keeps on at this rate. Don't hesitate to lean on me; and if you get very tired I will try another plan."

He was silent for a while after this, but, as the storm rapidly increased in its might, he glanced uneasily once or twice around him, and called to his servants to keep close. The sand was scudding before the breath of the blast stinging their feet and faces; the angry clouds almost seemed to touch their heads—so low, and dark, and thick, and close they gathered; the black waves lashed themselves furiously into whitest foam, and a deep, distant, sullen roar sounded like underground thunder.

"What *is* that noise?" asked Ruth; "it frightens me more than anything else."

"It is the water coming over the bar—the ground-swell. It *has* a mysterious sound, and it means mischief. But we are nearing the settlement now. I have not the honor of knowing you—where shall I take you?"

What made Ruth unwilling to tell her name?—anxious to remain unknown as the heiress of the great Desborough fortune? and what made her pleased to be able to answer in such a way that she retained her incognita?

"We shall pass the house presently."

She was very, very weary. Had it not been for his support, she would have fallen to the ground long before.

Mr. Gray felt the arm which had at first reluctantly and lightly rested on his, gradually leaning heavily; then, in spite of herself, her whole figure drooped upon his shoulders—she tried to keep up, tried to walk firmly; her skirts incommoded her; each flounce seemed weighted with lead, not lace; the wind fought her like a strong enemy—she sighed and almost gave up. "I—I—can't," she panted.

"Here it comes!" cried her companion.

Down poured the rain in sheets—in floods, and yet unconquered, the fierce wind drove it ahead, refusing to be stilled by even a deluge.

Mr. Gray passed his arm around Ruth's waist as he spoke, and carrying rather than supporting her, he encouraged her and soothed her terrors, as if she had been a frightened child.

"This is the house. We stop here."

It was a small unpromising mansion. Mr. Gray dashed up the steps into the piazza.

"Knock, Jim, knock like the Devil. The lady is fainting."

"No I am not," said Ruth. "I feel so glad to get here."

The door opened, and a grave old woman's face peeped over the head of the servant, who tried to close it again, when he found that the wind was affecting an entrance.

"Oh Ruth, Ruth," cried the old woman, "what is this? Aint you with—?"

"Hush," interrupted Ruth, "I left them and went to walk—very foolishly. Mr. Gray, wont you—?"

He was gone. She ran down the steps after him—caught him.

"Surely," she said, "you will go no farther in this storm. I believe I owe my life to you. Come in. I can scarsely speak."

She was gasping in the rain-tempest. Her voice could hardly be heard in the crash, and roar, and rush.

"Your servants too. Come in for Heaven's sake."

At last they were housed, at least for the time, but every gust seemed to threaten the wooden roof and walls with instant destruction.

"My cousin, Mrs. Price, Mr. Gray," said Ruth, introducing him.

The old lady courtesied. She was evidently no "high born hostess." She bustled about noisily.

"Did you get wet, Ruth? Do be careful. What will your pa say? Where did the gentleman meet you?"

"Pray be quiet, cousin Frances; you are louder than the storm. What a fusser you are." Ruth's voice was kinder than her words. "Make Thomas show Mr. Gray to a room—come with me first. Don't mention my name or papa's," she whispered as they got into the entry. "See that Mr. Gray has the use of all those antique suits of your absent boys, that you keep so thoroughly brushed and aired. Look after his servant; get some brandy—papa's best— and don't fidget me to death. Supper as soon as possible."

"Oh, yes, dear Ruth—but such a storm—and you are dripping wet, and I can't find my keys—. Oh, here they are. And why didn't you stay at Mrs. Clares'? And I believe the kitchen is under water."

Ruth was gone. She evidently had the habit of never listening to good Mrs. Price, who pattered away now on her different errands, talking incessantly.

CHAPTER II

In a half hour more, Ruth re-entered the parlor to which her new acquaintance had likewise just returned. She had taken off her jewels and wore a plain, darkish dress. Her abundant hair was put back carelessly as usual from her broad, full forehead.

A lamp was lighted, and stood upon a small table in the corner. Mr. Gray was advancing towards it, evidently in search of one of the numerous volumes which lay scattered beneath the light. Ruth spoke and he bowed. For the first time she saw him distinctly. Singularly handsome was the face that met hers—a straight Greek profile; clustering dark auburn hair; eyes so intensely blue that they seemed almost black; a proud, sweet mouth— feminine in its curves, color, and ripeness, but with a rare strength shown when it ceased to smile, and which disclosed, when the full lips parted, teeth, white, small, and even. The figure was slight, well made, nervous—the attitudes, graceful and unstudied. He had changed his clothes, and said, laughingly, to Ruth, as she greeted him:

"You see I have obeyed your orders as conveyed through your servant. I did not hesitate to don these respectable habiliments, when he said, 'Miss Ruth say you *must.*'"

"They are old-fashioned, but better than the newer ones which have passed through what we did. What do you think of the night?"

"It and the storm are just begun. Are you frightened yet? Pray don't attempt to open that window."

"Are we in danger here?" she asked.

"Shall I answer candidly?"

"Always, if one answers at all, it should be candidly."

"Then, I think we may be after a while, if the wind continues to rise with the tide."

At this moment the parlor door burst open, and a blast shook the house from rafters to foundation. In rushed Mrs. Price, followed by some terrified domestics.

"Oh, Ruth, the kitchen is gone. I just got out in time. The sea is upon us. Let us go."

"Where?"

"To the Fort."

Ruth looked at Mr. Gray. He answered her glance.

"If you wish to go, certainly. So far, I see no reason for removing. No doubt the Fort is already filled with people; if we can stand it here, you will be more comfortable."

"We wont go, cousin Frances, just yet."

"You can look out from that Southwest window—it is comparatively calm from that quarter. Would you like to do so?"

Ruth followed him. What a sight met her view! She had been conscious all this time that the house was rocking, the wind whistling through the venetian blinds of the piazza, and that a deafening, dull, continuous roar of mingled wave and wind never ceased; but she was quite unprepared for the grand and fearful spectacle before her.

The Island was at its narrowest width just beyond their house in the direction from which she looked. Billows, higher than she had ever dreamed the storm-god could heave them, now met from North and South across this space. Great logs of timber were whirled like straws in the incessant dash. The wind howled like a living thing, maddened with rage and pain; the rain had ceased; the sky was one unbroken plain of sullen, grey hue—such a color as a light would give if veiled by a thick cloth, which subdued, but did not extinguish. The full moon was behind that dark canopy, helpless to disengage herself.

A heavy "wind" every now and then told when the mighty force of the waters drove a piece of timber, like a battering ram, against the foundations of the house.

Ruth shuddered, and yet was fascinated by the angry majesty of the tempest.

Here and there a straggling group was seen in the space above, where the waters met, huddled together for safety, striving to breast the wind.

"Are they trying to cross to the Fort? Will they be able? Good God! what madness!"

"Not so much as you think. It is not deep there; the power of the waves is almost spent before they reach that point. To us it looks worse than it really is. If our piazza goes, and if these logs keep on pounding away at us as if they owed us some personal grudge, we must take up our line of march to that very spot. This is getting too sublime."

"Don't jest," said Ruth, gravely.

"Are you alarmed?"

"Yes, for the first time in my life. I have never felt powerless and dependent till this night. But for you—"

She paused, and caught his arm. The house fairly reeled, so tremendous was the blow dealt by one of those drifting, merciless timbers.

"We had better go," said Mr. Gray, emphatically and calmly. "If you have any valuables here, put them up in as small a bulk as possible. Don't be more frightened than you can help. Believe me, we will not be in absolute danger. Keep your courage—"

A wailing cry interrupted him. Mrs. Price came, weeping, in. "Oh, let's go; I can't stay here. Ruth, do you want to murder me?"

"We are going. Summon the servants. How many have you? Are these all?" A huddled group of terrified negroes were clustered in the entry. "Jack, Jim, no nonsense now. Jack, hold this lady's arm firmly when we start," he pointed to Mrs. Price; "and if you let her go, you may as well follow her. If there are any trifles here that you prize, secure them at once." He spoke to Ruth. "Get your thickest and least cumbrous wraps, and be quick, please."

In ten minutes they were ready. A package of silver-ware was tied up by Mrs. Price, with trembling hands, and she was preparing to move off, dropping spoons and forks at every step, as if she were planting them in view of a future crop.

Gerald Gray directed a halt; had them picked up, tightly secured, and put them in Jim's keeping.

"Oh, Ruth," whispered Mrs. Price, in the midst of her terror, "your pa's heaviest English silver—and who's this gentleman? and mayn't the boy run off with them?"

"Cousin Frances, you are too absurd," said Ruth, sharply. "Stay behind, and take care of the spoons if you wish. We are ready," she added, turning to Mr. Gray, and giving him a small square box; he slipped it in the pocket of Tom Price's overcoat, which he had likewise been obliged to appropriate to his own use.

"Now, we must keep together as closely as possible—walking in a body so as to present as large and solid a surface to the wind as we can manage. I will lead the way with you," to Ruth. "You are my charge. Mrs. Price, don't be frightened. Jack is strong and courageous. You, my man," addressing one of

Ruth's servants, "pick up that child; is it yours? wrap that blanket over head and all. Now forward, and wait till I put out the light in the parlor, and we will close the back door as firmly as we can."

Perfectly cool and deliberate, Mr. Gray inspired his little party with some courage and energy.

Carrying a lantern—which the wind immediately put out, and he then abandoned—his right arm firmly wrapped around Ruth's waist, they left the house.

"Keep close—no straggling. This way." His voice sounded clear and strong, and cheering in the wild whirl of desolation and comparative danger. The water was more than ankle-deep where they started, for the huge waves were breaking, as had been shown, upon the very steps of the house in front. It was very hard to keep one's feet; twice they had to stop to pick up Ruth's maid, who keeled over from sheer fright; "the wind talked too strong to her," she said.

As they neared the most dangerous portion of their journey, the water widening up to them to close with its new ally from the back creek, Gerald spoke almost tenderly to his drooping companion. She clung to him with ever growing confidence.

Fate favored them—or a kind Providence rather—by causing a lull just then, in the sweep of the blast. And yet, perhaps, the day was coming when Ruth would rather that every element had conspired at that moment to drag her into the mighty flood, and carry her a dead and drifting corpse far away to the great ocean, whose white waves lashed the shore!

But this was not to be. Safely they forded the perilous path, and safely they passed under the archway of the Fort, to be welcomed by crowds of acquaintances, who were ahead of them in seeking shelter. Everybody was so anxious about Miss Desborough; everybody was so glad to see her; everybody had thought of going in search of her. Ruth stood pale, and cold and silent, as usual, in the midst of this storm of words which she thought more unbearable than the one without. Mr. Gray had left her to see after some possible accommodations.

The barracks were filled almost to suffocation. The officers and their wives courteously tendered their hospitality, which was necessarily limited. The beds were given up to as many invalids and children as could be accommodated. People wandered about laughing and chatting. There was, as yet, no accident to cause gloom. Within the low, thick walls of the Fort, they defied the tempests, and it was more like an informal, impromptu picnic, or maroon, than a storm-wrecked party.

Phyllis Clare, a young lady of the highest fashion and spirits, soon dashed up to Ruth, with her petticoats pinned above her trim ankles, and her brown curls dishevelled most becomingly.

"Dear, dear Miss Desborough!" she exclaimed, seizing both of Ruth's hands, how alarmed we have been for you! Cissy and I nearly cried because papa would not let us go round by your house. He said that he was sure you were here already."

"Oh, yes," put in Cissy, "such a time we had; Phyl and I wanted to bring all our things. I have had just had such a love of a dress made, with a baby-waist, so becoming; not like most baby-waists, but a pointed band coming up like a stomacher; it just suits my figure—you know I am so full, ordinary baby-waists don't become me—and this is a choice silk of that delicate peach color; but papa wouldn't hear of it, and, now, robbers may get into the house and carry off every atom of our clothes. That peach color doesn't do for everybody, for, although I am brown, my skin is so clear,"—and Cissy passed her plump white hand over her lovely face, where if ever "milk and roses," "strawberries and cream," found their proper simile, it was there. She was beautiful with that beauty of flesh, and blood, and silkness, which men find so attractive; there were soft dark eyes, and red lips, and soft brown hair, and soft white shoulders, and soft round arms; indeed she was very soft within and without!

She looked so femininely gentle, too, beside Ruth's tall, angular figure, and stern, cold, pale face. Phyllis had more sense and less beauty; she went for style, grace and dash. Interrupting, now, Cecilia's flow of half-lisped words, she offered that Ruth should come and join their party; "all of *us* are at the other end of the piazza. There are some queer customers here." "I'm sure," in a loud whisper, "that's our butcher, who eats the largest half of his own beef. And that's Madame Butcheress, I suppose, talking to him."

"That's my cousin, Mrs. Price," said Ruth, with a grim smile.

"Dear! dear! so it is. But she is very eccentric, I suppose, and likes to—."

"She is a very humble person, as are all my family," said Ruth. "I come and board with her so as to help her live. Perhaps the butcher is my relation, too. I have a great many poor relations, who, strange to say, never thrust their attentions nor their society upon me, although *they* would have a right to do so."

Phyllis Clare colored; the stroke was too palpable, and even Ruth seemed to regret her unnecessary harshness.

"But, as cousin Frances is so taken up with the butcher's bovine confidences, I am more at leisure to go with you, only—," here she paused hesitating, "only—there is a gentleman—." She turned to look for Mr. Gray. He was unpacking a basket just behind him.

"Looking for me?" he asked. "Here am I, getting out some biscuits for a little shaver who is crying from hunger, not having, I presume, tasted one mouthful since his supper, two hours ago—poor, starved thing! Capital old lady, Mrs. Price! In spite of her terror she has put up provender enough in this champagne hamper to last us a week. How I do like a thoughtful woman of the Mrs. John Gilpin stamp! Here, young man, stifle your cries with that," and tossing a handful of wine-crackers to the child, and receiving a smile and word of thanks from its gratified mother. Mr. Gray rapidly uttered all this, rose from his seat, and presented his handsome face to the astonished gaze of the Misses Clare.

"Gerald!"

"Phyllis!"

"Gerald!"

"Cissy!"

"Where on earth do you come from?" asked both ladies.

"Recently from the hospitable, but at present dangerous, mansion of Mr. Price—just before that from Crane Island, where I went to shoot a white crane to make a fan for Cissy."

"Nonsense," pouted Cissy.

"Tell us the truth," said Phyllis.

"Truth to a woman, dear Phyl! Little ladies like you don't wish men to tell the truth to them; and even if they do hear it, they don't believe it, as, for example, now."

"And why did you not come to dinner today? Miss Desborough dined with us; but I suppose you desired to make her acquaintance without our help."

"Miss Desborough can dine where she pleases, and, as for making her acquaintance, that's partly as I please, and I have not made up my mind about it; heiresses are not to my taste."

"What?" questioned Phyllis, with her eyes and her mouth rounded into surprise, while Cecilia exclaimed, "mercy, me!"

Ruth had very soon recovered from *her* surprise. So Gerald Gray was some connection or intimate of the Clares. This was the nephew probably, whose absence at dinner pompous Mr. Clare regretted. If his name was mentioned, it had escaped her memory or only grazed her hearing. She stood quietly by, during the first exchanged sentences, then, when Gerald uttered his doubtful remarks about her, she smiled faintly, and immediately said:

"*I* am Miss Desborough." She had no idea of making a mystery of her identity, or rather of letting the Clares suppose she had done so.

Mr. Gray started, laughed merrily, and took off Tom Price's hat with a low bow.

"A thousand thanks for the introduction, and a thousand pardons for the apparently saucy speech just now."

Ruth briefly told her story. "After I left your house, Miss Clare, instead of going home, I fancied a solitary walk would do my head more good than any other repose. I never saw the storm coming—walked nearly to the end of the Island, and, fortunately met this gentleman, who, without knowing me, most kindly brought me back. To him I owe, most probably,—," detesting all expressions of sentiment, Ruth stopped, and "locked his lips." Phyllis was warmly delighted, and Cissy said, with just a shade of pettishness, "Very romantic indeed."

Then the conversation turned into other channels, and they discussed the storm, which was still, of course, a first object of interest. Ruth was not more communicative nor demonstrative than usual. The high wind could not blow away her reserve, nor the high tide wash a more genial spirit into her manner. It must take more than an outward tempest to shake her serenity. Nevertheless, she joined the aristocratic group of the Southwest corner of the staunch old Fort, where some played cards, some *talked* of reading prayers, and a few desperately tried to go to sleep, sitting bold-upright while the lamps swung overhead from their iron chains.

🦑 CHAPTER III

There was a good deal to see, a good deal to amuse. A pretty widow, lively and full of spirits, put her two little boys on a mattress with seven others; charged them to be quiet, and then establishing herself in the piazza, never ceased talking from that time till she went home the next day. She flirted, she jested, she ate sandwiches, she prescribed for one woman's sick child, and put another mother's restless infant to sleep. She sang a gay song in an undertone to her group of admirers, and left them to tie up somebody's head with vinegar; nothing came amiss to her, and her consoling words and light step were encouraging to the most despondent.

Then there were anxious wives sending after careless husbands, who would come, listen to all the "I wish you would see about so and so's;" reply readily, "yes, my dear—certainly," and walk off to resume the hand at whist, from which they had been torn.

Gerald Gray had a quick eye for the ludicrous and pleasant way of telling what he saw. He pointed out many things, and told many things to Ruth which made the long night pass more quickly than she could have supposed possible. Then, so singular had been their meeting, so curious its results, that an intimacy sprang up which was stronger than any Ruth had ever owned for mortal being. There was no time to pause, to consider. Gerald's manners were so high-bred, and yet so easy, he had overleaped all the barriers erected between herself and the world at large. Before her watch told her it was twelve o'clock on that memorable night, her acquaintance of six hours' date knew her better than those who had visited her for twenty-six years. And then he possessed one attraction, one attribute; he held one trump that must command the game. He had rendered her a service, a service of vital importance, without knowing her.

Dispossessed of all the prestige of that wealth she held so cheap, and which all others deemed her sole possession, he had come to her relief; she had seen in his eyes, his bold, beautiful eyes, that *he* did not think her displeasing or repulsive. He had met a plain, quiet woman, unconscious of danger and unprotected; he had come to her assistance; resisted her attempt to get out of his way, and had rescued her from her perilous position. True, any gentleman might and would have done that, but he had done more. However slight the indications, they were clear to her—his manner almost immediately had shown a nearer interest than that produced by the circumstances of the case. Ruth would have scorned the idea that she fancied "love at first sight" had taken possession of this handsome Gerald Gray for her, and, yet, there had been something in his manner; something vague, but meaning in his tone. In a word, he had understood her, he had established between themselves a kind of free-masonry, an electric chain of unspoken thoughts, strange, new, and not yet analyzed by the stern novice. Its charm was great and subtle; its influence she never resisted.

Phyllis Clare gradually withdrew from Ruth's side; she likewise carried away Cecilia, not so far as to isolate her cousin and the heiress, but far enough to give Gerald a chance for a tete-a-tete. Once or twice Phyl came back and joined in the conversation; once Cissy came with her and fixed her large soft eyes steadily on Gerald's face. He smiled affectionately and saucily at her.

"What makes you so silent, little Cis?" he asked, familiarly taking her white hand.

She snatched it away and said, "I am listening to you."

The tone struck Ruth; it was pettish and reproachful. Phyllis glanced at her sister, and then wound her arm around Cissy's waist.

"Cis is cross, Gerald," she said, laughing, "because I have been scolding her. She flirted outrageously all through dinner with Mr. Taylor."

"I did not," said Cissy, shaking back her curls; "you would seat him beside me. He is a tiresome goose. There! that's what I think of him."

"Oh, Cis," said Gerald, teasing her, "poor Taylor is dying for you. I am sure, by this time he is roaming the city. I presume he went back at 7, since I don't see him here—he is roaming the city, smiting his large forehead with his larger fist and offering incalculable sums to any boatman who will row him across the stormy water. 'A silver pound' feebly conveys *his* bribe, and, yet, cruel 'Lord Clare Willin's daughter' doesn't even wring 'her lily hands' in sympathy for her absent sufferer! Ah, women! women! our tormentors! our heartless executioners! why have we not the courage to cut our silken chains and be free!"

"I think you very rude and foolish," said Cecilia, walking away.

Ruth looked grave; Phyllis smiled uneasily, and Gerald put his head back and laughed heartily.

"What little simpletons girls are, to be sure!" he said; "now, there is Cissy, who is as proud of her conquest of Taylor as if she had, single-handed, stormed a fort, or, like Florence Nightingale, founded a hospital; and yet, because I her cousin, to whose attentions she was accustomed, before I went abroad, because I am not sighing at her feet like a good many others, she is peevish at my remarks about this conquest, and put out that I am not one also. These recognized beauties are perfect marauders. Nobody is safe." He paused.

"You are silent, too, Miss Desborough, and don't look satisfied? Did *you* also think me rude? Shall I go and make peace with my little cousin?"

"Surely, Mr. Gray, it is not for me to decide that question. I have never seen you with your cousins before. I do not know the intimacy which warrants—; it is no concern of mine." Ruth spoke as indifferently as if he had asked her opinion about the color of some woman's gown—dress being her detestation.

"Oh, pray, try and take an interest in this, for I fancy your judgment is good under all circumstances. What would you have felt if a cousin had so spoken—no, that's not it, for you and Cissy are not at all alike, nor are at all likely to feel alike—. What do you think about it?"

"I think that you are making a great deal out of a trifle. I should say—since you *will* keep on asking me—you had better tell Cecilia that you did not intend to wound her."

"And you will not let anybody take this delightful chair, which is 'as tall and straight as a pop-i-lar tree,' during my absence? Promise."

"I promise," said Ruth, half smiling.

Mr. Gray dashed off to his cousin, and, with his back turned to Ruth, spoke a few words. Cecilia listened at first with a pout, then she showed her dimples, and raised her eyes to the speaker's face—he moved directly in front of her, concealing her expression from the steady gaze of Miss Desborough. Then, with slow-turning head, laughing glance, and graceful motion, he nodded good-bye, and returned to his chair.

"It is all right," he said: "Cissy is amiable, with all her pretty weaknesses. The temptation to tease her is very strong, for I confess, Miss Desborough, that I *am* a tease—an inveterate one."

Ruth thought enough had been said on the subject; she did not like, somehow, the manner on either side. Was Mr. Gray frank about his cousin? Was Cissy's jealousy attributed by him to the true and only cause? Anyway, "it was no concern of her."

Wrapped in her plaid, she leaned out and tried to gain some fresh news from the sky about the progress of the storm. Mr. Gray began to tell her of a midnight tempest in Switzerland, during which he had been sorely buffeted. Then he talked of Rome, Florence, Naples, Paris, London—not the hackneyed, every day phrases, but his own fresh, clearly defined views, sentiments, thoughts. A few piquant personal adventures; a few "telling" mots; an anecdote here and there of people high in renown, either from beauty, birth, or position. He prefaced his talk about society, by saying, "I had some very kind letters of introduction to some very great people, and then I had, and always have, that fairy gift—luck. Things generally turn out well for me, which is but right, because no one has a keener appreciation. I do *enjoy* thoroughly. Now, those who are comparatively indifferent to everything, ought to have snubs and disappointments; the wrong woman always turning up at the right moment, for that walk, or that drive, or that waltz; and the wrong man boring you; and the book you want invariably lent out; and the souffle over baked; and your rival successful in love, war, or politics. *They* don't mind it, and you would fearfully; and as suffering is of course properly apportioned, like happiness, also, of course, you should have what you desire—I mean the fanciful—you representing, in this instance, myself—I ought to tread a path of roses."

"And do you?"

"Well—yes—and—no. You see my whole position is so peculiar—I may be a rich man, and may never have a shilling. My uncle, not my uncle Clare, but my father's brother, lives in New Haven, and has a good fortune—, but I am boring you with all this?"

"Indeed no, pray go on."

"Do you really know nothing about my belongings? for I don't choose to tell you some rather uninteresting facts, which most people have heard."

"I assure you, except having heard your name casually mentioned, and so seldom that, when you introduced yourself it was quite unfamiliar, I knew nothing of you. And don't be shocked at my confession of such unflattering ignorance. I so rarely take an interest even in the people that I meet habitually! I promise to treat what you say quite differently." This was an unusual warmth of speech for Miss Desborough. Had one of her "friends" heard it, it would have been considered more encouragement than any man had ever yet heard from those rigid lips.

Mr. Gray bowed with only a matter of course air, and could not have done a wiser thing.

"Thank you. My uncle, Mr. Norman Gray's wife, is a Boston heiress; her very large income is, by her father's will, divided between them equally, but the fortune goes to the long heir; if she survives him, back to her family; if he outlives her, it is all to be mine. They have no children. Her health is, and has long been, deplorable. No change can be effected in this state of things. My uncle is very kind to me, and, like Edmond About's twins, of the Hotel Corneille, I have thirty thousand dollars a year, because he has. Strange to say, my dearest college friend and chum is my aunt's nephew, holding the same place in her affections and intentions as I do in my uncle's. It is a queer, romantic enough sort of business."

"And is your chum likewise your aunt's sole heir?"

"Oh, no! he has a brother and a sister to share with him. I have a mother, but neither brother nor sister."

"That is so nearly my own case," sighed Ruth. "It is so very sad to feel so alone in the world. If I had a lovely younger sister to care for, or a brother to care for me, life would have seemed so much fuller and brighter. Papa does not heed me."

(Ruth Desborough, confidential!)

"Yes," said Gerald, softening his soft voice, "without my mother's love, and my consciousness of how necessary I am to her happiness, I would be sauntering about Europe now, objectless and dissatisfied. I ought to have a profession, to be earning my own bread; I feel it deeply, but my uncle will not hear of it. My aunt and himself tried to make some sort of compromise with her people, so that, in case of the fortune going legally to them, I might not be entirely penniless; but William Jesselyns (that's my friend Francis' brother), by no means adores me, and refuses to sanction any such arrangement. He prefers to run the risk. So be it. At any rate, I have still youth and health. I can drive, too, and groom a horse. Would you take me as a coachman, Miss Desborough? or even 'flunkey?' With a little training, I am sure I should form an impressive innovation upon the usual race of dark footmen who fill our Southern halls. Or, if I come to grief, I may give dancing lessons. You don't know how well I dance. If there were not so many people about, I would certainly favor you with an *echantillon* of my prowess in that line. Do you dance?"

"Dance! no," said Ruth, grimly; "I used to drag through quadrilles when I first 'came out,' because my father wished it, but 'graceful measures are not mine.' When did you get back from Europe?" she continued, abruptly.

"Three weeks ago I landed at Boston, embraced my New Haven relatives, and then rushed down here. I suppose it is about ten days since my return. By the way, how odd our meeting was! It was the merest accident that brought me just—to your feet. And to think that I had been carefully avoiding you all day!" He laughed mischievously. "You are sure you forgive me for my impertinence?"

"Quite sure. Do you know that to find a person who avoids me is a luxury I have never before wittingly enjoyed?"

"Alas! alas! for I cannot promise that I shall ever do it again." He leaned his head upon his strong, white hand, pushing up as he did so the short clustering curls from his forehead, and fixed his lovely, saucy eyes straight upon her. A flush slowly, yet not painfully, rose to Miss Desborough's sallow cheek. She could not meet his gaze unconcernedly, but managed to say with moderate indifference—

"Oh, now, you must know you will always be welcomed; my father must thank you for saving me."

"No gratitude, if you please; if you mean to establish a private Humane Society, and intend offering me a gold medal, I decline on the spot. But indeed I owe you an apology for all this rigmarole about my 'prospects,' which, after all, are anything but gloomy. I believe my poor aunt only too frail and broken in health. Besides, long may they both live, for the death of either would be an affliction that neither positive wealth could console, nor decided poverty deaden the sense of. The wind is rising again; do you hear it? and with the breaking of the dawn, will come the next tide."

The hours had indeed passed most swiftly; it was drawing towards daylight, and anxious eyes were again watching the waves, which had scarcely receded at the ebb. Faint streaks of dull light struggled in the East, and the water came pouring in from the back creek. Presently, the whole Island seemed covered like a vast lake; scarcely a foot deep in some places, four feet in depth in others. The poor, drowned poultry floated about on the surface, and horses and cows were led away to the highest ground that could be reached. But an overshadowing Providence mercifully protected man and beast. Seven of the most exposed houses on the front beach melted away like lumps of sugar dissolving in a tea-cup; the roofs settling down upon the wrecks with perfect propriety and great regularity; but not a life was lost. Trees fell here and there, and the picture of desolation was complete, so far as inanimate objects were concerned. About eight o'clock gentlemen wandered to their partially submerged houses, and came back reporting much discomfort but no farther danger. The refugees from the Ocean House beat a retreat from their hospitable military asylum; fathers summoned their households; and, although no sunshine yet illumined the gray sands, and the sullen roar of the wind still murmured hoarsely, every one felt that safety was proclaimed. Ruth was among the first to thank the officers and ladies of the Fort, and depart. Her servants reported Mrs. Price's house as still standing, and not looking much more worsted by the ravages of the blast than it had long been those by time.

"Cousin Frances" timidly proposed staying where they were until complete tranquility reigned. She faintly remembered some dreadful newspaper stories of robbers and murderers that had overrun that unfortunate Island in the Gulf, some years before, when the sea overcame the wretched inhabitants. Her suggestions met with a peremptory refusal; "besides," added Ruth, "we have already trespassed unmercifully upon the good nature of our entertainers."

"You might offer to pay board," hinted poor Mrs. Price. "Your pa wouldn't object."

Ruth's great eyes transfixed the culprit, who saw and "wilted."

"Money, money," Ruth muttered, half to her companion, half to herself; "we purse-proud millionaires think that everything can be done for money; and our dependents catch the tone. Will I never be free from such ideas?"

"A palpable hit," whispered Gerald, laughing; "very unkind of you to say that, when you recollect that the staple of my talk this night has been money."

Ruth smiled and shook her head.

"Mine was a shaft never meant for you. And now, good-bye, Mr. Gray. I see your cousins coming; they probably wish you. Need I say," she went on hurriedly, "that I hope to see you."

Before Gerald could answer, Mr. Clare and his daughters were beside them; the pompous, great man bowing low over Ruth's quiet hand, which lay in his patronizing grasp.

"My coachman has been unable to bring the carriage, or I should have been proud, dear Miss Desborough, to conduct you home. Most truly do I rejoice that my sister's son has had the privilege of serving my old friend's daughter; the young gentleman may well look happy at having secured such an honor. My girls told me some hours since that you were here with us. I should have come at once to pay my compliments, but my valued friend, Gen. Harris, had persuaded me to form a whist party in the mess room, and there we have passed the night; while, with you young people the hours have gaily sped in mirth up here. You do not seem to have suffered from our protracted vigils, my dear young lady?"

"Not at all," answered Ruth, passive and laconic.

"That is well. My mad cap, Cecilia, rejoices, I think, in what she calls a frolic."

There was little frolicsome in Cecilia's air or face. Phyllis, with pretty sisterly earnestness, was smoothing her *cadettes* curls, and chatting coquettishly with an admiring Mr. John Morris. On hearing her name, Cissy asked:

"What are you saying about me, papa?"

"I say that this storm has been quite a frolic to you, my pet."

"Has it? I am sure I did not know it. I suppose Gerald thinks it high fun, because he never enjoys anything half so much as seeing people uncomfortable."

"At me again, Cissy?" said Gerald, setting his teeth together, with a steady look from between his half-closed lids. "Come, be a good little girl. Let me wrap your shawl more closely around your pretty little shoulders and keep yourself warm—and cool," he added in a whisper.

Phyllis began to make a bustle and hurry of preparation, darting a warning glance at Cissy, and taking her papa's arm.

"Mr. Morris is waiting for you, Cis; and here is your other glove." In giving it, she pressed Cis' hand tightly. "Good-bye, Miss Desborough; we will send a dove from our ark soon to see how you are getting on. Gerald will take you home, I presume. We will have your room ready, Gerald, for they say that no boat can yet leave the Island, but I would not be surprised if, by night time, we all have to take shelter here again. Anyway, you know where you are welcome. Come, papa, Cissy is quite ready. We had better do as the others, and take advantage of this lull to get away."

Under cover of Phyllis' smiles, nods, and words, the party moved off briskly, soon followed by Ruth, Mrs. Price and Mr. Gray.

Little was said during the short walk; for it was occupation enough to pick their way through the pools of water, and over logs and obstructions.

The house was undergoing a little sweeping and setting in order; a fire was kindled in one of the out-houses still standing, and the savory fumes of a hot breakfast in preparation, were grateful to the nostrils of "Cousin Frances," who had despatched this *avant-garde* before she left the Fort.

"Stay and eat something," urged Ruth to Mr. Gray.

But he declined, saying that his Uncle Clare would expect him, and, moreover, if it were possible, he must return to the city and relieve his mother's anxiety.

"If I do not get away you will not be rid of me, for I must see how you are coming on, if you will permit me." He held out his hand; Ruth gave hers—they were standing just within the doorway—he, bright and beautiful as the morning star, with his soft glancing eyes, exquisite, mobile lips, soft, glowing cheeks, and all the airy, frank grace which distinguished him; she, pale and worse, careless in dress, looking much older than her years, with the strong, habitual reserve of her manner and face, struggling against the growing interest of this new acquaintance.

She faintly returned the kind pressure which he ventured, and they parted.

❀ CHAPTER IV

The storm was over, after three days of discomfort, damp gray sky, and nothing especial to eat. Happy those good heirs whose closets contained stores of tin canisters, from the warehouses Boden & Fils, of Bordeaux, and who could consequently regale themselves upon *pates and saucisses truffles* in place of the uncomestable beef steak and drowned chickens.

Mrs. Price rejoiced in her ample provision of hams and corned beef, kippered salmon and cariached fish. A box of sardines made the owner thereof very popular, to stray callers during the lulls of the sixty hours' gale—the housekeeper who possessed a supply of Boston crackers, might have trusted her reputation in the hands of her nearest neighbor, and *soi-disant* dearest friend. But that was all past now.

The sunshine glittered over heaps of sedge and rubbish left upon the beaches, front and back, and the waters tranquilly swept up not much nearer to their old landmarks, and looking as innocent as if they wondered what had done all the mischief, in the way of wrecks and ruins, which lay mournfully about. The wind was a mere murmur, soft as thistledown; in fact, it was "wind" no longer—only a gentle breeze, which carefully and slowly lifted the ends of the black lace scarf which Ruth Desborough wore over her head, and tied beneath her chin. She was looking out dreamingly from the window of her own room which faced the sea and the south-western sky.

Ruth's bed room did not look at all like a "maiden's bower;" it had few feminine trifles; a solid book or two, in solid binding, substantial, solid furniture, without one lounging chair, and on her dressing table ivory backed brushes and combs, and a large bottle of lavender or cologne water; not one essence *flacon,* nor a *polissoir* for almond shaped nails, no *pomade* for lips or tresses; nor Bohemian glass jars for powder puffs, or cold cream. All was orderly, neat, cold, uncoquettish.

The rays of the setting sun streamed in, lighting up the room, and resting on the head of its mistress as she leaned one supporting elbow upon the window sill, and her listless other hand held a small sized open note. Those beautiful, autumn southern skies! Her absent gaze was fixed upon the changing glories of their gorgeous coloring, but her thoughts were with the dozen lines in that note:

"Dear Miss Desborough," it said, "I find myself unable to keep engagement you kindly allowed me to make with you for this evening. You must guess at once that it is a matter of great importance which forces me to say this. Alas! it is most sad, as well as most important. My dear uncle, of whom I spoke to you recently—who was but a week ago a hale and hearty man, died suddenly of apoplexy, without warning of any kind. My poor aunt found him cold and lifeless by her side, on awaking. The shock was too great. In two hours she followed him—her feeble frame being an easy prey to such grief, and such a blow. This double misfortune necessitates that I should leave to-night for New Haven.

Your kind heart will sympathize with me in my great sorrow, and may I hope that, during my short absence, you will not forget

Your faithful servant,
GERALD GRAY"

Ruth read that note more than once. It was simple, unaffected, natural— written evidently in haste, and carelessly composed. Once she drew out her watch and calculated that in so many hours he would have started on his journey. *Did* he regret, she wondered, the informal engagement made to bring her a book that evening from town? In the midst of his sorrow and the confusion of his sudden departure, it was considerate of him to remember it.

Then she half smiled. How much more had other young men done in labored proof of their interest in her? Did not Charles Wentworth, while they were setting his broken arm, insist upon his sister leaving his bedside to inform Miss Desborough that while riding into the country to procure for her a certain black and tan terrier to replace a dead favorite, he had been thrown from his horse and seriously injured? But she had simply been disgusted with this "bold stroke for an heiress," and with civil regrets and hot house grapes, cold enquiries and exotic bouquets, gave Mr. Wentworth to understand that when her dogs died, her father could replace what he had once before given.

Then she remembered the water party at a famous picnic, and her admiration for some pond lilies, and John Barksdale's desperate lurch over-board in trying to get them. She had been but little touched by this act of devotion, and had severely snubbed the aquatic youth, when, three hours after, he informed her (originally) that he "would go through fire as well as water to serve her."

But these were notorious fortune-hunters—men who "went in" for every heiress-plate on the matrimonial turf—whereas Gerald Gray had studiously kept away from his uncle's dinner, lest he should be drawn into this golden circle.

"Pshaw!" exclaimed Ruth, at length, aloud, when arising from her seat, "this is too absurd."

She heard voices below her window—Phyllis Clare's sharp but lady-like notes, and Cissy's incessant laugh.

They were coming into the house—too late to stop them—the servant had already said she was at home; and moreover, Ruth felt herself inwardly confessing that she rather wished to see the Misses Clare.

"Oh! Miss Desborough," cried Phyllis, as she ran forward on Ruth's entrance, "isn't this dreadful about poor Gerald? Papa had a note from Aunt Ellen, written in despair. To think of Mrs. Gray not dying first—living just two hours too long! I can't think of anything else. Gerald would have been so rich and so happy, and now I suppose he has not enough to keep him in patent leather and perfumes. Wasn't it provoking of Mrs. Gray?"

For the first time, Ruth recollected what he had told her about the fortune and the disposition of it.

Phyllis went on:

"You know, of course, all about Mr. Norman Gray—everybody knows. Gerald has been brought up like a crown prince for expense. To all human knowledge, and everybody's expectation, he would have an immense estate. That forlorn, horrid Mrs. Gray was such an invalid nobody ever supposed she could possibly outlive her husband, but those two hours have upset everybody's calculations."

"It *was* very unkind of Mrs. Gray not to have died sooner. I don't know but that, as her health was so wretched, she ought to have been decently put to death some time back, and thus have relieved the anxiety of Mr. Gerald Gray and his friends," said Ruth.

"Oh! don't put in Gerald. He was absurdly attached to his aunt, and could not bear to hear me wish that the good lady were safely disposed of. It was only this morning, at breakfast, that he reproached me quite angrily for saying something of this sort."

"Did he know this morning, last evening, of this loss?"

"Dear! no. The telegram sent from New Haven came the first day of the storm—after he had come down here, and loomed off again, when I told him that you—that we—had a dinner party. His servant put it in his room—said nothing about it to Aunt Ellen, and there it lay during those two days that the gale lasted, and he could not get back to town. He *might* have gone up yesterday evening, by the first trip which the steamer attempted, but *he says* the boat left him, and it was just as well, for when he got back to us, about eleven o'clock, (I don't know where he had been,)" and Phyllis looked, as if she were trying *not* to look arch, "and it began to blow again, as if the roof would come off, we were *so* glad to have him with us. Gerald inspires one with so much courage—he takes every thing so coolly."

"Does he take his loss of fortune coolly?"

"Aunt Ellen says, in her note, that he did not appear to give a thought to that; all his grief was about his uncle and aunt, and his being down here, gay and careless, while they were lying dead in the house which has always been more 'home' to him than even his mother's."

"An amiable trait," said Ruth, stiffly, seeing that Phyllis paused for some remark.

"Gerald *is* very amiable," continued Miss Clare, "the most amiable person I ever knew. Cissy and I having never had a brother, have always regarded him as one. While we were in New York at school, Gerald used to come constantly from New Haven to see us. He always brought such lots of presents for us, and took us everywhere that Mrs. C— would let us go.

Then, when he went to Cambridge, we saw less of him, but his vacations were spent pretty much with us on the plantation, when we grew up, and came home. Cissy and I are deeply devoted to him."

"What is that about me, Phil?" asked Cecilia, who had been talking all this time to the inevitable Mr. Morris, the General's son, and their constant escort.

"I say that you and I have always looked upon Gerald as a brother."

"Oh! yes, he has *always* looked upon *both* of us as his *sisters.*" Cissy spoke again with the same asperity and intention that had before struck Ruth, and with great emphasis.

"You need not be so emphatic, Cis," Phyllis laughingly rejoined. "But I am forgetting the object of our stopping here—won't you come and walk with us, Miss Desborough? I am dying to see how all those houses look that have been washed down. Do you know Miss Fisher declares that her 'splendid jewels' were abandoned by her in her midnight flight, and are buried beneath these wrecks of the merciless sea? If we have luck, we may pick up a stray bracelet or so. True, nobody ever saw the 'splendid jewels,' which we only now hear of—but of course they are there."

Ruth wished to decline, but she had to give way to Phyllis' polite insistence; so they took a short walk, found no bracelet, nor did they strike out much that was new in conversation or ideas. Phyllis, several times, alluded to Gerald—his journey—his probable return. She did not ask Ruth how she knew that his relatives were dead, and himself *en voyage* before her visit. Ruth fancied her too heedless to think about it, and was only glad that no question should oblige her to confess (what she certainly would not have concealed) that Mr. Gray had written to her.

❦ CHAPTER V

"Don't turn yet, pray."

"Is it not time?"

"There is a moon."

"True; but it was just here a month ago that you quoted the moon as a reason for my turning."

"Ah, yes!" answered Gerald; "but then there were clouds fierce and black about us; and when I saw a poor, forlorn 'unprotected female' standing here, unaware of her danger, I rushed to her rescue. It was sublime of me, wasn't it?"

"Well, if not sublime," said Ruth, smiling, "it was very kind, and 'the poor, forlorn, unprotected female' was and is, very grateful."

"Of course she is, because she has the kindest and most grateful heart in all the world, and does not consider that by that little act of politeness I gained the dearest of friends. My luck again! Had we met in an ordinary way at my uncle's that day, you would have ranked me among the herd of young men who dance, talk, dine and die; but that important deity, luck, favored me, and here I am, elevated to the post of chief councillor and unworthy ally of the Great Miss Desborough, with a large G."

"The Great Miss Desborough will depose you if you laugh at her."

"Not she; she has taught me not to fear her, and from the pedestal of my position I only laugh at the envy of the infuriates who are jealous of me. But what a wretch I am to go rattling on in this way, when I have something to tell you which makes me very sad, and which I trust you will not be pleased to hear."

"What is it? Pray tell me. I would rather know it at once."

"Oh, there is no need to open your handsome eyes at me so wildly," said Gerald, with playful tenderness, and drawing her arm unforbidden through his. "Don't prepare for the worst; it is no very great matter after all. You must have conjectured when you first heard of my poor dear uncle's death, and of the changes that it would bring to me, that I could not stay idly here in our drowsy old city. I cannot live on my mother, who, dear soul, has just enough to keep up the style of existence to which she has been always accustomed. There is enough for her, but not enough for me. I suppose I *could* manage to eat, drink and sleep at her expense and get a place as a clerk on the Bay, which would ensure me a new dress coat every two years, and cotton gloves for the summer. Picture me, oh, my friend! 'driving a quill' under the jurisdiction of old Herbert, instead of driving my black mares under my own eyes!"

"Terrible!" said Ruth.

"And then marking cotton bales without the cotton gloves, mind you, and doubtful concerning the spending of half dollars, and patronized by attentions from fellows who have been all this time receiving mine, and worse than all, warned off by the sour looks of mammas who have hitherto encouraged my witticisms to their delightful daughters!"

"Halt there," interrupted Ruth, "there I am sure you are wrong, as mammas with us do not discriminate in that way about their daughters' partners."

"Don't they? Bless your innocent comprehension! Wait till you are a young man with fine prospects, and see how popular you will become with the very people who to-day think me an extremely over rated person, and very much changed for the worse since my European trip."

There was bitterness in Gerald's tone, beneath its careless outside ring.

"What are your plans?" asked Ruth gravely.

"Rather undefined. California is still a good opening for aspiring youths."

"But you don't believe that you will make a fortune in a year or so and come back powdered in gold dust?"

"No, indeed; I do not. I expect to pass many years there, and to have many ups and downs, to speculate and lose, speculate and gain many times, before I make one hundred thousand dollars. That is all I want."

There was a pause. Ruth's face was paler even than usual. Gerald suddenly looked at her.

"You are *very* kind," he said. "I believe you really regret my going away."

"Most sincerely," she faltered. "When do you think of going?"

"In three weeks."

"So soon?"

"Why not; if a thing *has* to be done, why linger putting it off?"

"True."

"Yes, it is true; and many other things are true, which are as true, but more foolish, and consequently one cannot speak of them."

"Such as—?"

"I said one could not speak of them. Would you be so little like yourself as to be indiscreet in asking questions?"

He forced a smile which met an answering one still less joyous than his own.

"Yes, for this once—and because we are friends."

"It is because we are friends and nothing more, that I dare not say what I would like to say. It is because your friendship is so precious to me, that I fear to lose it by confessing what you will treat with contempt—it is because we are friends only, that I would desire to make a confession."

"You speak enigmas," said Ruth, and she drew away her arm under pretense of fastening her shawl.

"Let me do it," said Gerald, gently drawing her shawl together. "It will not be the first time that I was more successful than you in securing the folds of this plaid of your predilection."

He stood facing her; his beautiful countenance quite divested of its usual *insouciante* expression, and as his hand touched her's in again taking her brooch to fasten the rebellious shawl, she perceived that it was as cold as ice.

"It is a 'plaid of predilection,'" said Ruth, in a very low voice. "I connect it always with the memory of that day I first met you. I keep few anniversaries, and that is not of very ancient date, but I don't think I shall easily forget it."

Gerald caught her hand. "Ruth!" he exclaimed impetuously.

She threw up her head. The old instincts were strong in her. No man but her father—few women—had ever called her by her Christian name.

Gerald dropped her hand gravely and with a low bow. "Forgive me. I forgot myself," and his small white teeth were pressed against his under lip. He offered his arm with a stately air—she took it. It trembled for a second, and then grew quite still, as he called her attention to a curious cloud of vivid crimson, shaped like a man on horseback.

"Very strange," said Ruth; "quite like one." She was looking far away from what he was pointing at.

"Does your mother approve of this?"

"Of this cloud? I doubt if she has seen it, and probably would not offer approval or disapproval about an affair which is palpably beyond her reach."

"Your answer, although meant to sneer at my question, is, perhaps, very near the truth?"

"What truth? What is truth, dear Miss Desborough? Have you 'a passion for truth,' as I hear people say, who show their reverence and affection by never approaching their passion. Not that I mean that you never approach truth, or that—"

"What are you talking about? Why are you going on in this frantic way?"

"I am frantic too, am I? Impertinent and frantic, and what else?"

"Unjust," said Ruth, quietly.

"Unjust to whom? Not to myself, surely? I give myself credit for being very just to Gerald Gray, Esq. I think him an unmitigated ass, and a very—"

"Pray, stop; you are unjust to me."

"To you! In what, pray?"

"In believing me to be unfeeling and insincere."

"My dear Miss Desborough! when did I accuse you of either of those rather common little vices?"

"If you do not accuse me of them directly in those words, you do so indirectly by your—. You know that I am deeply grieved by all that has happened to you—by your sorrow, by your loss of fortune, and now, by this necessity, as you consider it, to leave us all."

"Well?" He was trying to make her look straight at him. She was turning her head aside like a blushing girl of fifteen.

"Well?" he repeated, inquiringly.

"Is it kind, then, to behave so capriciously? To begin a conversation in which I was interested, and break it off with foolish phrases, uttered in a tone of irritation?"

"Pardon me: it was you that turned the tide of my feelings, and cheered my presumptuous words."

His voice was low and full of passionate earnestness. Presently he went on rapidly:

"I know that I *am* presumptuous. I know that you will probably meet what I dare to say with chilling looks and haughty words, yet how can I avoid it. You have guessed it already. You know that I love you, and that I must not tell you so. I, a man of broken fortunes, you, a great heiress. The interest with which you inspired me when first I saw you, and which then I had the right to feel, and in time utter, is now—would be now regarded by you as a desperate attempt. Pshaw! forgive me my *friend.* Forget what I say. Do you forgive me? Speak, dear Ruth—this once I *will* call you by your name—your gentle, Bible name—tell me you forgive my folly."

"It is folly," said Ruth. "How can I believe that, in so short a time, I, a cold, unattractive woman, have inspired you with love for me. No; I do not accuse you, believe me, I do not. I do not accuse you of any such mean motives as you hint at, but I do think that you misunderstand your feeling for me. We are speaking *a coeur ouvert*—I initiate the frankness with which you express yourself—your vanity has been flattered by my manner; my manner has a fictitious importance; you have been naturally pleased to be set above every-body in the circle which had chosen to make me a person of consequence; gradually you have accustomed yourself to fall into the belief that I am as worthy of admiration individually as—"

"Pardon me for interrupting you: *your* feelings I may not understand—my own, I thoroughly comprehend. I do not deny that I have seen women handsomer than you—more brilliant, more dazzling, more soft, more gener-ally attractive, but you are *you.* I have never flattered you. I never shall; but when I tell you that Ruth Desborough, with her stern and stately carriage, her frozen look, her icy tone, her repelling air, has for me a mightier charm than the most languid or sprightly, the softest or sauciest of her sex, believe me that I speak a truth as holy and as certain as God and Death."

"You have known me so short a time!" said Ruth, gently.

"How like all women is that speech! Do men often fall in love with the women whom they have met daily with indifference for years? Is not love *always* instantaneous, if only in the germ and unspoken."

"*What* do you love in me?" asked Ruth quickly, and raising her dark eyes to the beautiful face of her lover, with a glance which for the first time in her life, revealed the charm they ought always to have had.

"What do I love in you?" *Que sais-je?* I love possibly the heart and the inner nature which, if ever you could love, would be revealed to the man of your choice. I love the passionate depth of womanly tenderness which you have beaten down so skillfully, but which will spring up in floods if ever you permit it. I love the outward ice, as contrasted with the inward fire."

"I see you do not know me," said Ruth, blushing and subdued.

"I see that you know that I do know you," whispered Gerald. "You may deceive unobservant eyes, but not mine. From the first moment that we met, I never did you the injustice to suppose that you were the 'statue in lead' you would like the world to believe you—cool, hard, polished and grey."

"Yet you wish me to be the last."

"A pun! are the skies falling?" Gerald pressed her arm fondly to his side. "You have not answered me? Will you accept, then, that quality as your future name?"

"You have not yet asked me to do so! You told me you would *not* ask me?"

"Did I, dear trifler? Then, I humbly ask it now?"

"Give me time," pleaded Ruth.

"Time, again! I have a wise old aunt who is nearly a hundred, and she says, delays are dangerous."

"Resolves should go calmly, for repentance gallops; is not that a good saying, too?"

"No, indeed; for, if resolves went quickly, repentance could never overtake them. Ruth, dear Ruth, you cannot tell what an effort it has cost me to cast aside all those doubts and worldly terrors which I spoke of just now. To have you suspect me, and despise me—to have pitiful considerations of money come up between my heart and yours! You would not put me off with phrases and hesitations if you knew how sore I feel—how differently I would speak if our positions were reversed—how I would sue and plead, and wait, thankful for the merest atom of attention and hope; but now, if you do not pledge yourself freely and fully, my pride will rise in arms. You have everything to give—I, nothing. So, conscious of my unworthiness, I must have *all*, or reject all."

"A first rate reasoner!"

"You are turning coquettish on my innocent hands. Dear Ruth—*my* Ruth—answer me."

"First, answer me," said Ruth, suddenly grave.

She stopped walking, and seated herself on a log, drifted up a month ago by the tide.

"Sit here," she said, "by me. I do not know if I love you. I know I like you very much; and it may be that my affection for you, which I took to be gratitude and interest, is something deeper. Stay," she cried, as he caught her hand, "listen to me. I have always (the long always of a month, two weeks of which you were away,) I have always suspected that there was an understanding—a by-gone, or a present attachment between Cecilia Clare and you. I have been told so—vaguely by some persons—positively by one. I never questioned you about it. I had no right; but I own I would have given a great deal to know the truth. It worried me, this doubt; I, who never cared for anybody's concerns. It *frightened* me—the constant dwelling on this thought in my mind. Now, I have the right to ask, and to demand of you, on your honor, has Cecilia Clare any claim upon you? Was there ever any attachment on your side for her?"

"On my honor, no," answered Gerald. "Cissy was a pretty child, is a pretty girl; she is a favorite of my mother's—was a belle among boys of my own age when I was a boy. I have looked upon her, and treated her invariably as a sister, but I used to like to take cousinly privileges with her, and carry her off from other boys, just to tease them and amuse myself. But nothing more— nothing that went beyond this."

"She *is* very pretty," said Ruth, musingly.

"Yes, I think her very pretty, and very amiable, and all that. A good, industrious girl, too, with all her affectations. She has a sewing machine, and works it famously—keeps all those younger ones in the nursery well supplied with petticoats and pantalettes. Somehow the vision of Cissy, at her sewing machine, is commendable, but not attractive. And then her back—I own Cissy's back has always repelled me."

"What is the matter with her back?"

"Did you never notice it? It is a very defective back. Her spine is threatened, and her back is very ugly. Not crooked you know, but clumsy." He shook his head mischievously. "Whenever Cissy's back is turned, her attractions vanish."

"But look in her face and you forget her back?" asked Ruth.

"I did not intend to convey that idea. You asked me about a silly report, which some kind individual has made his or her business to tell you. Without circumlocution I give you the exact and entire truth. There is nothing to conceal, and I conceal nothing."

"Then, you do not love her?"

"Is your question an insult? No; I do not love her—I have never loved her; moreover, and to this, I likewise pledge my honor, I have never to any woman, until this day said, 'I love you.' I have had flirtations and follies to answer for, like every man; but I have never felt, nor owned, nor professed love for any woman till now. My passions have been aroused, my tastes gratified, my fancy aroused, but my heart has been my own. I have never dragged those sacred words in the dust of every idle whim, nor whispered them in every pretty ear, nor kissed them out close to rosy lips. They are yours. Heaven nor Hell can not rob you of them. Worthless they may be, but such as they are, I love you."

Two days later, Miss Desborough's and Mr. Gray's acquaintances learned, with surprise, that they were engaged, with the full approbation and consent of the destined bride's millionaire papa.

CHAPTER VI

Ruth was married on the 24th of November. It was not a long betrothal, but long enough to give time for the lawyers to draw up very liberal settlements, and for all the city to be exultant or despondent, as their fancy suggested, over the unexampled "good luck" of that favorite of fortune, Gerald Gray. Long enough for a magnificent *trousseau* to be procured, the ordering of which Ruth placed in the hands of her future cousin, Phyllis Clare, who merited this mark of appreciation not only by her rapturous delight at the match, but by her superlative taste in matters of dress.

St. James' Church was crowded to excess. Twelve o'clock was the hour, and a large number of those present were invited to the breakfast which took place immediately after the ceremony.

To many conventional eyes all brides are "lovely," but Ruth did not elicit this comment from the present audiences.

Her costume was as superb as lace and diamonds and *moire* could make it, but the dead white was very trying to her sallow skin; and her eyes, the really fine features of her face, (when permitted to be,) were steadily kept down. She showed no other sign of emotion, and repeated the responses calmly and in a low, measured voice.

Gerald was quiet, contented, very handsome; his manner and dress were equally correct and admirable. Everything that he had to do was done just in the right way, from the tie of his white cravat and the manner in which he carried his bride's bouquet, to the putting on of the ring and the endowing of her "with all his worldly goods."

There were no bridesmaids. Mrs. Gray and her brother, Mr. Clare, stood near the altar, on the right side of the groom. On the bride's left stood portly Jacob Desborough, stout, red-faced, jolly and delighted. His daughter was marrying an "*aris*-tocrat"; one of those good looking, gentlemanly, highty-tighty youths, who would know now which side his bread was buttered, and behave accordingly; and Ruth wouldn't die an old maid, as he had begun to fear that she would, with all his money left to charities.

The large drawing rooms were lighted, with shutters closed and curtains drawn. Porcelain and silver, and glass, and wax lights, and flowers, decked the long table, stretching through the lofty suite. Phyllis, radiant in pink silk, with the greatest love of a bonnet that *Laure* ever fashioned, fluttered about like a stray sunbeam that had slipped in through the chinks of the windows; and Cecilia looked very pretty and sober in blue; but she did not seem happy, and had little color and a red flush about her eyes; she had a headache from dancing too much the previous evening, she said. Mrs. Gray was a picture of middle aged triumph and mature enjoyment. There was a good deal of her brother's natural turn for pomposity about her, and as she swept through the rooms in her black velvet and dowager prints, her huge, stately figure and well cut *prononce* features were no mean addition to the splendors and varieties of the day.

Liveried servants, marshalled by a grey haired butler, (who might have been serving crowned heads since his infancy, if the dignity of his black countenance was the criterion of his life-long avocations,) were busily en-gaged in placing upon the table massive silver dishes, unmistakably English, and costly in their taste and fashion. Mr. Desborough had made but one stipulation with his daughter about the arrangements for the day—every-body must have a seat.

"None of your standing up, snatchy 'colations,' Ruthy, where, when you gits some oshters you have time to see them grow cold before you can scramble for a bit o' bread, or a dry sangvitch. No; give everybody a seat, comfortable like, since you new fashioned people won't have a dance and a setting down supper as folks did in *my* day. Don't have all those stuck up Clare and Cressingham; people say I begrudge them plenty to eat and a place to eat it in. They are your relations now; show 'em once and for all that I can give 'em a spread to look at."

So everybody had a seat, but for those who preferred a cozy time elsewhere than at the long board, where Mr. Desborough presided, there were small tables in odd corners, which proved extremely popular.

But just before Marcus, the magnificent, had bowed his white cravat with an astounding bow, before his young mistress, to pronounce "breakfast ready," Mrs. Gray led her son into the partial shadow of a brocade curtain and renewed her warm congratulations.

"Dear Gerald," she said, "I have always been proud of you; I always knew that you would be a comfort to me; that in you I should find ample atonement for the errors and misdemeanors of others—"

"Softly, dearest," said Mr. Gray, "She knows nothing of all that, and you must learn to be cautious about it."

"What! she has never heard? you have never told her?"

"No."

"Ah, my son, was that right—wisest?"

"I thought and think so. Best 'not distrust Caminara.' Why rip up old stories?"

"And her father! has he never heard anything about it?"

"I fancy not. He has always had something else to think about. He is not very wise, nor has he a good memory, except for figure and calculations. I think he must have been in China about that time, cheating the sons of the sun on the opium or tea question."

"For shame, Gerald," Mrs. Gray said, half smiling; "he is your wife's father."

"Don't I know it; am I likely to forget it? I rarely forget anything at anytime, dear mamma, but I don't talk at any time of much that I remember. It is not a bad rule, that; suppose you try it."

He looked a little impatient—just a little—just enough to give a slight, nervous quiver to his thin nostril.

Mrs. Gray turned to some other topic.

"Dear love," she said, "why have you not worn the studs I gave you, to-day? I should have felt pleased to see them glittering in that miraculous shirt bosom. I was so glad, I thought, of having them set for you. Once I came very near giving them to Cissy; poor little Cissy was so dying for diamond earrings."

Again the slight quiver was perceptible, and accompanied this time by a momentary compression of the sweet, almost feminine lips, that at once robbed them of the latter expression.

"Ruth gave me these," he remarked. "It was a *tenchene* [?] of hers; one of her few little romantic ideas. She had a watch which had been her mother's—the only thing I remember hearing her say that her mother had ever saved money enough, out of her wages as a nursery governess, to purchase—the only thing Ruth owned which she valued, and which had not been given her by her father. She went off the other day, sold the watch, and ordered these studs for me, with the proceeds. They are plain and handsome—a double G in the enamel their only ornament. See," and he turned up the delicate wristband of the "miraculous" shirt, "these are the sleeve buttons. After this sacrifice of hers, of course, I could do no less than wear them on the most important and sacred occasion."

"Of course, of course, my dear, and it was very pretty of dear Ruth, although I confess I don't quite enter into her motives."

"Don't you?" and Gerald looked listlessly around him.

"Dearest," said his mother, "excuse the question: are you very happy?"

"Intensely, sublimely, emphatically, and I see Marcus patronizingly bowing to my bride. Time's up, dear mamma. Any way, this long talk of ours looks suspicious to the eyes of this company. I fancy Mrs. Grundy thinks that you are discussing the marriage settlements with me. Here comes my respected papa-in-law."

"I believe, mar'm," said old Jacob, offering his arm, "'tis me that has this honor. Mr. Gray, will you please to lead out some lady. Your uncle has charge of Ruthy."

Mother and son were instantly transformed.

Mrs. Gray lost the affectionate look and intonation of voice, and became gracious, condescending and stately. Gerald smiled and put on an air of irrepressible, yet most becoming joyousness. His lot fell upon a former friend and patroness of Mrs. Desborough, in her early days—a good tempered, excellent, stout lady, of undoubted fashion, large appetite, capital lungs, and a well developed talent for laughter. They formed a merry couple; and from his seat at the middle of the table, Gerald sent his lively sallies right and left, with all the intensity of a school boy and all the good breeding of a finished gentleman.

Not far from him, but a little out of earshot, was one of those small tables I spoke of, occupied by two ladies and three gentlemen. It was a party in full tide of fun, flirtation and fault finding—but the latter quality spared the eatables.

"I pronounce this *salmi* quite worthy of the worthiest *chef* that ever sported the *cordon-bleu*," exclaimed Mrs. St. Clair; "try it, Bettina."

"I have tried it, but give the preference to these lobster cutlets. Some more champagne, McIvor," Mrs. Denham added, languidly holding out her glass to her neighbor. "Don't be so lazy or I will send you away; and don't make eyes at Bertha. She isn't looking at you and I am."

"He shall look at me if he chooses," said Bertha St. Clair, laughing. "Don't force from me that forlorn old adage about cats and kings. But on the whole, let us look for a moment at the bride, and prepare to drink her health; Mr. Clare is proposing it."

"Ladies and gentlemen, my friends," said Mr. Clare, with one hand on his ample white waistcoat, the other with the seal ring and its large crest, waving his brimming glass—"my very excellent friends, I trust you will not think what I am about to say is out of place or unwelcome. On the contrary, I am firmly persuaded that my remarks will fall upon pleased and sympathizing ears. It is by some deemed unnecessary, by others, inelegant, to propose toasts. I own that I am not of their opinion, in view of which, allow me, before proceeding further, to say a few words about myself."

"Oh!" groaned Bertha, and down went her head, seeking an unfindable truffle, and discovering what she really needed—concealment behind Mrs. Denham's shoulder, for the laugh which broke over her saucy face.

"I am an old fashioned man—a very old fashioned man," pursued the drawing room orator, warming to his subject, and rolling out his words with unctuous delight, "and I like old fashioned things and habits. I like this social board."

"My idea, sir," put in Mr. Desborough, "Ruth wanted a colation, but I said to her, says I, 'yes, and when you git your oshters, where's your bit o' bread'; but I am interrupting you, Mr. Clare; excuse me, sir," nodding his jolly head up and down; "go on."

"If those two old fellows keep up this mandarinic performance," whispered Bertha, as Mr. Clare bowed his head, and flourished back at the host, "where's our 'bit o' bread' and as for oshters, the venerable Marcus won't stir himself, nor permit one of those 'irrepressible conflicts' to move hand or foot while it is going on. Ah, here comes Mr. Clare again."

"Just so, my dear sir. Your ideas and mine have always been singularly alike."

"Except when old Jacob was director in the Mechanics' Bank, and refused that 'bit o' paper of yours,'" again interpolated Bertha, softly, to her companions.

"For many years I have watched with interest and delight the progress to womanhood of a young lady whose graces of mind and person none more highly appreciated. If I had a son I should have said, 'try and win her.' My nephew has succeeded in carrying off this prize. Nay, my dear Ruth," as Ruth laid her hand gently and rather nervously on his arm, "we are among our friends. I say, ladies and gentlemen, that I like old fashioned habits and customs, and none better than that of gay and festive scenes like this when a happy marriage, a suitable marriage, a marriage which we all rejoice in, takes place. And I like to drink success, and health, and prosperity to the couple, and above all to this couple, and beyond all, to my new niece, the bride."

"The bride!" was echoed from lip to lip, and Mr. Desborough cried:

"Git more wine, Marcus; fill the gentlemen's glasses; fill the ladies' glasses. Ain't any champagne in the house? Suppose you send around the corner and buy some." A joke very much appreciated by those who saw the uncountable bottles of the finest vintage, flowing like water in every direction, not to mention such decanters of Serchal, Amontillado, Tinto and Brown Sherry— such as, alas! the soils of Madeira and Spain no longer can furnish.

Mr. Clare sat down, and Gerald left off twirling his wine glass and looking annoyed. He smiled at Ruth and she smiled back at him.

Bertha St. Clair caught both smiles. She touched Mrs. Denham's arm, saying:

"Look there! Too late. You missed it. I saw Ruth Desborough beautiful!"

"Great Diana!" drawled Bettina, "can't she do it again?"

"Yes; I imagine that the same cause can again produce the same effect?"

"What cause?"

"Gerald Gray threw his whole soul into the blue of his eyes, his heart into the curve of his lips, and made her a present of the investment."

The young men laughed, and Mrs. Denham shrugged her shoulders.

"But how does that change her decidedly plain face into a beautiful one?"

"Because she lives only in his looks, and draws her existence and her whole appearance from him. She is now, and always will be, what he makes her."

"Pshaw! one of your fancies. Mr. Taunton, will you give me some of that *biscuit* before it melts? McIvor is star-gazing as usual today."

"What a little woman for pitching into innocent people you are, Mrs. Denham," said Arthur McIvor. "Here, give me your plate, you shall have the whole *biscuit*, if you wish it, at once, or by installments, greedy little thing!" This last epithet murmured close to her laughing face.

"Stop fighting, you two," said Mrs. St. Clair; "I can't hear what Mr. Taunton says. I have come to the conclusion that society is ruined by being composed of persons who have lived together all their lives, been sent to the idle bench in company when they were just out of petticoats, and just in a girl's school, and then continuing to associate on familiar terms. Witness the abominable behavior of my friend, Mrs. Denham, and that youth beside her. How can we expect them to conduct themselves like grown up people, when they have had their heads knocked together over the same primer so often! What were you saying, Mr. Taunton?"

"I asked if you thought this a real love match?"

"Do you wish the truth, as I believe it, without reference to considerations of what is 'due to feminine delicacy,' and the 'propriety of supposing attachments always mutual,' and 'deference to'—fiddlesticks and so on?"

"Yes."

"Then I proclaim this match to be, on the lady's side, one of the most insane and unreasoning passions; yet a love as pure, as self-sacrificing, and as devoted as ever filled a woman's heart and made up her life."

"And on his?"

"Ah, exactly on his! *Je bois, monsieur, a votre admirable sante.*"

"Nay, pray answer, dear Mrs. St. Clair. Don't you think he wished to marry her?"

"Certainly, or he never would have done it, if the penalty of not doing it had involved the skinning alive of his own mother and every other human being that walks this earth—except himself."

"Then, you think it is nothing, absolutely nothing, but her fortune that he wanted?"

"Or a pair of old shoes of Mr. Desborough's, with pointed toes, that are up the stairs on the shelf, in the right hand closet of the front garret, and which are too worn out for Marcus to accept, and lie there by accident, but couldn't possibly be asked for by any thing but a whimsical son-in-law," responded Bertha, quietly and gravely.

"What on earth do you mean, Bertha?" enquired Mrs. Denham, opening her great brown eyes.

"Mean, my dear, I mean simply that Gerald Gray wants only what he wants and what he wants he will have, be it great or small, trifling or of consequence, lovely or unlovely, sought by others or universally neglected. He has no rule to guide him, no fixed idea to follow. He wants it to-day—he will scorn it perhaps to-morrow; but while the whim lasts *he will have it*, if it is a thing to possess; *he will do it*, if it is a thing to be done. There is nothing too cowardly, too low, too vile in the way of means to accomplish his object. He would lie, steal, cringe, swear, cheat—murder, if necessary. He would trample under foot every tie, every moral obligation, run any risk, dare any possibility with the same calmness and indomitable courage as if he were sustained by an inward power, born of high aims and noble aspirations. He is almost invincible, because he is utterly unrestrained and perfectly unscrupulous; because in his pursuit, be it the countless thousands of an heiress, or her father's old shoes, or the gratifying of a vanity, or the piquing of his compeers, he puts his whole energies to work, and neither falters nor swerves aside, even should his path be encumbered by rocks of honor or rivers of honesty."

The speaker paused; her cheek was flushed and her eye bright; possibly her earnest tone had by its long continuance and the silence of her companions, in some way, struck the attention of the very subject of her remarks. Gerald Gray turned and looked towards the table. His glance met Mrs. St. Clair's; he smiled, bowed and raised his wine glass, without any hesitation; she returned the smile, the bow, and the glance, as easily and with as little embarrassment as if she had been discussing the hero of a novel.

"Oh, what a hypocrite!" said Mrs. Denham, laughing.

"Mr. Gray? Yes."

"No, you little wretch, I mean you."

"I am *not* a hypocrite. Why do you call me one?"

"Because you bowed and looked just now at Mr. Gray as if you admired him intensely."

"And so I do; I think him excessively handsome, and excessively clever. I think him so very much both, that my cowardice won't keep on good terms with him—personally.

> I have but the single way,
> I cannot call him a—field
> For woman's defence in open day—
> Man only can weapon wield.

Woman must 'only wield' smiles of an unalluring and insipid character."

Mr. Taunton shook his head.

"What means Mr. Taunton's ominous shake of the head?" continued Mrs. St. Clair.

"I disagree with you. You both underrate and overrate Gray."

"As how?"

"He is by no means so charming, nor so wicked as you describe him."

"My dear friend, you reason like a man talking of a man. I reason like a woman talking of a man. I grant you that although very handsome, I have seen men as handsome; and although very clever, I have see many a great deal cleverer; but, he has a sort of charm that, however indescribable, exists. Pshaw! facts speak. Look at Ruth," turning her head slightly towards the upper end of the table; "no you can't look at her; she has gone to put on her traveling dress, and it is nearly time for us all to say good bye; so give me some champagne and let me get on with my theory. Look at facts—look (mentally) at the late Miss Desborough. Was there ever a graver, colder, more able-to-take-care-of-herself young woman? How long has she resisted the attractions of Gerald Gray? Is it because he is so good-looking and so agreeable—because he had large, deep, passionate sapphire eyes and is quick at repartee, that he now stands master of this house and of that woman's heart? No. It is because he is thoroughly unscrupulous. He has found out her weak points, whatever they are, and has taken them as trumps to win the game. I know nothing about it, but I divine it all. Ah!" and the speaker slowly nodded her head, and fixed her eyes on her uplifted bumper of champagne—"I am terribly afraid of him."

"You!" exclaimed Arthur McIvor, who entertained a lively admiration for Mrs. St. Clair; "you afraid, and of Gerald Gray! What an idea!"

"Young gentleman," said Bertha, with mock gravity, while her bright eyes danced with suppressed amusement; "if Gerald Gray wished my hand from off my arm, or my nose from off my face, I should feel that they were no longer safe. He would bully me out of them, or persuade me, or lie to me, and I should end by being minus both or [wiser?], and thanking him for his trouble, and apologizing for their being no better!"

"You are too absurd, Bertha."

"You are prejudiced and unjust, Mrs. St. Clair," said Mr. Browne, the third gentleman of the group, speaking for the first time. "Pardon my saying so; you know my friendship for you too well to put harsh constructions upon such words. I only desire to set you straight about this matter. I have every reason to believe that Gerald Gray is not the man you take him to be. I have but one regret and one fear in this business. He is entirely loyal and true, but I fear that he has thought more of pleasing his mother, whose ambition is great, than of crushing an old sentiment which, although unreciprocated, (by his own confession to me,) was some time back very sincere. The lady *never* cared for him, but he was *once* very much in love with that lovely creature."

Mr. Browne motioned towards another small table at no very great distance.

"What a beautiful thing a man's friendship is, to be sure! Ah, Bettina, if women clung to each other and stood by each other as men do, how much stronger a body would 'the sex' be. Now, my love, do you think that *you* would have rushed to *my* rescue as Mr. Browne does to Mr. Gray's? No, indeed, you would have regretted the truth, and wished perhaps that it were less widely known. Hush, dear; I know you are going to contradict me, but it don't signify, and I am dying to see this 'lovely creature' of Mr. Browne's kind imagination and Mr. Gray's fond fancy. Which is she?"

"Miss Cecilia Clare."

"THAT!"

Was there ever scorn more expressive than a woman's face and voice can give!

"My good Mr. Browne!—my excellent and worthy Mr. Browne! a little simpering, silly, soft, and giggling girl! I retract. I take it all back, Bettina. I withdraw all that I said. Better any truth than invention like that. Your idea to Mr. Browne reminds me of a speech I once heard when Wm. Ashe married that forlorn wife of his—that dreadful woman. Somebody said that he had married her for her money—she had money—there was money somewhere floating in the family, besides madness. 'No,' contradicted a friend, 'he is in love with her—really in love.' 'Ah, that's bad,' said the first somebody—'very bad. The one would be want of principle, but the other is want of taste, and we all know which is most to be held in horror.' But the company is dispersing, and here comes the bride again. Let us make our adieux."

Ruth had changed her dress—was ready for their short journey to her father's country-place, where the honey-moon was to be passed. Her costume was strictly elegant and dark, and became her more than her bridal white. She lowered her veil as the doors were thrown open, and the gaudy sunlight flashed in.

A handsome carriage, stylishly appointed, and with four horses, was waiting for them.

Ruth kissed her father and her new mother. Mr. Clare led her down the steps and put her in the carriage; Gerald sprang in after her, and gave the order "go on;" while saying it, he waved a final farewell, his last look resting on Cissy's pale face, as she leaned upon Phyllis' shoulder in the door way.

Mrs. St. Clair did not lose this.

"Pooh!" she murmured to herself; "it cannot be. Come, Bettina, let us be off. The whole thing has been extremely well managed. Those four horses are rather excessive, but then they are necessary, which excuses a little display, even from so well bred a man of such quiet 'ton' as Gerald Gray! But—but—depend upon it, no good can ever eventually result from a palpable case of 'married for money.'"

CHAPTER VII

Honeymoons are the proverbial "stupid things, except for the parties concerned," unless, as in some cases, they are sad and dreary days, never remembered but with shudders, and seldom spoken of. Do you think that when pretty Emilia Jones was "persuaded" by her mother that to marry rich and devoted John Mason, whom she did not care for, was a capital and praiseworthy act, since Louis Martin, whom she loved, had, in a measure, jilted her—do you think Emilia likes to recollect those moonlight evenings of her honeymoon-trip to Philadelphia? Does she like to think of those prim streets and houses, like brick tombs, built for respectable grocers—every shutter a funeral slab, and the only escape for heart and eye up through the linden trees to the magnificent variety, the fitful wealth of color and light above, indelibly associated in her mind with that time? It was not the "stupidity" of her bridal tour that weighed upon that young spirit, destined one would think, for a higher fate, than the virtuous, and decorous, and prudent marriage which Mrs. Grundy applauds to this day. True, Emilia Mason is linked to a fool, an obstinate, jealous, tiresome fool, whom she don't love and can't respect; but he is "the father of her children," and she keeps her carriage, and Mason admires her very much—what more need she ask of this life? But we will pass over *her* honeymoon, if you please.

Then, I rather imagine Julius Brodie did not find his honeymoon a dream of bliss, or *only* "stupid." He wanted position and some money to keep it; he had a passion for intellect, and grace, and feminine softness, but—he was obliged, by the requirements above named, to win and wed such an ungainly, dull and affectionate young woman! I fancy *his* honeymoon was an awful trial, until his sturdy shoulders got used to the matrimonial burthen.

I need not ask that stately, proud, passionate, ambitious beauty, what her feelings were when she had accomplished her noble object, and led captive from the altar the little, insignificant, self-willed, old, ugly *millionaire*, whom she preferred to the honorable devotion and poverty which might have been her fate; before she had quite entirely put away the past from her well-regulated affections—before she had absolutely accepted diamonds and bankstock, place and power, as the proper substitutes for love and youth, sympathy and congeniality. I think she must have found *her* honeymoon a frightful experience.

And there is another style of honeymoon, an old, old story, which always fills my eyes with tears to think of—they were humble people whom it concerns—a pretty country-girl, poor, uneducated, one of many daughters, and her lover was like herself, penniless, but stout-hearted. He left her to try his fate in the West, to rescue from the primeval forest enough land on which to make his corn-patch or to build the little shanty which should call her mistress. Years passed—but they were both young and hopeful; every now and then "a letter came out"—as they expressed it—the spelling far from perfect, the writing anything but beautiful, but the faith and the affection unchanged, to find her the same. Then—of course, you are prepared for it—a long blank. No word, no news, no sign. A stray traveller, who had journeyed on those distant roads, and who had enquired concerning the young man, as they were from the same section of country, was told that his neighbors had reported him as dead; passing, accidentally, that way, this eye-witness saw the deserted log house, with its solitary, small window staring, shutterless, at him, and showing bare ragged walls inside.

The poor little girl, who had steadily hoped and waited, had no time allowed her for grief or tears—they were poorer than ever—"mother was sick," necessarily, and "father had taken to drink;" there were so many little mouths to feed and so many yellow heads to comb! She must help her older and younger sisters, and put aside her sorrow; but the pathetic face, with its paled roses, attracted more than one suitor; she was not only the beauty of the family, but it was well known that she could work as bravely as her plainer sisters. Then came the refrain of "Auld Robin Gray," and to cut my long episode short, the luckless girl was assured that there was no crime in giving her hand to a very well-to-do young man, who wanted to marry her, while her faithful heart was still full of the lost one.

The Squire tied the knot, and the few guests sat down to the humbly furnished hospitality of this marriage morn. There came a tramp of horses; a child looks out, the bride listlessly raised her head and did the same. A cry of mingled joy and horror broke from her lips. Leading a horse, (upon which a woman's side saddle was fastened,) mounted himself upon another, there came the dead lover to claim his promised bride, and to carry her away, as the custom then was, to his comfortable home, still farther West than his first choice, still richer land, but with postal facilities it seemed worse than none, for his letters, telling all this, had never reached their destination.

By the law, she was another man's property. Too late; just too late! Too late by ten minutes or by ten years, what matters it? Those fatal words, "man and wife," had been spoken. I might moralize for pages on them—so easily said—*never* to be unsaid, with decency, "until death do us part."

He turned his horses' heads and went back to his dreary forest home. Think of *her* honeymoon! But there are brighter sides than this—there *are* first days and weeks of wedded life unspeakable for their full delight, not from their bitter memory. In fact, I recollect meeting a couple once—the gentleman an old acquaintance—who seemed to entertain the most exalted opinion on this subject. He was a small, smiling, rather absurd youth, who lisped slightly, and had light curly hair, and a taste for painting.

"And so you are married?" I said.

"Yes; my wife is here."

"I shall be pleased to make her acquaintance, presently."

He bowed delightedly.

"How long since this charming event transpired?" I went on.

"Only four months—not quite four months."

"Ah! then you are still almost in the honeymoon?"

"Don't say that; I entreat you, don't say that; this is not the honeymoon surely? Is not this to be all our life? Don't make me miserable by letting me suppose that this must end. I fancied this honeymoon, as you call it, was our existence."

He passed his hands through his flaxen curls and seemed ready to cry; so I asked to be taken across the room to the other member of this delightful partnership. He frisked beside me, talking gayly.

"I am afraid you will find her 'new,'" he said. "She is very 'new,' quite young; but you will be lenient, she is so 'new.'"

The "new" young lady sat at a table, looking over some engravings; her back was to us, and, as her admiring spouse stood beside her, his head was just on a level with hers.

"Miss Mary!" he called, gently, "Miss Mary!"

Miss Mary turned round, and the introduction took place.

The usual preliminaries of how much she had heard of me, from her side; and on mine, of how much I appreciated the young gentleman whom she had so highly honored, were followed by my simple and natural question, as to the length of their stay in this country. I hoped that they would make it their residence, &c.

"We shall stay here about two years and a half," said Miss Mary.

"Oh! no! love, three years," amended her lord.

"Two years and a half, dear," persisted the lady, beaming into his face.

"Three years, my dearest; I *think* three years."

"Two and a half, love, only two and a half," insisted Madame, smiling, shaking her head, and gazing fondly into the fond eyes beside her.

"Three years, . . . ," surely, neither they, nor you, my patient reader, expected me to stand any more of that. I beat a hasty retreat, and have never seen nor heard of the "new" young lady or my old acquaintance since that moment.

Whether the honeymoon still lasts, or whether it turned acid about those disputed six months, I am unable, therefore, to say. He is the only decided admirer and unmitigated supporter of honeymoons that I ever met. Perhaps it is because people don't confide in me enough, or I have not sufficiently enquired into the matter. But I fear that many a *menage* which has since shaken down into shape, consistency, and tolerable contentment, began, perhaps, on both sides, almost always on one, with a restless looking back on what Whittier sings:

> "Of all sad words of tongue or pen,"
> The saddest are, "It might have been!"

And even in its happiest aspects, and with no such skeleton to teaze or terrify, how many a woman learns, with sadness and amazement, that the lover, to whom her will was law, has been suddenly transformed, (as he ought ever to be,) into the superior power to whom her feminine fancies must pay homage and deference? Is every young girl taught this necessary lesson? Is she always warned that if her happiness now fairly begins in the double life, for which God destined her, her trials also walk hand in hand with this happiness? She has become the one object of another's existence; with her rests his earthly comfort, but he is human and a man, he is her head and her master. Has it been earnestly and affectionately recalled to her, by those who first taught her to walk and to pray, that St. Paul writes: "The husband is the head of the wife, even as Christ is the head of the Church; . . . , therefore, as the Church is subject to Christ, so let the wives be to their own husbands in everything?" Surely, if those inspired words, by which we profess to live and be guided, if they mean anything, they do not mean such marriages as are daily made, and urged and commended. Think of it! We didn't think of it at all. In no point of really rational view, do we consider marriage, its fearful responsibilities, its awful risks, its fierce temptations.

Men see a pretty face in a ball-room, or a pleasing manner, or hear of a large fortune, and they ask no more; if it were a fine breed of horses they wished to procure, or a pleasant travelling companion for a summer's jaunt, they would look into the pedigree of the one, and reject "bad blood;" they would hesitate in the other case about the man's temper, his habits, his capabilities for making things "agreeable." Alas! alas! when it is only a marriage, only life, only salvation, perhaps, how lightly, how carelessly, how cruelly are these matters managed!

The parent who is trustee of his daughter's fortune, weighs, considers, examines; "he could never forgive himself if he invested Sarah's money, left her by her godfather, in some losing concern;" what about Sarah's heart and soul, given into his temporal care by her God?

Oh! would that my pen were dipped in immortal fire, and had the power to trace my weak words in every parent's understanding. I renounce the task of touching their hearts, but can I not open their minds to this subject and its importance? I am no advocate for foolish, hasty *love matches*, as imprudent fancies are sneeringly called; but even such would not be hopeless if both men and women, as boys and girls, were instructed in the duties and requirements and quicksands of matrimony, just as they are in Latin and Greek, modern languages, housekeeping, dancing, double-entry, "Shakespeare and the musical glasses." If girls were not taught that marriage is a necessity, and that "any marriage is better than none!" On the contrary, would that this truth were sucked in, with mother's milk; "any loveless single life is more respectable than a disunited, unloving, married life." To my eyes no spectacle is more degrading than the squabbles, the coolness, the mutual (or one-sided) dislike of two people, who, nevertheless, bring yearly a baby to be christened, and are said by their friends "not to live comfortably, but still they get on!"

I seem to have wandered from honeymoons, also, as I wandered from the thread of my story, but it is often from honeymoons that married disasters chiefly spring. George has been accustomed, perhaps, to see his mamma, who is well broken into harness, trot along calmly and contentedly under the guidance of the conjugal rein; he expects to see "his wife" in these early days, go through her paces as deftly. Louisa, *au contraire*, has been used to home, perhaps, to recognize "the grey mare as the better horse;" she tosses her saucy head and kicks over the traces when the bridle means right, and she means left. *If* George is a sensible man, he perceives the difficulty, and coaxes his pretty, dearly-loved, spirited little nag. Doesn't St. Paul tell him too, (for there are two sides to this and every question,) "So ought men to love their wives as their own bodies. He that loveth his wife loveth himself;" he should not show temper, but he *must* show firmness. And she, if her real education has been neglected, if she has never learned, that honorable submission is her lot, and is wisest so; or if, oh, miserable woman! she married with the perfect conviction of a sad truth, known equally to herself and to her friends, that this George, whom so recently she swore to honor and obey, was not capable of inspiring either sentiment—shut the book of their lives. She will learn to "manage" him, (hateful word!) or they will fight for supremacy, or she will be sullenly "conquered," or ingloriously conquer him, and so live, "till death do them part!"

What, says Phoebe Carey about that tremendous clause in our Episcopal service, murmured every day as thoughtlessly as if it had no more significance than the "very humble and obedient servant" of a formal note?

> "Promise to *Love!* why woman thinks
>   To lose a privilege, not a task;
> If thou wilt truly take my heart,
>   And keep it—this is all I ask.
>
> "*Honor* thee! yes, if thou wilt live
>   A life of truth and purity;
> When I have seen thy worthiness,
>   I cannot choose but honor thee.
>
> "*Obey!* when I have fully learned
>   Each want and wish to understand,
> I'll have the wisdom to obey,
>   If thou hast wisdom to command.
>
> "So, if I fail to live with thee
>   In duty, love and lowliness,
> 'Tis Nature's fault, or thine, or both,
>   The greater *must* control the less."

Which is all very well, if spoken before hand; but one is not permitted to interpolate "ifs" in one's marriage vows, and, unluckily, it has not yet been satisfactorily decided, that the failure of one party to keep his or her share of this solemn compact, exonerates the other from its weight. And, yet, this, *the* bargain from which there is no withdrawal, to which no bounds are assigned, never to be honorably dissolved, either by "mutual consent" or the "terms of limitations;" this is the firm which is most easily arranged—into which either or both partners plunge with a reckless indifference that Satan must smile to see, for it surely brings him, over and again, his richest harvest of human and unhappy souls!

I turn from the sad pictures, which here present themselves, to a brighter scene. Was there ever so happy a honeymoon as Ruth Gray's? Did ever bridegroom wear a serener brow, or bend eyes more beautiful and bright upon the woman who worshipped him than did Gerald? Beauchamp is a lovely spot. As its name indicates, the house stands on a fine field of level ground. The river runs between low banks, about forty yards from the marble steps that in a stately double sweep lead up into the large, two-storied, handsome house, of which the servants' apartments and various offices occupy the ground floor, and you enter through a broad piazza into the drawing-rooms and halls on the first story.

Of course, there are live oaks, old as the river almost, with great "gnarled trunks," standing in the informal beauty of their forest growth and not in stiff avenues of cultivated grace. You see no fences nor stone walls; to the right, in the distance, there is a low, broad gate, and stretching away on either side, you can catch glimpses of a hedge, (higher than a man's head,) of the impervious Cherokee rose; in the spring it will be covered thick with the white four leaved blossoms, mingled with the long sprays of the yellow jessamine. This forms the enclosure; the drive winds prettily in a smooth gravel path, around and about the trees, from that gate to the front entrance. Don't take the little Gothic building for a lodge; it is the chapel, where, every Sunday afternoon, there is service. The stables are to your left; do you see the small pond on which the rays of the setting sun are shimmering through the boughs of that over-shadowing oak? Mr. Desborough has a fine stud, and the grooms are leading out the horses now in detachments, and watering them; you can hear the tones of those unmistakable African voices, faintly ringing through the clear, crisp air, as the men laugh and joke with each other and lazily get through their tasks.

Ruth and Gerald are sauntering by the riverside. His arm is around her waist, his other hand holds one of hers.

They are quite silent; presently she lifts her dark, wistful eyes to his face.

"What are you thinking of, darling?" he asked, gently.

"I am trying to discover why you first loved me. It is that old, provoking question; one that I asked you before."

"Indeed?" and he smiled and pressed her hand, which clung so fondly to his grasp.

"Yes. I know that most people would think me a great idiot for not instantly deciding upon the most natural solution—that you don't love me at all, and that you marry me for my money."

"Ruth!" said Gerald, gravely.

"Don't interrupt me, dear. *I* have never doubted you for one instant. If the whole world maintained such or such things against you, from your own lips, only, would I believe them. It is your truth that I love in you. Your frank sincerity; ah, darling, if you could but guess how weary of falseness and hypocrisy and double-dealing my twenty-six years of this life have made me!

No, don't guess it. You would not like to find me such a withered, wilted, worn-out worldling."

"Alliterations' able ally, I see you are."

"Do you recollect," pursued Ruth, "that very first evening of your return from New Haven, when papa came into the room, as you were asking me to read that long letter, that dear and precious letter, the diary you kept on your journey and during your absence? He glanced at the voluminous manuscript, and you said, 'I am asking Miss Desborough to read my college valedictory.' No sooner had he left us than you started up with an exclamation of pain, and turning to answer my eager demand as to what ailed you, I saw your face as pale as death, and actual anguish working every feature—."

"Hush, dear child, don't recall all that," said her husband, raising her hands to his lips.

"But I must; it was then the blow was fairly struck that brought me for life to your side. 'I have told a lie,' you said, with bitter emphasis; 'I feel it *here*, like a red-hot mark upon my forehead.' Gerald, from that instant I adored you. God forgive me! but it is true, I adore you."

"My sweet worshipper!" said Gerald, smiling half ironically, and very tenderly kissing the mouth that trembled with passionate feeling.

"Yours was the jealous love of truth that I had so long been seeking. Now, I was satisfied. Unlovely and unlovable as I know myself to be, when you said to me, 'I love you,' on that star-lit beach, I did not for one second doubt it; so it is that I want to know, not *if* you do, but *why* you do?"

"Perhaps it *is* for your money," said Gerald, teasing her; "I love your lands and that house and the one in town, and the 'irrepressible conflicts,' and— your beauty," he slowly added in a different tone.

The tears started to Ruth's proud eyes—ah, me! with "the full happiness of her double life had come the trial" of tears. I wonder who ever saw Miss Desborough cry? Why is it? why must it ever be that the fountain of our perfect joy lies always next to that briny source? When she "walked through life," bitterly alone, her eyes were as dry as they were cold.

"You are laughing at me!"

"Dear child," said Gerald, pressing her to his heart, "how have I wounded you? Oh, Ruth, what a silly, dear, little goose you are! Of course there are lots of women handsomer than you; it is not for your looks that I love you."

"I should hope not, even if I were a red and white beauty, like Cecilia Clare. I should as soon be loved for the land and houses and 'conflicts' as for my skin and eyes and hair; at least the former are more lasting usually."

"I agree with you entirely, but, at the same time, I must insist on being a better judge than you of your appearance. Can't you see that your eyes and mouth are beautiful?"

"No."

"Candidly?"

"Was I ever uncandid, Gerald?"

"True; well, then, to impress upon your bewildered understanding that they are, and promising that I should love you just the same if they were not, which, perhaps, will help to answer your almost unanswerable question as to the 'why' of my love for you, listen to a little verse that came into my mind just now. You can tack it on to the end of that pretty ancient ballad we read yesterday, 'Her I Love.' How does the original go?

> "I know a little hand,
> 'Tis the softest in the land.
> And I feel its pressure bland,
>   While I sing;
> Lily-white it seemeth now,
> Like a rose-leaf on my brow,
> As a dove might fan my brow,
>   With its wing.
> Well! I prize all hands above,
> This dear hand of her I love!
>
> "I know a little foot,
> Very cunningly it is put,
> In a dainty little boot,
>   Where it hides;
> Back and fore it glides—

(No, that's wrong; help me, Ruth, when I stumble; ah!)

> Like a shuttle it flies,
> Back and fore, before my eyes,
>   As it glides.
> Well! I prize all feet above,
> This dear foot of her I love.
>
> "I know a little heart,
> It is free from courtly art,
> And I own it every part,
>   For all time!

Ever it beats with music's tone,
Ever an echo of my own,
   Holy time!
Well! I prize all hearts above,
This dear heart of her I love!

Now, these lines are very charming; but listen to what was suggested by the bright smile and your actually speaking lips, as you sat silently beside me last evening, not uttering one word, yet saying a volume:

I know a little lip,
Where a bee would love to sip,
Like the honeysuckle's tip,
   Is it sweet.
Parting now with ruby glow,
Arching, too, like Cupid's bow
Weaving smiles of joy, I know,
   When we meet.
Well! I prize all lips above,
This dear lip of her I love!

"Do you like that, *miladi?*"

"Very much," said Ruth, blushing with pleased attention. "So you are a poet, too?"

"*Comme me voyez!* Not exactly destined to be *the* author of the Great Epic of the Day, nor shall I attempt 'to snatch at the bays' of the Poet Laureate over the water—but enough to be your poetaster in ordinary, and send you 'pomes' on your birthday when you are good. And take care that I don't have to add another verse about 'an eye, that dearly loves to cry,' belonging to 'her I love.' My darling, tears are my terror! I saw a 'glistening drop' trying to make its way from under your long lashes just now. *Pas vrai?*"

"Yes, I am very sorry," said Ruth. "You should forgive it for its novelty. I did not use to be given to the 'melting mood.' However, as my smiles were once quite as rare, and you have taught them to me, why you must, I fear, take their sisters along with them. But it is growing cold. Let us go in."

The sun had sunk far below the trees, and the twilight had deepened into night. The cheerful blaze of the great wood fire sparkled through the undrawn curtains of the drawing-room windows. How luxuriously comfortable it all looked, as the wedded lovers paused upon the lowest step, and

Gerald said, resting his arm upon the pillar of the balustrade, and as if to finish the conversation before they entered the house.

"So it was that fib of mine which won your stubborn heart?"

"No," said Ruth, smiling, "it was your agony of remorse for having told it, you obtuse Gerald."

"And if I should ever be detected in an unremorseful one, an unconfessed prevarication, would you unlove me?"

"Yes." Ruth's voice was almost as harsh as in her loneliest days, when she uttered this monosyllable after a silence of a moment.

"Well, you need not fear it," he said. "But I always fancied that it was the beautiful handwriting of that diary that gave you to me—and the spelling! Dogberry was wrong, it is 'spelling' that 'comes by nature.' My poor uncle used to be in despair about my erratic mode of vanquishing orthography. I never 'cave in' to it, but I make its rules submit to my powerful pen."

"Yes," said Ruth, laughing. "On one page, you appeared suddenly struck with the curious look of some marvelously lettered word. 'That, I am sure, is not right,' you wrote, pathetically; 'do you think, dear friend, that it is ig—, with a dash and a final e, a trouble which makes me play such fantastic tricks with Johnson and Webster?"

"I am sure," said Gerald, again drawing his bride near enough to lay his beautiful Greek head upon her shoulder, as she stood on the step above him, "you may as well acknowledge it; you wished for a full-grown scholar, whose knuckles you can rap."

"I wished, most earnestly, to show him that I believed in what Pope wrote to Martha Blount, and Mrs. Pioni quotes in her shrewd old age, to her baronet friend—what was his name? She had got a melancholy letter from him when he was beset with family anxieties, and she cites this autographic scrap of Pope's: 'My poor father died in my arms this morning; if, at such a moment, I did not forget you, assure yourself I never can.' Mrs. Pioni concludes that *her* friend, also, really loved her, to write when he was busy and unhappy; when I read those hasty letters you wrote me, and that longer diary, full of thoughts in which I was present, was it strange that I came to the same conclusion?"

She softly bent her head and timidly, almost, laid her lips on his white forehead.

"At all events, Ruth," he said, "you do not regret your choice, just yet?"

"My darling! I am *too* happy. You stand between me and Heaven. I am a new creature with you; there is new blood in my veins; a new sun, moon and stars in the sky; all life is changed since I met you. I no longer regret my poor mother, as I used to do. But, on the other hand, I am more tolerant, I hope, of ordinary people." She paused. "Can you believe it?" she added with a little laugh. "I find Cissy Clare less insipid than skim milk, because I love you."

I fear honeymoons *are* stupid things, except to the parties principally concerned, and that this conversation is no exception to the adage.

🐚 CHAPTER VIII

Mr. and Mrs. Gerald Gray bid fair to be the most popular couple in their very fashionable circle. Why not? It was the most natural thing that could happen. Gerald's indolent, pleasant, gay manners, were always attractive; he had always been permitted to take more liberties, say more saucy things, and be more quoted by men, and petted by women, than anybody. He was good-naturedly selfish. Provided he had everything he wished, he grudged no human being taking their share of the good things of this life; he would even invite them to partake of his own superfluity. If he had four "weeds" in his *porte cigares,* and the softest-cushioned sofa in the club-room, he would willingly tender one of the Habanas, (his "smoke" never exceeded three,) and point to the next best seat in the room to the first agreeable man that entered, would amuse the new-comer by a thousand funny stories, and leave the pleasantest impression of his social qualities on the mind of his companion, when he sauntered away. He paid his bills scrupulously; however much he was given to jokes against other people, permitted none to be launched against himself; was free with his money, and was called "very high-toned."

Their home was gay and hospitable. Mr. Desborough gladly retired from an active share in its honors. Tight shoes, and what he called "his stuck-up manners," were thankfully and almost permanently abandoned for a country life, varied only by visits to his daughter at quiet seasons, when balls were over and dinners few. He admired his son-in-law vastly; Gerald thoroughly understood what his *beau-pere* had called "which side his bread was buttered"—he showed no eagerness about spending money, (he knew that Ruth would take the coat off her father's back, and "put it up the spout," to supply her idol with a full purse); he was very polite to the old man, and they got on extremely well together. Beauchamp and the town house were virtually theirs already, and Mr. Desborough retired to Bellair, a small place near the city.

And Ruth! Ruth was the happy victim of the most delicious and soul endearing delusion. She fancied that she had married an angel with a silky moustache, a cameo profile, a strong sense of religious duty, (with no great practice about it) shiny boots, excellent principles, the sweetest temper, and the loftiest ideas of truth and honesty. And this perfect being loved her! Had not he, the apostle of that goddess always down a well, had he too not moralized with her, over and again, upon the strange yet beautiful chance which had kept his heart absolutely untouched, until that ever blessed storm, whose driving wind had sent him straight, by so mere accident, to her side? Had he not from the moment when she placed her hand in his, and led him up those ricketty steps of Mrs. Price's house, had he not felt that virgin heart thrill to the touch of those fingers, unconscious then, of their miraculous power? Oh silly, silly woman's love! Was there ever anything so blind and so foolish as a devoted woman? Ruth Desborough had more sense than half her sex—Ruth Gray was intensely absurd. Ruth Desborough weighed and judged, hesitated and doubted—Ruth Gray looked at everything through her husband's blue eyes, and placed her reasoning powers in the alembic of his mind, from which her ideas came forth as he willed them.

But she was very happy. I only can wish to every feminine soul whose earthly comfort I pray for, that they may pass through life with the feelings that made up Mrs. Gerald Gray's wedded existence.

Of course there were some clouds in this marvelously blue sky. Its otherwise monotonous azure would have wearied the gaze, perhaps. Light white,

> "Argosies of summer, wrecked and drifting,
>   Floated,"

occasionally up to the zenith, and once or twice a positive thunder-cloud, black and threatening, sent out its "forked tongues" of flame, and the rain drops fell, fast and furious. Mutterings of thunder rolled from marital lips, and the "cloud" was apt to put on its beaver and quit the home in the sky, leaving the shower to dry up, uncrushed. But how lovely the "cerulean vault," after all this, when the sun shone again—and explanations were given—and Ruth's proud spirit, having gladly stooped to ask pardon, for his having given her offence—how graciously her imperial master passed over the crime of *lese majeste!* There was no Vashti in the Gray *menage;* but Esther was always bending low before Ahasuerus, and praying him to allow her to speak her submission. Jealousy was the skeleton in Ruth's closet: she scarcely would acknowledge that she saw it. She hid its dreadful old bones as well as she could, and never willingly unlocked the door. She was better off than I would allow Mr. Thackery to give me credit for being, when, one evening, the lower press beneath a book case in the library, where we were supping, *would* fly open with a bang every two minutes, just at my back. Again and again the servant closed it—the key would not turn. I rose up and jammed a piece of paper beside the lock—"you are very anxious about that door," said Michael Angelo: "is the skeleton there?" "Ah!" I sighed, "that small spot would not hold half of *my* skeletons."

Ruth had but one: sometimes it took the visible shape of one woman, sometimes another. Gerald would spend hours at a ball, lazily chatting with some girl, saying nothing probably that as Ruth's property he had no right to say, but looking a great deal, and making this young heart, (he liked them young and fresh,) dance with gratified vanity. Or he would devote himself, in an obscure corner, to some old flirt of his, some daring-eyed, gay-spoken woman, and Ruth would, as she passed, catch whispers and low laughs. Then, he would disappear at the theatre, and her anxious lorgnette would discover him in a private box, sitting on a low stool at the feet of some desperately attractive woman, playing with her bouquet, and looking as little like a married man as a perfectly disengaged one could represent. But, oh, bitterest of bitter pangs, was to hear of her beloved from others. To be told that at that ball where she did not go, Mr. Gray was the life of the evening. "He and his cousin, Miss Clare, got up a new dance—what was its name?"

Ruth did not know: but she knew well the sickening sinking with which she asked, "which Miss Clare? Phyllis?"

"Oh, no; Cissy. You know Mr. Gray's favorite was always Cissy."

There is no instinct in these things. Ruth had a dread of Cissy Clare. Gerald always spoke of her as frankly as possible: no *reticence* apparently, in word or action. She was his cousin; his early playmate; his mother's god-daughter. He even made a merit of never noticing Cissy before Ruth, when Ruth commented upon it.

"Darling," he said, "I know you have an idea that I was in love with Cissy; I can't get it out of your precious head—what then must I do? I can't absolutely neglect poor little Cis, who is a good, amiable, harmless little creature—so, I never dance with her, or talk to her, where it will wrong you to see me. If you bid me speak just the same, when you are present, I shall do it."

Of course, Ruth was ashamed, and begged pardon.

Then his other flirtations: "What would you have, Ruth, dear?" he would say; "recollect we are married, not lovers. We are living one life now. You would not wish that I should keep on talking only to you in society, and following you around with my eyes, as I did in my courting days? I must talk to other women."

"Certainly; but you talk to *one* woman."

"Cissy, again?"

"No—but all last week, at every party; in the street; at the opera, you were laughing over Eugenia Hopes' luxurious shoulders."

"By Jove! Ruth, they were luxurious. I wonder if anybody will ever rouse that girl. I should like to do it. Stop, darling, don't go off. Listen to me. Don't you know that I would rather talk to you than to anybody—but you must learn to understand me. I only care to do what you call 'devote myself' to some one indifferent woman at a time. You must learn to understand my temper, and I don't always wish to do what I prefer doing. That is the key note to my wayward ways that vex you sometimes. And then you are jealous."

"I know I am," said Ruth, gravely and sadly. "I wish I had some vanity; I think I should be happier."

"You are not happy then; you have made *me* so happy, and I cannot make you so?"—Gerald fixed his eyes upon her troubled, averted face.

She turned, and threw herself into his arms.

"I should be an ungrateful wretch, if I said or thought so. No, Gerald; these are but trifles after all, and are my necessary crosses. I must learn to bear them."

But there were occasions when such merely passing outbursts were superseded by the dark storm charged clouds of which I spoke. One such occurred about five months after their marriage, and may perhaps be looked upon as the final thunder clap which, severer and longer-rolling than its predecessors, sounding in our very ears, and seeming to threaten entire destruction, dies away harmlessly after all—echoing from the distance, faintly and more faintly still—till the rainbow is seen spanning the fair sky, and proclaiming that peace has really come at last.

Gerald had been more wayward, and more obstinately bent upon smiling demonstrations of a disagreeable nature than usual. He had worried poor Ruth as remorsely as a powerful child can torment a helpless kitten. Kitten gets *cattish* and shows her claws, and the child is then justified in knocking it about the head till it understands that "velvet paws" alone are admissable for the weaker party. Kitty submits, and blows cease; but her fur is rubbed the wrong way, her whiskers are pulled, her tail is pinched—all in fun, you know—just playful nonsense, but the impatient and not perfect-tempered feline specimen darts out the sharp defenses again, to be again summarily dealt with, and so on, and so on, *ad libitum*.

Gerald had a select party to play "draw poker," or "lanquenet," or some pleasant card deviltry of a delightful nature and gambling tendency; this was rather aggravating, because his wife, like most true women, had a profound aversion to games of chance. He had not exactly promised her to give up such things, but he had distinctly and voluntarily assured her that he meant to do so—and had been very much commended and thanked by her for his virtuous resolve.

The morning after this party, she casually found out that his pockets were empty, and her mild remonstrance was met by a contemptuous desire to know if she were trembling for her future. Immediately she repented, and felt humiliated at her own want of delicacy—but to teach her more prudence, Gerald told her carelessly, in the evening, that he was going to a supper, at the house of a lady of whom she justly disapproved, and whose very decided and marked attentions to Mr. Gray formed many a bone in Ruth's skeleton.

To ask him to give up going was, she found, a sure method to make him go; but she tried it, and produced the satisfactory result—a distinct assurance that nothing should prevent his keeping his engagement, but likewise he laughed very kindly at her fears of Mrs. Redbum's attractions.

The more affectionate his words, the more she hoped he would change his mind; but off he went, leaving her more irritated than she had ever been against her chosen lord and idolized master.

The next day she had quite lost her temper; she injudiciously asked him questions about his supper, and tears came to her eyes when, after he had given her vague and thoroughly evasive answers, he left the breakfast-room with a cool "good morning," and bade the footman tell his mistress that he would dine at the club.

In the afternoon, when Ruth was taking a solitary dine, her husband's drag passed her with Cecilia Clare seated beside him, looking excessively handsome, dressed to perfection, and both in the gayest spirits. *Les convenances* escorted them in the same shape of the groom in the dickey; but my unhappy heroine, a prey to the deepest melancholy, ordered the coachman "home," and passed the sad hours till bed time in restlessly pacing the floor of her drawing-room, alternately indignant against her absent darling, with herself for sending him away by her injudicious behaviour.

"He is right;" she murmured, "I cannot tie him to my apron string; we are not sighing lovers, but two people who have their separate duties to perform, and who, though united by the strongest bonds to each other, are not disunited from all the world. Because I care for no society but his, it does not follow that he should care for none but mine. And yet—it is cruel of him. Is it my fault—is it a crime that I regret each hour he gives others in needless, and to me most annoying, attentions? Why not have left me where I was? Why awaken in me this overwhelming love for him, this unreasoning delight in his presence, and then forever rob me of it." A passion of tears followed her almost inarticulate words.

"How silly!" she thought, recovering her old grimness of expression, and seating herself resolutely in a chair near the reading lamp. "Let me find my old self once more. I'll read."

A few pages were listlessly looked at, and then the book was thrown aside—10 o'clock struck—she drew the *buvard* and inkstand near her, seized a pen and wrote a few lines:

"Dearest Gerald," she said, "great resolutions come sometimes very suddenly. I remember your telling me—oh, *so* long ago—it was last October, was it not?—that if resolves went as quickly as repentance, the latter would never overtake the former. So, tonight, I have decided upon a great and sudden act. You will hear of it tomorrow. I am so tired of annoying, so helpless to prevent it. The childishness of my love for you, inexplicable as it would be to most people, *you ought* to understand. I was never really young, and certainly never happy, till I knew you. But the penalty I pay for the deep joy of my love, is too much for me. I have hit upon a plan, which I am sure will meet with your approval. And *may* [it bring] loving peace to both of us—to you, whom I so incessantly disturb with my jealous fears of—I know not what, and to me, who am now, and will be to my last breath,

> Faithfully yours,
> Ruth.

"I lay this on your toilette table; I can't bear to go to sleep with you fancying, probably, that I am angry."

She folded and directed her little note, and went off to her own room, first passing into her husband's dressing room, and depositing the loving message among the gold-mounted bottles and jars systematically arranged before his mirror.

Who could have recognized the Ruth Desborough of a year back, in the yearning-faced woman, who paused to look with such a long gaze of tenderness upon the manly belongings of that room? His riding whip lay upon a chair, she took it up and almost stealthily carried it to her lips; a pair of old boots, carelessly left near the wardrobe, were *his,* and fondly looked at for *his* sake.

Indeed, I don't think that the silliest girl could have behaved more foolishly—human nature is certainly very absurd—and monotonous.

Her maid was hastily dismissed, and the outer door locked as usual, but she did not know that she had carelessly pushed the bolt of the dressing room door—and worn out with the long tension of her mind, the sleeplessness of the two previous nights, and her tears, she presently fell into a deep slumber.

It was daylight when she awoke, and her eyes told her that she was alone and that there was a strip of paper pushed under the dressing room door. She sprang up and seized it.

"My own heart's darling, I write this with tears in my eyes. Oh, I have behaved shamefully to-night! I stayed at the club for no earthly reason but because I was angry. When I came home, your door was shut; you had bolted it. I scratched and scratched at the panels, but no answer. I lay down on my sofa really unhappy, and wishing so much that you would wake up. I tried again to make you hear me, you usually sleep so lightly, but in vain. Then I saw your dear little note, lying so white and still among my things, and a strange shiver seized me; I hardly dared to open it. Darling, I do and can love you so much; why is it, *why is it*, we do not get on well? At that stupid party I went to last night, I kept wandering about, caring to speak to no one. I missed my Ruth's loving look; and yet, this morning, I was cross to you, and continued so all day; but my anger has gone to the winds now. And your poor, little, good note. What plan is it? I am half tempted to arouse the house; you are so still. What should I feel to know that this door—but sleep on, dear child; I put this under the sill. I hope it will catch your eye at early dawn."

I don't essay to describe Ruth's deep delight as she read this note; her eyes devoured the contents, and then she flew to her husband, who was lying awake upon the sofa. On her knees beside him, with her happy head upon his breast, she thanked him for writing such a wondrously clever and brilliant production. I fancy no pen, to her mind, ever traced sentences so perfect.

Never was Gerald more truly her lover than in the grey dawn of that April morning; he had evidently been shaken by a tender remorse for his victim. It was the turning point in their lives. Ruth's real happiness dated from that day; Gerald had been seriously alarmed; and it had awakened all the best feelings of his nature. He had been vaguely uneasy about Ruth's note; he had been thinking about her "wealth of devotion," and he felt how very dear she had made herself to him, over and above the fact which we cannot doubt, of his never having loved anybody but herself, except his own self, probably.

"And what is that mysterious plan, my darling?" he asked.

"Let us off to Europe for a year or two; we could easily persuade papa to spare us. I think it will do my temper good."

Gerald smiled and kissed her.

"Your's is a very nice plan, and I have not one objection to offer."

In May they sailed.

✿ CHAPTER IX

The Grays were two years absent. Mr. Desborough did not miss his daughter enough to hurry her back again, nor was she disturbed by any visions, which constantly filled the anxious minds of her fellow-citizens, who more than once provided a step-mother for Ruth, and a fine family of half sisters and brothers to share her patrimony.

She wrote very regularly to him, and he was very proud of the letters; dwelling with great satisfaction upon her presentation at two courts, her admission into very high circles both in England and France, and accepting, as a master of secondary importance, but still pleasant enough to know, the fact of her conjugal happiness, which, even to his rather obtuse comprehension in such matters, was clear enough.

Gerald wrote sometimes, too; one of his letters from Paris contained the gratifying information of the birth of an heir, and what was not quite so expected, of an heiress also. "Ruth named them at once; and is so determined upon it," he wrote, "that although you may naturally think, dear sir, that she is too fond of almost perpetuating my cognomen, she *will* have both of our babies called for me—Gerald and Geraldine; therefore, they will stand in their baptismal record, and very fine little monkeys they are, I can assure you. Ruth is doing wonderfully well, and will write so soon as her stately professional attendant will permit her to use her pen."

Another letter, some two months afterwards, had best be given in full:

Paris, April 10th, 18—

My Dear Sir:

I have the pleasure of announcing a piece of intelligence that is very well worth telling. You may remember to have heard me say that one of my late aunts, Mrs. Norman Gray's nephews, has been from my boyhood my closest friend. His name is Francis Josselyn; he, with his elder brother, William, and a sister, became heirs to my aunt's fortune by the terms of her father's will, and her marriage settlements. At the time of that sad blow when I lost both of my most kind and most partial relations, Francis was traveling in the East, exploring the centre of Africa for aught we knew, or setting up as a private Arab citizen, with a house, a palm tree, and a tent of his own. It was very long before any intimation could reach him of the change in his pecuniary condition, and when it did, he merely sent word that he would come home after a while.

Since I left America, nearly a year ago, a sort of fatality seemed to follow the Josselyns; Emily, who had married very well, with as strong settlements as her aunt before her, but only with regard to herself and her possible children, died last December, of typhoid fever, some weeks before her expected confinement; and not ten days after, William would drive a horse warranted *to* runaway, which *did* so, dashed him out of the buggy, and killed him on the spot.

He was unmarried, and, consequently, my friend Francis became sole heir, and his presence absolutely necessary. He was fished out of the desert, or wherever he was, and got to Boston by some circuitous and eccentric route best suited to his taste.

In looking over the packages and letters accumulated for him, there was one always considered too weighty to be sent by post to Arabia, Vetria, or Timbuctoo, for it was a desk of our Aunt's, carefully sealed up, and directed to him. In it he found an earnest and urgent appeal to share his portion with me, if ever fate should put in his power; a duplicate letter to myself, asked the same of me, in the other case. Our beloved aunt added a few joint words to the effect that we were equally dear to her, and she was satisfied that the affection of each would rejoice to serve the other. Now, as Francis had seized the earliest chance to send me from his own generous heart a like proposition, when first he heard of our uncle and aunt's death, he triumphs like the great souled creature he is, over what he considers the legal and authoritative necessity for me to accept; especially as the address of the desk to him was her last living thought.

He argues that this is a will of our aunt's, which, if the law ignored her right to make, justice requires us to honour.

I have yielded to his most generous persuasions, in a measure, leaving the management of our affairs to him; ostensibly, during my absence abroad, but, in reality, never intending to have a division of the property, unless I find out that he lets me draw more than my share.

It is in vain that I argue with him that by your liberality, Ruth and I "fare sumptuously every day," and "purple and fine linen" are week day clothes. He says, and it is a truth I have always forcibly felt, that I shall be more satisfied when you are not my sole banker; although the consciousness that I have now a very independent and handsome income, will never make me forget that your generosity of spirit, as well as of purse, has never for one moment caused me to remember with pain that I brought so little in worldly goods to my dearest Ruth.

As for her, were I a prince, and she a beggar, she could not more systematically, and as if unconsciously, try to make me feel that everything is mine, and she, my dependent.

The little ones are fat and thriving, they are no longer only snow balls with a dash of red upon them, and Valencienne lace, (I think that is the article,) running all over their small bodies in flounces and frills. They begin to sit up and look like Christians; one of the *bairnes* almost shook her cap off her head this morning, with a toss of indignation, because I refused to believe that Gerald, jr., can say "mamma," and Miss Geraldine lisp "papa." It all sounds bah! bah! to me.

But I leave this kind of talk for Ruth's letters. Party spirit runs higher than ever in our State, I see by the papers. The —— comes occasionally to me— fire-breathing and foolish as usual. The lack of brains and the excess of arrogance that distinguish that journal, fill me with deep delight—that I am not there, and forced to look to its pages for my breakfast-table views of politics, at home and abroad.

In our obscurer districts are the people still voting for C—— for Congress, although his tombstone can be seen any day! Just as in some northern counties, it is said, votes are constantly dropped in the electoral boxes for Washington, maintaining that the report of his death is only got up by jealous rivals anxious to supersede him.

But my second sheet is filled. Ruth's love.

I am, dear sir, yrs. faithfully,
GERALD GRAY

Another year passed away without any particular event to mark it; but when the third early spring of their absenteeism began, Mr. Desborough grew impatient to see his grand children. Such feelings must be very natural, because we constantly witness them; and parents, by no means doting upon their immediate offspring, are frequently quite wild about their grand children. I suppose that the instinct of paternity, like madness, sometimes skips a generation.

The Grays promised to make their arrangements to return in the autumn. The twins needed sea air; they were going to Biarritz. Gerald wanted to visit Baden again, and Ruth had agreed to meet some friends afterwards at Pau.

Ruth *had* friends now; she numbered not a few Duchesses and Countesses among her allies, not to mention pleasant English women, and some slightly foreignized Americans, like herself. But, I will not describe my heroine as she looked to those who only knew her as she was now. I prefer to bring her home, and, let her be framed in the old *cadre* of the first twenty-six years of her life. However, I will just lift the veil before she leaves Paris, for one small glimpse of her.

Rue des Vieux Augustins

12 Oct., 18—

Dear Mrs. St. Clair:

You guessed as rightly as you usually do, when you decided that to hear from you and to execute your commissions would [give] me great pleasure. Gerald was quite proud of your confidence in my taste.

I took your measure and your directions to Vegriou; she understood perfectly, of course, but still these people constantly are guilty of mistakes; so I was careful to make her go over everything with me. Your ball dresses I chose of materials as light as a married woman can wear. Gerald can't bear to see heavy silks dancing, and you know how correct his notions are. We decided that a new shade of that eternal *mauve* would suit you for a dinner dress, and I have had it trimmed with white lace. I *had* determined on black *chantilly*, but Gerald chanced to be struck with the lovely combination of color and a suit of *point d'alencon* worn by Madame de Boisvoger, and called my attention to it, so I instantly rushed off and countermanded the first order. I am sure you will approve.

Clara Daix has the honor of furnishing your velvet bonnet, but I prefer Laure for your lighter ones. The *maison Gagelin* promises me a *manteau de velours ravissant* for you, and *Tilmaun* actually has the most elegant *coiffures* of anybody. In *that* department nothing would tempt me to try Vegriou again. Last winter, at a birth-day *fete* at Madame de Villeneure's, Vegriou sent home my dress at the last moment; Gerald wanted to be early, and so I had scarcely glanced at myself when I pronounced that I was ready. He screamed out when he saw me, that I looked as if I had been got by Madame R., in old King street! Such a wreath to be sure!

He dragged it off my head, and scolded at Val[er]ie, who, in vain, protested, as was perfectly true, that Madame would not listen to her assurances when putting it on, *que cela allait fut mal, et etait du plus mauvais gout.*

I humbly listened, as in duty bound, to Gerald's reproaches, while Valerie, almost sobbing from wounded taste, smoothed my disordered hair and replaced the *detestable guirlande* with diamond stars. But the next day I went after Vegriou, and told her that Monsieur would choose another *modiste* for me if there were a repetition of this crime. "Monsieur!" she repeated, with great amazement, but the fact is, I know so little after all about dress—it was only the dread of Gerald's railleries that ever made me think of such things. He knows this; so he takes the greatest interest in my toilette, and *helps* me wonderfully.

I cannot tell you how lovely my children are; you must forgive my pride in them. Of course, they are very much alike, but still Geraldine is the most beautiful. Already, she is a miniature of her father. I long to show them to you, since you ask so kindly about them. But I fear that they will be terribly spoiled; Mrs. Gray will not be able to help it, because they are Gerald's; and my father, who seems so anxious to see them, cannot resist, I am sure, their attractions. I shall have to be very severe. Somebody (I am really ashamed to mention my husband so often,) says that I may as well announce I mean to murder them. He is looking over my shoulder, as you may conjecture from this, and desires to convey his most respectful and admiring homage.

We sail by next steamer, this day week, from Liverpool, so that my letter will only be a little in advance of

Yours, very sincere,
RUTH GRAY

When Bertha St. Clair received this letter, she laughed, with genuine pleasure, over its contents.

"Love, the mighty master!" she exclaimed to Mr. Taunton, who dropped in to see her, (no very unusual thing,) on the evening of the day whose afternoon mail brought this missive. "I mean to have Ruth's dissertation on dress framed and hung up! Do you remember what sort of gowns Miss Desborough used to wear?"

"Perfectly."

"Does the mirror of your memory reflect the outline of her bonnets—the hang of her skirts?"

"I think so, faintly."

"Pray try and make it distinct, for by the mere force of contrast, I think you will enjoy seeing our fresh stepped from the-Journal-des-Modes towns-woman. It was a hazardous experiment to rely upon John Hutchinson's vivid account of Mrs. Gray's present perfect dressing, and send to her for my winter supplies, when it is comparatively so short a time since the heiress' awful toilettes used to disturb the eyes of her perforce silent friends; and yet, you dared, at their wedding breakfast, to tell me that I over-rated Gerald Gray!"

"What has he got to do with it? Can't his wife put herself in the hands of the French milliners without his being answerable for it, or credited with it?"

"Oh, out of my decided and misplaced friendship! haven't you read the lady's letter? Do you not see that she dresses *for* Gerald, *at* Gerald, *through* Gerald. He is in a hurry to get to a ball and the foolish creature don't see what she puts on! At that moment 'dressing for Gerald' was secondary to the horror of 'keeping Gerald waiting,' and the woman, who, I make no doubt, studies combinations of colors, slopes of sleeves, and *bavolets* of bonnets, was rushing off with some monster of a thing on her head, rather than that her liege lord should ask twice, if 'Madame were coming.' If you can name to me a greater work performed by mortal man than the transforming of Miss Desborough into a well-dressed woman, taking an interest in her own costume, and careful for the commissions of other people in that line, pray name it!"

Mr. Taunton laughed.

"I still believe," he protested, "that it is the force of surroundings, and not the power of love or Gray."

"Very well; let us wait and see. Already we know that her outward ornaments are revolutionized; what strange up-settings of character, manners and habits, (quite secondary matters!) may we not look for!"

CHAPTER X

"Half-a-dozen people sup with me to-morrow evening, the 'objects of the entertainment,' (unlike those at the wondrous party given by the D——'s ages ago, when we had no tea nor coffee, and Anna counted the 'forty-legs' that in some strange way, walked over the mirrors, all evening and we perished for lack of entertainment of every sort, first, and then nearly died afterwards from too much, in the shape of *that* magnificent feed,)—heavens! what a parenthesis—well! the 'objects' of this entertainment are Mr. and Mrs. Gray.

I have seen her!

I say no more; only this, you will not know what to say, when you have seen her too.

B. St. C.

Charles street, Wednesday, 6th Nov.
To Roland Taunton, Esq."

"You did not name any hour, so I came early," said Mr. Taunton, as he entered Mrs. St. Clair's drawing room.

"You were right," she answered, shaking hands with him. "But I ought to have said 9 o'clock, and, in fact," looking at her watch, "it is very nearly that now."

"And how do you find our foreign friends?" asked Mr. Taunton, lazily dropping into a chair beside his hostess.

"Very pleasant."

"Need one ask after the twins?"

"I advise you, if you wish to stand well with their mama, not to forget them. They are dear little things."

"And the papa? How is he?"

"As handsome as ever."

"Looks *married?*"

"Very."

"Seems happy?"

"Perfectly."

"Are you aware that you are cutting off your slave with strangely laconic replies?"

"Yes."

"*Parceque* . . . ?"

"*Parceque*—I warned you that I was desirous to let you decide for yourself the great question of my knowledge of character; so not one word more of Mr. and Mrs. Gray. Have you been reading Owen Meredith's poems? Don't you like them?"

"My dear Mrs. St. Clair, he says just what everybody has been saying since Solomon, and he does not say it as well as Byron. He howls too plaintively all the while. . . ."

"And you are too utterly prosaic to appreciate him. Of course, he says what everybody has been saying; how can it be helped? We are all feeling every day just what everybody has been feeling, but is our love commonplace, our sorrow meaningless, our hatred, and envy and malice, alas! of no consequence, because they are such old sentiments? The feelings of which he writes are as old as the hills, but his words and similes are new, I protest; and then his verses are not transcendental, shadowy, vague, but plainly expressed and *human*. I don't know if he is very desolate really, this young Bulwer, as his poems might lead one to believe, (in fact, I *have* heard that he is a very gay and jolly youth,) but, if the simplest of my friends wished to tell me that he or she had loved blindly or unfortunately, had been deceived and forgotten, had lived recklessly and repented, their hearts could not speak more plainly to my heart than in those pages."

"Well! as I have never loved blindly or unfortunately, been deceived and forgotten, had lived recklessly and repented, they are to me, only morbidly sentimental."

Bertha turned, and took from the table beside her the little blue and gold-bound volume, and, with her charming modulated voice, read:

"The more we change, the more is all the same,
     Our last grief was a tale of other years
Quite outworn, 'till to our own hearts it came—
     Wishes are pilgrims to the vale of tears
Our brightest joys are but as airy shapes
     Of cloud that fade on evening's glimmering slope,
     And disappointment hawks the hovering hope,
Forever pecking at the painted grapes.

"Why can we not one moment pause, and cherish
     Love tho' love turn to tears? or for hope's sake
Bless hope albeit the thing we hope may perish?
     For happiness is not in what we take,
But in what we give. What matter tho' the thing
     We cling to most should fail us? Dust to dust!
     It is the *feeling* for the thing—the trust
In beauty somewhere, to which souls should cling.

"My youth has fail'd, if failure lies in aught
     The warm heart dreams, or which the working hand
Is set to do. I have fail'd in aidless thought,
     And steadfast purpose, and in self-command.
I have fail'd in hope, in wealth, in love; fail'd in the word
     And in the deed, too, I have failed. And yet,

Albeit with eyes from recent weepings wet,
Sing thou, my soul, thy psalm unto the Lord!

    . . . .

"For now the fulness of its failure makes
My spirit fearless: and despair grows bold.
My brow, beneath its sad self-knowledge aches.
  Life's presence passes Thine a thousand fold
In contemplated terror. Can I lose
  Aught by that desperate temerity
  Which now leaves no choice but to surrender thee
My life without condition? Could I choose

"A stipulated sentence, I might ask
For ceded dalliance to some cherished vice,
Or half remission of some desperate task;
  Now, all I have is hateful. What is the price?
Speak, Lord! I hear the Fiend's hand at the door—"

"No, you don't; it is mine," said Arthur McIvor, entering.

Bertha put down her book, and proclaimed that both the new-comer, for breaking the speech, and Mr. Taunton for laughing at it, were utterly unworthy of hearing any more poetry then, and of her favour, forever.

A few minutes afterwards, all the guests had appeared, except the "objects," but before Mrs. St. Clair's patience and politeness were too much tried, they entered.

Gerald Gray was the same handsome, Greek-faced, saucy-eyed creature as ever; a trifle more dandified in his air, and perhaps not so boyish in his manners. But his wife! *Was* it Ruth Desborough?

Beside him stood a tall and shapely woman, in a magnificent dress of violet velvet, with rich sunset gleams of crimson about its heavy folds. Neck and arms were bare; falling away from her smooth clear shoulders, masses of lace relieved the solidity of her gown's material, and were confined over the bust by a bouquet of golden grapes with deep green leaves. Braid upon braid of black and shining hair were rolled about her head, and low at the back a wreath of the same style as the cluster upon her *corsage,* fell almost to her waist, its long tendrils giving a singularly graceful *abandon* to every movement of the wearer. Strictly beautiful no one could call her, but her fine eyes wore a look of such pure and perfect repose and intelligence. They had such a light of deep thought, passing words! Her lips, once so colorless and *set,* were now of a healthy red, with mobile curve playing about the corners. Her complexion had lost its sallow tinge; her figure had gained its natural proportions, and without challenging the sculptor's chisel, its lines were full and feminine.

She was, in fact, what our English neighbors call "a fine woman." Conversing, as she now was, with Mrs. St. Clair, she had more of the latter's coquetry or "passional attraction;" her sentences were clearly uttered, calmly composed, with a certain nameless, *insaissable* coldness of tone; but her husband spoke, and, on the instant, a kind of rosy shadow, more outward than inward, softened and warmed her look and accent. There was a lingering caress in each word she used towards him, as if her great heart enveloped each phrase destined for *those* ears in a certain intonation never bestowed upon the public. There was nothing fulsome, nor obtrusive, nor conspicuously affectionate, in either phrase or voice, but to a close observer it was sufficiently plain.

He was her sun; from him she drew the warmth and radiance of her existence.

Does any one remember the difference between Ellen Kean's acting, when she was upon the boards with no matter whom, and when Charles Kean appeared?

Supper was announced; this was Mrs. St. Clair's favorite meal. She pronounced suppers infinitely more agreeable and conducive to sociability than a dinner, where the continual presence of servants, and the constant change of courses, interrupt conversation.

After the first few dishes had been discussed and removed, the "domesticity" retired, whence the touch of the silver bell beside the lady of the house could easily recall them, and the conversation grew both animated and sparkling.

Unlike her former self, Ruth took part in all that was going on, and was even betrayed into quite a long speech about the error into which Americans fall, concerning Paris, its manners, morals and customs.

"I know nothing so belied as French women," she said. "We are led to believe that there is no wedded happiness in Paris; that every *menage* has separate interests and pleasures; that gentlemen habitually neglect their wives, and women care only for dress and flirtations. I assure you it is not so; there are as many happy marriages in France as in England or America. I am not prepared to defend the way in which young people are *fiance* there, but in consideration for my many charming friends, who are Parisians, born and bred and married, I protest against condemning their entire households. I would not approve of our inaugurating '*marriages de convenance,*' here, but I cannot let any one say that they *all* turn out badly.

"Then you still stake your faith on love-marriages?" asked Mrs. St. Clair.

"I do," answered Ruth. "Ours is a love-match. . . . but," and she colored, with a smile which lent a real beauty to her face, while her eyes glanced for one second at Gerald, who was watching her with evident pride and admiration, "we are narrowing down this discussion to a very personal one, and I am having it all to myself."

The light faded from her cheek, and she turned to listen to Mr. Taunton's question about a Paris acquaintance. But not with the grim and grave politeness, or endurance rather, of Miss Desborough; but, no, with a stately suavity and a quiet attention as charming as it was natural.

But a certain determined Miss Charlemont, who always enjoyed asking questions, preferred to exercise her mission just here.

"And you actually believe that there are thoroughly happy marriages, Mrs. Gray?"

"I should be sorry to disbelieve it," Ruth smilingly answered.

"Do you believe in their actual existence, or only in their possibility?"

"In both, under certain circumstances."

"For my part," put in Mr. Taunton, "I should the more readily subscribe to what Mrs. Gray says if those certain circumstances mean that marriages should be arranged as Dr. Johnson suggested, by the Lord Chancellor. Suitability of fortune, position, and so on, forming the foundation. . . ."

"For shame!" cried Bertha. "If ever the *libre arbitre* should rule, it is in the choice of a life-time companion. I would trust the choosing of my wardrobe to a judicious taste," she bowed to Mrs. Gray, "but for a husband, permit me to suggest that I can myself best tell what kind of man I should find it easiest 'to love, honor, and obey.'"

"Well, a single life for me!" said Miss Charlemont, tossing back her long, fair curls, with all the *aplomb* of a beauty not yet twenty-five, and sure that no one doubted her power to make it a double one whenever she pleased to do so. "I have known a great many married people, and I hope those present will excuse me for thinking that I consider myself a great deal better off than any of the wives I have studied."

"Oh, Lizzie, don't be so severe upon us poor women!" exclaimed Bertha, putting up her fair hands.

"Spare *us*, Miss Charlemont," said Gerald, "and leave some hope to your adorers."

"Oh, I don't say that either men or women are entirely to blame," remarked the young lady, with the calm self-possession of an American girl, who belongs to the school called "fast." "I only mean that—present company, of course, excepted—I should find it difficult to name one couple whom I consider happily married."

"What says Mrs. Gray to that?" asked Mr. Taunton, with quiet malice, as he looked upon Miss Charlemont's remark as a complete refutation of Ruth's belief.

"I regret Miss Charlemont's sad experience, but can, at the same time, congratulate her that her ideas are not founded upon a personal knowledge."

"Such profound discrimination, and such clear proof don't convince you?" pursued Mr. Taunton.

"They do not," said Ruth, who could not help smiling. Then leaning slightly forward with a graceful bend of her stately figure, she addressed Miss Charlemont with sweet gravity. "I do not know, of course, from whom you have drawn such unflattering and such discouraging convictions, dear Miss Charlemont, but, in the name of that time-honored sisterhood to which I belong, let me suggest that if the wives, whose condition you deplore, entered 'lightly and unadvisedly' into their wedded state, neither you nor they must be surprised that the result does not bring happiness. Or, if uncongenial elements are brought together by third parties, and are expected to mingle—what then? If I pour that finest oil of Lucca, excellent in itself," touching with her fan the flask from which Mr. Taunton had deluged his oysters, "and this purest spring water together, shall I make them combine, simply because I imprison them in my tumbler? Scarcely; and yet, all these are perfect of their kind, and, the glass, especially," lifting with her round white arm and gemmed fingers the beautiful Bohemian goblet, "is exquisite, you must admit. But the oil and the water would make, at their best, only a muddy compound, whereas. . . ." she smilingly extended the glass towards Mr. Taunton, and looked at the champagne he filled for her. She added water from her caraffe, held up the ruddy crystal towards the light, till her hand seemed bathed in the glow, then touched it to her lips with a bow to the young lady, and set it down.

With all her stately gravity, it was coquettish, and certainly very pretty.

"I shall never see a tumbler again without thinking of getting married," said Arthur McIvor.

"Only, if you feel as weak as water, be sure about the Champagne, and avoid oil, my little Marquis," said Bertha, who was much given to making a pet of this boy.

"Well," said Mr. Aubrey, "even in opposition to Mrs. Gray, I am forced to assure her that I have seen people who seemed as dissimilar as oil and water agree perfectly in the long run, while some spirits which appeared as likely to rush together as Champagne and Adam's Ale, made a confounded mess of it. Is it the beauty of the glass, the symbolic ceremony that Mrs. Gray considers perfect in itself, which makes occasionally the former miserable?"

"To drop that metaphor, that illustration," said Ruth, slightly coloring, "and to speak plainly, I cannot believe that what Almighty Goodness considered the highest and last blessing bestowed upon Adam is to us, his children, only a necessary evil. It was that which I disputed with Miss Charlemont, and which she has kindly permitted."

"Besides," added Bertha, swooping down to the rescue, "dangerous experiments are not peremptorily unsuccessful. I have a friend who prevails in filling a camphine lamp while the wick is still alight. She has not been blown up. I own I always leave the room, and expect to hear the explosion—am prepared to go in afterwards, pick up the fragments, and preach a sermon over the remains, to the text, 'served her right.' It has not happened yet, but I am none the less unshakably convinced that she is frightfully imprudent; and when some accident does happen, she shall not have my sympathy, for I will be sure that she got what she deserves."

"Which implies, . . ." said Mr. Taunton, who liked to make his hostess talk.

"That when man or woman with open eyes and without deception practised, marries unfortunately, I give them my heartiest pity, my sincerest wishes, my warmest sympathy; but if some mercenary motive, some unexampled carelessness, some wilful obstinacy, prompts the step—if it be 'an establishment,' a pique, or *ennui*, which has brought about what ought to be so solemn and sacred a bond, and they find it unendurable, don't look to this severe speaker for comfort."

"Mrs. St. Clair has aptly supported your views, dear Ruth," said Gerald, "but . . ." and he held up his watch.

Everyone was amazed at the hour, and they all rose from the table; carriages were called, and the ladies retired to be hooded and shawled.

"Mrs. St. Clair tells me," said Mr. Taunton to Ruth, as she waited in the hall for Gerald to find his *chapeau gibus*, which had gone astray; "Mrs. St. Clair tells me that you have two of the prettiest children that ever made a mother proud."

"My babies," said Ruth, with a bright smile. "They are to my eyes very beautiful, because they look like my husband."

"Come, come, Roland," cried Gerald, "you are going quite too far in your attentions to this lady. She is so insanely vain about those infants, that if you were the most disagreeable of men, she would pass the whole time on our way home now in commending your amiability, your frankness, and general good qualities. As it is, you are far too charming for me to permit such strides in my wife's good graces." And Gerald, laughingly, shook hands with him and drawing Ruth's *burnous* more closely around her, gayly marched off.

"Well?" enquired Mrs. St. Clair, with a saucy sparkle in her eye, as Mr. Taunton came to wish her good-night.

He kissed her hand.

"Never, oh, puissant princess, will I again dispute your most extravagant persuasion! You are right. I am ready to take off my hat in humble admiration of Gerald Gray, if, in return, he will permit me in all companies to express my even greater affection of the wife—whom he has created."

"Oh! you needn't testify to my judgment by falling in love with her," remonstrated Bertha, with a laughing *moue.* "Fall in love with her! Why, even if I were in that *devergonde* spot, Paris, in whose *devergondage,* or *disme* [?], the radiant Ruth does not believe, I should know that it was 'mere midsummer madness' to fall in love with her! I should be like the noble lord who bought Punch and took him home, sans the showman, thinking to find the *manimette* amusement without the wire-puller."

"Yes; or, like Rosamond, of the 'Purple Jar,' the willful little girl of whom Miss Edgeworth tells us, who would buy said jar to put flowers in, and when she had got it all to herself, lo! the lovely color came from the liquid contents which she had had taken out."

"Yes, Mrs. Gray is a part of Gerald Gray— and *apart* from him, she would tumble to pieces, grand as she looks now."

"Grand, indeed!" put in Arthur McIvor; "how the woman dresses too! I recognize her *solitaire* ear-rings, but they don't *limp* in her ears as they used to do, when her father 'had them out' on state occasions. And did you see her hands? Such brown, ugly things they used to be!"

"Oh, I fancy she owns and rejoices in *pate d'amande* and mother-of-pearl nail polishers, and all such dainty trifles, which, *dans le temps,* she scorned. But, go home, good people, before I yawn my head off. My politeness won't permit me to let you see me gape."

"One instant, dear Mrs. St. Clair: do you think Gerald is really in love now, or was it all the time?"

"I think—I think—that I don't know. Where is that little idiot, Cissy Clare? You needn't any of you, answer. Good night."

The question asked by Mrs. St. Clair seemed to be one of small importance to Mr. Gray. He casually remarked to Ruth, after their first dinner at his uncle's, that Phyllis was faded, since her marriage, (she was now Mrs. Ralph Fordyce,) and that Cecilia had lost her color, but was very pretty still, and then appeared to think no more about either.

He had met both of his cousins with the same jesting, half-teasing manner, habitual to him, had rallied Phyl on Mr. Fordyce's wig without the smallest consideration for her conjugal pride; and had pressed Cissy to sing "The Wind and the Beam loved the Rose," and then laughed at her absurdly affected style, and gave imitations of it, and he seemed not at all overcome by her telling him that if he had learned to think the ballad foolish, and her singing absurd, he need not tell her so.

Ruth came to her assistance.

"What is Gerald doing, Cissy?" she asked.

"Only teasing, I suppose," remarked Phyllis.

"Only asking me to sing a song he used to consider very beautiful and that he now laughs at."

"Not the *song*, Cissy," said Gerald, saucily.

"Well, the singing, then," said Cissy, very good-humoredly; "you used to like it too."

Gerald vowed that her present performance was not at all that of by-gone days.

"It is just what it always was; it is you who are changed," remarked Cecilia.

"Perhaps so; you see the grand opera has made me a connoisseur. But I protest, Cis, that if I have heard better singing, I have not seen better temper."

Cissy's dimples broke over her smiling face at this compliment, and soon after the Grays' carriage was announced, and they went home.

A few days more and business called them to Beauchamp, where they were to stay until race week.

Ruth enjoyed vastly her return to her own home; and even the gayeties of Paris seemed for a time banished from Gerald's mind by the duties of a planter.

Mr. Desborough came to spend a week or two, especially to enjoy the society of his grandchildren, whom he considered the most marvelous specimens of juvenile humanity. He would walk about half the morning leading each stumbling little baby, and followed by the *bonne,* or sitting under an oak tree, would alternately help to dress Geraldine's doll or set up Gerald's tin soldiers. He wished to have these two-year-olders "assisting" during the whole ceremony of dinner, but the wise mamma forbade their appearance until dessert, when he was allowed to administer an occasional bit of preserved ginger, or a savory biscuit, to the youthful tyrants of his old age.

One morning towards the middle of January, Gerald received a letter which seemed to fill him with anxiety and concern. It was brought by a messenger on horseback from his mother.

He went off with it to the library, wrote a hasty answer, despatched the servant, and returned to find Ruth, who was eagerly waiting for him in her dressing-room.

"I have something to tell you, darling," he said; "something that is grave and terrible."

She started up with a smothered cry.

"Have you time to listen to me?"

"Time to listen to you?" she repeated; "oh, Gerald, what a question! What is it? I would not go out of this house, after seeing your look a little while ago. I fancied that you had something to tell me; what is it?"

He sat down, and drew her back to the sofa beside him, holding her hand.

"Dear Ruth," he said, "do you recollect my telling you once that there was something connected with my life that I might one day be forced to reveal, but I thought it best to let it alone and unsaid, until there was a necessity for doing otherwise?"

"Yes; it was long after our marriage, and I told you then, that I *ought* to know all that concerned you, and *had* hoped that I did."

"Just so, dear, but I thought differently. The moment has come when I must tell it. Ruth, did you never hear of my father?"

"Your father?" repeated Ruth, with astonishment; "Your father! yes; I heard—I always supposed—I took it for granted—that he died when you were a child."

"He did not, but I have not seen him since I was a child. *Your* father was in the East Indies, I believe, when the event happened which virtually widowed my poor mother, and he was reported to have died; and the scandal of the whole thing passed away in fresher tales, and as you never listened to gossip, and Mr. Desborough's acquaintances are business men, and cautious men, and our engagement took place almost before we were known to be acquainted, no one had then the hardihood to speak of it before him or you."

Ruth's face grew into a faint semblance of its old lines.

"Was it absolutely necessary to hold back this mystery, whatever it is, from me?"

"I told you just now that I thought so."

She toyed with her wedding-ring, twisting it round and round upon her finger with the thumb of the same hand—a motion familiar to her when annoyed, and her eyes gazed straight ahead. She evidently was thinking more of the concealment than of what was concealed.

"Do you not take an interest in what deeply concerns and distresses me, darling?"

"Do you doubt it? I am waiting till it is your pleasure to speak."

"My father," he went on, and as Gerald spoke, he placed his wife's head with gentle force upon his shoulder, and made her look up at him; "my father was a very handsome, dissipated, reckless man—a careless husband, and an indifferent parent. He gambled and did everything a man can do, and still keep his place as a gentleman, till, one day, his evil star brought him, face to face, with a person whose home he had made desolate, and then abandoned his victim. They say it was a fair enough fight—both were armed—but one fell forever, and the other escaped.

Ruth started up—"and my children," she said; "you have given my children such a lineage as that?"

"They are *my* children, Ruth; are you ashamed of *their* father?"

"I should have known this; you should have told me: you spoke openly enough even on the first day we met, of puerile, pitiful money matters; *this* you withheld—not only then, but always."

"I did it, darling, for the best. I did it to spare you a knowledge which could only grieve."

"You knew then, as you know now, that there is no grief which, to my mind, ought to be spared with the one you love. And was it to spare me a grief, or to spare yourself a refusal, that this was withheld?"

Gerald set his teeth together, and the dark flame burnt in his blue eyes.

"As you please," he said, and turned away. "I come to you beset with troubles of no common order, and you talk to me of your feelings, with neither sympathy nor interest for mine."

"They ought ever to have been the same," answered Ruth, more gently; "our feelings, should have had no divided line. But go on."

"My father escaped from the hands of justice, and four years ago, we *did* think that we had tidings of his death—this time positively, and not like the rumors which were skilfully put about in the first instance, that he had been drowned in one of our own rivers, just after he got away. But we were wrong then, as the world was fifteen years ago; he has come back to his native city."

"Oh!" groaned Ruth, and she moved nearer to him.

"The letter from my mother is written in despair; he has been to see her; he trusts in his changed appearance, and in the lapse of time that has passed since the — death I spoke of. But we know the Jernigham's brother avowed solemnly, on the dead man's body, to avenge him—he will be recognized— the whole wretched history brought to light again—another murder, or a trial—God knows what." He started up and paced the room.

"My poor darling," said Ruth; she had put aside her displeasure, and the sense of broken confidence. "See," she continued, "I will say no more about what you ought to have done. Let us talk now of what you ought to do. What are you going to do?"

"I have ordered my brougham [?] wagon and 'Midnight.' I shall drive at once to town, see my mother, and decide upon my plans. So far as I can judge by her hasty, unhappy note, he has come back penniless, attracted by the *news* to him of my uncle's death and my marriage. He has been in Australia, Cochin China—the devil knows where! God be thanked, Francis' liberality of heart and means enables me to provide for him; but it shall be on one condition—that he returns whence he came. If he refuses now or breaks his word afterwards, I shall put him in the clutches of the law without hesitation."

"Then, you don't require to consult with me?"

"No, darling, I seldom need to consult with anybody. Even if their ideas are better than mine, I prefer my own. Didn't you know that? Need I remind you that 'my own' is better than anybody's 'own'—my own wife, for instance, my own love, who began just now, by tormenting me, and ends by putting her two dear hands in mine, and accepting all I say, as 'wisest, virtuousest, discreetest, best.'"

He bent his lips to hers; all was peace again.

"I will give you this undeniable praise, darling: you never oppose me, nor dispute with me, nor assert yourself, except just long enough to show that you have a will of your own, and ideas of your own, but that they always give way to mine. There comes the waggon—ring for Valerie and let her put a couple of shirts, and so on, in my valise. I will run off and kiss the babies."

In five minutes he was back, as lively as if he were starting on a pleasure excursion. Ruth could not help saying, when Valerie had disappeared with the valise, and was heard in her shrill French accents, down stairs, ordering it put under the seat of the *voiture:*

"My dearest Gerald, what wonderful spirits you have! How do you manage it?"

"They manage me, darling. If it were not for this eternal spring of nonsense and lightness that I have within, such an errand as this would be fearful. Instead of wondering about my spirits, you ought to be thanking God that I have them."

"I do, but when will you be back."

"My child, do I ever answer a question like that, even if I knew the answer myself?—which, in this case, I do not. I shall write continually, and return just as soon as I can—of that rest assured. Good-bye, darling, my good little Ruth; God bless you; keep up a brave heart. Take care of my namesakes, they are both asleep; and, oh, by the way, make some excuse to your father for me. Give him anything but the true reason, steer clear even of my mother in speaking, and don't fret. Once more, good-bye."

She saw him off, so handsome he looked, so brave, so bright; he was just gathering the reins from his servant's hand, and casting a laughing, cheering, loving, last glance at her, when the spirited horse gave a bound and a prance. How the beautiful lip lost in one instant its playful smile, as it proudly curved over the white teeth, and he tightened the rein, and showed "Midnight" that a master's hand was on the bridle.

And Ruth gazed after him till the great gate clanged behind the waggon wheels, and the waggon and the loved one, and the black horse and the groom in the rumble all swept behind the hedge and were lost to her view.

Left alone, she began to think over this most unhappy resurrection of what she had supposed to be a long buried father-in-law; but the first shock passed, did she greatly blame Gerald for its being an entirely new source of disquiet?

Not in the least; she was busy considering if he had taken clothes enough, if he would find the sun very warm in his long drive, if he would be able to succeed in getting his father quietly and safely away, if it would keep him many days from Beauchamp, if she had best go to town herself, what she should say to her own father, so as to protect the secret, and yet not be a falsehood. All this she pondered about long and silently, walking, as was her habit, when in thought, up and down her room, with folded arms and downcast eyes. Not once did she remember the possible agony of poor Mrs. Gray, not one thought of pity for the once brilliant man of fashion wandering back to his home, repentant perhaps, but destined to be thrust forth again among strangers and to a foreign, far-distant land.

Was she not selfish? Her whole heart, its sympathies, its affections, its life, were given to Gerald only. Why? Because she hoped for his in return, in the first place; and because she couldn't help it, in the second.

She loved her children because they were Gerald's children, far more than because they were her own; but had he seemed fonder of them than of her, I should not like to answer for the consequences.

Alas! alas! here was a great-hearted, honest, thorough woman, the first part of whose life had caused the stream of that life's human hopes and fears and wishes and aspirations to be dammed up by the bitter curse of suspicion and lonely wealth; and the latter part, by the sudden flood pouring impetuously without check and without reason into one man's keeping—lies absolutely at his mercy.

Her heaven was here; she asked no other light now or hereafter than that which beamed from his dear eyes; she wanted no guide but his firm hand; she needed no support, no counsel, no help but from that wayward, strong man, whom she had sworn to love, honor and obey. And she was happy. She thought herself very, very happy.

❦ CHAPTER XII

MY DARLING;—I got to town safely; Midnight went the distance like a trump, never turned a hair, and landed me in Locust st. in time for dinner. Pretty good work, that! But you know nothing about horses, you dear little goose, and I make no doubt fancy that your fat bays could do the same, if you would let them. Mamma is awfully cut down; looks ten years older. I shall see *him* this evening. I write this to send by the morning's mail, and to relieve your anxiety. Kiss the toddlekins for their precious papa, and don't let that young man take everything away from my young woman as you constantly permit; it is not you and me, all over again.

God bless you. Your G.
Wednesday evening, Jan. 23

January 28th.
DEAR RUTH:—Got your letter safely. Matters progress more slowly than I like. Write to me every day if you can; I miss you dreadfully. Since my last of the 25th, *he* dodged us, but now I have been obliged to take detective Shorter into the secret; he found *him,* and I have a bad piece of news for you—I must

go to New York and see *him* off. We have discovered a man who is trustworthy, and wants to go to Australia. I settle a pension of $500 a year upon this man so long as he keeps *him* abroad. Dallas (the man), seems honest and reasonable. It is the best we can do. My father—well, he is my father, and still so handsome and, Lord! how clever he is, sharp, quick—well, he does not want to go, and we have got to make him. Go he shall, never to return while my head is above the sod. I settle $1,000 a year on him, and we all four, Dallas, Shorter, *he* and I sail from Savannah on the 1st of February for New York. I feel gloomy about it. I know you will be thoroughly wretched, and I don't intend to trust myself to come and tell you good-bye, because it would end in my letting D. and S. go without me. Duty, darling; a thousand thanks for the draft you so thoughtfully enclosed in your last. It is very acceptable, for I don't wish to attract too much attention to myself by doing too much bank business. My regards to your father. Be sure to switch Gerald if he imposes on Geraldine. I see you doing it!

God bless you, little woman. Your G.

SAVANNAH, Feb. 1st.

It is very late, my darling, and I have had a long drive, and must in a very little while go on board. We were told that the steamer could not leave till tomorrow, and as I met Tom Albyn, who invited me to go out and dine at his place, and seemed surprised at my journey North, and inclined to ask questions, I thought it best to go with him, and by my usual *degage* manner put him off the scent. He is not at the hotel with me, but is with D. and S., some where else, of course.

We had not been an hour at Montcalm, Albyn's plantation, when, who should come tearing out but Shorter, with the news that the steamer would sail this evening; so they scrambled up a hasty sort of lunch for me, and Albyn had out another bobtail, and drove me back to the city in fine style. A cool evening, a rising moon, a song or two, some poetry and a couple of Havanas, made it pleasant enough. Speaking of bobtails, do, my darling, make Jim attend carefully to my poor nag, with that cut on his eye. But I need scarcely worry you about that, for Jim was in tears on the subject when I left mamma's house. I heard him mournfully saying to her coachman, "T'aint the cost, but the style of the animal, I regret, sir."

Shorter reports *him* as pretty quiet. We have had some funny times, which I will relate if I escape the dangers of the sea, &c., and return in safety to the *heaven* where I would be.

Recollect my last urgent advice to you. Come to the city, at the appointed time, go to the races, &c., look cheerful, happy, if you can, my poor darling, enjoy it all,—good-bye to such things for me, forever.

> "The day wears on, the storms keep out the sun,
> And thus the heart," and so forth.

This northern visit of mine will grieve you terribly. I think my mind dwells more on that than on anything else. There is no use for you to deny that you have visions of (by me) long-forgotten New York belles, whom your vivid fancy will picture, knowing by instinct of my arrival, and waiting on the wharf with siren arms to welcome me. Well, I am grave now, have no fears; independently of the sad errand I go on; my heart and fancy are irrevocably fixed, and it seems humiliating that I should be obliged to swear to her whom I so passionately love and respect, that I am hers only.

But time is up. Good-night, darling; kiss our babies for me. Think of me all the time, and, oh, should you be tempted to say harsh things of people, or to be suspicious, and to relapse into your old severity of look and manner, remember you are so dear to me. I am so unwilling that you should do anything or say anything unworthy of the real sweetness and nobleness of your character. And if these should be my last words to you, which heaven forfend, remember what I say for the sake of your

G.

And so Ruth Gray did as her absent lord desired, and to the delight of many young ladies who feared that there would be no ball at the Gray's in consequence of Mr. Gray's absence, the great windows of the drawing rooms were punctually opened four days previous to the Wednesday of race-week, (the commencement of "the season" in that Southern capital of which I write), and Mrs. St. Clair, *l'amie de la maison* confidently predicted that there would be plenty of pleasant doings in that spacious mansion.

"And what has taken your cousin away just at this time?" asked Arthur McIvor of Cecilia Clare, with whom he was waltzing at a ball and discussing dancing prospects.

"To meet Mr. Josselyn, of Boston, whom he has not seen for years, and who behaved so beautifully about Mrs. Norman Gray's estate, I believe."

"How beautifully?"

"Don't you know? Why, he insisted upon sharing the fortune with Gerald, although he wasn't at all obliged to do so."

"Well, by Jove! some people are born to too much luck. Look at Gerald! No matter what happens, he always falls on his feet. Old uncle drops off with apoplexy and leaves him penniless; the richest woman in the State, who turned up her nose at every man in it, marries him as soon as he asks her—instantly."

"Yes, he is very fortunate, especially in his marriage."

"Exactly, especially in his marriage," pursued McIvor, who was quite unconscious of Cissy's half-sneer, "most men marry a pretty woman, and before you can say what a lucky dog he is, what happens? Why, she is old and faded and forlorn. On the contrary, Gerald marries a downright, plain woman. Don't I remember how Miss Desborough used to look? the woman couldn't dress." Mr. McIvor was great on dress; "she couldn't dress, she wouldn't talk, she was sallow, and pale, and thin; she had nothing to make her endurable but her money, and as I didn't want her money, I couldn't endure her. He carries her off, and look at her now. She is a handsome woman."

"Handsome?" said Cecilia, with a little laugh of disdain, and showing all her lovely, soft dimples. Cissy always laughed outwardly if there was no corresponding merriment within.

"Well, if she is not regularly handsome, she is a grand-looking woman. Here she comes, let's speak to her. What a superb silk that is, and how it fits! Good evening, Mrs. Gray. Will you allow me to tell you that I have been admiring your dress?"

"I feel very much flattered, Mr. McIvor," said Ruth, smiling gently. "Good evening, Cecilia; is Phyllis here?"

"No, I came with papa."

"When will Mr. Gray be back?" asked Arthur.

The rather indifferent expression gave place to a bright look. "Thank you, in two days I hope to [see] him."

"Where is he?"

"In Boston, I fancy. Our cousin, Mr. Josselyn, was at the West when we came home from Europe, and it was necessary that Gerald should go North now. He will probably induce Francis to return with him—a conquest for you to make, Cecilia. I have often heard Gerald say how handsome and charming he is."

Cissy gave her the usual twittering laugh, and Mr. Taunton, on whose arm Ruth leaned, said something about the impropriety of Miss Clare being allowed further pasturage for her inhuman treatment of the ruder sex. Then they all four bowed and parted, and Ruth went to speak to Mrs. St. Clair, who looked very brilliant in one of the Paris dresses of Mrs. Gray's selection.

"Don't come near me," cried Bertha. "I am making a great effect while you keep on the other side of the room. I don't wish to have my *toilette elegante crasse* by your magnificence. *Qu'elle est sublime cette ariane,* with her Theseus departed!"

"Very well," said Ruth, laughing; "if you talk in that way, I shall grow malicious, and ask if your friend, Mr. Berrian, is near—he who wanted to know if that lady spoke English with French quotations, or French with English quotations?"

"That lady is far too amiable, or she should have made one of her admirers brain Mr. Berrian with his own ledger. But if I say that you look like Penelope pining for Ulysses—"

"No, thank you, my Ulysses has found no Calypso, I trust, and I just look like Ruth Gray, who wants to know if you will take a seat in her carriage tomorrow for the race course?"

"Certainly, and be delighted, provided you don't array yourself like the Queen of Sheba. How I hate diamond necklaces!" pursued the saucy creature, drawing up her white neck, and looking in her friend's eyes, as she whirled off in the waltz.

"What a light heart she has!" exclaimed Mr. Taunton.

"Do you think so? I should say she had light spirits. But I never talk of Bertha. It is a rule with me, and one I wish her other friends would follow. If one praises her, it seems somehow as if the most flattering words get turned into a different meaning when repeated, as they always are, and if one hazards a syllable, ever so slightly indicative if dispraise, it grows into a monstrous slander an hour after its birth from one's unconscious lips. I have learned to know this, and I love her too well, therefore, to talk about her."

"But to me? There is no one who cherishes a kinder regard for Mrs. St. Clair. I see her faults, of course."

"Just so," put in Mrs. Gray, gently; "and even if you did *not* see them, I should still keep to my rule."

"Have you always been so partial to her?"

"No, I remember, years ago, disliking her very much. But I found out her best quality."

"And that is—"

"You know her faults so well, and don't know her best quality?"

"I had no idea that you could tease," said Mr. Taunton, laughing; "You have caught that from Gerald."

"Perhaps I have, but I caught my liking for Mrs. St. Clair through Gerald, too."

"Indeed!" and Mr. Taunton remembered the wedding breakfast and Mrs.

St. Clair's not very flattering comments upon the bridegroom, and the idea passed rapidly through his mind, how often it was that those appreciated *us*, of whom we think least.

"Yes," continued Ruth, "and since you *are* a friend of Mrs. St. Clair, I will tell you something which I got from my husband, and which first turned the tide of my feelings toward Bertha. He—a gentleman of his acquaintance had a vast admiration for Mrs. St. Clair—liked to talk a great deal to her, dance with her, visit her, and pay her much attention, privately and publicly. The gentleman had a wife who adored him—she was, what you know is very shocking, but still—"

"She was jealous."

"Very. Mrs. St. Clair saw it. The next time this gentleman approached her, she fixed her true yet laughing eyes upon him and said, "That idle and disengaged young men should entertain me and amuse themselves, by sending me bouquets and turning around the circle of my crinoline; very well! As the navvy said to his neighbor who wondered why he allowed his wife to beat him with a spade, when he could so easily master her, 'It pleases she, and it don't hurt I.' 'All baggage at the risk of the owner,' is my motto with such butterflies. But, that a woman should be made unhappy through me, however unreasonably; and that I should lay unconscious or violent or gentle hands upon other peoples property, heaven forbid!" She made him one of her sweeping courteseys and—that is all."

"And who told this; she or he?"

"Gerald told it to *me*."

"And the gentleman's name is—?"

"So intimate as you are with Bertha, ask her," said Mrs. Gray, with a polite, slight sneer.

But Mr. Taunton smiled so good-naturedly, and began to praise Mrs. St. Clair so warmly, and Gerald's words coming forcibly into her mind about "her old severity of manner," she resumed her suavity, and talked of the next day's races.

Mr. Clare came up to greet her, and she dropped Mr. Taunton's arm with a cordial yet stately bow, and gave her uncle-in-law the supreme satisfaction of walking her up and down the room. Mr. Clare flattered himself that they made a magnificent display, and that the finishing touch was given to Mrs. Gerald Gray's grandeur of appearance when she had his support.

Mr. Taunton came to a conclusion extremely shrewd, very commonplace, and entirely wrong.

"Gerald has made a merit," he thought, "of Mrs. St. Clair's *verbage*, and under cover of this confidence, they mean to flirt as much as they choose. Of course, 'he is the gentleman,' and she is laughing with him, and twisting the wife round that remarkably pretty little finger of hers."

Decidedly Mr. Taunton was a great friend of Mrs. St. Clair. Did he not dine with her twice a week? And was not her pleasant chat and saucy ways the chief things that kept him alive at dull times? But then, you see, he knew her faults. From our intimate friends, who know our faults, and so delight in mentioning the fact; and the faults, good Lord deliver us!

Before the short season of ball room gayety was over, Gerald was back, looking particularly well, and quite ready to dance at parties, or play billiards at the club, or toss his children higher than his head, or watch Ruth, as she allowed her two small darlings to crush every atom of *friandise* [?] out of the toilette which Valerie had just superintended; and then—go and make it all over again, lest her large darling's eyes should be afflicted by the sight of a *chiffonne* collar and crumpled sleeves.

"And you have told me so little about Francis!" said Ruth, the evening after his return, when the romp was over and the children were in bed. "How glad I am, that we are going no where to-night!"

"And so am I," Gerald said, as he threw himself lazily on the sofa, and she took a low seat close beside him. "But I will tell you what I am more glad of: to be back with you—to be quiet in my own house, with my faithful, loving, loyal love."

The tears swam in Ruth's eyes; delicious tears, tears of gratitude that he should so care for her, this great, beautiful, wayward creature!

She took his hand and pressed her lips to it, the tears gathered and fell. He lifted her head caressingly.

"My darling, we don't behave 'like married folk;' one would suppose that we were lovers still, only, in those days, it was *I* that sat at your feet, and kissed your hand, as I do now. But I like these days best—it is very comfortable to play 'grand seigneur,' and have you think of nothing but pleasing me. Particularly, as that seems to be your idea of happiness too."

"Yes."

"That being the case, let me remind you that you are positively forbidden to show one tear."

"But I am not crying," protested Ruth.

Gerald shook his head.

> I know a little eye,
> And it dearly loves to cry,

God knows the reason why,
All the day!

"For shame, Gerald; I never cry now. What an idea! I did indulge in such follies when I was first very happy—and very unhappy—but we have gone through that stage."

"Have we? Then I am sorry, because in my mind and thought, the verse goes on,

"From *her* heart the tear-drop wells,
To *my* heart its story tells,
And it holds me in its spells
  By this way!
Well! I love all eyes above
This dear eye of her I love."

"Oh, dearest Gerald, that is the same ballad you quoted and added to in our honeymoon—let me write it down."

"Write down Mother Goose, you ditto!" cried Gerald, catching her by the sleeve as she sprang up. "Sit down you unreasonably vain woman! eager after anything that praises you. Proud now of your power to cry—why, the twins could beat you at that any day."

"Let me thank you, then," and she bent over and kissed him.

"Don't crowd the monkeys," said Gerald playfully, and putting up his hands before his face, after tenderly returning her kiss. "Do you know, Ruth dear, that I don't think cart ropes could have kept me longer away; and it was so hard to act upon your nice suggestion and take a row to Boston, which simplified my Northern visit to all enquiring minds."

"Yes; it was effectual, too—for no one appears to trouble themselves further about it. And Francis?"

"Will you be so good as not to interrupt my train of thought? I was so glad, too, that you should not know exactly the day of my return—to come home, when you were at that ball and slip snugly into my dressing room, charging Joe and Valerie not to tell you, when they let you in. I watched your quiet, indifferent face, through the door, which I left ajar, on purpose. Valerie kept her counsel with all the tact of her nation, and was proceeding quietly to unlace your dress, without a word. You were listlessly unclasping a bracelet, when your eyes fell upon my gloves and penknife, that I had laid on your pincushion. Ah! then came the flash of marvelous light into your great eyes, the bright, overwhelming joy of your expressive face. Two quick words—'*c'est assez*,' to Valerie, and you almost thrust her out of the room, as she was smilingly and respectfully disappearing. In one bound, you were beside me, close to my heart, dear treasure, speechless and panting, and as I folded you in my longing arms and sat down, though you were in your favorite attitude, on your knees, with as little concern for your beautiful blue and white crepe as if it had not been *the* dress of the evening."

"And you?"

"Oh, I was not much better; I had not seen you for a month, remember, and I was pining for you. It is, indeed, when sorrow and trouble come, that a man learns fully to understand his dependence upon the single-hearted woman who loves him. I thought I loved you very dearly before—I only seem to know it now."

> "The world is filled with folly and sin,
>   And love must cling where it can, I say,
> For beauty is easy enough to win—
>
>   But one isn't loved every day,"

quoted Ruth.

"Ah, Mrs. St. Clair has taught you to read Owen Meridith, has she? How is that fair creature?"

"Very well."

"Who is she victimizing at present?"

"Mr. Taunton, I believe."

"Oh, that's an old story. Francis says—"

"Ah! Francis at last. *A la bonne heure,* pray go on about Francis."

"Isn't that like you? Interrupting me to ask me to go on. Francis says—"

"Dear Gerald, won't you tell me what Francis looks like?"

"Go away, Mrs. Gray—Gooseling. I won't say another word. I am fast asleep."

"Please forgive me," said Ruth laughingly, "I was very stupid, that's the truth."

"Well, Francis says—that when he comes on this spring to see us, we must make up a pleasant party at Beauchamp and have Mrs. St. Clair. He understands that she is more charming than ever, and he caught a flying glimpse of her years ago, and liked her hugely."

"So Francis is really coming on? I am *very* glad."

"If he does not start for Central Africa or Central America—if he does not propose fitting out a new expedition to the North Pole, or a sail of observation to the Southern Seas, I think he is booked in his own mind for a visit to us. But you must not reckon on him without those contingencies."

"And may I ask, now, how he looks and how he seems?"

"You may, my love. He is a great six-foot-two, splendidly built man. I think he has grown several inches since I saw him last, but as you never saw him at all it will be easier for you to credit his assurance that he has not. He has ordinary features, of the usual number, with a great mustache, at which he pulls constantly in a sort of savage way, and his eyes being of very light grey, and his skin and hair so dark, it gives a peculiar look to his face; but he is a handsome, bold type of a traveler."

"He never means to marry?"

"What on earth would Francis do with a wife? Unless she were an Indian, and used to the tramp, or would like a husband whom she saw for ten minutes every ten years, I don't think he would suit her."

"And who is going to look after your common fortune?"

"Ah! that's the point; as I live at the South and he lives in spots, we are to have an agent, who, I presume, will live on us."

"How shocked papa would be at such recklessness!"

"Of course, my darling. At college we used to be called Sir Francis Reckless and Sir Gerald Wayward, and college *sobriquets* have a deal of keen sense in them always."

"I wish you would not pride yourself on being wayward, Gerald."

"Well, I won't, dear. And about this party to Beauchamp. Shall it be as Francis says?"

"As you wish, of course. When do you think he will come, if he comes?"

"In about three weeks,—middle of March."

"To stay—?"

"As long as he finds it pleasant; but I think we had best appoint the second week in April for the party, and ask them to spend a week—who shall it be? Mrs. St. Clair, McIvor, Taunton—who else?"

"Your friend, Mr. Browne?"

"Oh, Browne is such a muff—but he is a good fellow—swallows anything—let's have him."

"Shall we invite Mrs. Denham?"

"Yes, she will do very well—talk to Browne. She don't mind who she talks to. She will rattle away with that beautiful face of her's all aglow, and her straight black brows giving such decision to her regular features, and not caring a button whether it be Tom, Dick or Harry who is listening to her."

"Well, those are enough, I suppose," said Ruth. "If any decline, we will fill up."

"Not half enough, my child. You ought to have some 'demoiselle'—some girl to make music. Think of somebody."

"I know so few girls at all intimately or socially," said Ruth.

"Why, there is Cissy—why not ask Cissy? And Phyllis and Fordyce. They haven't been there yet, and ought to be invited sometime."

"My darling, Cissy is so affected and so dull!"

"Better then take her when she can be diluted with others."

"Diluted! Can we dilute insipidity? Dilute cistern water?"

"Ruth, dear, what did I ask you? Not to be harsh, was it not! And Cissy is my cousin—a favorite niece of mama's—a little inoffensive, sweet tempered, good girl—whom I look upon as my sister."

"Did she look upon you as her brother, do you think, Gerald?"

"Are you going to open up that old question? My love, have I ever deceived you?—judge by what I say now. I verily believe that Cissy 'did' care for me more than I dreamed of—I fear that she has never married because she was disappointed. I fear mamma encouraged an idea in her mind that my attentions to her were other than Cissy herself, of her own knowledge, knew. Can you suppose for one instant that I would, by word or action, re-awaken in that innocent-minded girl an interest in me, when my life and heart are irrevocably and happily and fully engaged elsewhere! Do you think so meanly of me? Can you love me as you do, and think me so vile? It seems to me that if you were to see or hear me showing or expressing the utmost attention to Cissy, you would understand that my reason for so doing had nothing unworthy in it."

"I believe you, Gerald," said Ruth; "I was wrong. We will write Cissy and Phyllis and Mr. Fordyce. And never will I again utter such suspicions."

"That is my own perfect darling."

❀ CHAPTER XIV

It was a gala-week at Beauchamp. The old home—once belonging to an English master, who had built it in those first days, when the lordly British gave that aroma of good birth and breeding to our State, on which we still pride ourselves, with or without cause—often added to and renovated, but now quite divested of its gentlemanly air of antiquity, was ringing now with gay laughter and made the scene of genuine and gracious hospitality.

The weather was beautiful; just cool enough to permit a little fire in the morning, but necessitating open windows all the day long. Not too warm to be out of doors; yet with a sun so bright, and a sky so blue, and an air so balmy, that it was no wonder that Francis Josselyn proclaimed Italy a humbug in comparison, and vowed that if ever he had the patience or power to settle himself anywhere, it should be on a neighboring plantation, with just such trees, just such a Cherokee rose hedge, and just such an out-door canopy, as those of Beauchamp, exquisite Beauchamp!

"Pooh!" exclaimed Mrs. St. Clair, as she sat upon the low balustrade of the stone steps, and switched with her riding whip at the violet bed on her right hand. "You are so impetuous! Such a ridiculously impulsive creature! and the worst of it is, you really believe what you say and fancy for about two days, or two hours, or two minutes, that you are eager to *be* what you say—the lord of a Southern domain, for instance."

"Why is that the worst of it? It ought to be the best of it."

"No; because some day you may set your fancy upon something where others are concerned, and it may not suit them to change their minds as quick and as easily as you do."

"Then—they have a safeguard against one, as I would have against my-self—my sense of honor. If I carried off man or woman on the whirlwind of my fancy, as you are pleased to call it, the fact that I implicated anybody else would steady my resolve, instantly, and *fix* my plans."

"A—a—h!" drawled Mrs. St. Clair, bending down her head, and taking up the train of her *amazone* to examine a speck of dirt upon it. "You and Mr. Gray are really not cousins, are you?" and then she suddenly lifted her eyes and fixed them on the face of her companion.

He smiled in the most unconcerned manner, and folding his arms upon the same balustrade, and resting his chin upon his wrists, as he seated himself so as to bring his eyes almost on a level with hers, he said, slowly.

"You mean something by that very 'inconsequente' question. What is it?"

"I never meant anything in my life," answered Bertha. "Here come Mrs. Denham and Mr. Browne; he has out-gallopped you this time, my friends; where on earth were you lingering? What a magnificent leap, Bettina. Indeed, it *is* a frightful pity that you were not permitted to follow the bent of your natural genius and be a circus rider."

"It is so," answered the pretty widow, patting her horse's glossy sides, as the groom came to lead him off. "Good-bye, my beauty. You went like a love to-day. Fancy me, Bertha, flying round 'the ring' with Festus as a 'trained animal'—saw dust in profusion—brass band blowing its curses away—and I butting my head through six successive hoops of coloured paper, amid the acclamations of a bewildered audience!"

"Won't you try it some day for a limited but most enthusiastic crowd?" asked Francis.

"Unfortunately, as you heard Bertha remark, I was not permitted to go into that line. But you asked what kept us—I saw some delicious chickweed, and I persuaded Mr. Browne to gather it for my parrot."

"Oh, that parrot! didn't I rush wildly into your room this morning, thinking I heard you say 'come here, Bertha, come here,' as if an assassin had you by the throat; and behold! it was that wretched bird sidling up and down your dressing table, and looking at himself in the mirror like a hooked nose demon."

"Did you?" laughed Mrs. Denham. "Why, he is improving."

"Do you travel always with a parrot for a protector?" asked Mr. Josselyn.

"Make her tell you how she tamed this one—a series of pitched battles. Bettina, with two pairs of beaver gloves and a crooked poker, to help her, always managed to come off victorious."

"I should like to have seen it," said Mr. Browne, gravely; "it must have been very pretty."

"Here comes something pretty," said Mrs. St. Clair. "I think you told me that you and Mr. Gray are not really cousins, Mr. Josselyn," she added in a half whisper.

Advancing from the woods, where they had been strolling, Gerald and Cecilia Clare now emerged through the great gate and sauntered towards the house. He was in his shooting jacket and carried his gun; her face was almost hidden by the broad brim of her garden hat—her hands were full of wild flowers. He did not notice his four guests till he had nearly come up to the steps, but his cheery voice saluted them as soon as his eyes saw them.

"No birds today, Mrs. Denham!—I am very sorry—but I did my best."

"Did Cecilia go to bring home the game bag, and sing of your prowess?" asked Mrs. St. Clair.

Cissy looked up blushing and very pretty; her light curls were stuck full of blossoms and leaves.

"No," answered Gerald; "I met Cissy all alone, poor thing, as I was coming home."

"So you pocketed her, determined not to return without something to show as your morning's work."

"Yes; and I think a man who could bag Cissy for life, and show her off as the captive of his bow, would merit to be crowned himself, instead of crowning her—as I did, with all these jessamines and things."

Gerald spoke as openly and as unconcernedly as if Cecilia were his sister. Not a shade of discomposure, not the smallest vestige of a "flirtation" in his tone.

"Has Ruth not got back?" he went on. "It must take Fordyce a long time to embrace that relation of his that Phyllis and himself carried off Ruth to visit."

"It is nine miles to Mrs. Armstrong's," put in Cissy, "and, of course, they had to eat lunch, and all that."

"Of course, and spoil their dinners by lunching at three o'clock, when we dine at five, having previously eaten something here. Well, it is now after four—and there goes the dressing bell."

"Where are the other gentlemen?" asked Mrs. Denham.

"Gone in by the back way; McIvor returned hours ago; Taunton and Aubrey left me to come back and take a sleep."

"Lazy wretches!"

"Were you up at six o'clock, fair lady?"

"Not more than I credit that they were; but we *must* go and dress; what a dawdling way one gets into!"

"And here comes the carriage now."

In a few moments it drew up, and Gerald was helping out his wife, and asking Phyllis for how much she expected to be set down in Mrs. Armstrong's will, after this superhuman effort.

"Oh, Gerald! such a dear old lady!" said Ruth; "I am excessively glad I went. She asked so kindly after you."

"What a stretch of goodness!"

"And she makes so much of the twins!"

"Of course she does; the whole country is crazed with a desire to see them!"

Ruth laughed; "well; I wish to see them now, at any rate; and as we have but little time to spare, I shan't lose a second, or dinner will be ready before I am."

"Don't you believe that Gerald and I ought to be 'real cousins'?" asked Mr. Josselyn, following Mrs. St. Clair up the staircase.

"Wait till I know you better, and see if you deserve—to be so traduced," said the smiling lady, as she nodded and closed the door.

While he dressed, Francis was turning over these scraps of remarks in his mind.

"Does she mean anything?" he thought. "Pshaw! I see what she means—and it is nonsense. If women are not just at the moment bent on mischief themselves, they are always fancying that others are. That is why the bitterest scandal always comes from the ugliest and most uninteresting women. A real belle has her hands too full of her own affairs to be concocting stories about her neighbors. Positively, if I were of the softer sex and wished to lead a quiet life, I should establish myself among the flightiest and giddiest of the lovely beings—with not the smallest reference to their 'reputations.' The worse they are, the more chance for mine."

He tied his cravat, and settled his chin comfortably in the shirt collar.

"Ergo—if I wish to keep Mrs. St. Clair's eyes from following Gerald, I must try and make them follow me—for a different motive. Can't I persuade her that I am madly in love with her! No. Not unless she first falls in love with me—and that don't appear to be in the least likely."

The coat was now put on.

"It is an abominable thing, to get up such ideas—put such notions in one's head. I think very badly of the St. Clair for doing—but stop!—what did she put in my head? What did she say? What thought did I already have, however vague, which made me guess at once what she was driving at? I'll try and have a quiet talk with her this evening. Upon my soul, I think Ruth is the finest woman in the world, and she is more thoroughly in love with that fortunate rascal that I ever supposed a woman could be. For it is only men who really love once and forever."

He sighed deeply, and walked down stairs.

☢ C H A P T E R   X V

"We are tolerably punctual, after all," said Ruth, looking at her watch, as they took their places at the dinner table. "Only eight minutes after five o'clock."

"What is this reason for this eager pursuit of punctuality, may I ask?" said Francis. "Is there to be an execution immediately after the meal, that we are not to lose?"

"Oh, no!" answered Ruth, "but Gerald can't bear to wait for his dinner."

"You spoil him," remarked Phyllis, from her side of the table. "Don't let Mr. Fordyce hear you."

"Since when, Gerald, have you grown such a martinet about hours?" asked Francis.

"I'll tell you," cried Mr. Aubrey; "since Mrs. Gray humors all his caprices."

"Go on, my friends," said Gerald calmly. "I like this sort of thing. I assemble you together and you preach insubordination to my wife."

"I have a personal spite in this matter," said Mr. Aubrey, sending away his soup plate and helping himself to wine. "One day Gerald was engaged to dine with me—a select party—two very precise Englishmen—and we had to wait three quarters of an hour for this punctual young prince, who finally strolled in, as calmly and as composedly as possible—had been playing billiards, or driving a new horse, or amusing himself in some way—and 'there he was at last,' he seemed to say, and we ought to be so glad to see him at all, that he should be made much of, not abused."

"Well, that was very bad, I admit," said Gerald;" quite unpardonable, and now that I have eaten that dinner, and have this one in prospect, I can venture to hint that I ought to have been turned away from your festive board and put into the hall, just where I could see what was going on, but not partake. Could vengeance go no farther?"

"Oh, nothing can be more just and formidable than your strictures upon yourself, after the mischief is done, and the penalty impossible."

"Did you ever hear of an adventure I had once about a dinner?" asked Mrs. St. Clair; "if not, I'll tell it."

"You might as well, being Jenny Lind, ask if, having heard a certain song, we wished to hear it again," said Mr. Taunton, gallantly.

"I consider your question too vague, Bertha," put in Mrs. Denham; "You have had more than one dinner adventure, have you not?" and she looked mischievous and meaning.

"Tell it, any way," half whispered Ruth; "the next course seems dilatory; *une histoire, madame, les plats nous manquent.*"

"After that, I almost dare not," said Mrs. St. Clair, bowing to her hostess, and raising her finger threateningly at Bettina, "but all I had to tell was this. It was the last day of race week, and I was to dine with the Everards to meet a certain distinguished lecturer, whose name is very familiar to us all. I had engaged my cousin, Miss Turner, to send her carriage back for me after she got there, and had invited a 'really' punctual gentleman to take a seat with me. Tired and dusty when I got back late from the course, I nevertheless was ready in time, and as the five minutes to the hour arrived—with it, in walked my friend, Mr. Mayne. No carriage—five o'clock struck—five minutes past. Mr. Mayne grew impatient in a gentlemanly way—said he wasn't, but looked pitifully at his watch. He would not desert me, and the carriage would not come. Useless to think of sending for another—everything that had four legs had been occupied in conveying everything human to the races; before I could get tired horses harnessed up again it would be anyway too late."

"Were not they dining very early?"

"That's the worst of it. After appointing his own day, our Humorist friend had agreed to give another lecture that very evening, which would necessitate his leaving the table at half past six; from the beginning, therefore, it was all wrong—but to cut my story short, (for here come the dishes, she said softly to Ruth,) I decided to start on foot. Picture me, then, at twenty minutes past five o'clock on a bright afternoon, in an apple green satin with black lace flounces, a white opera cloak, and a white 'molie' thrown over my otherwise bare head—said green satin held up out of the dust—trotting along beside Mr. Mayne, in his dress coat and white kids! We took every bye-street that we could, but I think we met everybody I ever saw. One woman that I had gone to school with, and had not laid eyes on since, passed, and stared at me—as well she might."

"Well, I suppose you were received with acclamations, when you did get there?"

"I am not so sure; Mary Turner *was* miserable, I am happy to say, because there had been such a mistake about the carriage—but the lecturer towered in his wrath! I think if he could, he would have had me sacrificed on the door sill! You see he had an uneasy consciousness that his after thought about another lecture, was not polite to his entertainers—then, by my absence, he was losing still more of his possible dinner; but, unlucky me! it was destined to be a day ever memorable for its *contretemps*. What possessed me to be so tactless, those gods alone know that preside over the conversations of foolish women!"

"Why should such deities interfere with *you?*"

"Listen: I mentioned with all the exaltation of the Lady Castleton, who was so proud of knowing a literary *dessous des cartes,* that the Harpers had just written me that no greater proof could be given of the poor standard of public taste, than the fact that the 'Wide, Wide World,' sold better than 'Vanity Fair.' It was all up then! How glad we were when 'Charity and Humour' left for his 'estrade.' [?] *We* were charitable enough to forgive his ill-humor—when we ceased to suffer from it—but he has never forgiven me, I fear—if he remembers me at all—to this day!"

"What a cross creature he must be!" said Phyllis.

"Cross or not, he is *my* author," said Bertha, "and there are some books of his—some words of his—that ought to be framed—taught in schools, hung up at cross-roads, switched into boys and pounded into girls. I drink to his health!"

"You are so enthusiastic," drawled Mrs. Fordyce.

"I should hope I am," said Bertha, curtly.

"Enthusiasm in a woman so often leads into mischief," said Phyllis, pensively, "it is a great responsibility. I admire it very much, but I shouldn't like to have it."

"Anybody would suppose, Phyl, that enthusiasm was a gown or a new-fangled ornament, or an animal to care of," said Gerald.

"Indeed, I appeal to the gentleman," said Phyllis; "we all know that Mrs. St. Clair can do anything, and be trusted with anything. She has gifts that few women could manage; but for us,—the majority of us—is it not best that we should have less enthusiasm—be less impressible?"

"Ah! *pattes de reloin* [?]!" said Mrs. St. Clair, in an under tone, to Mr. Josselyn. "The malicious meaning there! Shall I thank her and pretend I don't see?"

"If you ask my opinion, Mrs. Fordyce," said Mr. Taunton, "I should say you are perfectly right. Weak women had better have weak qualities, but Mrs. St. Clair should be enthusiastic; and when you get to more names, I shall continue to answer yes or no, as long as I am permitted."

"I like everything that is genuine," said Gerald. "Genuine enthusiasm, genuine simplicity, genuine—"

"Wickedness?" asked Mr. Aubrey.

"Not exactly. But even genuine wickedness is better than disingenuous goodness. I hate pretenses of all sorts. I would not care to be, for one moment, other than I seem to be. I would not—"

Mrs. St. Clair was looking steadily at him.

"Did you speak, Mrs. St. Clair?"

She shook her head.

"Oh! you were a theoretical man always," said Aubrey. "How much religion have you, pray? and yet, would not any one think, to hear you talk, that you were of the most strictest sect."

"Of the Pharisees," said Francis, laughing.

"For shame!" exclaimed Ruth. "How can you say so, Francis? Gerald don't laugh when he talks so."

"You and I have not been asked our opinions, Miss Clare," said Arthur McIvor. "Shan't we put in one word?"

"Oh, dear, no!" said Cissy, with her eternal simper. "I never dispute with gentlemen, and in fact, I know my opinion is quite worthless."

"Why?"

"Oh, I have never thought about enthusiasm, either as a pretence or otherwise. I take it for granted that people are just what they seem to be. And some things suit some women and wouldn't suit others. You know that,—in short, Phyllis and I think exactly alike."

"Most satisfactorily reasoned," said Gerald. "You have only contradicted yourself and involved your statements, Cis, in the most bewitchingly, unreasoning manner. Never mind, you are not a strong-minded woman, and don't care a button for all this. Let us leave it to Phyllis and Mrs. St. Clair, and follow Mrs. Denham's example; she has been eating her dinner and 'talking horse' with Browne, like a sensible creature. Won't you ride Mountain Mary to-morrow? And shall I make them give you some of this duck with olives?"

CHAPTER XVI

"Mr. Josselyn, pray come here," said Bertha, as the gentlemen joined the ladies in the drawing room. "I want to say something disagreeable. Not about you; don't start back and scream!"

"Oh! I am infinitely relieved, and you may make it as disagreeable as you choose."

"Thank you. I think Phyllis Fordyce the most intensely atrocious woman—so *maniere*, so false, so thoroughly pretentious, and so absurdly humble-minded!"

"Well, that is a mild, friendly sort of criticism. How gentle you are in your strictures!"

"Am I not? I knew you would think so. And now, having said it, I feel much better."

"What do you think of her sister?"

"Cissy? Oh, she is a little gabby, that's all."

"Gabby? Shall I marry a gabby? for I am thinking seriously of trying to win Cissy."

"Are you?" said Bertha. "I think it a capital plan. I am sure you will like it very much."

"I am very glad you approve. When do you think I had best ask her?"

"Oh, I wouldn't ask her at all, if I were you. Get Mr. Gray to ask her for you."

"Well, that is not a bad idea either. He has known her so much longer than I have—seen so much more of her. He thinks so highly of me, too, that he could put my qualities in a more favorable light than I could myself."

"Exactly. I am sure he would plead your case with ardor, and then I think the less you see of her the greater your ardor would be."

"She is so pretty—Cissy!" said Francis, pulling at his moustache; "such a simple-minded, beautiful girl; not clever you know."

"Oh, dear! no! no such evil quality as that about Cissy!"

And then these two began to laugh, and both sipped their coffee, till Francis resumed:

"Mrs. St. Clair, I am going to be serious now."

"Seriously serious, or playfully serious?"

"Seriously serious. Without circumlocution, I think Gerald is making an ass of himself, and I wonder who else sees it besides ourselves?"

Mrs. St. Clair drained her cup, set it down, leaned her head upon her hand, and bit her lips.

"Not Ruth, certainly," she said, at last.

"Shall we try to stop it, before she does see it?"

"Can we?"

"At least, we can try."

"You can command my services. What do you think of doing?"

"I am going to flirt with Cissy."

"*Bon!* And I?"

"You must flirt with Gerald."

"Pleasant, but *very* dangerous. My dear Mr. Josselyn, don't you know that I am terribly afraid of this delightful Gerald? Ah! you ought to have heard me hold forth on the subject at his wedding breakfast. Really, my own eloquence quite filled me with surprise. *Je me admirai tant* that I was quite shocked at the feeling."

"You must not find fault with doing yourself what all the rest of the world does."

"A truce to *fadaises*. Conspirators don't waste their time paying each other compliments. When are we to begin our arduous undertakings? I am unfiegnedly sorry for *you*."

"This very minute."

"Very well; like a true Knight, posting to the battle-field or the Tournament, I shall put on my armor at once. Is my hair smooth—quite smooth?" Francis nodded. "And how are my eyes? Clara Wheeler has a way of blacking the lids with a hairpin held over the smoke of a candle. Shall I try it? It gives an oriental languor and brightness. Or shall I borrow a little of Phyllis's *rouge* that she never uses?"

"What makes you so malicious this evening?"

"I don't know. Evil associations perhaps. Well, we have no especial programme, but we are to compare notes, I suppose, and carry on the war vigorously."

"Yes."

"Then, let us begin. Goodbye. Spread your nets, and I mine."

Bertha sauntered off, looking bent on mischief, but, as she left, Ruth took her seat.

"What are you and Bertha talking about? both looking as wicked as possible."

"Floating in a sea of small-talk."

"You like Bertha, don't you?"

"Very much. She is what Gerald talks about—genuine. Her defects are genuine, but so are her virtues. Her likes and dislikes, her figure and fancies, her feelings and complexion. She is genuinely pleased and genuinely displeased. She is genuinely naughty, when the humor is upon her, and genuinely good, when she *is* good."

"She is perfectly sincere," said Ruth.

"Too sincere, for she can't conceal anything. I never saw such an ostrich, nor ever heard a greater misnomen than to call her 'a thorough woman of the world,' as some people do. She would be a vastly more popular person if she were a woman of the world. But if she is hurt, she *hollers*, like a baby, and if she is glad, she enjoys it, like a child."

"Yes, she lets people see that they worry her."

"Which, of course, in a Christian land, is an invitation to everybody *to* worry her."

"And they drive her wild sometimes, with their stories, and comments and injustice."

"And they will continue to do so, till she is indifferent to it."

"That will be only when she is in her grave," said Ruth. "Poor Bertha!"

"Not a bit of it. She will have the sense some day to turn where such things can't pursue her."

"Right," said Ruth, gravely.

"Ruth, why don't you ask Miss Clare to sing?" began Francis, after a pause.

"Oh, Francis! do you like to hear her?"

"Excessively. She is so pleased with herself when she is at the piano. It does one good to see the air of triumph with which she seats herself—gives a sort of hump to her back, turns up her eyes, opens her mouth, and 'wobbles,' as Mr. Yellowplush says."

"For shame! I don't think it is proper to ask the poor girl to make herself ridiculous."

"She won't thank you for not giving her the opportunity."

"Very well; I'll ask her."

Mr. Josselyn followed Mrs. Gray, and added his entreaties, which were not needed, to Cissy. She was knitting a purse, seated near the lamp. At the table next her, Phyllis was reading, and on the other side, Gerald was in his usual lazy, lounging attitude on the sofa, talking to both his cousins, for Phyllis' book did not seem to be very engrossing.

As Cissy went off, Bertha sauntered up to look for something on the same table, and a merry interchange of nothings took place between herself and her host, which ended in her ordering him to the other end of the sofa, with all the cushions if he choose, but to give her the side nearest the light and between him and Phyllis.

Before Mr. Fordyce had been dislodged, with his candlestick and newspaper, from the piano, and required to go and take refuge beside his wife, which at once entailed upon her the privilege of listening to scraps of news she had already read, and not hearing what Gerald and Bertha were saying, these two had embarked in a jesting conversation, which sank into lower and lower tones, as Cissy began to sing.

On she went, from one bravura to another, plied with flattery by Francis, and amazing him with the variety of grimaces and blunders that she executed.

But presently there was a laugh from Gerald in the very midst of some pathetic note, Cissy colored and looked around. Bertha was holding up her finger, as she looked at Gerald's outburst. The song came to an abrupt conclusion.

"Have you not skipped?" asked Francis. "Don't cut me off in that way."

"I will sing something else," said Cissy, turning over the leaves of her music-book. "I don't know the Italian words. The person who copied the notes for me only put the English ones; but they are very pretty, Rossini's music.

> No loving word was spoken,
> Calmly and coldly we parted;
> I knew thee too false-hearted
> To waste regret on me!
> I felt the chain was broken,
> To bind us more, ah! never!

And parting e'en forever,
Sought no farewell of thee!
In vain my heart, forsaken,
Thy treachery now remembers,
For love's undying embers
Still burn for thee alone!
Ah, yes, for thee alone!

A dead silence fell upon the room. Cissy got up and walked away from the piano. There had been something too marked in her voice and the words not to attract attention. Phyllis colored, looked intensely annoyed, and then said:

"How absurd English words to Italian music always sound."

"Do you think so, Phyl," asked Gerald; "now, I think there is a good deal of sense in Cissy's song. I wish to learn them words; I shall keep them to launch at Ruth's head, if ever she purposes to run away from me. Or shall I sing them to you, Mrs. St. Clair, when you leave Beauchamp? How do they go?"

And then he set up an imitation, and shaking himself out of his lounging seat, he went after Cissy, making grotesque *roulades*.

"Cis, my dear, I admire that vastly; I want you to teach me the words."

"Go away, Gerald," she said, a little pettishly; "you always tease me."

"But you don't mind being teased, do you?"

Her back was turned to him, and she seemed deeply interested in some engravings. Conversations recommenced. Mrs. Denham began playing waltzes; the chairs were pushed aside, and they began to dance. Francis went up and invited Cissy.

"Mrs. St. Clair is waiting for you, Gerald," he added.

Ruth was leaning back in a great chair, tapping her lips with a paper-folder; she seemed watching the dancers.

Bertha stopped near her, and then offered a turn to Mr. McIvor. Gerald leaned over the high back of the chair and spoke to his wife:

"Do you feel badly, darling?"

"No."

"You look worried."

"Yes."

"All this row bothers you, and Cissy's music."

"Yes, Cissy's music."

"It is rather poor. Has it given you a headache?"

"No, a—"

"Heartache, perhaps?"

Ruth was silent.

"You silly Ruth! Are you going to allow Cissy Clare to annoy you?"

"No; Gerald Gray annoys me."

"At least, you are candid. Most women would conceal absurd and unfounded jealousy."

"I don't compare myself with most women, any more than I do you with most men."

During this colloquy, Bertha rapidly whispered to Francis: "The storm is brewing."

"All hands to reef sails, then," he answered. "Who is tired of dancing?" he called out. "I am. Let's play some *jeu innocent*. Mrs. Denham will thank me, for I am sure her fingers are stiff."

"Yes; what shall it be?"

"What were we playing two nights ago?"

"Oh! something new, let's have," said Bertha. "Suppose we try that game that is mentioned in 'Daisy Chair'—that High-Church novel that you were pouring over, Ruth? One goes out, we choose a word, which each must insert into a story that each must tell."

"Original story?" cried Mr. Aubrey. "I have no invention."

"Then remember one; only be sure to bring in the word. Who shall go out?"

"Let two go out together," said Francis; "it makes it easier for the guesser. I vote that Mr. and Mrs. Gray retire to the dining-room and be the first victims."

"Carried unanimously."

"Choose something easy: recollect we are dull," said Gerald, as they left the room. "Bless Francis for that idea, my darling. Look at me. What troubles you?"

"That silly song of Cecilia's."

"Confound Cecilia! Can I prevent her from being silly? She doesn't know what she is doing. She sings die-away ditties with the air and tone of a victim. For heaven's sake, don't notice her. I don't know what possesses her to be so foolish. I don't like to startle her innocence by letting her or anybody else see this sentimental set at me; and you observe how I treat it. Instead of helping me, it worries you."

"But ought not Phyllis to interfere?"

"Phyllis did speak to her, and poor Cissy was quite shocked, and really has no idea of how much nonsense she shows. She really don't care two straws for me. She is a perfectly good, well-principled girl; but you know,—mamma's ideas,—all that—she fancies that I;—in fact, poor child! this is her notion of *revenge* for my short-comings."

"We ought never to have asked her here," said Ruth, decidedly.

"It was my fault," said Gerald, "and it will be mine if it is ever repeated. Now, you are all right, my nonsensical darling, ain't you?"

"Yes."

"Ah! there's a monosyllable that I like."

"Come in! come back!" called out the voices from the drawing-room.

✿ CHAPTER XVII

"Who begins?" asked Gerald, entering.

"Mr. Fordyce."

"I heard," said Mr. Fordyce, "that there were excellent mushrooms to be found in the old field—"

"Dear Mr. Fordyce," interrupted Phyllis, "what sort of story is that?"

"Mrs. Fordyce to pay a forfeit if she interrupts Mr. Fordyce on *this* occasion," said Gerald.

"In the old field adjoining the next plantation," went on Mr. Fordyce. "I knew that my amiable host would not object to having some, nor throw any obstacle in my way, if I even carried off Plato from some knife-cleaning duty to help me in the search. I started when I first got up, armed with faith, perseverance and a stick, not to mention Plato. I walked myself tired and hungry and came back, without seeing a single mushroom!"

"Perseverance!" said Ruth and Gerald, both together.

"Oh, no! no!" they all cried.

"Very well done, indeed, Mr. Fordyce. Now to the next."

"Some people think," said Mrs. Denham, "that everything is to be accomplished by faith in your own powers. I will relate a small anecdote that upsets such ideas. This winter I had set my heart or my head, I don't know which, on the conquest of a young gentleman, and I fancied that if I only believed that I could,—had faith in myself—it would be an easy matter. There seemed to be no obstacle to interfere. He was young, and foolish, and conceited. I talked to him, laughed with him, flattered him, and was rewarded by his saying one day: 'Mrs. Denham, you are a charming woman. Faith! if I wasn't so much younger than you, you would have great trouble in getting rid of me!'"

"Oh, that's too easy," said Gerald. "Faith! Mrs. Denham, you might have done better. Take my place."

The answer was a burst of laughter.

"Mrs. Denham has treated you as the *toreadors* treat the bulls, Gerald," said Francis; "she shook the red rag in your eyes, and held the dagger in reserve."

"What is your guess, Ruth?" asked Bertha; "only one for each permitted."

"Heart?"

"Your head runs on hearts. Do you remember any mention of hearts in Mr. Fordyce's mushrooms?"

"His heart was in the business, but he did not say so," said Arthur McIvor. "Now, Francis, 'tis your turn."

"Once upon a time there lived in a city, which shall be nameless, a youth, who madly loved a maiden. That's a famous beginning, but it doesn't go on so well. He was poor; she wasn't rich. Those are obstacles to the course of all true love. He went away; not to forget her, but to work for her. That is an everyday occurrence. They wrote and wrote to each other. He was as true as steel and thought her truer. On the last page of her last letter, she said:

'And so I write to you; and write and write
For the mere sake of writing to you, dear.
What can I tell you that you know not?'

"He didn't know that with the same pen that traced those lines she answered 'yes' next day, to the booby with ten thousand a year, whom she married in a month, and who asked her that evening to do so. But she took a night to consider about it—twelve hours; in fact, sixteen, to consider whether she should cast off the man who loved her so deeply and passionately. That was a hesitation he should have been proud of; and so I told him, for

Women's hearts change lightly;
(Truth both trite and olden;)
But blue eyes remain blue,
Golden hair stays golden,

and there are as good fish in the sea as ever were caught or lost. Now, guess the word."

"Obstacle," said Gerald, a little gravely.

"You have guessed it," Francis said. "Take my seat. Come, Ruth, you are not released until you guess for yourself."

"Do you think that is a true story?" enquired Phyllis, as the door closed on Francis and Mrs. Gray.

"My child, all stories are true about something. There is nothing new under the sun. We may read of an imaginary Mr. Johnson's sufferings, but depend upon it, a real Mr. Thompson has had something very like it to experience. What some Margery in a book is said to have felt, depend upon it, a Mary in actual life is undergoing and suffering, or feeling and enjoying. We can't strike out new sensations to wring us or make us happy, any more than the book makers can. 'Everything is new; everything is old,'" said Gerald.

"But," persisted Phyllis, "do you suppose that this story of Mr. Josselyn's has any relation to himself?"

"No more that through his relationship to Adam, and consequently the whole human family."

"Ah! I thought—"

"Phyl, thinking is the most dangerous thing anybody can do. Nothing would induce me to think."

"Well, it strikes me it would be as well to think about the word we are going to choose," said practical Mr. Browne, "and not keep those two waiting all night."

So the word was chosen, and Ruth and Francis summoned.

"Begin, now, at Mrs. St. Clair," said Mr. Aubrey.

"Eighteen months ago," began Bertha, "I got a note from a friend of mine, (she glanced at Mrs. Denham,) telling me that she was, at the very moment of writing it, undergoing the pleasure of a visit from a widowed 'landed proprietor' of our common acquaintance, who had come with an extraordinary prayer—a plan to propose for our approval. That we should select a party of ten ladies and ten gentlemen, to go into the country on the Monday week following. We were to carry—"

"How long were you going to stay?" broke in Gerald; "for I suggest cradles."

"Gerald!" cried Ruth, reprovingly.

He held up his hands, and looked provokingly handsome, while the young men laughed, and Bertha went on, vainly trying not to smile.

"We were to carry horses and fishing lines, and ball dresses, and to stay a week. I wrote in reply, that unless the plague were to break out, I feared we could have no excuse for this little entertainment, and so, I suppose, by way of revenge upon my lukewarmness, when these Bo—, when these unlimited ideas resolved themselves into a *fete,* given by said landed proprietor, at his ancestral Hall, he never invited either of us at all."

"I can't guess anything," said Ruth, puzzled. "Gerald put me out."

"I was listening to Mrs. St. Clair's story, not picking at her words," said Francis.

"Which only means," said Bertha, "that you both wish to conceal your dullness. The word came—"

"You mustn't tell," exclaimed Mr. Aubrey. "You spoil my chance of escaping detection. I am going to quote. I warned you I couldn't invent. Listen to moon-rise from Fort Sumter:

> Slow-climbing from the abyss of dread,
>> Beneath the horizon's mystic line,
>> The August moon begins to shine,
> A sullen orb of angry red!
>
> Still upward! Lo! the lurid glare
>> Commingles with a purer sky,
>> And softlier on the gazing eye
> A shield of rose illumes the air!
>
> Up to the Zenith!—Silver bright
>> The stainless splendor swims, below,
>> The tremulous ocean seems to grow.
> One pathway of celestial light!
>
> From doubt and anguish, and despair,
>> I watch my clouded future climb!—
>> Look up! from yonder arch sublime
> Its glory floods the gaze of prayer!"

"Very pretty and proper;—whose?" asked Gerald.

"I found them in Mrs. St. Clair's album," answered Mr. Aubrey.

"Did you, indeed? They evidently emanate from the pen of a virtuous and right-thinking young person. Name the author, Mrs. St. Clair, and if he is present let's crown him."

"Oh, there are other verses in Mrs. St. Clair's album," said Mr. Aubrey. "What do you think of these, surmounted by a bunch of faded hearts-ease?

> See! faded my flowers low dropping in sorrow,
> Afar from the bosom they die to adorn;
>> Let thy sweet lips but press them,
>> Thy fair hand caress them,
> And the grief of the night beams with joy in the morn.
> Sweet flowers! go, tell her *my* heart's ease has faded,

Like you, on that bosom I die to recline;
But the sweet lip disdains me,
The fair hand restrains me;
Ah! sleeping or waking, but sorrow is mine."

"Mr. Aubrey! Mr. Aubrey!" cried Mrs. St. Clair, as well as she could for laughing; "what do you mean by this? You interrupt the game and wish to throw my little Marquis into confusion, by quoting the verses he sent me wrapped in sugar-plums at Christmas!"

Gerald's color had risen, and he darted an uneasy look at Aubrey.

"*I* write verses!" exclaimed McIvor. "It's my opinion that Aubrey wrote the first and—"

"Hush, hush, my child; you needn't be ashamed of them, and if you put in another disclaimer, I'll smother you with wreaths myself;" and Bertha launched into a laughing, jesting skirmish with her boy-admirer, and drowned his protestations in a torrent of nonsense.

Josselyn understood at once that Aubrey had quoted himself, and that Gerald had written the sentimental *madrigal.*

"This is all very well, and Mr. Aubrey recites admirably," he put in; "but what is the word? Do *you* guess, Ruth?"

"Not in the least. They must condense more."

"And not deal in episode."

"Go on to Browne—he may help you," said Gerald, who seemed in no wise anxious to descant on the merits of album poetry.

"Prayer," said Mr. Browne, clearing his throat.

"Oh! prayer," exclaimed Ruth; "that is it! Bertha spoke of the landed proprietor and his extraordinary prayer."

"Yes, I thought you would guess it then; but Mr. Browne is more considerate in his aid than myself."

"Well, I thought we never would guess it at all," said Francis. "I am not good at guessing, and things must be very plain to strike *me*. Nothing more obscure than what I have just heard hits the range of my intelligence. Browne's help was absolutely required."

The entrance of the supper tray caused a cry of surprise—no one had fancied it half so late.

Francis poured out a glass of curacoa for Bertha, and smiled meaningly as he handed it to her.

"That dates five years back," she said, answering his look; "but I had not supposed that Mr. Aubrey knew its origin, and would seize it as a weapon. Did I not tell you that I *knew* how saucy Mr. Gray could be? It is for this reason that I want you to let me off. The creature has such eyes! and is so fearfully saucy. I think I could always resist the encroachments of his beauty upon my peace of mind, but I am powerless against his impudent nonsense."

"But you know you are not really to attend him—only *dis*tract him from feeding his vanity and tormenting Ruth."

"What a monster you are! Then you don't consider my feelings at all. Seriously," she went on, ceasing to smile, "I wonder if we shall do any good?"

"We can't do any harm, and our object is certainly commendable. I trust implicitly to your tact. Just get this girl out of the house without letting Ruth see that—"

"That what?"

"That Gerald has not been frank with her. I sincerely believe that he loves her now; but, I fancy — and so you have not finished reading '*Rouge et Noir?*' Ruth"—she was beside them—"send me something to read, please. I can't go to sleep before the small hours as you primitive people do. Good night."

"Have you and Gerald talked yourselves out?" asked Ruth, "and will you read a sober book of my choosing?"

"You had better come and take a hand with us," suggested Mr. Aubrey.

"Oh, these cards—detestable cards," cried Bertha. "Why will men so waste time and money—sitting up all night shuffling and dealing? If I were you, Ruth, I should forbid the 'devil's books,' after a certain hour, in my establishment. Wait till I get a country seat."

"Then you would never have your friend, Mr. Leonard Germayne, as a frequent guest, Mrs. St. Clair."

"Why not, pray?"

"He would not like to go where limits are set to turning up the king—and a mighty pretty way he has of doing it too. The only thing he does better is—turning up the ace."

"For shame," said Bertha, indignantly.

"Well! ask Browne. Browne is our informant."

Mr. Browne shook his great Teutonic head, (his mother was a German,) and smiled meaningly.

"Come, out with it, Mr. Browne. If what you hint is true, say it—if it is false, deny it. Don't stand there looking as if you might disclose volumes—and then after all have a mouse exit from your mountain."

"God bless me! Mrs. St. Clair, you are so hard upon a man."

"No, I am not; but I hate innuendoes, half-words, which are meant to mean whole sentences of condemnation, and so on—stabs in the dark from those who would not scratch with a pin by daylight."

"Bertha," said Mrs. Denham, warningly.

"Oh, nonsense!" cried Bertha; "Mr. Germayne is my friend. I like him—I like his wife, and I should scorn to sit quietly by and hear slanders of him—none the more fatal because half-syllabled. If Mr. Browne means that he has seen Mr. Germayne cheat at cards, let him proclaim it. If he is not sure of it, let him never hint at it again. It is dis— it is outrageous."

"You take up a fellow so quickly, Mrs. St. Clair," said Arthur McIvor.

"Yes, I do," said Bertha, shortly. "I despise underhand dealings. It is not the first time that I have heard such talk as this, and I don't like it, and in my presence it shall never pass unnoticed."

"Why, my dear creature," said Bettina, "you don't imagine, do you, that the Germaynes don't know that such things are said, and that it is quite useless for you to break lances in this manner for them?"

"I know nothing but this," answered Mrs. St. Clair, "that they are my friends, and, as such, I owe them a sacred duty—"

"They will fall off from you, just like others."

"So be it; truth is truth. *Fais ce que doit, advienne ce que pouvra. I* don't believe what had been said; that is sufficient for me. Am I not right, Ruth?"

"Yes," and Ruth then whispered, "but a little fierce."

Bertha broke into a light laugh and held out her hand to Mr. Browne.

"Pardon me," she said, with her softest air of contrition; "and of our conversation only remember this, that were I to hear you accused behind your back, I should be just as energetic to the speaker."

Mr. Browne took the fair hand, bowed and said something unintelligible, but the cloud remained sulkily on his brow.

Ruth, Bertha and Francis stood together in the hall. Francis shook his head, with a look half amused, half sad.

"Don Quixote, *en jupes,* Mrs. St. Clair."

"And after all," said Ruth, very low, "I fear Mr. Browne is right. Gerald has a horror of gambling; he never touches a card now, unless obliged to play for politeness, and he says that Mr. Germayne's society is not agreeable to him, because that gentleman is so devoted to play, and is too—lucky always."

Bertha's upper lip trembled with suppressed amusement, and then a shadow of sadness darkened her expressive eyes.

She looked earnestly for a second in Ruth's calmly happy face, but only said, "Good night, dear."

Francis Josselyn kissed Bertha's hand. "True, reckless and doubting" was his thoughts, and then he took Ruth's. "True, cautious and unsuspicious," he went on. "And there is a deal of semblance between these two women, and neither they nor the world will ever know it." All he *said* was:

"Good night, sweet ladies."

🙵 CHAPTER XVIII

"Well, this is our last day here," said Mrs. Denham, as she drew her chair to the breakfast table.

"Yes, and it is fortunate that it is so bright a one, for we will take advantage of it to go and see the old Church, shall we not?" asked Mrs. St. Clair, turning to her hostess.

"I wish you would all consent to remain a little longer with us," said Ruth, politely.

"I don't see why you hurry off in this very punctual manner," Gerald said, taking up the strain.

"Of course," said Bertha, laughing, "you have done now the right and proper thing—we are pressed to stay, and I, for one, decline, but with the pleasant feeling that I have not overstayed my welcome."

"I would gladly remain," remarked Phyllis, "but we are expected at my mother-in-law's by to-morrow afternoon's train, and she would think it a breach of decorum for us to put her off."

"Does Cissy go with you to Mrs. Fordyce's?" asked Gerald.

"Yes; some of the Rutford girls are asked to meet Cissy. She is such a favorite with every one, that I was not surprised to have Mrs. Fordyce urge me not to let her forget her promise to come, with the suggestion that the dear old lady would do everything in her power not to make it too great a sacrifice, for one so young and so much admired."

Nobody took up the strain, or expressed the natural desire of everybody to secure Cissy. Mr. Browne did say something, which was swallowed with the mouthful of waffle that he was at that moment mastering, and a second after, Cissy herself entered, looking very fresh and fair.

"Now let us discuss our plans," said Taunton, who had had a headache the previous evening, and retired very early from the company. "Are we going to the Church?"

"Yes."

"Nice road?"

"Well, it is rather shady, which will be an advantage with so warm a sun. Those who don't like rough travelling had best go on horseback, perhaps. Mrs. Gray will take the carriage, for she never rides."

"Who will go with me?" asked Ruth.

"I will," said Phyllis; "my riding dress is not with me, and I like the carriage just as well, and don't mind jolts."

"I shall ride," said Bertha.

"And I," added Mrs. Denham.

"Are you going to try Mountain Mary, Cis?"

"Oh, yes, if she is very quiet."

"Quiet as a rocking-horse, and it would be just as hard to make her runaway."

"Then that is settled," said Mrs. Gray, rising. "We had better start about —" and she looked at Gerald.

"About 11 o'clock."

It was a gay and frolicsome party which took its way through Beauchamp woods to the deserted and dilapidated Church.

Mr. Browne had finally decided to drive Mr. Fordyce in the trotting-waggon, which came to the door, with Midnight in such prancing spirits, that the timid elderly lawyer, was half inclined to back out, and take refuge in the carriage with his wife; but being earnestly assured that "it was only his fun," by the admiring groom, who held the head of the handsome "fast-trotter," he, a little reluctantly, hoisted himself up to the seat, beside Mr. Browne.

"I say, Ruth, do you ever trust yourself in that wagon with Mr. Gray?" asked Bertha.

"Frequently," answered Gerald for her; "but I have to take her again. What is the use of driving so insensible a woman behind such a nag as that! Do you know, Mrs. St. Clair, that one afternoon, after having recently exhorted my wife to pay a little attention to Midnight's good points—after having forced her to confess that he was the most splendid horse she had ever seen, what do you suppose she did? I had some thoughts of buying Tom Trenton's milk white mare, and had her to try, and asked Ruth to go to drive, without mentioning the mare. We got in and went off. Ruth gazes at Snow with the air of a *connoisseur*, and says to me in a little patronizing air, assumed tone, "It must be admitted that Midnight is a superb creature; I never saw him better?"

"Of course that story is true!" said Ruth, joining in the laugh against her.

"Of course it is," said Gerald. "Now let us be off. The carriage had better go ahead, for Jackson knows the road better than any of us. Aubrey, you go in the carriage, I believe?"

Mrs. Denham had Mr. Taunton for an escort, and Mrs. St. Clair, seeing that Gerald was determined not to quit Cissy's side, exchanged a rapid glance with Mr. Josselyn, which ended in the latter falling back to form a trio with the two cousins, while Arthur McIvor escorted Bertha.

Bertha could not help enjoying the sight of Gerald's provoked countenance, when he found Francis persisting in helping him to teach Cissy in which hand definitively she should hold her reins. Mr. Gray could find no excuse to get rid of Francis, who was so placid and so pleasant, paying outrageous compliments to Cissy, who smiled and simpered and colored, and was as inoffensive and pretty as a large wax-doll.

Through the grand old primeval forests, which, except for the worm fences here and there, and a very indifferent road, looked as if neither the hand nor foot of man had ever come near them before, they went for several miles.

"Who does all this land belong to?" asked Francis.

"I don't know exactly where Mr. Desborough's interest ceases, or Taunton's begins," said Gerald. "The dividing line is not of very great consequence. It is not cotton land; and it is very poor corn-land. Take care, Cissy; don't jerk her so."

"Of course; that is always the cry—corn or cotton; and now the introduction of the first named article is an innovation on a *gentleman's* consideration. You Southerners never will be the people you ought to be till you leave off thinking it derogatory to your dignity to cultivate anything but cotton or rice. When some of you planters turn farmers, it will be a great thing for you all."

"I make no doubt; and I have not the smallest objection to their doing so."

"Miss Clare, would you refuse to dance with me if I grew and sold potatoes, beans and turnips? That only will deter me from it, when I settle as Gerald's neighbor."

"Oh, well, I don't know. It is not the custom, you know."

"That decides me," said Francis, firmly. "Adieu, ye shades of gathered 'produce,' that have never yet been planted! Miss Clare disclaims ye, and I disown ye!"

"Did the first settlers here, the English gentlemen who owned these lands," asked Cissy, "did they plant beans and things for market?"

"No, I fancy not; they were for the most part men of fortune, and the chief of their time was given to laying out their grounds and digging fish-ponds, instead of ditching and draining their lands. There was an immense amount of labor given to ornamental work. As Tom's father, old Trenton, says: 'You can see that niggers then only cost fifty dollars apiece, when their services were wasted in that way!'"

"These places have all passed into other hands, have they not?" persisted Francis, obstinately bent upon being agreeable, and making Gerald instructive. "The descendants of the first colonists have not kept to the old sites?"

"No, there are strange enough places to be seen about here; not very long since, there was a house which had remained for years and years deserted. It belonged to the M— family. The young English bride brought over by the last occupant from her cheery British home, was miserable in the midst of the black faces and the solitude. They seemed to have rushed off one day, with scarcely any preparation or packing up. Mr. Desborough told me that when first he bought Beauchamp, twenty years ago, he went over to visit this queer, neglected place. Two ancient negroes still tottered about the premises. There was a harpsichord open, a book turned down upon its leaves, as if just being read, pictures upon the walls, faded carpets on the floors—a strange haunted, weird look everywhere. The old negroes didn't 'know rightly' who owned the place. Roses still bloomed in the ragged garden, and the fish pond was choked up. Not long after the woods were on fire, and the house was burned down, and the old negroes straggled off and died."

"And who owns it now?"

"What? the house that was burned down? My dear Francis, I have been amusing you enough. Cissy don't care a straw for old burned down houses."

"Yes, I do; and I think that a very interesting account. Tell us about somewhere else."

"No, I won't, because while listening, you have let Mountain Mary pull and pull at the bridle until she had got her head between her forelegs and looks like a cart-horse."

"Ah! there we are," cried Francis, "arrived! There is the carriage, and the ladies have got out."

Under the porch, through the always open door into the old Church, where the British arms above the altar saved the building in the Revolutionary days. The Lion and the Unicorn had been freshly gilded and touched with red, a year or two before, when an attempt had been made to get up a congregation and a clergyman, which failed through lack of funds, fervor and farmers. Gerald suggested the first reason, when said attempt was soon discussed, Ruth hinted at the second, and Francis boldly stuck to the third.

"Who was to make your congregation?" he enquired. "If all this waste land were in the hands of tenants, broad-shouldered, hard-fisted, working men, planting corn and beans and turnips, do you hear Gerald? corn and beans and turnips; how much better it would be."

"For country doctors, yes; for you are reckoning without fevers and such things. You Northern people never cease being afraid of our climate, and yet never consider that it is this peculiar soil and climate which keeps us from spreading over our country and filling it up, as you do with yours."

"The ground would be filled up with the bodies of victims fast enough," said Mr. Taunton, quietly.

"Not here—I don't believe it. In the swamp lands, necessarily," said Francis. "But, take this land into cultivation, drain, manure, clear—. You would soon see."

"Whoever saw an a-c-h-i-e-v-e-m-e-n-t pronounced hatchmen, and much mentioned in Mrs. Gore's novels, and other instructive works?" cried Mrs. St. Clair, from the gallery over the door. "Not you travelled people, but we republicans and sinners?"

"Not I! nor I!" answered several voices.

"Then run up here instantly."

There was a scrambling for the narrow stairway, and a clambering over old worm eaten seats, till they stood before the black wooden board over which was painted the coat of arms, &c., of perhaps the last person in this country who followed the lugubrious and yet time-honored custom. It had been hidden away behind a bench.

"How queer and distant this little nook of a place seems from our times and people?" said Bertha, as she leant over the railing of the gallery and talked to Francis. "We are so new; those monuments yonder, on either side of the chancel, would be almost modern in an English Church; they have only been there a little over a hundred years, to us they are antiquities; yet, I don't think ten people care about them! If one could flip up this small, grey and to me perfectly interesting old Chapel, and plant it safely where it could be entirely renovated and used, half the world of our world would prefer a staring, just-built edifice with not an association about it."

"Progress, dear Mrs. St. Clair! This Church is not comfortably built; and what awkward little pews!" put in Mr. Aubrey, joining them.

"Precisely," said Mrs. St. Clair, saucily; "you are one of the world I speak of."

"New things for a new country," suggested Francis, languidly.

"But eternal newness is immortal vulgarity," said Bertha.

"That sentence is so much like you, Bertha," said Mrs. Denham, laughing at her. "Sounds so fine and means nothing!"

Bertha made a rush at the speaker, who caught up the folds of her riding habit, and disappeared down the staircase, followed by Mrs. St. Clair, and when the gentleman came up with them, Bertha had revenged herself by taking possession of a superb wreath of jessamines which Mr. Taunton had gathered with great difficulty for Mrs. Denham, and winding it around her own black plumed grey *mousquetaire* hat.

They passed an hour deciphering inscriptions, and making wonderful discoveries about family connections.

"Why," said Phyllis, "who ever dreamed that Mrs. Turner, that red-faced, horrid woman, (however, she is dead, poor thing!) who ever dreamed that she was a niece of the Rutfords?"

"I didn't dream, but I knew it," said Mr. Fordyce.

"Why didn't you tell me? I never would have snubbed her so, if *I* had known it, and when we were at Catoosa Springs together. Here is her tombstone."

"See how important it is for us to get up *our* Debrett!" exclaimed Mrs. St. Clair. "How much more easily poor Mrs. Turner would rest now under that stone, if Mrs. Fordyce had only known that her mother was a Rutford!"

"I don't think we ought to jest about a death so recent," said Ruth, gravely. "Let us go farther off."

"You are right, Ruth," whispered Mrs. St. Clair, "and it was very naughty of me, but Phyllis does put me out of patience. I think she would strike sparks of indignation from a cold potatoe!"

"Has Mrs. John Gilpin brought anything to eat?" asked Gerald, as he came towards them.

"Yes," said Ruth, "our lunch is in the carriage; but let us get outside of the enclosure. *This* is consecrated ground."

"Right again," said Bertha. "I fear we have shown more curiosity than reverence in our visit, so far."

Presently they were all sitting under a great tree, and the contents of the hamper were happily brought to light.

Old jests and new were bandied about, and Bertha began to moralise in her usual flighty fashion.

"Don't you think," she said, "that people really grow better if they live in the country?"

"They grow fatter, usually," said Mrs. Denham, helping herself to some more *pate*.

"But," persisted Bertha, "do they not grow better? How little excuse one can make to one's self for evil thoughts of one's neighbors, malice, and uncharitableness, when one lives away from all the petty annoyances and invitations of society."

"On the contrary," said Mr. Taunton; "they grow self-satisfied and intolerable, from having nobody to rub their own opinions against; they form erroneous judgments of people and things."

"They become intensely selfish," said Gerald.

"I thought you had never lived in the country till now," cried Bertha, innocently.

"Mrs. St. Clair, your remarks are personal. *Do* you think me selfish?"

"I am no judge," said Bertha; "I am so selfish myself," smiling into his eyes with mock humility.

"Who says you are selfish?" broke in Arthur McIvor; "I don't think so at all; I think you are a very nice woman, which you wouldn't be if you were selfish."

"Young gentleman, come hither," said Bertha, solemnly. She took off the jessamine wreath from her hat and wound it round Arthur's curly head, as he knelt before her, taking care not to derange the perfect "parting" right in the middle of his forehead. "I crown you my knight henceforward and forever. Rise, Sir Arthur, and give me some chicken."

"Bertha, what is the use of abusing yourself?" asked Bettina; "there are so many to do it for you."

"I like to follow *la mode*," said Bertha.

"Is it the fashion?" asked Francis; "alas! can I never hope to be fashionable here? What is your crime, dear Mrs. St. Clair?"

"Upon my word, I have never exactly found out," said Bertha, carelessly. "Sometimes I hear it is because I am so satirical—because I say sharp things. But I have set traps occasionally for my best friends, like the lawyer and his client, and have found out that once more it makes all the difference in the world 'whose ox it is that was gored.'"

"I don't quite understand."

"Shall I explain? Well, for instance, I am embarked in an encounter with somebody, and a skirmish of words ends in a mutual drawing off, which is called 'one of Mrs. St. Clair's quarrels'—all the odium rests on me. In vain I protest that the provocation came from the other side. 'Oh, impossible!' My fault has only been to resent. 'Oh, that cannot be!' At last I tell the story, reversing the actors, attributing to the other party my speeches and my actions, and *endossee*-ing theirs. A chorus of exclamations: 'Of course, don't you see? You were palpably wrong; nothing was done to you; you were needlessly fierce! poor so and so, no wonder that they are wounded.' 'You think so, really?' I say. 'Most assuredly, nothing can be plainer,' 'I am heartily glad,' I answer; 'because I have exactly reversed what happened; 'twas *they* that did such and such things, and *I* who had the other side.' 'Ah! well, let's hear it all over again,' if I am weak enough to accede."

"What?"

"I find out that 'it makes all the difference in the world whose ox is gored.'"

"From which state of things you conclude—"

"Two. First: that Aesop is ever fresh, and that naughty wolf, my world, is always having the stream at which it drinks seriously muddied by this innocent little lamb far below the current; and, second: that it is the fashion to think me always in the wrong;" and then she made a courtesy *a la Fontanges,* and proposed that they should all go home.

CHAPTER XIX

"Mrs. St. Clair, may I come in for an instant?" said Ruth, tapping at Bertha's door.

"Certainly," cried Bertha; "is anything the matter? Sit down."

"Nothing very alarming, only I will venture to consult you. I have just got a note from my father, as we entered the house—but don't stop arranging your hair, you can listen just as well, and it is near the dinner hour, and I know you don't like being hurried."

"Thank you, your father is not ill, I hope?"

"No, not exactly, but he writes that his head gives him some uneasiness, and adds," reading from the note in her hand, "unless I grow worse, I will start for Beauchamp on Wednesday morning." You see, he has not come; this note ought to have been here yesterday. Of course, had anything very serious been ailing him, my cousin, Mrs. Price, with whom he stays now, when I am not in town, would have sent for me; but still I am a little worried."

"Of course. Are we in your way this evening? Would you go at once if we were not here?"

"Oh, not to-night; it is already after four o'clock. But you and Mrs. Denham meant to go to town by the twelve o'clock train; would you mind going instead with me in the carriage *very* early? It is now later in the day, but by starting at six o'clock—can you calmly contemplate six o'clock?—we shall have a pleasant drive, and I can return when I please."

"It will suit me perfectly. But the luggage?"

"That and your maids can still take the train."

"If we are not in your way, I think the plan a very agreeable one, and I am glad you have spoken so promptly and without hesitation."

"Thank you, my dear Mrs. St. Clair, it was exactly what I knew you would say."

"Well, it is exactly what I wish you wouldn't say, when you address me as Mrs. St. Clair. Pray call me Bertha, as you sometimes do, and as everybody else always does."

"Bertha, then," said Ruth, smiling, and stroking the bright dark hair which her guest was rapidly braiding; "I am by nature very formal and stiff, you know."

"By education you are growing very much the contrary," said Bertha, as she looked up at her.

"Yes, Gerald is my teacher, and it is easy to learn from one who practices what he teaches. You will pardon my foolish admiration, when I say, that his graceful ease of manner is to me perfectly charming; but I always think that my efforts to imitate him are very like the donkey's labors in the lap dog line."

"I think you are getting a style of your own which is even more attractive than his."

"Oh!" said Ruth, blushing faintly: "I shall make you one of your own courtesies for that. But the fact is"—she paused; "the fact is, my present anxiety about papa is a little based on an evil conscience. I fear I am too much taken up with the study of Gerald and his perfections to be able to pay the attention I ought to papa. I have an uneasy, vague presentiment of some coming evil connected with my dearest feelings. Have you ever had such silly fancies?"

"Dozens of times; very seldom with any result. It is quite reasonable that you should wish to go to Mr. Desborough, and I think it is right, but I make no doubt you will find nothing to alarm you. Either he is only still ailing, or else he has changed his mind about coming. Perhaps he has heard that you have a house full of noisy, chattering people, and keeps out of their way."

"Perhaps so," smiling. "At all events, I think I had best go; and you are sure that Mrs. Denham will not object?"

"Quite sure. What becomes of the gentlemen?"

"Phyllis takes Mr. Browne with them to the Fordyce's, by the up train in the afternoon. Mr. Aubrey and young McIvor go over to the Tauntons' to hunt, and pass a few days. Mr. Taunton goes in his own waggon, after breakfast, to his sisters, whose place is sixteen miles across the river. Francis remains here with Gerald."

"Mr. Gray does not go to town with us, then?"

"Oh, no! he stays to see the Fordyces off, and, of course, I leave him to look after the children."

"Of course."

"'Twas his proposition that I should suggest your going with me, and thus reach town so much sooner. Now, good-bye; I must hurry up Valerie. Your hair looks like plaited satin, and to think that I can do nothing with mine, except put it in Valerie's hands! Gerald always says when I attempt to arrange my hair myself that it looks as if I had invited the furies to pass a leisure moment in brushing it."

"So 'twas Gerald's proposition, was it?" murmured Mrs. St. Clair, as Ruth closed the door. "Humph!"

In half an hour there was a rustling of silks down the stairs, as the ladies assembled in the drawingroom, and immediately after dinner was announced.

The variable climate! This evening it was like the last of May; windows were thrown open, and in the coming twilight without, everything looked so cool and still, while around the plate-laden table, where flowers in profusion bloomed, the tall silver candlebra were not yet put to use. When the dessert and the children appeared, the candles were lighted; and if among the many stereoscopic views which flood the civilized world, this room could have been transferred to cardboard, the result would have had a great sale.

The women were all in their different styles, worth of admiration, from stately Ruth to smiling Cissy. The gentlemen were, some of them, singularly handsome. Mr. Fordyce would only have lent a little shade to the colors. Then the two lovely babies in their white embroidered dresses, and shoulder knots, and sashes of bright, broad ribbon. They had *mignonnes* heads with long curls, and such pretty, foreign-accentuated voices and ways; their skins like ivory and roses, and their plump little bodies so well shaped.

Gerald at first clung to his mamma, burying his fair head on her shoulder, and refusing to look up, while Miss Geraldine, standing on her papa's knee, had seized his face between her two little chubby hands and was kissing him without ceasing, coquettishly pretending utter uncognizance of Mr. Taunton's efforts to draw her attention towards him.

Presently, however, she let her large, blue eyes wander in that direction, and before very long, was sharing an orange with him, and chattering away in her little half French, half English jargon.

"Did you see the papers, Mr. Fordyce?" asked Gerald. "They were late in coming to-day, and I had no time to skim them over before the dressing bell."

"Yes, I read one or two."

"Anything new?"

"A fuller report of the X— case."

"Ah, indeed! Is it decided?"

"Yes; verdict against him—marriage pronounced valid."

"From what paper do ours copy?" asked Mr. Aubrey.

"From the London *Times*."

"Didn't you read it?" enquired Mr. McIvor; "I did."

"What case is this?" Mrs. Denham asked.

"A case to prove a marriage," answered Mr. Aubrey. "A certain dashing British officer, wishing to put off a lady's claim to bear his name and possible title—not to mention that he has performed the ceremony recently with a No. 2."

"Ah, yes! I remember seeing something of it. Poor woman!"

"Poor woman, indeed!" said Francis, quietly. "Don't waste your sympathy on an adventuress, dear Mrs. St. Clair."

"Don't be harsh in your judgments, Mr. Josselyn. Why call her an adventuress?"

"Read her own confession; she followed him to the Crimea; she ran him down, she—"

"Stop; she may have done so, and that was very naughty, and unfeminine, and there I abandon her. We all of us will admit, won't we, madames, that a woman who runs after a man is an unnatural monster? So far, we have not a word in her defence. But he, he acknowledges, does he not, that she would not live with him on his own terms, however much she may in the first instance have run after him?"

"Yes."

"Then she had principle, if not great modesty and decorum of manner?"

"Not she; she wanted his name, and the position that it would give her."

"How do you know?"

"Let's hear the story," said Bettina.

"The bare story is very simple," said Francis; "a pretty and attractive girl meets a handsome man above her own station in life; he is struck; she is flattered, still more by his rank than by his admiration."

"Recollect this last is Mr. Josselyn's own conclusion. Stick to facts, oh, prejudiced traveller! and tell her story, not his."

"Very well. They part; they correspond without meeting, till he gets to the Crimea, and there she goes at once as one of the band of volunteer nurses; sends after her admirer, and he falls again at her feet, but tells her he can't marry, first, because he had no money, and secondly, because his relations won't like it. So she then proposes a Catholic ceremony, not binding in law, but comfortable for her conscience, and it takes place."

"He assuring her," interrupted Bertha, "in every possible way of his affection, and now pursuing her as steadily and as persistently with his devotion, as she ever did him in her thoughts, discussing with her the impossibility of legal marriage, but ready to go through any religious ceremony she choose. He gave her a ring—"

"He gave her a ring, and a priest blessed them, that's true."

"But the gallant Major don't believe in priests. In a year or so, when he grew tired of her, he left her, and without explanation or preparation, or apparent change of feeling, he marries a rich widow, doing it all as secretly as possible at first, so as to prevent the interference of his real wife."

"But, my dear Mrs. St. Clair, what sort of woman can she be? That speech to the Irish mob after the verdict in her favor!"

"My dear Mr. Josselyn, I am not defending the woman; I am indignant at the deed. Were you to murder the meanest man in the world, I should not the less consider you a murderer. The honorable Major had to pay a certain price for a certain piece of property, and it matters not whether the value received were at all proportionate to the sum disbursed. It was a *prendre* or a *laisser* on positive conditions. He didn't wish to *laisser* it, and when the payment grew burthensome, he denied the debt."

"Come with me, Gerald; I'll show you the pretty picture," said Cissy to the little boy. Cissy's feelings were in the process of laceration from this discussion.

"What is your opinion, Ruth?" asked Mrs. St. Clair.

"Entirely with you. There is no excuse for him. I agree with the sergeant, who, when he answered a question 'upon his honor,' cried out 'upon your oath, sir; I do not want your notions of honor.' I am heartily glad to see her righted."

"Why, Ruth, where have you been studying the X— case?" asked Gerald, smiling.

"The papers came before we left; while waiting for all of you in the hall I saw them."

"Dear Ruth," said Francis, "how can you be so hard upon the rougher sex? Indeed I thought you would come to my assistance against Mrs. St. Clair."

"In the cause of strength and his, against weakness and truth, never! I may have thought Major X— unfortunate, if his fancy, being his master, had led him blindly to sacrifice his life and fortune to an unworthy woman; but a gentleman's plighted word, his sworn faith, can never be gainsayed, simply because he wearies of his bargain."

"Do you recollect that beautiful sentiment in the *Roman d'un Jeune Homme pauvre?*" said Bertha; "*Il vaut mieux outre passer l'honneur que de raster en deca; en matiere de serments, tous ceux qui ne nous sont pas demandes sous la pointe du couteau ou a la bouche d'un pistolet, il ne faut pas les faire, ou il faut les tenir.*"

"*Voila mon avis,*" added Gerald, finishing the quotation, and bowing at the lady.

"What, you too, old fellow? I thought you would be with me," said Francis; "well, I suppose I may as well give up the defence, which I was, I beg Mrs. St. Clair to believe, only doing to bring out her 'enthusiasm,' and I am glad to proclaim in my natural character, that the honorable Major X— is a dishonorable scoundrel."

"Why should you suppose, Francis," enquired Ruth, "that Gerald would side with you? Why suppose that any gentleman would uphold a creature who is a disgrace to his name and position?"

"Ah, here comes an avalanche," cried Francis, playfully, holding up his hands. "Don't throw your plate at my head, dear; you will certainly break the plate. Don't you know men always stand by each other? Mrs. St. Clair says so, and I say ditto to every thing Mrs. St. Clair says."

"Gerald would never stand up for deceit and falsehood in any shape. I should disown him if he did," Ruth said, smiling proudly.

"Well," put in Phyllis, "I think allowances should always be made for gentlemen when they fall under the influence of designing women."

"Yes, poor things!" said Bertha contemptuously; "poor, helpless men! I am so sorry for them. They go through a great deal of danger."

"I shall be very much obliged, therefore, to you two excellent ladies if you will kindly protect me, a tender creature, from the vengeance of that 'designing female,' my cousin, Mrs. Gray, who will perhaps poison my coffee presently," said Francis, laughing.

"Don't you know, Francis, that Ruth permits no slur [?] on my perfections except from her own tongue? There is written upon me, invisibly but indelibly, a 'notice to quit,' addressed to all human kind. 'Stick no bills here.'"

"I see it," said Bertha, "on your noble brow," raising her hand.

> Range undisturbed among the hostile crew,
> But touch not Gerald, Gerald is *my* due."
>   (Signed) RUTH GRAY

Ruth laughed and said that she supposed there was no use to disclaim; so all rising they adjourned to the drawing room.

CHAPTER XX

Passing through the hall, they stopped to look at a large trunk.

"Oh," said Phyllis, "that is from dear Mrs. Armstrong, for me. From your aunt Charlotte, Mr. Fordyce. It is full of old brocades—things ever so old. Dresses and coats, and all sorts of head gear. See, how beautiful!" She lifted the lid, and presently everybody was upon their knees examining the rich silks and embroidered velvets of an ancient date.

"Wasn't it good of her to give them to me? Here is the lovely pink and silver which she selected for you, Cissy. I wish we were going to have a fancy ball to wear them."

"Why shouldn't we have a fancy ball to-night, all to ourselves?" said Arthur.

"Yes, that would be great fun."

"Would you be willing to lend these treasures, Phyllis?" asked Ruth.

"Oh, certainly."

Then began a scene of fun and laughter quite indescribable. Cissy, of course, had her pink and silver, and Phyllis set her eyes and hands firmly on a certain gorgeous yellow, covered with humming-birds. But to choose for the others was no easy task. The men especially were bent upon getting the best of the habiliments, and as there were but two handsome coats, there was quite a scramble for them.

Finally, a moderately just division of the spoils was made, and after a whispered colloquy between Mrs. Denham and Arthur McIvor, every one went off to dress; each promising not to be more than an hour in the robing process.

"But rouge!" exclaimed Bertha; "where shall we get any rouge? and if we powder our heads without rouge, we shall all look like grey owls."

"Mrs. Fordyce eagerly joined in; "Ah, yes! rouge! that is a great difficulty. What shall we do? Of course nobody has any."

"I have," said Ruth.

"My dear Ruth, don't expose the secrets of your dressing-case," said Gerald in a loud whisper.

"And of your color," said Bertha, reproachfully.

"I defy you all," answered Ruth, "but I condescend to explain that I saw only yesterday a pot of Lubin's finest bloom, still among my 'effects,' where it has been since I went *en marquise* to a French ball last year."

"Ah! honorably acquitted!"

"Valerie shall start on an excursion around the house with the article in question, for the use of both ladies and gentlemen. Oh, Geraldine, what a little monkey!"

Miss Geraldine came running towards her mamma, dressed up in a waistcoat, of which the flaps made a train for her, hotly pursued by Mr. Taunton, who was destined to appear in it presently himself.

Such peals of laughter began now to resound through the house; sudden dashes were made from room to room, and loud calls for curling-tongs, and Valerie, and rouge.

Valerie was in her element; so full of importance and suggestions, and pearl powder; modestly veiling her coffee-colored French eyes, and mincing her words; whisking through the passage with her cap strings streaming behind her, and her trig little figure darting in and out wherever summoned.

At length, about nine o'clock, they began to re-assemble. Ruth, having been deprived of her maid's services, was almost the last to appear. As she entered the drawing room, she was greeted with quite a burst of admiration. Her dress, being one she had already worn, was more *soignee* in its appoint-ments than the others. The powdered hair had artificial curls—the *bandeau* of brilliants and the graceful plumes became her vastly; so did the very rich colors of her skirts and train. The lace she wore was magnificent; her stately carriage suited the sweeping robes; her dark eyes were doubly lustrous from the effect of the softly tinted cheek. Three black patches gave a coquettish charm to her smile, and she wielded her fan with the perfect nonchalance benefitting her toilette.

She was essentially of the type *grande dame.*

"Why, you are lovely," cried Bertha, sailing up in red and white, with oceans of old blonde flowing over her, and large coral beads around her white throat.

"The same to you," said Ruth, smiling.

Phyllis looked very handsome with her humming-birds, and her darkened eyelids, and Cissy was charmingly pretty in the pink and silver.

"But where is Mrs. Denham?"

"Not down yet," answered Mr. Taunton, who was admirably got up. "Both she and McIvor are missing still."

Messrs. Fordyce and Aubrey now came forward, leading between them Mr. Browne, whom they protested they found trying to hide from his own knee breeches.

Of course this was fair game for Gerald, who joined in the comments for and against Mr. Browne's legs.

Francis touched Ruth's arm; she was gazing intently at Gerald, and started.

"Own that you think him perfection and nothing more," said her nominal cousin.

"Certainly I do," she answered frankly.

"I think Browne should petition the government to force everybody back into tights," said Gerald. "I predict that Browne would make a brilliant marriage if his calves had a chance."

"He would be a greater lady-killer than our friend X——, whose case we have been discussing."

"I go for what is in my head, not for what carries it," said Mr. Browne, good-humoredly.

"I protest against resuming the discussion of Major X——," said Bertha; "unless every body agrees that he ought to be hanged."

"I don't at all agree," said Mr. Browne; "I think he is a plucky fellow, and behaved very naturally."

"Indeed!"

"Yes, no man *can* love a woman long, to whom his is not legally united;" and Mr. Browne rounded his eyes and looked solemn, "Every woman ought to feel that."

"That is your opinion, is it? But you likewise believe the converse case, that he always loves one to whom he *is* legally united?"

"Of course."

"How astute! I wonder from what you argue? Not from anything you ever said, surely. It never occurs to you that because marriage forces a man to stand *outwardly* by his word, inwardly he is not any the truer? Believe me, one who would be false to a love *only* binding in honor, and which, by your creed, can be broken, will never keep any better the vows legally sworn, and which, in a measure, therefore, he must seem to respect."

"Not my creed; God forbid!" said Mr. Browne, backing down before the indignant flash of Mrs. St. Clair's eyes; "I have no opinion on the subject."

"No experience, you say," said Gerald mischievously.

"*My* opinion is," said Bertha, "that you had better leave off being proud of either your head or your heart, and accept even your legs instead!" turning her look upon him.

"That is one of Mrs. St. Clair's hard speeches," whispered Francis.

"I know it," said Bertha, candidly. "Poor Mr. Browne is not aware that he is taking part in a comedy, and getting the sort of treatment, mentally administered, which, in Ravel pantomimes, passes for wit—hard kicks."

"Do you think that Gerald suspects that we are lecturing him over everybody's shoulder?"

"Not in the very least. I do believe that he is sweetly unconscious, or else he plays into our hands with calm impertinence."

"Yes, he helps us more than anybody."

"I think Mr. Fordyce will have a fit, if I launch any more plain phrases at the X— case. He looks upon me now, why—see that."

The door was thrown open with a flourish and two figures entered. The first was a little old lady, with a cap and wrinkles and black mittens and powdered hair and spectacles, and eyebrows like two strokes of Indian ink. She leaned one hand on her gold-headed cane, and the other was firmly linked into the arm of a tall young creature who swam vivaciously by her side with a huge fan and innumerable graces and airs.

The old lady stumped her way up to Ruth and introduced her daughter: "My beloved Adeliza," she said, "an unsophisticated bud, of which in me you see the full blossom."

Then groaning and puffing she sank into a chair, while the "beloved Adeliza" by turns fanned her afflicted parent and made wondrous eyes at the gentlemen.

Of course they were immediately recognized—and Arthur McIvor as the "bud" played his part as well as his venerable mamma, Mrs. Denham.

His pretty, boyish face, with its short curls and wreath of roses, was infinitely funny; and the way in which he managed his petticoats and hoops, and bridled and smiled, and looked and hesitated, did great credit to his powers as an actor.

Presently was heard the tuning of a violin, and in the entry appeared the plantation fiddler assisted by a friendly tambourine player from an adjoining estate—while at the open windows "going" upon the piazza, sundry heads with bandanna handkerchiefs proclaimed that the trimly maids were enjoying a sight of the fruit of their labors.

The evening grew into quite a frolic. Gerald's gay spirits, never needing much impetus to set them going, were at their highest pitch. Mrs. St. Clair was not far behind him, and Francis matched them both.

"No quadrilles to break the 'proprieties' of your brocades and powder!" exclaimed Ruth.

"Of course not," said Gerald, "may I ask the favor of the fair Adeliza's hand for a minuet?"

"Who knows the minuet?"

"Oh, it is all bows and courtesies and any time," said Gerald recklessly.

"Well, it will be so for this evening. Mrs. St. Clair and I will 'lead the measure,' and make the figures as we go; but I think the 'Lancers' danced very slowly with extra salaams will save our time."

"I don't think old Joe is up to the 'Lancers.' Can you play the 'Lancers,' Joe?

"Nebber year of such a ting, Maussa," responded Joe; so he was then requested to perform his slowest and best known tune, and Gerald led out *the* young belle, who tripped back several times to her mamma and whispered, and trembled with modesty before she could make up her mind to leave the maternal side.

Phyllis fell to the lot of Mr. Aubrey, and Mr. Taunton danced with Cissy.

In the midst of the gay laughter, and the many absurdities, Ruth gradually forgot the anxiety which had weighed upon her since receiving her father's note.

Her voice frequently joined in the lively sallies which flew from side to side: the sage sentimentality of Adeliza's mamma and the daughter's affectations; Gerald's bright and saucy face was by itself enough to amuse her. Unconsciously, she, after a while, ceased speaking to Mr. Fordyce and just watched the dance with happy eyes and a half smile. Mr. Fordyce finding that she was silent and inattentive to him, began to fidget about the table near which they were sitting. He had quite a taste for drawing, and thought he would sketch the scene. Ruth grew alive to her neglect of the little lawyer, and opened a drawer to find a sheet of thick paper. She gave it to him, and beneath was an envelope with "good advice" scrawled on it in Gerald's hand. Taking it out, she found a slip cut from a newspaper, and reading the title "Jealousy," remembered the very evening on which her love had given it to her. The smile deepened as her thankful heart recalled how sad she was in those early days when Gerald and she were first learning to understand each other. "Did I ever need such advice in very truth?" she thought, quite forgetting that only on the previous evening there had been a slight spasm of the malady—but then it was but slight, whereas in those bye-gone days the case seemed fierce and chronic. Yet she sighed, too, as she glanced over these words of Dickens:

"Jealousy is as cruel as the grave: not the grave that opens its deep bosom to receive and shelter from further storms the worn and forlorn pilgrim who 'rejoices exceedingly and is glad' when he can find its repose; but cruel as the grave is when it yawns and swallows down from the lap of luxury, from the summit of fame, from the bosom of love, the desire of many eyes and hearts. Jealousy is a two headed asp, biting backwards and forwards. Among the deadly things upon the earth, or in the sea, or flying through the deadly night air of malarious regions, few are more noxious than is jealousy. And of all mad passions, there is not one that has a vision more distorted, or a more unreasonable fury. To the jealous eye, white looks black, yellow looks green, and the very sunshine turns darkly lurid. There is no innocence, no justice, no generosity, that is not touched with suspicion, save just the jealous person's own. And jealousy is an utter folly, for it helps nothing, and saves nothing. If your friend's love is going, or gone, to another, will your making yourself hateful and vindictive stay it or bring it back? If it is *not* leaving you, is there no risk in rendering yourself so unlovely?

Commend me to all bereaven bears rather than to a jealous person, especially a jealous woman. There is neither reason nor mercy in her when once thoroughly struck through with this fearful passion. She renders herself altogether repulsive by it—an object more of dread than affection to those who have loved her best. And if she regain not her self command and return not to her senses, she frequently destroys utterly the attachments she most prized. Her friend may, indeed, refuse to forsake her, but it will be duty that bids him stay; and never will he be able to forget what an abject thing she has once appeared.

But let not any too rigorously judge the conduct of a jealous woman or a jealous man. Remember that the maniac *suffers*. To be sure, the suffering is from selfishness—often it is without a shadow of a cause; but still it is suffering, and it is intense. Pity it—bear with it. You may yourself fall into temptation. It is a sorer curse, a more certain and fatal blight to the heart on which it seizes, than it can be to those against whom its spite is hurled. Then while none should bend too far to the whims of jealousy, all should be patient with its victims; and also should be watchful and careful that it enter not their own heart."

The music—if the scraping of Joe's fiddle and the clatter of the tambourine can be called music—had ceased. Some one laid a hand on Ruth's shoulder—she looked up, and Gerald enquired:

"What are you studying, darling?"

"A mastered science—the symptoms of a cured malady—the 'diagnosis' of an almost forgotten case."

He looked at the paper.

"You remember it?" she asked.

"Oh, yes, perfectly; weren't you naughty in those days? And haven't you improved since!"

"In everything?"

"Everything; vanity especially. I see why you so readily gave in to the notion of this *travesti*. That dress is charming—it suits your figure, style, face, air! And do you know that you were never so handsome in your life, my love, as to-night?"

Ruth's eyes sparkled with a tender lustre, she said, almost shyly:

"Thank you. I think the angels in Heaven are not more beautiful than you, Gerald."

He laughed.

"I think you are as great a goose as usual," he said. "But we must not stand flirting here in this outrageous way."

As he nodded at her and went off, she rose and stood for a second motionless beside her chair.

In that moment there came a great rush of thought through her mind—her lonely childhood, her solitary girlhood, the luxury and the lack of sympathy in which she had passed her days till he came. But for him, what would she still have been? His sweet and dear affection had made a new world for her. Could she love him enough? But there was a weight upon her spirit, nevertheless. What could it be? The dark cloud that rested upon her was almost inexplicable. "Is it papa?" she thought. "Is he ill?"

"Why, Ruth, you should have an artist here to sketch that *pose*," said Francis.

"What is the matter?"

"Don't move; put back your hand where it was, now look in that mirror and tell me what you see?"

She saw a magnificent figure, gorgeously arrayed; one full, round arm resting with drooping hand and pendant fan upon the back of the chair; the head partly turned over the shoulder, and the small throat proudly rising above a beautiful bust, closely imprisoned in its jewelled stomacher. The large, bright eyes looking steadfastly clear, and the softly chiselled lips just parted, broke now into smiles as she saw what he meant.

"You and Gerald wish to make me quite foolishly conceited, I think," she said.

"You will be petitioning the legislature, too, as well as Browne. Certainly, powder, patches, trains and rouge are your slaves, and you were better than a *Watteau* as I first saw you standing there. It was a delicious *tableau vivant*, and might have been lithographed as '*La Reverie.*' Of what were you thinking?"

Before she answered, Mr. Aubrey, who was hovering near, caught at the idea of tableaux. He proposed that they should get up a few, then and there.

"But we should have no audience," said Phyllis.

"No gauze screen," said Mrs. St. Clair.

"Oh! we shall not be so fastidious as to demand all the accessories of preparation," said Mr. Aubrey. "And the audience will consist of those who are not at the moment acting."

"That is, some of us will look our prettiest to be gazed at by the others till their turn comes to do likewise."

"Just so; and that bow window will be a capital spot. Let's arrange the curtains so that they can drop across the entrance, and be withdrawn immediately; pieces of string will do it."

In a very short time the tableaux were formally inaugurated by the simple process of congregating all the lights upon an *etage* within the curtain of the bow window, and thus darkening the drawing room.

"Mrs. St. Clair was deputed to lead the way and perform the first picture. She thought a few moments, and then selected Josselyn and Mr. Taunton to accompany him.

Gerald and Mr. Aubrey stood at each side, ready at a given signal to draw back the curtains. The word was spoken, and with only a slight hitch, the draperies parted and disclosed Bertha sitting in one of the high-backed *fauteuils*, Mr. Taunton kneeling at her feet and in the very act of kissing her right hand; while the left was receiving from Francis (who peeped cautiously from behind the chair) a very palpable love letter. "A coquette to the life!" was exclaimed, and warm plaudits, of course, were duly given; twice was the scene exhibited, and then Mrs. Denham being called upon asked for the aid and presence of her "daughter" and Mr. Aubrey.

The venerable dame was soon seen in a state of evident anxiety about this young creature's occupation. The listening attitude with partly bent head and uplifted hand, showed that her eyes no longer did their office, for very near stood the culprit—her waist encircled by Aubrey's presumptuous arm, and only half defending herself from the kiss which was threatening her rosy cheek. It was perfectly apparent that the blind grandmama suspected the smuggled presence of the young lady's lover.

This picture was succeeded by the "Dull Lecture;" in which Phyllis figured as fallen asleep while listening to Mr. Fordyce reading. There was a general smile at the aptness of the representation, and Phyllis took the occasion to inform her lord that her choice was intentional, to signify that political news and law cases always wearied her.

Lastly, it was Cissy's turn; "what should it be? She had no sort of invention. Would not Ruth take her place?"

"No; Ruth had from the first begged off—she was so stupid at such things."

A general dearth of ideas seemed to fall upon the company; at last somebody said "The Inconstant," that's a pretty picture and very easy.

"Oh, yes: the old story—you know, a fair and dark beauty, and a man," said Ruth.

"Extremely comprehensive!" said Mr. Aubrey. "It is Gray's turn or Browne's."

"Not mine," said Mr. Browne; "I plead my right to choose, and I have a private tableau to finish off with."

"Very well, then I will sacrifice myself," said Gerald. "Take this cord, will you, Browne, and play scene shifter," then turning to his cousin: "Cissy, who will you have?"

"Ruth, if she will consent."

Ruth again declined, but there was an outcry against her; so she yielded, and the three retired behind the curtain.

In a few minutes they were disclosed; Gerald was in the foreground whispering to Cissy and holding her hand to his heart; behind them, with a look of dismay and indignation, and anguish, Ruth stood transfixed. It was the best picture of all, yet it gave least pleasure to some of the lookers-on.

"*La reste n'est pas toujours bon vin,*" said Bertha in a low voice to Mr. Josselyn.

"Let us hope that it is only a 'might have been,'" he answered.

As the applause died away, and the trio emerged, Gerald said laughingly to Ruth, drawing her close to him in the darkness of the drawing room, "Darling, did you feel as fierce as you looked?"

"Not quite," she said. "I am cured of all that, I trust, forever. Although I heard them saying 'Mrs. Gray's expression is capital,' I could not but feel that some time back I could have better looked the character of a jealous wife."

"What a trump you are darling! But you leave me now not a fault to peck at!"

He dropped her hand as the curtains parted once more, and Mr. Browne was seen kneeling on a cushion, with a telescope to his eye, pointed at the group, while a large placard on his breast proclaimed him "The real, original, drawing-room astronomer."

The lights resumed their places, and supper was declared inevitable and necessary after all these varied efforts.

"This is our last regular meal under this hospitable roof!" exclaimed Mr. Aubrey, as his glass was abrim with sparkling moselle. "I devote this bumper to the happiest wishes, Mrs. Gray! May we all meet again here some day."

"It rests with yourselves," said Ruth courteously.

"Yes; since we have proved that you can spend a week in so dull a spot as this without cutting your throats in despair at so wasting your time, or ours, for bringing you here, let us trust that Beauchamp will get up a good name and become really popular."

"Become! you are too modest, Mr. Gray," said Bertha. "It *is* popular."

"It has been one of the pleasantest weeks of my life," said Mr. Browne soberly.

"Well, mesdames," remarked Mrs. St. Clair, rising, "I don't know what your sentiments are about the hour, but *I* know that I start for town at six o'clock, A.M., and I have at least six pounds of powder to brush out of my hair—so, very reluctantly, I say good night, wishing you all the luck to get rid of this beautifying, but very troublesome adornment, as quickly as possible."

CHAPTER XXI

"I will say goodbye to you here," Ruth said as she put in her head at Gerald's door.

"Come in, my child; why that doleful tone? Any one would suppose that we were parting for several years. Tie this cravat, there's a love; I never saw such an obdurate piece of silk. Oh, what a bow! Get away, you worthless woman. There! how do you like that?" He turned his head round to her with his chin in the air. "But, what ails you, Ruth?"

"I don't know that anything ails me; what is it?"

"Why you look at me as if you were taking an inventory of my features. You will find them just the same to-morrow, believe me."

"I hope I shall. Kiss me, dear, and let me go."

"I am sure you are not well, Ruth. You had better give up this journey, even if your father is ill."

"I wonder which of us is more absurd; I, for feeling as if we were parting for years, or you, for talking of my drive as a journey."

"As if anybody could ever be as absurd as you! But don't stay longer than you can help; if you don't return to-morrow, I shall come for you. You know how I will miss you."

"Do you really, really miss me?" asked Ruth.

"Do you really, really need to inquire?" said Gerald affectionately. "You know, darling, how I dislike to be forced to express my feelings; but this I will say, that never was man blessed with a love more true than yours for me, and never was love more thoroughly appreciated. How then can you doubt that your presence is absolutely necessary for my complete contentment? And it seems so strange for you to ask me such a question in this gray morning *apropos* of nothing.

"And feeling perfectly sure as I do—never so sure—in all our wedded lives as now, of the wise provision which made me link my life with yours! But I hear Mrs. St. Clair's voice in the corridor. Goodbye my own darling."

He folded her in his arms and strained her to his breast. Her whole soul was in her eyes as she bent back her head and looked with tenderness unspeakable into his face. "Oh, my God! how I love you!" she murmured passionately. In the dim light her countenance was radiant yet solemn. "Goodbye," and she was gone.

When Gerald followed to the dining room, the early party were hastily breakfasting. Mrs. Denham was feeding her parrot on toasted waffle, and exhorting him to eat like a Christian, and Mrs. St. Clair was descanting eloquently on the delights of rising with the dawn.

"It is such a cheap and easy to be had pleasure," said Francis, "why don't you oftener indulge in it?"

"Simply because it is a habit which renders the possessor insufferable! How entirely I agree with Elia in his view! An early riser thinks that in performing that virtuous act he exonerates himself from doing any other, and is at liberty from that pedestal to lash the vices of all mankind—and spare his own."

"Yes," said Francis, "just as severely virtuous women think that the exercise of that decency puts them at liberty to commit any other excess."

"Not to mention," said Gerald, "that half the vinegar-faced females who are so hard upon their sisters, and so soft upon themselves, had better remember the Spanish proverb and be humble: 'Impregnable is the castle that never has been stormed!'"

"Scandal before sunrise!" exclaimed Bertha. "What a picture to carry away of life at Beauchamp."

"Is this what is called scandal?" asked Francis innocently; "upon my word, the devil is not by any means so black as he is painted. Have I been scandalous, Ruth?"

"Scandalously brilliant for such early hours. Don't keep it up, or Bertha will run down before we start, and Mrs. Denham and I expect her to be very entertaining."

The carriage came to the door at this moment, and there was a general move.

"I trust, Gerald, you will not forget to have lunch at 12 o'clock for your cousins. Pray, Francis, remember that Mr. Fordyce always takes brandy and water, and always requires to be pressed about it—make Gerald think of it. And when you dine by yourselves to-day don't let Gerald give the children anything at dessert that they should not have," said Ruth, "and"—

"And be sure, Francis, that you pin my napkin well over my shoulders, and see that I don't drink more than—how many glasses of wine, Ruth?" broke in Gerald, catching his wife by one end of her shawl.

"I understand, my dear," said Francis. "This precious creature shall be made to do all that is proper, so you can leave him with a tranquil conscience."

"Adieu Beauchamp!" cried Mrs. St. Clair, stretching out her arms towards the fair lawn and the old oaks.

"*Au revoir,* you should emphatically say, dear Mrs. St. Clair. May we hope often to see you here."

"What! are you really off!" exclaimed Arthur McIvor, rushing down stairs. "Am I not to be permitted to embrace my honored mamma at parting?"

"You lost your filial privileges when you doffed your skirts," said Mrs. Denham, springing into the carriage, and looking excessively coquettish.

"Ah! then he had them when he wore crinoline?" asked Gerald impudently.

"Did I positively imply it?" retorted the pretty widow.

"Don't forget *me,* Mr. Josselyn," said Bertha, meaningly.

"Is this a spot for such tender suggestions?" ejaculated Gerald. "Hide your blushes behind me, Francis, while I whisper your reply to this imprudent lady."

"Not a bad idea that the answer should come through you," said Bertha, glancing at Francis, who with bare head and pulling at his moustache, stood smiling beside their host.

"Well, there is nothing more to be said, drive on."

Scarcely had the carriage rolled twenty yards upon the smooth gravel than there came a cry of "stop," and Gerald arrived breathless at the window.

"You did not say, Ruth, whether Francis was to send a boy with me to carry my gun when we go shooting to-morrow morning—what do you decide?"

He looked so handsome and so merry. His wife, as if involuntarily, touched his head with her caressing hand, and then blushed intensely as his laughing eyes reproved her.

"Decidedly, have the boy, unless you promise not to load the gun," she jestily replied.

"Certainly, Mrs. Gray," Bettina said, as they once more drove on, "you can boast of owning the handsomest creature in the world!"

"Yes, he is very handsome," Ruth agreed frankly, "but he has more than looks. Seldom has there lived any one with such a temper and such spirits. Don't let me speak of Gerald. You know how foolish I am."

❀ CHAPTER XXII

"Well, Gerald!" exclaimed Francis, lighting a cigar and setting himself into his chair; "do you know I think you a monstrously happy fellow?"

"I am not complaining of my lot, am I?" responded Mr. Gray, leaning across the table for the decanter of Madeira. "But what at this instant elicits your remark, may I ask?"

"It is by no means the first time that it has struck me, but I feel in the humor for confiding to you my sentiments on the subject, and it is the sort of weather in which one feels like airing one's private convictions. Besides, except for that hasty day in Boston, it is, I verily believe, the first occasion of a *tete-a-tete* that we have had."

"It is so. We have had no chance for one of our long, by-gone talks. Ruth and you are such cronies, and she has learned to endure smoke so patiently, that it has been a *vie a trois* ever since you have been here."

"God bless her!" said Francis, heartily. "What wouldn't she endure with patience?"

"I think *I* know a thing or two that she wouldn't endure," said Gerald, half smiling. "Throw away that cigar, Francis, and try one of these of mine. You always are torn by conflicting emotions, between your love of good tobacco and your natural economical propensities. Upon my word, if I were not afraid to speak plainly, I should say that you are the d—dest stingiest fellow, to yourself, in the world."

Francis playfully made a dash at him with his fist, which Gerald parried with the extended cigar case. Josselyn helped himself and walked to the door, which opened on the piazza, to throw out the maligned Havannah.

"You were always extravagant, and I have always felt obliged to save for both of us. The fact is, I have been taking care of you so long, and feel such a property-right in you, Gerald, that it would be very hard to bring myself to the consciousness that to seek to guide you, and scold you, is an interference."

"An interference! why you are in a condition to need a straight waistcoat, young man, when you bring forth such nonsense as that. What are you diving after?"

"Gerald the second's top, which you were quite willing to let him set as a pinnacle to that mould of jelly just now, had I permitted it. He must have dropped it when his *bonne* carried him off."

"Geraldine filled my coffee cup with a whole tea set of ancient acorns I think."

"They are beautiful children."

"Yes, pretty little monkeys."

"I like that. You are as proud of them as their mother is. You don't deserve to have such babies, if you undertake to speak so dispassionately."

"*I* like *that*," retorted Gerald. "In the name of Malthus, are you setting up for a connoisseur in children? Since when have you been seized with this mania?"

"Since I began to envy you the possession of such a wife and such children."

"Envy is an evil passion," said Gerald solemnly.

"Seriously, Gerald, I wonder if you comprehend the extent and value of your blessings?"

"Seriously, Francis, I do," said Gerald, yawning.

"Look at your position," Francis went on. "What more could earth give you? You have youth, health, wealth, friends, intellect, good looks, education,—"

"No corns, and never a headache."

"A wife, who is the most admirable of women, and two children—"

"Who seldom cry."

"What more could you have? What is there for you to wish for? Answer me, and don't look so doubting."

"Contentment," said Gerald, shortly—"forgetfulness."

"Contentment? Forgetfulness?" repeated Francis, with surprise. "Ah! true! That sad business across the water. Yes, that is a bitter drop in your cup; but I did not think it enough to spread its taste through all the draught."

Gerald was silent.

"You have had no bad news recently?"

"No news at all. I presume all is right. There has been scarcely time to hear anything."

"I fervently trust that neither your mother nor you will be made further unhappy in that quarter. Do you mean, Gerald, that—"

"Don't let us talk about it," said Gerald. "You know me of old, and my way of taking things. I never speak of what weighs upon me; nor do I ever let any one see its effect upon me. Do you recollect that time at school, when I was unjustly punished and accused—when for so long I had to bear averted looks from our uncle, who believed me guilty, and I was denied every possible pleasure. I felt ready to murder everybody, except you, and yet, did I not look as placid and cheerful, and didn't I play as many pranks, and seem as unconcerned as if I had not a care?"

"True. And when I wanted to condole with you and comfort you, you drove me away from the subject, with sarcastic sentences and practical jokes."

"Precisely. I don't understand the thing which is called 'sympathy in trouble.' The way I behave to my troubles, is to ignore them utterly, or treat them, if possible, as a sort of gloomy fun."

"Let me ask one question about this: How did Ruth take his coming back?"

"She had never heard of him till he returned."

"Good God! And what did she say to you?"

"Three syllables of reproach, and three hundred of tenderness."

"She *is* a trump!"

"She is a very noble woman," said Gerald, calmly. "Shall we have candles? They will not bring them till I ring, and it is quite dark."

"No; I like this soft twilight."

"As you please. I wonder if we shall have good sport to-morrow in the Taunton woods. You will find it hard riding, Francis, and yet you get so restive at the idea of keeping to your stand. The underbrush is perfectly uncleared. Old Josiah Taunton is a curious specimen of the uncultivated aristocracy. Just before you came, his brother, (Louis' father) and himself, had a dispute about the hunt, and Josiah vowed that his idea was the best as to the course they should pursue. 'Drive the deer through them woods!' he said, scornfully. 'Do it! I swear, Bro. Tom, no use for skin 'em after you git them through.'"

"Young Tom Taunton is an admirer of Cissy Clare, isn't he?" asked Francis, carelessly. "She was engaged to him?"

"Not she," replied Gerald. "She refused him."

"I doubt it."

"What can you know about it?"

"Rather more than you do it seems."

"Pooh! nonsense! I tell you she refused him."

"I tell you she accepted him, and she would have married him, but Phyllis did not think him rich enough, and made her father make Cissy give back his ring, and ask the return of her heart."

"It is an infernal lie that somebody has been foisting upon you," said Gerald, angrily, "and I don't believe a word of it."

There was a silence of some few minutes, and then Francis said:

"Gerald, you and I are more than brothers to each other. If you saw me on the edge of a precipice, would you not risk your life to point out my danger to me?"

"I suppose I would."

"Shall I not, then, risk your anger in pointing out a moral precipice to you?"

"Francis," said Gerald, with closed teeth, an unfailing sign that the devil within him was rising; "it is a dangerous thing to meddle too much with even a brother's affairs, unasked,"

"I am silent then," said Josselyn; "but I am bitterly mortified. Pray pardon my intrusion."

"Oh, hang it all!" exclaimed Gerald, impatiently, but more good-humoredly: "say your say; have it out. You know I never could oppose you."

"Thank you, old fellow," and Francis grasped his cousin's hand warmly for a second. "Let's get it over quickly. I think you are going too strong with Cissy Clare, and she—"

"Don't breathe a syllable against her if you wish me to listen to you. She is just as good, and as innocent, and as child-like as—"

"As she can be. My dear Gerald, I don't blame her in the very least. I blame you."

"For what, pray?"

"I will go no farther back than this morning: Your manner, from the time they breakfasted at 8 o'clock, till they left at 2. Had you chosen to look at your cousin, Mrs. Fordyce, you would have seen plainly her disapprobation."

"Phyllis had grown fretfully impatient of the attentions that Cissy receives from anybody."

"You are mistaken. Mrs. Fordyce is a perfectly prudent, proper woman, and you may be sure that she will never bring her sister back to Beauchamp, to be exposed to your very compromising although it may be perfectly innocent, devotion."

"Well, perhaps she is right." Gerald jerked out his words, and filled his glass.

"Then, another thing," Francis went on, not heeding, apparently, what the other had said. "You were gambling with Taunton and Aubrey almost every night while they were here, after the ladies had gone to bed, and I found out unintentionally and accidentally from Ruth, that she believes that you never play, and that she supposed you to have been sitting smoking and talking with me, instead of being engaged in interminable games of 'draw poker' and 'faro' with those men."

"She chose to think so, and I did not contradict her."

"My dear fellow, why take to so fast a pace? You have the brightest present, the most unclouded future, the least embittered past—"

"Fair and softly Francis. What if I tell you that I am utterly and irretrievably wretched."

"I will tell you that you are entirely mistaken."

"Very well, then; listen to me. You talked just now of this being an evening for unrestrained confidence. You shall have mine. Much good may it do you, since you *will* persist in knowing my faults and follies. Where shall I begin? Oh, yes! You know as a boy, I was spoony about Cissy Clare."

"To my amazement, always."

"That is neither here nor there. I don't think any of us ever fail to be amazed in some way at our neighbor's infatuation, while our own is possibly no better. I don't think that Julia Otey was much cleverer than Cissy, and certainly she is not as pretty. You need not start up! We are fencing without foils, and you began it. Well, I played fast and loose with Cissy for years. I liked her well enough to like nobody better, and yet not sufficiently to give up my liberty, for her. She is about my own age, you know, so we had a long siege of it. Just when I found that I was getting too nearly caged, I would haul off; but then, if any man came about her, I would immediately cut in and drive him from the track."

"Extremely creditable conduct," said Francis.

"Wasn't it? Tom Taunton's attentions carried me further than anything else. I did get jealous of him and questioned Cissy pretty closely. It was then she assured me that she had never been engaged to him; that she had refused him instantly. Had she ever thought of accepting him, I should have lost all faith in her."

"She knew that very well, and answered accordingly."

"Francis!"

"My dear Gerald, you are surprised that you, who could deceive her, were deceived by her."

"I did not deceive her. I never have deceived her. I behaved atrociously, but I was only too open, with *her*, poor child!"

"Go on."

"Not long after this conversation with Cissy, I went abroad. (When we crossed together, you remember, and you started for the East, and we parted, to meet under different circumstances!) I was absent twenty months, and came home in August; it will be four years this summer. Mamma wanted to see me, so I only staid a day or two at New Haven, and then came straight home. The Clares were on the Island. Uncle Clare had lost some money, and was economizing, and cutting the girls down in their expenditures; and Phyllis was thinking that some of them ought to marry, and as Cissy's chances that way were greater than hers, and she was always a capital manoeuverer, she took the earliest chance of consulting me, and asking me to make Cissy marry a Mr. Taylor, who was dancing attendance about her. I told Phyl that I was the last person to whom she should apply for such a purpose, as she knew my feelings, &c. I don't know whether I was quite in earnest when I began, but between teasing Phyl, and my real fancy for Cissy, I ended by saying a good deal.

"'Gerald,' said Phyllis gravely. 'This must cease. You must make up your mind one way or another. It is no use to keep up this sort of thing. Between your own behaviour and aunt Ellen's encouragement, Cissy is acting very improperly. She will never marry while you are unmarried, and you are never going to ask her to marry you.' 'But,' I said, 'do you wish to make me believe that Cis wants to marry me?' Phyllis nearly grew angry. 'I only mean that you are treating her shabbily, and that she is very foolish to permit it; and I intend to put a stop to it.'"

"She was very right and I commend her," put in Francis.

"Of course she was right, and I knew it, too; but *I* did not wish to put a stop to anything, so I took Cis to drive that afternoon, and laughed and talked nonsense to her, and enjoyed her pretty feminine folly, and thought her dimples, to look at, better enjoyment than the cleverest woman's conversation. Phyllis' face was dark as a thunder cloud when we came in, but she smoothed it off and began to talk about a dinner party they were to have the next day, and—Miss Desborough."

Gerald's voice lowered at the name, and he drank another glass of wine. The pale moonlight stole in through the open doors and windows, otherwise the room was dark.

"Ah!" said Francis.

"Phyllis first gloated over the riches appertaining to that lady; then she spoke of her *hauteur* and her indifference to everybody. 'There is a conquest worth making, Gerald,' she said, as we sat apart and together, after tea; (for she settled poor Cis down at backgammon with uncle Clare, and out of my reach.) 'If you could carry off that prize, you would do well; but not even you, invincible as you think yourself, could storm or undermine that castle!'

"I was highly entertained at this effort to pique me, and showed Miss Phyl that I was too old a bird for such chaff; but, nothing daunted, she went on with shrewd hints about Ruth's weak points and habits, introducing them as if merely in discussion of her character, and saying nothing further about my having an interest in the possibility of bringing them to bear upon the person in question. I was to go to town in the early boat; so, on bidding good night, Uncle Clare hoped that I would return to dinner and be introduced to Miss Desborough. 'An excellent match for you,' said my venerable relative; 'and with your expected fortune, she could not suppose you actuated by mercenary motives, which is her hobby.'

"Cissy looked so sadly and sweetly at me that I answered, very decidedly, that I did not think it at all possible for me to dine with them, and finding an opportunity, I said to her, at the foot of the stairs: 'Miss Desborough and I may one day be good friends, for I like strong characters; but I shall never try to marry her, Cis; of that, rest assured.'"

Gerald paused, and buried his head in his hands.

"Now, I am going to tell you something horrible, Francis."

"Out with it. Better make a clean breast at once, and forever."

"Better bury it forever, and not dig up the body, as I am doing now. Francis, we shall both repent this conversation. You will think worse of me than you ever dreamed of doing, and I may begin to dislike you for knowing my weakness."

"Not a bit, Gerald, and you know it. Nothing could make me think ill of you. I might mourn, sincerely, over some unexpected *escapade* of yours, and sing penitential psalms with you, and wear a mental white sheet, sprinkled with the ashes of a repented error, but that is all. I could no more quarrel with you than I could with my own right hand."

"We are told to pluck off our right hand if it offends us."

"If said right hand, by its offenses, leads us into sin; but I want to lead this right hand out of sin and folly."

"Probably it does not wish to be led," said Gerald, shortly.

"Let me judge," Francis rejoined. "Tell me the story, just as it comes. Just as you used to pour out all your college and school deviltries to me, easing your mind of the burthen of them, and putting me under the necessity of setting all straight."

"You can't set this straight."

"Go on."

"Well," said Gerald, in a harsh, rapid voice, and striking upon the table as he spoke, with the handle of his fruit knife; "I got to town very early—before breakfast. I went to my room. There lay a telegram on my dressing table. I opened it. It was dated the previous day. It contained the news of our double loss. It was from Mr. Lord,—short as telegrams usually are, and distinct as a lawyer generally is. But three lines, and yet, I entered that room a man with the world before him, and the contents of that brown envelope told me that I was irretrievably a beggar, or very near it. You guess the rest, don't you?"

"Go on."

"For a moment I was stunned; but I swear to you, Francis, that my first thought was *not* the fortune—my second was. My third, the devil whispered!—it was a woman's name,—. How soon my plan matured itself, I don't know. I think it was done in half a second. I deliberately sealed up the telegram in another envelope—made a moderate imitation of my own name from the back of the original for the address, and put it my pocket. We breakfasted, and I told my mother that I was going again to the Island, but not to dine with the Clares, who were to have a party for Miss Desborough. I borrowed her coachman, and took my own boy, Jim, put on my shooting clothes, and started for rice birds at Hutter's point. You wonder what that all meant? Phyllis had told me that Ruth's habit was to walk always late and alone on the beach. I had two notions: one was to come in and find her still at the Clares, and pique her, if possible, by my indifference of costume and manner, or to make her acquaintance in some accidental fashion, during her walk, if she took one that evening. On the way to the row boat, in which I intended going to Hutter's Point, I stopped a small boy; pointed out the house, bade him ring the bell, and deliver the re-sealed telegram. I knew it would not be opened till my return. Confess, Francis, that you are disgusted?"

"Not in the least," said Francis, calmly. "I wish to know how it all turned out."

"As most things do when satan takes them in hand, and so long as he is permitted to guide events, devilishly well. I killed some birds and cooked them for my dinner in a lovely grove of live oaks, with tangled swings of wild grape vines interlacing their old trunks, and then I took a fancy to see if I could find a crane on one of those uninhabited islands opposite Rutledge-super-mare. By this time the wind was pretty high, and I thought things began to look unpromising. No woman would venture to walk out under such a sky, but I preferred not being on the sea myself; so, feeling anything but gay, and full of dissatisfaction with myself and everybody, finding great difficulty in making the passage, and decidedly as much out of sorts with the world, and as melancholy and as wretched a rascal as ever breathed, I landed on the beach, far up at the east end. By Heaven, Francis! there came a rush of amazement and audacity over me, such as successful villains in every line of crime must feel, when the most sanguine and unlooked-for hopes are fulfilled by that unseen agency which often baffles our comprehension, by its strange playing into our hands. A figure stood three yards from me, motionless and silent. I approached it, and recognized a person, whom I had often seen, but who, it appears, had never noticed me—Ruth Desborough."

❀ CHAPTER XXIII

As Gerald here paused, Francis lit another cigar from the stump of the old one, and asked tranquilly:

"You spoke to her?"

"Of course. And then something infernal and powerful stirred within my breast—a recklessness surpassing every sentiment of the kind I ever before experienced. The part I had to play became a real pleasure to me. I was interested in my own acting and—I did it to perfection. Knowing Ruth as I since have done, I see that it was a wonderful effort. Phyllis had given me instructions that were very useful, but with luck favoring me, I walked over the course in a manner that surprised even myself; although, without modesty, you who know *a little* of my career, I may say that I am not unused to facile conquests. But everything went for me. This was the evening of the last 'great storm'—an equinoctial gale that lasted three days, tearing down houses and frightening the people more than they were hurt."

"But you did not stay on the beach?"

"Scarcely. On the contrary I offered my escort to the unknown lady immediately, and urged her to hasten home. Poor Ruth! poor dear Ruth! how stately and indignant she was when I accosted her! She has told me since how unspeakably impertinent she thought me! and in fact but for the fierce wind and the furious rain, I don't think I should have made any progress at all—but she grew grateful when she saw her danger; and, finally, the cards of our game were death, and I seized the four honours, and made the odd trick besides."

"Your game, not hers."

"Oh! she played her part too, poor soul, although comparatively a very innocent one. I soon perceived that she did not wish to be known; she was keeping dark as to her name—my own, I had instantly disclosed; but it was plain that to her it was the name of a stranger."

"Perhaps she had her concealments, too?"

"Who? Ruth? My dear fellow! she *said* that she had never heard of me before. You understand her very little, if you suppose that any statement, the most seemingly problematical, could be false when coming from her lips! No! her morbid suspicions were swept away by my admirably performed ignorance of herself, and my interest in this unknown woman. We were obliged, finally, to take refuge at the Fort, and there, as I expected would be the case, came the denoument of the drama. I found myself in the presence of my two cousins, and Ruth discovered that this was the young gentleman who had refused to make her acquaintance at their dinner that day."

"Had Phyllis told her of your refusal?"

"Not exactly; but it transpired in a manner *not* unprovoked by me, and helped on by Phyllis, who looked like a triumphant conspirator when she saw me. To this day, Phyl has never guessed the truth, but thinks that to her skillful innuendoes and her wise provisions, are owing the circumstances of that evening. You may well imagine that her delusion has never been made clear to her, and when the blow of my uncle's death fell upon them, Phyl's excessive delight in her prophetic judgment was really amusing."

"And Cissy?" said Francis, indifferently.

"Poor Cissy!" Gerald repeated with a softened voice, "I was cruel to her as only a man can be cruel. I did not spare her one pang. Before her eyes I threw myself headlong at Ruth's feet, and treated Cissy with a careless impertinence that was disgraceful, but *necessary*. This was my most difficult part. Ruth suspected the existence of some understanding between Cis and myself, for it must be confessed that the poor child scarcely concealed her jealousy and her indignation. Phyllis tried to carry it off with a high hand, but the mine was nearly sprung once or twice. A word of indiscreet explanation would have shattered my hopes, for I read Ruth thoroughly even then. An unoccupied heart she might believe herself capable of filling, but to suppose it possible, for a man attached elsewhere, to seek her, except for her fortune, she would never credit."

"What did Cissy do?"

"Oh, a dozen silly things, and she looked so sweet and mild and fair—it was abominable of me—but the die was cast, and I was bound to conquer my own feelings and Ruth Desborough's. My pride was aroused, too, in a very little while—almost instantly. My attentions were public—it would not suit me to pass for a baffled wooer of the heiress."

"And had you no pity for Ruth?" asked Francis.

"She had and has no need for pity," said Gerald, "she has never known, she shall never know, by what dubious paths her happiness came to her. Miserable I may be, but she is happy."

"It will not last. Sooner or later such a deception must come to an end, especially when you bring Cissy beneath her very roof, as if to invite her observation. Has Ruth never been jealous of your attentions to your cousin?"

"Dozens of times!"

"In the beginning?"

"From the beginning."

"Did she question you?"

"Ah, there it is! Before she would engage herself to me—when I saw that she loved me—she made her acceptance hang on the balance of that question. That came hard upon me, Francis. There is something in a downright lie that goes against the grain dreadfully. But she asked me, 'on my honor,' had I ever been in any way plighted or entangled with Cissy."

"And you answered—?"

"You see, things were desperate with me. Without being in love, I ardently desired to marry Ruth; I liked her. I had determined never to think of Cissy again, and those grave uncompromising eyes of hers which permit no halting, were upon me, I answered, on my honor, no."

"Humph!" said Francis. "She believed you?"

"She believes in me with the simple faith of the child in its mother, of the Christian in his God."

"Gerald, how can you help loving her?"

"I do love her. I love her very dearly; I respect her nobleness of character, her singleness of purpose, her truth, her faithfulness—but she never was and never can be, not the woman I love, but the woman who *is* my love."

Gerald did not see the curl of contempt which settled on Josselyn's lip, but gave no shade to his tone as he enquired:

"And in all this time she has never grown on you?"

"Sensibly; in fact, I lost myself during those two years, and more, that we were abroad. I think I had no regret, no remorse, no recollection while we were absent. It is on coming back here, it is on seeing again that faithful and unhappy child that I am overwhelmed by the thought of my fatal rashness! Had I but been patient. Think of it! Situated as I would have been—with the comfortable fortune, which I owe to your generosity, Francis—and with that pretty creature whom I loved since my boyhood, what a different man I should have been!"

"Very different, I think!" exclaimed Francis, significantly. "Do you mean, old fellow, that you are really in love now with Cissy Clare?"

"I mean that she has a place in my heart that nobody has ever filled."

"Allow me to say that it is the most unhealthy sentiment I ever heard of—I believe as utterly unreal."

"As you choose."

"And do you confide your feelings to her?"

"Certainly not. I respect Cissy as much as I love her. And—"

"Do you, for one instant, fancy that she could ever love you with the intensity and utter unselfishness of your wife?"

"Unselfishness! surely Ruth's love for me *is* selfish. Would she be willing to give me up, do you think, to secure my happiness at the price of her own in me?"

"My dear fellow, that proof of her love would be as supremely unhealthy and unreal in your present mutual conditions as the sentiment you think you have for your boyish fancy. But answer—do you for one moment suppose that Cissy Clare cares for you, or could care for you, as Ruth does?"

"No; I believe no human being could be more utterly devoted to another, soul and body, than Ruth is to me. 'Tis her own fault; I had loved her better had she less loved me. She is always on her knees to me—now, I adore the woman who requires you to be incessantly on your knees to her. My spoiled, petted, capricious Cissy, good natured and sweet-tempered, but used to adulation and loving me, would have made just the little household idol that I should have worshipped."

"And the agreeable and sensible companion, and the judicious mother of your children—"

"Yes," said Gerald, shortly and decidedly, "Cissy is not brilliant, but she is perfectly sensible and judicious. If I want brilliancy I can seek it in books or out of doors—but this is idle talk. What is, is. What has been done, can't be undone. I made a mistake—I acted with duplicity, and I bear the consequences."

"You *don't* bear the consequences, and ah! how many men would give their right hand to have your consequences to bear! Don't regret your confidence, Gerald, it has taught me a lesson, it will teach me to endure my lot. Our happiness lies within ourselves most truly, since a position such as yours is not by itself capable of making one so. But I entreat you, by virtue of our long intimacy, put aside this foolish fancy, which [is] the most utterly unreasonable source of disquiet. Would that you could see Miss Clare with my eyes, then I could be quite content to let you see Ruth with your own. That she should be overshadowed by such a shape as that!"

"We have said enough," said Gerald, rising, "more than enough."

"One word more; for God's sake conceal from Ruth forever all that you have told me. You do blind her successfully, but 'ware the day she discovers the merest suspicion of the truth."

"To whom do you tell it! My life would be a pleasant and tranquil one!" exclaimed Gerald, laughing and stretching his arms. "Come, I am tired by all this gloomy retrospection. I hate talking about disagreeable things which can't be bettered. If I were being led to the gallows, you know I should jest with Jack Ketch. Let's have a game of billiards."

"Your life a tranquil one! Yes, I think so," said Francis, "a very tranquil one so far as Ruth was concerned. You should know her best; but it strikes me that were she *to find out for herself* that she has been the victim of this long series of deceptions, her course would be plain and undeviating."

"In what way?"

"She would never forgive it, and she would leave you."

"Ridiculous!" said Gerald, laughing disdainfully. "Nothing could separate Ruth from me—but I should have a wearisome time, striving to set things straight again. And I should be very seriously sorry to make her unhappy."

"Oh, Gerald! you say so, and yet you run the risk every day of your life. Be just, be generous. I scarcely know what to advise—perhaps to tell her all would be the best—even to the length of confessing your sin from the first guilty beginning—even to telling her the truth about the telegram, and all that—and pouring into that faithful heart all your follies—telling her how you have learned to love her and to mourn the unworthy commencement of your acquaintance. She would be, perhaps, your best help against any renewal of this sentimental nonsense. . . ."

"Tell her then what is just as untrue as anything I have ever told her," interrupted Gerald. "You don't know, Francis, how much it will cost me to pursue the path I have marked out as the right one—but although I never intend to see Cissy again—never intend to trust myself in her society, I cannot forget her, nor speak of her to Ruth as you would have me. It would be false—false as all the rest. Don't you see now that I am driven into all kinds of dissipation by the misery of my position? What but this has made me spend hours with those men, gambling? What but this makes me drink a vast deal more than is good for me. . . ."

"Oh, by Jupiter! Gerald, that is coming it a little too strong! You have a natural turn for gentlemanly potations. You know that two glasses of whisky punch, judiciously administered, would make you confess a murder—or commit one; and as for cards, my dear fellow! . . ."

Gerald broke into a laugh. "Yes, I am afraid if I were at the gates of Heaven, and St. Peter looked agreeable to the notion, I might pause to propose a hand at 'poker' before entering. But for all that, it is only too seriously true, that when I remember where I am, and where I might have been, I am ready to hang myself, and as a solace, fly to Barclay's or the bottle."

"Very well," Josselyn said, heaving a great sigh. "If a man is bent upon making a fool of himself. . . . Let us take a game of billiards, as you propose."

"What a beautiful night!" said Gerald, going towards the piazza.

"Promise me, old fellow," said Francis, following him, and laying his hand upon his shoulder just as they reached the doorway, "promise me that no inadvertence on your part, no more foolish attentions to Cissy, will awaken Ruth, by any chance, from her happy slumber."

"Your warning comes too late, Francis. I am here," and Ruth stood before them.

"Ruth!" cried Josselyn, springing to her side. He took her hand and looked her into her face. The hand was cold and rigid, and lay passive in his grasp; the face, seen by the pale moonlight, was set like the face of a corpse; like the face of one who had passed away in agony and in despair.

Gerald leaned against the door post, motionless and haughty; a slight, contemptuous smile played about his lips. Lucifer was unchained and defiant.

Ruth's great eyes were fixed upon Francis, and slowly, deliberately, harshly, her voice broke the silence.

"Why did you beckon to me, Francis? I do not regret it, but I don't understand it."

"Beckon to you!" He thought her reason had gone.

"Yes," she said. "The horses were restive. I got out and sent them round by the stable entrance, and walked up the avenue. You came to this door, looked at me, and signed to me to come here, instantly disappearing. I fancied some plot of yours. I knew not what—I felt so gay, so joyous; my visit to town was all a mistake; my father wrote Beauchamp when he meant Bellair; it was a slip of his pen. 'Twas to Bellair he went on Wednesday; I hurried back from town; I—I did what I supposed you intended. I stole quietly into the piazza—Oh, God! Oh, God!"

The cry of anguish seemed wrung from her against her will. Gerald advanced towards her:

"Dear Ruth," he said, "this is—"

"Don't let that man speak to me, do not let him touch me!" she exclaimed hoarsely and fiercely. "Protect me from him, Francis. You are of his sex, but not such as he. This house is mine: he must quit it."

"Let him speak to you—let me leave you together," whispered Francis imploringly. "This is most unfortunate—"

"Unfortunate!" repeated Ruth scornfully. "That is the word you use! Yes; even you an honorable and God fearing gentleman, you find no word but unfortunate to bestow upon such an act as this. Had this person been detected concealing an ace at cards, or had his hand shaken with terror if standing up to be shot at, you would have turned your back upon him, disowned him, loathed him, but it is only *unfortunate* that he should be a liar, a schemer and a smooth-faced, smooth-tongued villain—because I am a woman."

Vehement and energetic as were her words, her voice was not raised nor did she move. Slowly she uttered them, as if each were a sword thrust sent deliberately to its mark.

"Ruth, I beseech you to listen to me—to listen to Gerald. You throw away your whole life at this moment. It is my fault, it was my fault. I insisted upon an idle confession of an idle fancy. There is no reality in all this. For God's sake, speak Gerald—"

"I threw away my life when I thought I had found it, on that 24th of November, when I stood at the altar."

"Those whom God hath joined together, let not man put asunder," said Francis softly.

"Aye! If God *hath* joined them together. But as well say that if you ask a blessing on a murder it becomes a sacred act, as say that such—. Let this end at once and forever. I am no child, no idiot pining away in grief. Look at me, Francis. Is there *sorrow* in my face?" She brushed back the dark masses of hair from her ghastly white cheek and brow. "Is there any soft influence at work, think you in me? You have heard of me as cold, hard and fierce; you met me—what I shall never be again. My old self has arisen within me. I thank God for it. No gentle word nor thought shall ever again have the mastery. I leave such things to my fair *rival*—to the beauty whose image has never left the faithful heart—oh! that such 'a mere white curd of asses milk' should have such power! Power to rob a man of decency and honor!"

She turned and left them. Her steps echoed down the piazza, and a great silence followed.

"What will you do?" asked Francis at length.

"Nothing."

"Leave matters as they stand? how can you?"

"I think I have already informed you this evening that I never yet saw the earthly good of interfering or ripping up old things. Your diplomacy has had a good result. I don't know what you contemplate. By the way, Ruth says you beckoned to her; perhaps you have prepared all this, and wish to bring me on my knees to my wife?"

"Gerald, you need not try to quarrel with me. You need not knit your brow, nor set your teeth. No insult you could offer me would move me now. I am too profoundly wretched. I try to understand what she means—ah, yes! I went to throw out my cigar, it must have been then that the motion of my hand and arm she took for a signal. Great Heaven! don't stand yawning and stretching yourself there. Of what stuff are you made?"

"Flesh and blood and bones, I fancy. At least it looks so."

He rang the bell for lights. "Will you go to the billiard room now, Francis?"

"No," said Francis vehemently.

"My dear fellow," said Gerald, after a moment, and leaning his elbow upon the chimney piece of the empty grate, "You have brought an immense *ennui* upon me, have the goodness not to increase it by looking as if the world had tumbled to pieces, and the accident was destroying your comfort entirely."

"Are you mad, or simply unfeeling?" asked Francis.

"Neither. I regret what has occurred more than you can do. When Ruth is cool, I will make it straight—but I have tough work before me."

"Very. So tough that—. I tell you Gerald you over-rate your power with your wife, and you shock me by your indifferent air. For God's sake go to Ruth, try to console and reassure her; yet—"

"Yet what?"

"I fear it will be unavailing."

Gerald slightly smiled. A servant entered, brought more candles, and stood expectant before his master.

"What the devil do you want? What are you loitering for?"

"The coachman sent to know when you wanted the carriage, sir?"

Gerald bit his lip, and the dark flush of his cheek and bright flash in his eye were dangerous to see.

"In a half hour," he answered, and as the servant left the room he brought his clenched fist down upon the marble of the chimney with a heavy blow. "She orders me from her house—she will find it difficult to bring me back. It is a false move, for she must make the next herself, and that must bring her to *my* feet."

Francis slowly shook his head.

"Are you for a midnight drive with me?"

"No; I stay with Ruth. I shall not desert her."

"Try and bring her to reason, then," said Gerald sauntering out of the room.

"Is this my life-long friend," mused Francis; "is it thus that the light hearted, a little selfish, but noble boy ends in the man? Is this what I called his *insouciance,* his happy temper?

"Heaven have mercy upon this household, for Satan's clutch is upon it just now!"

Restlessly he paced the piazza. "How will it end? How *will* it all end?" And the gentle moon looked down upon the placid scene; wealth and nature combined to make Beauchamp a residence for a prince, and all evil passions were at work to render it a desert.

CHAPTER XXIV

Ruth Gray's bedroom was a luxurious and charming one—with its lace lined curtains, the rose colored silk flushing through the delicate meshes— the white enamelled walls almost panelled with pictures—pictures of flowers and children, and shepherdesses. The *Duchesse* mirror had upon its draped toilette-table the gold topped contents of a superb dressing box. Large *armoires a glace* flanked it on either side—deep comfortable chairs and low cushioned seats were in every direction. The basin and ewer were marvels of porcelain beauty—within the draped curtains of an alcove beyond, was the bed with its *couvrepied* of lace likewise, and its great French pillows in their richly bordered cases.

It was the apartment of a Parisian coquette transferred to the banks of a Southern river, a view of which might be had from either of the two windows which opened upon the piazza. The Venetian blinds were closed now—the room was darkened—not a sound was heard—yet it was not unoccupied.

Ruth was seated motionless and alone; her hands were tightly clasped around her knees—her eyes were fixed and tearless. So had she sat for hours—since she had silently given breakfast to Francis, and looked to her children. She was not restless, nor impatient, nor angry—she was only stony. She did not seem to feel sorrow or regret, or anxiety—she seemed to feel nothing. The life was taken out of her—it was the shell of a woman.

There came a low knock on the door—twice repeated. She rose and opened it—Francis stood there, with his kind, manly face.

"I fear I am in your way, Ruth," he said; "I shall go to town, and have come to bid you goodbye."

She held out her hand without a disclaimer. "Goodbye," she said, as if mechanically.

The light in the corridor fell full upon her haggard eyes, her wretched, blank face.

Francis paused. "May I come in?"

She hesitated, then moved aside and made way for him to enter. He sat down.

"My dear Ruth, let me be a peace maker—it is my right—it was I that made the mischief—"

"You!" she repeated, "you made the mischief? 'Twas you that made him a liar and a dastard?"

"Hush, my dear, dear Ruth—you are his wife—"

"No!" rang out her harsh, metallic voice. "In the sight of man, I am his wife, but in the sight of God I have never been. No miserable wretch who parades her painted charms in the public street is less the wife of her temporary companion, than I am the wife of Cecilia Clare's husband. His heart, his thoughts, his wishes, his hopes, his life were hers—what makes a marriage?"

"Ruth, you are not reasonable—"

"Spare me," she interrupted. "I respect and admire you—spare me commonplaces. Gerald Gray," she shuddered as she spoke his name, and how could Josselyn but remember the lingering caress with which she used to utter it! "Gerald Gray is the father of my children. God have mercy on them, innocent sufferers by another's crime! They are mine, but they have no longer any parent but me. He will not dare take them from me—if he does, the law shall judge between us."

"Will you not let him justify himself—speak for himself—?"

"Are you mad? or do you think me so! Is there any peace or life possible between two people—and have you forgotten his last reply to your urgent request? Am I so abject in your eyes that you see no bounds to my weakness? Cease to urge me. The man for whom you plead is unworthy of your pleading, and I am not so unworthy as to be touched by it."

"Do you really think that Gerald does not mourn this fatal secret coming to your knowledge as it did? Do you not *know* that he feels it bitterly? That pride alone keeps him from you now?"

"Have you forgotten Major X?" said Ruth bitterly. "Had my marriage been illegal, how long since would it have been disowned and annulled? Question for question, Francis; and now leave me, I implore you." She looked like some wild animal at bay; her head turned restlessly from side to side, and she half rose from her seat.

"Oh! dear Ruth, be the true woman that you are—the woman who always forgives *quand meme.*"

"You remind me of what I would give worlds to forget," cried the poor, tortured creature, springing to her feet. "Forgive! what have I not forgiven? What would I not forgive save the knowledge that he sought me without loving me, and lied to me from first to last! Oh, Francis! I could reveal such a tissue of systematic falsehood—such a dark record of unflagging deceit! such blind worship on my side! such unutterable tenderness lavished on the man who *endured* my affection, and pined for the caresses of Cecilia Clare! I thought I had no vanity—and I am one *throb* of wounded self-love to the core of my heart. I would grieve for my lost lover, for my wasted passion—and I can only think how I loved him! I ought to be overwhelmed with sorrow, and I am fierce with anger. In a word, I have been duped—duped from first to last—duped in my only belief—duped by the only thing I absolutely trusted! Don't pity me—I am not entitled to pity or sympathy, for it is my pride which is in the ascendant—my pride which has been humbled. I am not a deserted wife—I am a tricked woman!"

"Dear Ruth, I know what you suffer—only too well I know it. But have patience—every thing will come right. I don't believe in this retrospective admiration of Gerald's—don't tear your hand from me—think of what she is, and can you believe that any man in his senses could sincerely prefer her to you?"

"He may be a madman then—it matters little to me, but—so much the worse for my children."

"Think of the *esclandre*. For those children's sake, be patient."

"Enough," cried Ruth; "you speak as a man. You speak by the rules of your *caste*. Further words are useless; you do not understand me; you do not comprehend that were he to begin to love me from this hour, I could never love him again. What did I love? The truth, the honor, the nobleness of his character. I saw a shadow in the water and caught it to my heart of hearts. I loved what never had a substance within *my* reach. I held intangible, unexisting air. I crowned myself with a breath of idle wind, and fancied I was a queen. Is there anything to love in that man? I don't know what it is! He has blue eyes—but there are plenty of blue eyes in this world; he is amusing—but any actor of a French theater is more so; 'tis a bundle of rags on a scare-crow at which for four years I have looked with reverence. Your hand gave the flaunting deceit a fillip, and lo! I am cured."

"Yes, my hand! I wish it had been withered ere it performed so senseless an act."

"Why so?" asked Ruth, sinking into her chair, and speaking with a monstrous hard tone; "recollect what you said, sooner or later it would come. So desperate a passion could not be long concealed or controlled. A man could not live in the same atmosphere with such a syren without succumbing to her charms. True, he concealed it well. How he has spoken slightingly of poor Cissy to me! Francis, you see how weak I am—I am sneering at that insignificant girl who has had the luck to blast my life. Listen to my request—don't draw me on to further folly. Farewell; you are—"

"Dearly attached to you, Ruth; your warm and faithful friend."

"If I ever believe in anything again, I will believe that."

"Believe it now, I entreat you, and give me one word, one token to carry to Gerald, that may guide him through his darkness."

Ruth looked fixedly at him, partly opened her pale lips, closed them, turned away and walked to her writing table. Her back was to him. She placed her left hand before her. There was her wedding ring. Twice she turned to take it off and her courage failed—one wrench and it rolled on the desk. With firm pen and steady fingers she wrote:

"I wore this ring as a pledge of the sworn love, honor and faith of a gentleman; I return it to the giver knowing him now to be a liar, a trickster and a scoundrel."

It was soon done, the ring enclosed, the envelope sealed.

"Should he ever wish to explain himself, *this* will assure him of my reception," she said to Francis.

He took it doubtfully. Like a brother he folded his arm about her and pressed a kiss upon her forehead with a murmured "God bless you and comfort you, my child!"

A slight shiver ran through her whole frame; she said nothing more, and stood there like a statue; cheek, brow and hands deathly cold.

As Francis closed the door she sank upon her knees, and with her left and ringless hand passionately held to her lips, she tried to stifle the great sobs which convulsed her.

🧠 CHAPTER XXV

Francis was extremely unhappy and uncomfortable when he left Beauchamp, his first thought, of course, was to hunt up his cousin. He found Gerald at his mother's, with the most provoking look of calm indifference upon his very handsome face. No trace of a sleepless night nor an evil conscience disfigured those regular features and beautiful eyes.

He welcomed Francis as unconcernedly as possible. Josselyn was not gracious nor amiable.

Mrs. Gray was evidently quite unaware of anything unusual having happened, and enquired why he had left Ruth and the children?

"Gerald told me that he had to come away on account of some business—"

"Because I had to come, mamma. I did not tell you why," Gerald put in, smilingly. "How women will jump to conclusions and fill up sentences."

"Yes, my child, but of course, some business brought you, and you were quite content to leave dear Ruth under Francis' care, and now, here is Francis running to town, too! I have a great mind to go to Beauchamp myself, since you outrageous boys are so careless."

"Better not, you will meet Mr. Desborough, perhaps, and that will bore you intensely."

"Ah! Mr. Desborough is there! Why didn't you say so at once, and save me all my conjectures?" Upon which, Mrs. Gray rose to leave the dining room, adding, "Really, Gerald, you have a way of keeping back things that is perfectably unaccountable."

"Gerald," Francis exclaimed, as the door closed behind Mrs. Gray; "what are you going to do? It is useless trying to put me off. I brought on this business and it is my place to get it all straight as possible."

"When Ruth sends for me, I will return—not sooner."

"She will never send."

"*Tant pis pour elle.*"

"Do you think it will be *tant misere pour vous?*"

"Perhaps."

"Pray let me understand you. Are you pleased at the prospect of a rupture between yourself and Ruth? Is it this which gives so bright a look to your countenance?"

"I am intensely pleased to leave off acting—to be myself. I never could have had the *hardness* to tell Ruth, but since she chose to go eaves-dropping, and you chose to go prying, and you both heard the exact truth. I feel lighter at heart than I have done for years. I am very much attached to Ruth; I don't desire to quarrel with her; I regret most intensely that I ever deceived her about the reality of my feelings, and I am quite determined to avoid the society of other people. If all that doesn't satisfy her, why she can sulk as long as she pleases."

"And you are not grieved, not sad?"

"Not in the least. I can look men honestly in the face to-day, a thing I have not been able to do to my own satisfaction, this long while. Moreover, I wonder you are not surprised as I am, at my gentleness. If I were not full of kindness towards Ruth, I should find it difficult to pass over her words and manner and actions last night. She counted upon my good temper, or she would never have dared to order me out of the house, and this will show you how much inclined to bear with her I am, that I should soon pass over such an outrage."

"You should write to her, at least."

"Francis, have you never heard the old proverb about coming between the bark and the tree?"

Josselyn sighed and said no more.

Days passed and not one word or sign came from Beauchamp. These were miserable times for Francis, who felt restless, uneasy, unoccupied. He watched Gerald and discovered no visible mark of unhappiness or relenting. Mrs. Gray spoke constantly of Ruth and of the children; wondered that she had not heard from her daughter-in-law, and returned to question Gerald as to what was said in his letter from home. As usual he gave her evasive answers. Josselyn did not dare to enlighten her, and did not care to press Gerald further.

Frequently he thought of going back to Beauchamp and seeing if he could effect any change there, but he felt that such a step was utterly useless. Everything must come from Gerald and one might as well have tried to melt a sea of ice by talking to it, as try to make an impression upon that serene young gentleman. He did not like to deliver up the envelope with which he had been charged; the contents were plain enough to the touch, and he feared the words were not conciliatory. He had a natural dread of precipitating matters in a final outbreak, and lingered from day to day, hoping that Gerald's paternal affection might bring about a change in his intolerable cheerfulness. He encouraged Mrs. Gray to talk about the twins, and Gerald joined in with animation and delight; then the grandmother hinted as grandmothers sometimes will do, that a few details in their bringing up might be altered to advantage; but Gerald instantly took up the cudgels for Ruth, and protested that the children were perfectly managed.

Francis caught himself looking gratefully at Gerald, and could not but consider how absurd was his position—thanking the husband and his oldest and dearest friend, for speaking justly of the wife whom he had never seen till a month ago.

A week had gone by and Francis had almost fixed upon a day for leaving the South. He was carrying a heavy heart with him, and felt that his visit had been the cause of a misfortune that the laying down of his life would not now avert or conjure away. He and Gerald had ceased to speak on this all-important topic. He began to fear that perhaps he had already spoken too much. Left to themselves this couple might come to an understanding. He trusted to those holy voices healing the wounded depths of poor Ruth's heart; the desire to see them might exorcise the demon of pride from the mind of the offending party.

Francis could not blame Ruth. He could not think any step she might take too harsh or too hard, he might pray that she should be all softness and forgiveness, but he felt that she had been tricked, outraged, insulted.

If the confidence he had forced from Gerald had remained only with himself it would have appeared a lighter crime. Things that are not widely known, will, to the best of us, seem less damaging, than a smaller matter more generally circulated. We are called upon to bear the indignation of others, as well as to air our own.

Francis, however, (shocked as he was) while listening to Gerald, did not so fully appreciate the cowardice and meanness of his friend's action, till he found expression in Ruth's lips. But Gerald was correct in saying that this unhappy conversation would bring disunion between them. Never could their intimacy be again what it had been. Francis felt himself Ruth's champion—her sincere partisan. If their marriage no longer united Mr. and Mrs. Gray, there could be no question in Josselyn's mind as to the side on which he must range himself. If he must choose between them—justice and inclination were equally in the balance of the duped and unloved wife.

He was very sad about it; the genial, boyish, frank brightness of Gerald was irresistible and charming. His saucy fondness for Francis apparently untouched and unaltered, (unless they grazed the now tacitly forbidden ground), had always been Francis' delight. The gay nonsense and shrewd good sense, the sparkling folly and keen satire, the outward carelessness and the apparent under-current of affection in Gerald were rare and great gifts. Left early an orphan with an elder brother, morose and indifferent, and a sister as uninteresting as she was selfish, Francis had from their earliest days, attached himself to his "sort-of-cousin."

With the exception of one woman already hinted at, Gerald was the single being that his affectionate nature had fastened itself upon. And there was no possibility for him to respect Gerald as he had done. It is wonderful that he felt his Southern visit a failure—wished to end it, and hoped that apart, the old feelings would settle back after awhile to their former condition everywhere. It was evident that his presence did no good to himself nor to anybody—his absence might be more serviceable.

He announced his intentions to Gerald, who urged him not to go.

"I will stay on one condition," said Josselyn, hastily.

"My dear Francis, living among those woods so long has blunted your perception; you used to know me, once upon a time."

A servant entered with a note, which he handed to Josselyn; "From Mrs. St. Clair."

Gerald looked at his cousin and smiled knowingly.

"Tell Mrs. St. Clair's servant to wait, Tom. Ah, has the bewitching Bertha returned? She left town in another direction just after the visit to Beauchamp. Any secret?"

"None, whatever; she wishes to see me."

"Wishes to see you! What the devil does she wish to see you for? That woman runs every man—"

"Well, at least she never ran after you. I think the running was the other way, wasn't it, Gerald?"

"What do you mean, you smiling serpent?" asked Gerald, smiling himself.

"You can ask her," said Francis, pocketing his note and walking off with a nod, while Gerald laughed and aimed a book at his head, dropping it as his cousin disappeared and letting the gayety die out of his face, like a mask suddenly discarded.

🐚 CHAPTER XXVI

Bertha looked unusually grave and worried as she welcomed her guest. "Tell me what this means?" she asked.

She put in his hand a letter directed Francis Josselyn, Esq., and with it a note to herself.

"May I ask of your kindness, dear ("Mrs. St." lined out, and Bertha written over it,) to give the enclosed, with your own hands to its address. He may explain if he will—all that he chooses. If he does, don't be grieved for me—any more than you would be for yourself, had you dreamed a pleasant dream, and then waked up to life."

"There is no signature—but I know the hand as Ruth's—of course. It came yesterday—I only returned late last night. I could not guess where you were—I had supposed at Beauchamp—and I sent to the town house and found that both you and Mr. Gray were in Locust street—so I immediately wrote in search of you. What *does* it all mean?"

Josselyn opened the letter, while his impatient companion sat watching him eagerly. Having finished reading, he told her all that had passed.

Bertha was shocked, indignant, distressed; not so much surprised as he anticipated, for she said at once, "I guessed from the beginning that there was foul play somewhere—I never quite believed in Gerald Gray's disinterested attachment. I am not amazed to find that he married her for her money, and that alone—but I *am* astonished at his fancying himself in love with such an empty-headed insignificant doll! Truly, you men are strange beings!"

"Have you no hope of an adjustment of all this wretched business?" she went on presently.

"None. I fear that Ruth has taken her stand firmly, and I cannot find it in my conscience to urge her farther. How can I ask of her what in my own case—Mrs. St. Clair, these matters have brought us very near each other. By Ruth's implied request I have told you the whole story—it is her secret more than anybody's. She is the real sufferer, and has the right, therefore, to make what confidante she pleases, if by so doing it can ease her weary lot of one future or present pang. I will go beyond this." He got up and walked twice around the room. "You remember that evening we were telling stories—playing that game at Beauchamp; you recollect what I said perhaps—the man who went away to make a fortune, and was so cruelly jilted and deceived by the woman he loved—it was part of that programme you and I had laid out to open Gerald's eyes and close Ruth's. It was a tale commonplace enough, but Gerald knew both the hero and the heroine. I wished to recall to him the misery he knew that I had endured—to awaken some consideration lest he should plunge his wife into the same sort of grief [from] which he had sought six years ago to arouse me. I was the man of whom I spoke. That lady I found on my return last year, a rich widow, childless, handsomer than ever, wondrously improved in manner and person from the young girl to whom I was engaged when I was a college boy and she, a bright-eyed, unformed, simple little creature. She speedily succeeded in meeting me. My heart leapt with a momentary joy and triumph when with modest and yet passionate words, she continued to let me see that she could yet be mine—that she mourned sincerely a rash and foolish act—that my absence and her mother's persuasion had overcome her constancy and truth. Did I waver? Not for half a second. She had been false—she had lied—she had deceived me—there could be no trust again between us two. I believed her to be sincere now—but that did not wipe out what she had been. Her vanity can be content to know that I love nobody else, that I am true to the innocent and dear child to whom I plighted my faith so many summers since, but the lofty and lovely widow who usurped the nature of my lost love, shall never replace her. We could not be happy; I should make her miserable, for she could never command my esteem."

"Ah me!" sighed Bertha.

"You see," pursued Francis, speaking quickly, "it is a grievous thing to say, but Ruth no longer respects Gerald—she can no longer believe in him, nor trust him. The most that they could do would be to drag out a wretched existence of external politeness and inward chafing."

"He would not care," said Bertha shortly.

"No—he would not care," Francis repeated. "I am thinking of her. She will be like a machine with some damaging rust, some obstructing object introduced among its wheels and works; it will run awhile longer, but only by jerks and starts, and presently the whole thing will break with a crash, or just come to a dead lock and stop."

"Yes; as you first saw her, he has made her; now, she will neither go back to her former self, nor yet remain as she is."

"Perhaps her children may do her a world of good."

"Perhaps so," said Bertha, despondingly. "And her letter to you? What is it?"

"You can read it," Francis said, handing it.

MY DEAR FRANCIS:

Briefly I would thank you for your kindness and sympathy. Never fancy that I reproach you for what you consider your unhappy interference.

My father is with me; he consents (without entirely approving,) to my plans and wishes. I shall endeavour to be a better daughter than I ever yet have been. My children are well.

I have received this note; have the goodness to return it to the writer. It is evident that you have not executed the commission with which I charged you. It is my deliberate intention never, so long as life last, to exchange speech, look, nor written word with him.

For the future, my lawyer shall be my medium, if annoyed.

God bless you, Francis. When I believe in any human creature, I shall believe in you. Farewell.

Ruth.

"So he has written to her," said Bertha.

"So it seems; the letter is unopened. It appears to be short." Josselyn shook his head sadly. "It is a miserable business. Would to God that my conscience could acquit me of having aided in it!"

"Would to God that Gerald Gray had been less a scoundrel!" cried Mrs. St. Clair, indignantly. "And to think that she, the sufferer, will be blamed, canvassed, discussed, picked to pieces, and condemned, while that wretched creature will get off with hardly a word of remark."

"I cannot think so," said Josselyn.

"Perhaps not," Bertha added more quietly. "After all, Ruth is very rich, and that does cover such a multitude of sins!"

"You have not a very high opinion of your fellow beings, Mrs. St. Clair," said Francis, half smiling.

"I have the most ardent desire, believe me, to think well of them, but upon my word I can't find the opportunity to do so. All these weary years that I have plodded through this wicked and beautiful world of ours, I have tried so hard to find people whom I could admire, esteem, love. Is it my fault? is it theirs? I don't discover any that I can do more than put up with—very few even of these."

"You are not misanthropic, *pourtant?*"

"Very far from it—I have such credulity and such unfaltering 'faith in goodness some where,' that I am forever in pursuit of what I ought by this time to know, that I, at least, will never find."

"Happily, you please others more than they can please you."

"Do I? I doubt that extremely—and so would you if you knew better, not me, but those who surround me. For instance, I am called presumptuous and inconstant, because I have an opinion of my own on most points and because I cannot choose but give up the society of those whom I find to be false or treacherous. I have no doubt I appear to be both presumptuous and inconstant in the eyes of that majority with whom conformity passes for modesty and a fluent egotism, for constancy. Besides, let us admit a sad truth. If I wished to be, not exactly understood, but considered reasonable and right, I need only get in a decently honest way, twenty thousand dollars a year! Even the wisest and noblest, most just and generous people are liable to this moral affection. It can't be helped. If I were wise I would not quarrel with it—if I were very cool, I should perhaps admit its justice—being only what I am, it chafes and angers me. But it gives me hope for Ruth. She can never fall very low in the estimation of her fellow-citizens, and of the world at large so long as Mr. Desborough pays such an enormous State and city tax."

"You are bitter."

"Very—but consolatory, am I not? Think what a chance you run of always running right in your neighbor's eyes, no matter how zig-zag your path! I see you know, you and all the rest of *les gens riches*, doubling and twisting, now here, now there—now making a curve, and now flying off at an angle, but followed by admiring looks and the cheerful cries, 'How straight he walks!'"

Josselyn smiled.

"Oh, how frightfully matter-of-fact you have driven me into being. Disclaiming against money-worship! I shall owe you a grudge for ever and forever."

"Pray don't. I am to tell you good-bye for a great while now," and he rose.

"You are leaving the South?"

"Yes—leaving it sadly, reluctantly and yet willingly. You will not desert Ruth? She likes you——?"

"Desert her, never."

"She may take this blow quietly after all, and settle down into a calm, woman-of-the-world."

"How well do you understand her," said Bertha, a little scornfully. "I should recover from such an experience, and in time wonder at my folly—give balls, ride over people's heads, travel, educate my children, and be a very important member of society. But Ruth—her life is ended here. You see Heaven's gifts *are* equally apportioned. The gay coquetry, the sparkling wit, the imperious attraction of some women"—here the speaker slightly colored and turned away her eyes, for Josselyn, with half sad playfulness, bowed to her—"are wanting in our Ruth; but *en revanche* she has what is much rarer—a steadfast heart," and Bertha, in her turn, bowed to her companion. "A heart like Ruth's loves but once, and in ceasing to love it almost ceases to live. It has pleased Providence to give over this treasure to the keeping of a man who has acted very much like the cock in Aesop who found the diamond when he was seeking for a grain of corn. Gerald Gray don't care for this sort of diamond. He scratched and scratched in that *tas de fumier*, this world, till Fate brought the luck, he could not appreciate. True, he clapped his wings and crowed mightily at first—but—well! if ever he gets his grain of corn, I hope she will choke him in the swallowing thereof!"

"I hope he will never have the opportunity."

"Amen," said Bertha.

"I will ask a favor of you. Will you grant it? Should anything occur, however slight, in this matter, write me. Here is my address at Boston—wherever I may be, your letter will follow me."

Bertha promised, adding, "We are baffled conspirators, but at least we do not throw the blame of our failure upon each other."

✿ CHAPTER XXVII—AND LAST

Mrs. St. Clair to Francis Josselyn:

BEAUCHAMP, April 20, 1860.

My Dear Mr. Josselyn:

I wonder where these pages will travel before you open them! I might speculate for a while upon their possible journeyings, and almost write, "The Adventures of a Letter" in anticipation, were it not that I seldom guess aright, and so, might simply expose myself to your ridicule, instead of awakening your amazement at my prophetic genius.

Ah me! you will be as little of a wizard as I am of a witch, should you conclude, from this commencement, that I am in a gay mood and have bright news to tell. You see my date—Beauchamp—"beautiful Beauchamp," as we called it last year, when mirth and music echoed through its stately corridors, and charming women dotted the lawn towards sunset, making the old oaks bright with their presence and their sweeping skirts. How like a dream of long ago, seems that time, as I stand now each evening watching the slanting rays coming through the low-hanging boughs, and feeling sad and sick at heart.

What a changed spot it is! Ruth has been very ill—so ill that it is a matter of wonder that she should still be alive, and likely to live. Her cousin, Mrs.

Price, an elderly, well-meaning sort of woman, very considerately let me know of her danger. I came up at once, and have been here more than six weeks. It has been an anxious, wretched time. Mr. Desborough is not a man of much sensibility nor of very strong feeling, nor of any delicacy. His returning to live permanently with his daughter, has I make no doubt, been a terrible ordeal to her, patiently borne but very *wearing* to soul and body. His incessant allusion to her domestic misery, his rough ideal on the subject, his efforts to bring about a reunion, have, I fancy, done more to produce this fever, than she would admit, or he understand.

How strange it is that among some of the noblest men, and some of the otherwise purest-minded women, there should exist such extraordinary ideas of marriage—ideas so foreign to common decency of thought and life, that one listens with never-ending surprise to their words, and watches with something very like disgust their actions! Knowing this, why should I wonder that poor Mr. Desborough, who is so scantily gifted as I *hinted* above, should urge his daughter to live with a man whom she has long ceased to love. My limited acquaintance with human nature has taught me, therefore, a fact, which does not raise said nature in my estimation—viz. that almost all men, and very nearly all women, think that if a husband is content to endure the society of a wife, no matter in what light she holds him, she must thankfully accept her position, and consider herself highly virtuous and respectable while occupying it! Heaven help such virtue and such respectability! I'd rather see myself breaking stones upon the roadside—or, what is nearer my views of the fit depository for such pinchbeck qualities—beating hemp in Bridewell! (Is hemp still beaten in Bridewell?)

For the honor of womankind be it said, our dear Ruth was never likely to accept such sentiments, nor to model her life upon the *soi-disant* proprieties, as set forth by Mrs. Grundy. She had in honesty and truth given herself to a man utterly devoid of principle; it was a fatal mistake, but remediable so far as her honor lay. Her happiness had gone, but not her sense of decency; and although her father might urge every possible reason of policy and prudence, and although Mrs. Gray wrote her long strictures on a wife's duty (!), and although Mr. Clare once undertook to appeal in his most grandiloquent way to the fact of her children, threatening her with the terrors of "society," and winding up with that original phrase of exhortation, "let the dead past bury its dead"—they only had the power to harass and annoy, not to shake her firm resolve.

And Gerald, you will naturally ask, what of him? Probably he writes to you, possibly his letters are as frolicsome and gay as—the bells which dance on the top of a fool's cap. If so, they are perfect exponents of his countenance and manner. It is delightful to see so happy-looking a creature! "His good conscience," say his friends. Surely "the devil does take care of its own till—." I mean to write a moral tale with that title some day, and Gerald Gray shall be my hero. I used to think once that he *must* wake up to the value of what he has thrown away.

> Le prix d'un coeur qui nous comprend;
> Le bien qu'on trouve a le connaitre
> Et ce qu'on souffre en le perdant,

But any such fancy soon melted away before the fact of that cameo profile in its smiling calm. He may suffer sometimes, but it would be from indigestion not remorse; and I think he feels—a long run of ill-luck at faro.

I have never heard that he has made any especial effort to be reconciled to his wife. I am told that he "speaks forgivingly and kindly of her, and never suffers a harsh word against her to pass his lips!" Heaven does not grant me patience, when I am forced to listen to such speeches as this. (You were always so amused when I exclaimed "Heaven grant me patience!" You said I went so far from my actual condition with my petition,) and certainly among the preposterous, *enraging* things of this age of *simulacres* nothing surpasses the humbug of such remarks. Oh! the delicious satire of Thackeray when he writes, "What more can one say of the Christian charity of man, than that he is actually ready to forgive those who have done him every kindness." But so it is, and I make no doubt that there are plenty of people who look upon Gerald Gray as a martyr of mildness, because, after having lied to and cheated an unoffending woman—after having gone out of his way with infernal skill to break her heart and ruin her life, he does not sum up his career of *successful* villainy for has he not still the fortune she gave him?—by abusing her at street corners, or taxing her with infidelity.

Ruth's illness was slow in developing itself; it is still slower in leaving her. She is wrecked soul and body—the former, I still fervently trust, will recover its healthy tone, the latter is gone forever. It is pitiable to see her; I am sure you would not recognize her. Her beauty of expression, her clearness of skin, her roundness of proportion, have disappeared. Two great desperate eyes look out on vacancy from a ghostly white face—two poor thin arms are crossed over her sunken chest, and the bony fingers pluck restlessly at her sleeves, or else hang drooping and listless beside her. This physical change is painful enough to witness, but it sinks into nothingness when one studies the fearful ravages of her grief as shown in the deep lines which furrow a face that one year since, was bright, soft, feminine, and *so* happy. Do you remember—did you ever notice a certain sunny-sweet look, a kind of earnest radiance with which Ruth used to glance up into the eyes that were, alas! the eyes of her idol? It was, I think, the most beautiful, imploring, confiding, touching, loving look that ever lived under human eye-lids. It pleased me to watch for it, as I would for any perfect thing in nature or art, but several times then I caught myself murmuring, "Little children, keep yourselves from idols." I often recur to that all-absorbed look when I sit by Ruth now. She seldom speaks—she hardly seems to breathe. Gradually under one pretext or another, she has divested her bedroom of its pretty, coquettish air and there she lives, with bare walls, and a still, solemn tomb-like primness hanging over everything. I always feel on entering, as one does when the extreme hour has passed and he or she lies in the last sleep, while we, with "baited breath" and slow step come in gently and reverently, as if we feared to awaken or disturb the dearly loved whom no earthly sound can now reach. There is the same stillness and hush ever present in Ruth's room—not the quiet bustle and noiseless movements of a sick-chamber, but the silence which is felt only in the presence of Death.

Her children seem puzzled about her and half afraid of her. When Geraldine—over coming the first awe which always appears to paralyze them on visiting their mother—when Geraldine begins to speak, and says saucy things with all her wretched father's careless grace, his merry laugh, and a certain indolent shrug of her plump shoulders, I have seen the unhappy mother shrink from her with a sort of horror; while the little one, startled and half-crying, runs to me for protection.

Gerald has more of Ruth's own disposition and I fear may grow into a morose and reserved man, under the sad influence of his home. He has her eyes too, and is less like his father than the girl; and yet, of course it is so, I am sure she loves best the one whose appearance affords her the most constant pang, the keenest dart of memory.

The only change ever visible on this human mask, is when she sometimes fixes a gaze of agony upon the unconscious baby sitting at her feet, and then perhaps a single tear will roll down the poor wasted cheek.

Fortunately, their real names are not often mentioned—they have been so long called *Mimi* and *Petit Gros*. I would not dare utter the disyllable Gerald before her. Once only has Mr. Gray threatened to remove these children; he was met by a perforce peremptory announcement from Mr. Desborough that Ruth would apply to the law for her protection. The court might decide against her, but the scandal and the exposure he did not care to face.

So matters stand, as well as I can see them and read them. Dreary enough they are, and detailed as I have made them, I fear they are not clear.

How *can* I describe the desolate look, the weary restlessness, the stony calm of this tortured and stricken woman. No one could thoroughly comprehend it, unless they had in some degree suffered as she suffers. If she would only be angry, or cross, or indignant—be *something*—but she simply seems to have no life except a consciousness that—. I was interrupted here by a message from Ruth—a circumstance so rare that I hastened to her, throwing down my pen in the middle of my sentence and not resuming it till two days after. With a lighter heart, I take it up to tell what has transpired. We are going abroad, to Switzerland for the summer, Italy for next winter. Dr. Meadows orders the change imperatively. I hope many things from it. Ruth was very obstinately opposed to moving and sent for me, trusting, I believe that my unwillingness to quit her would induce me to be on her side—but she argued incorrectly. I offered to accompany her. Perhaps others of us wear shoes more or less tight, and hope to ease the pinching by walking on new roads.

I told her that I was writing to you; a faint color flushed into her face as she raised her sad eyes to mine. "Give him my—," she hesitated and added slowly, "tell him I have not forgotten him, and hope that he is well and happy. He is kind and good," she went on in an undertone. Then turning her head half impatiently, as if forcing herself to speak what she did not wish to utter, "Tell him I valued his letters, although I never answered them. When last he saw me," and a shiver ran through her wasted limbs, while the flush grew and settled into a dark red spot on each cheek, "I was mad and fierce. My pride and anger must have shocked him by their unbridled expression— it was not sorrow he saw, but frenzy." I stooped and kissed her without a word; she caught my hand and whispered, "Tell him I will try to pray—to forgive my enemies—some day—but not yet—not yet."

The flush faded, and a deathly pallor over-spread her face, she fainted in my arms, and was very ill all that night. Yesterday, she rallied again, and to-day she is decidedly better.

Our preparations have begun. I leave Beauchamp to-morrow to arrange my own affairs—a troublesome business, for we do not know how long our *exile* will last. There are dark mutterings in the political heavens, and some wise people talk with apprehension of "secession" and "civil war." God avert such calamities! but if the North forces them upon us, we will meet the storm, and quit ourselves like men—like the descendants of those great and glorious spirits who won our first independence. Abolitionism has "waxed fat and kicketh." "The negro" is found to be as good political capital as any other whim or ism, for unscrupulous demagogues, and I greatly fear that even among those to whom we might naturally turn for wisdom and sound policy should such a crisis arrive, we will discover that there is something stronger to their minds than honesty—something mightier than real patriotism. To go with the tide is so much easier than to stem it. When madness rages at the North, who will be found to breast the tempest? Assuredly not your admiration, Hon. E.E., of whom one of his and your Boston fellow-citizens wrote me some time since: "You people of the South may think as much as you choose of the 'Pet of the *Ledger*,' but I advise you not to trust in him. *We don't.* He has no back-bone." But I hope no such frightful contingency will arise. Should the South secede, it cannot be but that there will remain enough common sense among our ex-brethren to understand that gunpowder will not cement a Union, nor the bayonet bring about fraternal relations. Meanwhile Mr. Desborough has transferred large sums to England and France. He is a very prudent man, and if these United States becomes one vast lunatic asylum, we shall not starve abroad. Recollect, however, that I am intensely Southern; and as you value my good opinion hold yourself aloof from the (truly) "vain doctrine" of coercion. The society of my native State is not congenial to my feelings nor my taste—how should it be? Is there a spot where a fierce crusade could be waged unceasingly against this poor little woman who answers to my name?—but, nevertheless, I am proud of my people as a people, and I will stand up for them to the last hour of my life. I could not understand the existence of a traitor to the soil; and man or woman, born among us, who lifts sword or voice in defense of a dissolved Union, against my, his or her State, I should look upon as a blot, a renegade, a wretch not worth the cord with which I should like to see all such hanged! But I do not believe in the possibility of this winding-up of our model Republic. Separation *may* take place—war, never! With every confidence in the folly of the Northern Demos, he can scarcely push it so far as that. *Qui vivra verra.*

One word in conclusion now, of your friends in this part of the world. Bettina Denham is married. Mr. Browne is the happy man, and she looks very handsome and perfectly contented—but he has already suppressed the parrot and pronounces Arthur McIvor to be a dandy, and very uninteresting. Messrs. Taunton and Aubrey are as well dressed and as agreeable as usual. I trust that one of them, at least, will be profoundly overwhelmed by my departure. I am indifferent as to which, but my vanity demands the inconsolable condition of one. Mrs. Fordyce is the proud mother of a son—I can't find out if it is "the softened image of its sire," but I presume that it is as yet wigless.

The fair Cecilia is fairer than ever; but has the trumpet of Fame been silent about her? do you need me to inform you that she has at length rewarded the constancy and *courage* of Tom Taunton? Even so; a year ago when this business was first whispered in polite circles, some eyes looked askance on smiling Cissy, and prudent Phyllis brought her powers to bear on matters generally.

The doors of Castle Clare were virtually and virtuously closed upon their cousin, and much fierce skirmishing took place, I make no doubt, both inside and outside of those respectably painted portals. But Cissy soon dried her tears. In the first place such an innocent young thing (only twenty-six years of age,) could not but feel horrified at meeting a man who was separated from his wife, although necessarily her pure mind could not take in the idea that she had had anything to do with it. Mr. Clare played the role of the "indignant father," when it leaked out, as such things will, that his hopeful nephew fancied himself in love with Cecilia, and acknowledged to having married Ruth simply for an establishment. I could not help speculating as to what would have been his behavior if the news had been followed by Ruth's death, and the liberty of the afflicted widower to choose her successor; for I am afraid even a divorce would not have been considered a fatal and insuperable divider of these two faithful hearts, in the opinion of that respectable old humbug.

But Ruth's grief did not kill her, and divorce was not possible, so Tom Taunton was encouraged and swallowed the bait. To do the bride justice, she looked like a white lily, and had more dimples than I could count, when I saw her in her white and silver finery. She was simpering and giggling with all the intelligence of one of Maëlzel's automata, and from a distance Gerald was watching her, when my eyes intercepted the glance. He had the grace to color slightly and turn away. I did not see him speak to the fair, the inexpressive "she," who seemed serenely satisfied and deliciously inane. I do not doubt but that she will be a very admirable wife. Her feelings could never prey upon her looks, nor interfere with her duties. She was born to marry somebody—she meant to make a good match—she has done very creditably after all, and will settle into a comfortable, well-disposed matron.

I wish her much happiness and a great many children.

Mr. Desborough speaks of joining us when we are settled. Dr. Meadows goes with us now. In spite of his sixty years, he has all the vivacity and energy of a youth, and we shall fare admirably under his guidance. Without him, I should have feared to undertake so responsible a charge.

Looking back over the many pages of this letter, I am shocked to see their number; but yet if you will consider them as the winding up of a story in which both you and I have been actors, you will acknowledge that it could not have been shorter. It is almost a romance, is it not? the history of this past year, since the day we first met at Beauchamp, until this one, when I am telling you good-bye before quitting my country for an uncertain period. What will be the ultimate fate of the heroine? Neither you nor I can guess. If I dream a future for her, I cannot but reject the solitary life it naturally promises; and in spite of the useless folly of such retrospection, I think of the only man worthy of her, and sigh because they never met, when meeting might have secured their mutual happiness. How useless indeed! Just because they *are* suited to each other, they never would have found it out. Adieu. In all sincerity,

Your friend, faithfully,
BERTHA ST. CLAIR

THE END

Jane H. Pease and William H. Pease are Professors Emeriti, University of Maine, and Associates in History at the University of Charleston. They are the co-authors of *Black Utopia: Negro Communal Experiments in America; They Who Would Be Free: Black's Search for Freedom, 1830–1861; The Web of Progress: Private Values and Public Styles in Boston and Charleston, 1828–1843;* and *Ladies, Women, and Wenches: Choice and Constraint in Antebellum Charleston and Boston.*

Library of Congress Cataloging-in-Publication Data
King, Susan Petigru, 1824–1875.
[Gerald Gray's wife]
Gerald Gray's wife ; and Lily : a novel / by Susan Petigru King ; with an introduction by Jane H. Pease and William H. Pease.
Includes bibliographical references.
ISBN 0-8223-1407-X. — ISBN 0-8223-1411-8 (pbk.)
1. Women—South Carolina—Charleston—Fiction.
2. Charleston (S.C.)—Fiction. I. Pease, Jane H. II. Pease, William Henry, 1924– . III. Title: Gerald Gray's wife.
IV. Title: Lily.
PS2179.K36G4 1993
813'.3—dc20 93-15632 CIP